LEV TAHOR

A HEART REDEEMED

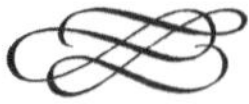

ANA WATERS

For new releases, special promotions, announcements, and ordering information:

Facebook @ anawatersauthor
Instagram @ anawatersbooks
anawatersauthor@yahoo.com
linktr.ee/anawaters

For Maggie. You are seen. You are loved. You are precious in His sight.

At this, those who heard began to go away one at a time, the older ones first, until only Jesus was left, with the woman still standing there. Jesus straightened up and asked her, "Woman, where are they? Has no one condemned you?"

"No one, sir," she said.

"Then neither do I condemn you," Jesus declared. "Go now and leave your life of sin."

— JOHN 8:9-11 NIV

CHAPTER 1

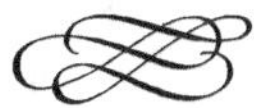

"Oh, come on Carly, spill it," my roommate, Monique Lawson, said. "What's his name?"

I blushed. "Stop it, Mon. I have to get to work." I nudged past Monique and into our shared bathroom.

She trailed behind me, her long blonde hair bouncing in a topknot. "You know I'll just beat it out of Courtney."

"Leave her alone," I said, already envisioning our timid, third roommate buckling under Monique's interrogation tactics.

Kelsey O'Connell, the fourth in our housing quartet, appeared with a toothbrush in hand. "I could hear you two all the way down the hall. What's up?"

Monique glanced over at Kelsey like the cat who ate the canary. "Carly's got a boyfriend," she sing-songed.

"I do not." I glared daggers at her. "Can you just drop it, please?"

Kelsey's eyes lit with excitement. "Oh, was it that guy we ran into at the farmer's market? I mean, he's older, but you can tell he used to be really hot."

I shook my head in disgust. "Ew, Kelsey! That was my coworker, Ted. He is very happily married, and his wife used to work in my job a million years ago. She's also really nice. I would never do anything like that to Rebecca."

Monique's green eyes expanded to twice their normal size. She raced into my bedroom and pulled Rebecca Margolin's book, *Tabula Rasa*, from my nightstand.

"Is it *this* Ted?" she asked, holding it up for Kelsey to see. "You actually work with Mr. Smolderingly Delicious?" Monique looked ready to swoon as she quoted Rebecca's fictionalized memoirs.

I snatched the book from Monique's hand. "Yes, okay? These are real people, and the mighty Margolin is still Culver's top, east coast producer."

"What about the golden eyes?" Monique said. "Do they sparkle like that in real life?"

Coolly, I replied, "I wouldn't know, Mon. I don't go to Culver to ogle my coworkers." If there were any pair of eyes I might admire in real life, they belonged to the hero of another book, and I'd only ever seen Joe Trautweig in passing.

Monique huffed. "Don't be so sensitive, Carly. I was just asking. The guy is a walking meme now."

"Find you a man who looks at you the way Ted looks at Rebecca," I said, quoting the latest round of *Tabula Rasa* .gifs circulating on social media. "I just hope his kids never see it. That would be so embarrassing."

Kelsey waved us off with her toothbrush. "Enough about this Ted guy. I want to know about your mystery man, Carly."

Monique yanked out her scrunchie to take "just woke up" selfies in full makeup and perfectly cascading tendrils. In between pouty poses she said, "I saw you guys coming out of

Burger Palace with a big group of people last night. He seemed totally into you."

"Whatever," I said, rolling my eyes.

"His arm was around your waist."

"It was a group photo, Mon."

Monique glanced conspiratorially at Kelsey for help. "He didn't look too sad having his hands on you, Carly. I mean, I'm not shipping you guys or anything, but you did look like a happy couple."

Kelsey leaned against the bathroom door frame watching me. "If it's not a big deal, Carly, why are you acting so weird about it?"

Exasperated, I said, "Because you guys are picking at me and reading into something that isn't there. Anything I say to defend myself just makes you think I'm hiding something. I promise I'm not."

Kelsey considered my words, but Monique smelled blood in the water.

Repositioning a curl, she added, "I was just surprised because it seems like you're still hung up on Dylan."

I sucked in a breath at Monique's cruelty. I wondered how someone who called herself my friend wouldn't hesitate to throw my past back in my face.

"Oof!" Kelsey exclaimed, noting my expression. "Carly, you're going to have to let him go if you ever want to move on."

"It's not that easy, Kel. He was the love of my life, and I ruined it." I squeezed my eyes shut, not wanting to revisit the shame of begging Dylan to take me back. I didn't want to think about Dylan and the rebound girlfriend who had recently become his fiancée. I didn't want to think about my own stupidity or the next three toads I'd used to fill the Dylan shaped void in my heart. Over two years had passed since Dylan rightfully dumped me, but it felt like no time at all.

Monique already seemed bored. "Don't get mopey, Carly. You're wasting your life over some guy named after a '90s teen soap opera. What was it again? *California 90204* or whatever?"

"Back off, Mon," Kelsey said, seeing the catlike sneer on our roommate's face. "You're usually the one breaking hearts, not dealing with them."

Monique shrugged and eyed herself in the bathroom mirror. She pushed at the tip of her nose then inspected the rest of her twenty-nine-year-old face for nonexistent wrinkles.

Kelsey frowned. "Sorry for prying, Carly."

I waved her off. "It's fine."

She nodded, then smirked at the sight of Monique lost in self-reflection. For Monique, that meant admiring herself in the mirror rather than doing any legitimate soul searching. Life seemed easy for someone tall, blonde, and beautiful. Monique also had no shortage of company in her bedroom next to mine. Earplugs had been a godsend.

My willowy roommate lost interest in my love life once she started getting likes and comments on her latest selfie, and I hustled through my morning grooming to make it through my thirty-minute commute to Parkview.

I entered my corner office with a bit of a frown, the topic of Dylan always sending me into a funk.

My coworker, Poppy Levine, looked up from her computer monitor nursing a cup of *Vincenzo's* coffee in her hand.

"What's up?" she asked, looking me over. "Was the date a total bust?"

I burst into tears. "Oh, Poppy!" I moaned.

She jumped from her seat to embrace me. "Sweetie, it's okay. You have to stop beating yourself up."

I shook my head. "I don't think I can."

"There's forgiveness in Christ, Carly. He's not up there waiting to sling some hammer down on you."

"You know what I did," I whispered.

"So does He," she said gently, "and He still loves you."

"It's not the same."

She looked at me patiently. "You've read my book. I know you've read Rebecca's and Taylor's too," she said, referring to another former employee at Culver, Incorporated. "All of us have a past, and all of us know we're loved by Jesus."

I had to grin at Poppy's earnest pleading. "You might just be the craziest Jewish person I know. Not even the kids from my old youth group talk about Jesus as much as you do."

Poppy smiled broadly, and I understood why her husband, Jared, seemed to worship the ground she walked on. Knowing Poppy's story personally and in print, her re-marriage to Jared Levine was nothing short of a miracle. I couldn't fault Poppy for loving Jesus after all she had overcome. I also knew that Jesus considered my sin unforgivable. At least according to my mother.

"Come on, Carly," she said, putting an arm around me. "Have some biscotti with me, and then we'll tackle the nightmare project the mighty Margolin just dropped off on my desk."

Sniffling, I took the tissue she handed me and blew my nose.

"Talk when you're ready," she said, picking up her coffee cup and taking a deep drink. "And you grab as much biscotti as you need, okay?"

I glanced down at my stomach pooch that had grown more pronounced with another round of Dylan depression.

"Stop," Poppy said. "You're going to have to forgive yourself for what happened."

"How can I? I'm not Rebecca or Taylor or even you," I said,

gesturing at her. "I knew what I was doing. Don't tell me it wasn't my fault because we both know it was."

She sighed. I knew she understood better than most. I had been hesitant to share my story with Poppy, especially after I devoured her own fictionalized memoirs. I had expected judgment or condemnation, but she had shown me nothing but kindness instead. I resented her characterization of me in her book as flighty and man-crazy, but I couldn't fault her for that perception. I knew the persona I had embraced after things fell apart with Dylan. It was easier to play a role than face the lives I had destroyed, including my own.

"Don't tell me to write it down," I said, seeing the wheels turn in her dark brown eyes. "I don't want people feeling sorry for me or using what I did as an excuse to do it themselves."

Poppy held up a recent employee benefits guide I had designed for one of our Fortune 500 clients. "Carly, you have a gift with words. You managed to take some of the most boring and recycled content on the planet and transform it into a fun read. Kacie and Wanda said their clients won't stop gushing about the huge difference from their old broker's booklet. I had to disappoint Joe Trautweig when he asked if I designed it."

Butterflies stirred at the mention of his name. I had developed an unhealthy infatuation based on Poppy's book, and the idea of real-life Joe Trautweig knowing my name made me blush. He had stopped working at Culver long before I'd been hired, and his brief, romantic entanglement with Poppy had been the cause. Although things had been tense for a while afterward, I knew Poppy considered him a dear friend. "How did Joe see my document?" I asked.

She smiled back. "Margolin Bible study. Ted invited Zach Perkins last Sunday."

"Oh." My mouth immediately dropped into a frown.

"Zach was really excited about the response to your benefits guide, and he showed it off to Kyle and Joe after Bible study."

"Are you kidding?" I gaped. "Why would Zach do that? I know Kyle and his wife are good friends with the Margolins, but what about trading secrets with the enemy? Kyle and Joe both work for Cooper & Jaye."

Poppy raised her eyebrow at me. "Was the date with Zach really that bad?"

"It wasn't supposed to be a date at all! Zach invited me to a concert at the Parkview Pavilion. It was him and a bunch of his friends from church. They acted like we were a couple, and it was just weird. Plus, all of the girls looked like clones."

"Did he try to kiss you?" she asked.

I glanced over to the Amish inspirational romance peeking out of Poppy's purse. "I got less action than the chicks in your Puritan novels."

She laughed. "Fair enough. I was impressed that Zach stopped admiring you from afar and finally asked you out."

"Why would you be impressed? I was shocked."

Poppy cocked her head and pursed her lips at me. "Have you looked in a mirror lately? You're gorgeous, and Zach seems like a pretty bright guy."

I rolled my eyes. "I'm pretty sure all Zach sees are blue eyes and an oversized chest. Besides, weren't you the one who wrote how office romances don't usually end well?"

"Jared said that," she corrected, "and all of that feels like a lifetime ago. My husband was also jealous at the time."

"But was he wrong?"

The smile slid from her face. "You didn't need to go there to make your point. Everybody has moved on, including Joe."

Unable to help myself, I asked, "Are you sure? Things didn't last very long with that realtor you said he met at church."

"Why? Are you interested or something?" she snapped. "Don't tell me you've still got that book crush on him."

Shamed into silence, I looked away. The lead weight of depression threatened to pull me down once again.

"I'm sorry," Poppy said, exhaling a heavy sigh. "I didn't mean to take your head off. Will you forgive me?"

I nodded. "I'm sorry too."

She offered a motherly smile. "Why don't we get started on work, and we can just table the conversation about Zach Perkins?"

"Thanks," I whispered, blinking back tears.

Poppy took note but said nothing. I watched her lips silently move as she worked on Ted Margolin's latest Request for Proposal. Instinctively, I knew she was praying for me, and I cringed.

I wasn't sure if I wanted anyone praying for me or that God would even care to listen.

CHAPTER 2

AFTER A QUICK BOWL OF MICROWAVE SOUP IN THE
break room, I made my way to the covered walkway separating
the Culver high rise from the parking deck. Referred to as "tornado alley" when the wind picked up, the bolted-down benches
kept the furniture from flying. On a whim, I'd decided to grab
some frozen yogurt from Let it Fro-yo, my favorite little shop
situated outside the parking garage.

I spooned the comfort food into my mouth as I studied
Parkview's finest trek between the two buildings. I often found
myself inventing backstories about the locals just for fun.

"So, you're a fan of the taro flavor too?"

I glanced up to see Joe Trautweig in the flesh. Even more
handsome up close, his well-trimmed beard accentuated a
strong jaw, aquiline nose, and a full mouth. A mound of purple
frozen yogurt sat on top of the waffle cone in his hand.

I managed a small smile, still stinging from Poppy's accusation. "Looks like."

"I've seen you around with some friends of mine, so I

figured I'd stop by and formally introduce myself. Mind if I join you?" he asked.

I shrugged.

Joe sat down and met my eyes. "Japanese sweet potato is a very popular choice with Culver employees past and present. I applaud your good taste, Carly."

I temporarily forgot about Dylan, Zach, or the three toads in between. Joe's innocent remark landed like high praise, and my stomach flip flopped. I blushed and looked away.

"I don't bite, I promise. My name's Joe."

"I know who you are," I said quietly.

"Ah, so you've read the books." He rubbed the back of his neck with his free hand. "Kyle Goldstein says to embrace it as an opportunity to share about Jesus, but I'll admit I'm not quite as open with my past as he is."

"They did change your name," I said, glancing back at Joe. "I mean, for anybody that knows you guys personally, it could be a little awkward, I guess." My eyes drifted to the oblivious Parkview workforce as they walked past us. "Most people around here just see a businessman with an ice cream cone. I think your secret identity is safe."

He exhaled a soft chuckle. "I can't remember if it was Rebecca or Taylor who gave me that ridiculous last name."

I genuinely laughed this time, and Joe's expression altered. His gaze shifted from humor to curiosity, and my stomach flopped again. He studied me for a moment.

"Carly, how much of what Poppy wrote about you is true?"

Taking the opportunity to hide from his scrutiny, I scooped another bite of yogurt into my mouth. "None of it," I answered honestly, "but that's my own fault."

Joe raised an eyebrow over pale, wide set eyes. Nothing in Poppy's memoirs had been fictional about the intelligence and intensity of that jade green gaze. The brief thought flickered that there might be life outside of Dylan and my perpetual mantle of shame. Shaking off that wishful line of thinking, I stared down into my yogurt cup. "I had a bad breakup. I didn't handle things so well after. That's what Poppy saw."

"Ah," he said. "How long ago did things end?"

"Too long. Everyone keeps telling me to get over it, but it's not that easy."

"Don't let anybody ever tell you how long you need to recover from trauma. If you rush the process, you'll wind up hurting yourself even more. Nobody has the right to judge the pain you've been through, especially if they've never experienced anything like it."

Touched by his words, I smiled at him. "Thank you. I have a couple friends who probably need to hear that."

He smiled back. "There's a lot you learn when you get to be my age. Getting old has its advantages."

"Old?" I asked, figuring that Joe was still a few years younger than the mighty Margolin. "I'm sure they invented the wheel before you were born, right?"

His eyes sparkled in amusement. "Please, tell me you know better than to eat laundry detergent pods."

"That's Gen Z, not me."

"Ah, a millennial. Society's new favorite scapegoat."

"Okay, boomer," I retorted, sticking my tongue out at him.

Joe gave a hearty chuckle. "My parents are actually baby boomers. I fall under the Gen X category, or maybe an Xennial. 1981 was a good year."

"Got it. Grunge music, teen angst, and a lot of flannel."

"Mountains of flannel," he said. "Enough to keep any lumberjack or hipster millennial happy."

I smirked. "Poppy says she doesn't understand why girls my age want to dress like the *before* in a '90s teen makeover movie."

I expected Joe to laugh again, but a strange look crossed his face. Ruefully, he said, "For a minute there, I forgot the connection between the two of you."

"Is everything cool in that department? Poppy says it is."

"Jared Levine has nothing to worry about. I've made peace with everything other than my own regrets."

"Funny you should say that," I said, feeling my defenses lower at Joe's admission.

"Really? Why?"

"I struggle with regret too."

He offered me a sympathetic smile. "I guess it's not relegated to any one age bracket."

"Definitely not. I may not be as old as you, but I feel like I've made enough mistakes to last a lifetime."

"That's surprising," he said, studying me. "You have the face of an angel."

"Hardly," I muttered.

Joe raised that same eyebrow again, drawing my attention to his jade stare that continued to unnerve me. "I hope you figure out a way to make peace with your past, Carly. When you do, please fill me in on how you did it. I'll take all the help I can get."

I exhaled a short laugh. "I thought Jesus was the catch-all solution for you Jewish Christians—or whatever you guys call yourselves."

He sighed and leaned back against the bench. "Real life is more complicated than the sunshine and lollipop gospel being sold in a lot of churches."

Intrigued by his answer, I took my own opportunity to study Joe. He caught my gaze and seemed taken aback by it.

Shifting my focus away, I saw that he hadn't touched his yogurt since he'd sat down. "You're dripping." I motioned toward his melting cone. Purple droplets had migrated inches away from his suit jacket sleeve.

"So I am," he said. "Be right back."

I took a deep breath while he entered the frozen yogurt shop. I wanted to shake my head clear of my confusing reaction to Joe Trautweig. Doing some quick math, I realized he must be at least ten years older than me. I had just turned thirty-one, and I assumed Joe was somewhere in his early forties. Figuring the age gap would be enough of a deterrent based on his comments, I immediately dismissed thoughts of our conversation being anything more than two strangers getting acquainted. It helped calm my attraction toward Poppy's former admirer.

Joe winked at me as he exited Let it Fro-yo holding a large cup. His upended waffle cone peeked from the top of his new dessert container.

"That's one way to fix it," I said, amused.

He broke into a full grin, suddenly resembling a man much closer to my age. I gulped, dismayed by how deeply I felt drawn to him. To make matters worse, the one person I wanted to confide in would probably put the kibosh on the mere thought of something happening between the two of us.

"You okay?" Joe asked, returning to his previous seat.

"To be honest, it's kind of surreal talking to someone I've read about in a book. Part of me feels like I know you already, but sitting with you face-to-face just reminds me that I don't really know you at all."

Joe ate a scoop of yogurt before responding. "I gave Poppy permission to write about our...relationship," he said, hesitating over what to call their time together, "but it's not easy reading about yourself in print. I suppose I should be grateful she changed some of the details."

"What about your ex-wife?" I asked, too intrigued to keep my mouth shut. "Is that what actually happened with Catherine?"

Joe's expression looked pained. "I'm not sure if I should be flattered or terrified that you know about my past. Everyone gushes about Poppy and Jared and their miracle marriage. I didn't think too many people paid attention to my part of the story."

"I never should have said anything." I blushed and looked away.

He reached out and touched my hand. "Sorry."

I looked over in surprise. "I should be the one apologizing. This is none of my business. I had no right to ask about something so personal."

"No need to apologize," he said, his hand still on mine. I looked down at our joined hands and then back at Joe, my heart pounding in my chest.

He also looked down at our hands. I saw the same confusion mirrored in his jade eyes. His lips parted to say something, but nothing came out.

Forcing myself to breathe, I slipped my hand out from under his.

"I...uh," he stammered, his eyes still locked with mine.

"Hey guys," Zach Perkins said, approaching us from the parking garage. "Carly, I didn't know you were friends with Joe." His tone carried a note of wariness. "Did you tell Trautweig about the concert we went to last night? All of my friends loved meeting you, by the way."

Joe glanced from Zach to me, piecing things together quickly. He stood up and gestured for Zach to take his seat. "I had to introduce myself to the woman responsible for the benefits guide you showed to us. It was a pleasure to meet you, Carly," he said warmly. "You are a woman of many talents, and I'm sure you'll find a solution to our common problem."

Zach glanced back and forth between the two of us, his brows drawn together in confusion. "Common problem?" he asked Joe.

I stood up, taking a step back from both men. "Joe, it was nice to meet you too. Zach, I'll see you in the office. I'm buried under a bunch of October renewal documents, so I need to head back."

"I'll walk with you," he said quickly, brushing past Joe and coming alongside me.

Ignoring Zach, I felt those pale green eyes on me before I looked up to meet them. I was jolted once again by their effect on me.

Joe's resigned smile turned slightly mischievous as he saw Zach take a step toward me while I took a larger step away.

"Maybe I'll see you around some time," I said to Joe.

Inserting himself into the conversation, Zach blurted out, "You could always come to Bible Study with me, Carly."

"Oh, I, uh, I don't really do that stuff anymore."

"What about last night?" he asked, trying to pull my regard away from Joe.

I pursed my lips. "You didn't tell me it was a Christian band. I feel like maybe you left that part out on purpose."

Zach blinked a few times, seemingly caught in a lie by omission.

Glancing between the two of us, Joe said, "Why don't I leave you kids to hash through your date? Zach, I'll see you at Bible Study on Sunday. Carly, while I'd love for you to be there, I'm sure you have your reasons for not going. I've been there myself. There's no judgment here."

"Thanks," I murmured, wishing I could say more without Zach hanging onto every word like a hawk.

"Maybe we'll see each other the next time Let it Fro-yo calls my name," he said.

"I've heard that taro is a very popular choice," I replied, "beloved by many."

Joe didn't conceal the spark of humor in his eyes, nor did Zach bother to hide his growing resentment at being ignored.

"Carly, I thought you said you needed to get back to the office," he said primly.

"She did," Joe answered before I could, "and both of us are clearly keeping Carly from her work. Zach, if you've got a minute, I wanted to ask you a few questions about that fantastic benefits guide."

Zach looked caught between a rock and a hard place, and I smiled in gratitude at Joe Trautweig. He tossed me a quick wink before engaging Zach in conversation and ensuring my escape.

CHAPTER 3

I sat in bed poring through Taylor Horner's memoirs, *Ex Nihilo*, reading and re-reading the part where her husband, Ian, first confessed his feelings for her.

"So good!" I moaned and clutched the book to my ample chest.

My third roommate, Courtney, poked her head in my doorway. "What is?"

I held up the book for her to see.

"Ah," she said, entering the room.

"What's up?" I scooted over on my queen-sized bed to make room for her.

"Monique found me."

I rolled my eyes. "What did you tell her?"

"Thank God, I didn't have anything to share. You know how she is when she thinks you're withholding information."

"She's relentless. I also don't understand why she's so interested in my love life."

"Because you don't let her bully you like she does to

everyone else. Also, I think Monique has always been jealous of you."

"Jealous?" I gaped. "You're kidding, right? Monique is the one with a new boyfriend every week."

"She had a crush on Dylan before you guys started dating, but he was never interested in her. I remember the look on her face the night we all met. She was hanging all over him, but he ignored her. He only had eyes for you, Carly."

"I remember," I said quietly. "Mon told me later that she was happy for me, but I never really believed her."

Courtney's high ponytail bobbed as she nodded. "Monique is used to being the center of attention, and she couldn't understand why Dylan didn't fall for her like everybody else."

For once, the mention of my ex-boyfriend's name brought a smile to my mouth. "Nobody was ever going to tell Dylan what to do, including Monique. I think it was one of the first things that made me fall in love with him." My smile fell, remembering how nothing I said after my horrific mistake could convince Dylan to work things out.

Courtney sighed, already knowing the direction of my thoughts. "Now, do you believe me?"

"I guess so. I just have a hard time believing she would still be jealous about that. All she does is put down Dylan and then ridicule me for wanting him back. I mean, look at me." I glanced over my figure and mentally compared it to my willowy roommate. "There's really no competition here. Monique can have any guy she wants."

"That's kind of my point," Courtney said, her gentle voice full of both compassion and intelligence. "Carly, you may not see yourself the way the rest of us do, but that's because of your mom."

Only Courtney could deliver a painful blow like that but still leave me feeling loved. My mother had been a faithful member of Bernard Ivy's church, First United of Hillcrest, for over thirty years. She had dragged me there as a little girl, and I had vague memories of Rebecca Ivy long before she became Mrs. Ted Margolin. I had known something wasn't right with that place a full decade before First United was forced to close its corrupt doors.

At my lengthy pause, Courtney said, "I'm not trying to hurt you, Carly."

"I know, but it's hard to shut off her voice in my head. Every time I try to move past what I've done, I hear my mother screaming at me that she'll never forgive me, and neither will Jesus. With the way things have turned out, I can't help wondering if she's right."

My roommate emphatically shook her head. "I know I've said this before, but your mother has a really warped view of God and the Bible. Pastor Ivy got sentenced to nine years in prison, but she was still protesting outside of the courthouse when he took that plea deal. Your mother has always sounded more like a cult member in love with her leader than an actual Christian."

"She and the other church board members saw Bud Riley's confession of all the illegal activities," I said, "but my mother still listens to audio recordings of Pastor Ivy's sermons. I just don't get it. Why does she talk about God's forgiveness and grace for what Pastor Ivy did, but she tells me that *my* sins are unforgivable?"

Thoughtfully, Courtney asked, "Do you ever wonder if that's why you ended up working at Culver?"

"What do you mean?"

She glanced over to the stack of books on my nightstand. "Carly, you have access to people who can tell you firsthand what a crackpot Pastor Ivy is. Didn't Ted Margolin say that Rebecca would be willing to meet you for lunch?"

"Yeah," I drawled, having forgotten that detail.

"I know you probably won't go to Bible study at their house, but maybe it would help to talk to Rebecca in person. She's one of the few people more abused by what Pastor Ivy preached than you were."

"Maybe," I hedged.

"Just think about it." She smiled at me encouragingly. "I'm not asking you to believe in anything. I just want to see you free from that place and from all the damage it's done to you."

"I know," I said quietly, "and I appreciate it, Court. Truly."

My roommate placed a gentle hand on my shoulder. "I know you have your reasons for why you won't go back to church, but I just wish you wouldn't think of your mother every time you think about Jesus. They're not one in the same."

"I've tried to read the Bible," I said, watching Courtney for a response, "but I would be lying if I said I didn't hear my mother or Pastor Ivy in my head."

"I'm so sorry. I wish there was something I could do to help."

"The fact you haven't turned your back on me says a lot," I told her truthfully. "I can think of a lot of Christians who would have dropped me after what I've done."

"Jesus forgave the men who drove the nails into His hands and feet. What makes you think He couldn't forgive you too?"

"My mother calls what I did an abomination."

"Your mother calls not giving ten percent of her paycheck to the church an abomination too. She has no shortage of *abominations* to go around."

I smirked at Courtney's sly wit. "True. She'd probably call my chest an abomination if it didn't look exactly like hers."

"From all of the news reports, it sounds like Pastor Ivy had a million side chicks. Do you think your mother's just overcompensating to cover up her own sin?"

I shrugged. "My mother is way too uptight for something like that. Her universe centered around that church. I think she's just in massive denial."

Courtney didn't look completely convinced, but she dropped the subject. "So, how did the date go with that Zach guy from work? You said he's kind of cute, right?"

"He didn't tell me he was inviting me to a Christian concert, and I felt ambushed by all of his friends from church. I think they call themselves 'Growing on the Vine' or something like that."

"Okay, so the music wasn't so great, but what about after? Monique said she spotted you guys at Burger Palace. Was the rest of the time lame too?"

"Everybody acted like they already knew me, except *Zach* doesn't even really know me. I think he's been stalking my social media accounts."

Courtney grimaced. "Oof! That's gotta be tough. Having Monique grill you about it probably didn't help either."

"Nope," I said, placing *Ex Nihilo* back on my nightstand with some other books. "She had to throw Dylan in my face too."

Courtney shook her head. "Don't let it get to you anymore. Monique only brings it up because she knows it's a trigger. She belittles you for still being upset about it, but she plays dumb about what she's doing. She gets off on making you feel bad about yourself."

"She's supposed to be my friend. Why would she go out of her way to hurt me like that?"

Courtney leveled a steady gaze at me. "Carly, in the four years that we've known Monique Lawson, have you ever met anyone so petty or capable of holding a grudge? She's not exactly kind to Kelsey when her back is turned either, and they're supposed to be best friends. I'm telling you, she's jealous."

I frowned.

"Look, I know we can't afford anything closer to Parkview, but maybe we could try to find an apartment together in Danbury. The commute is a little longer, but I'm really starting to hate living here. I feel like I'm constantly walking on eggshells with Monique."

"Why didn't you say anything sooner?"

She paused. "I was scared you'd pick her over me. You've defended Monique so many times, and I was beginning to wonder if maybe it was just me who had a problem."

"It's not just you," I said, "and Kelsey isn't blind to Monique's faults either. It's just that they've been friends since they were kids."

"What do you think about apartment hunting this weekend?"

"I won't miss needing these," I said, picking up my earplugs. "Sometimes I wonder if Mon is extra loud on purpose."

Smirking, Courtney said, "It wouldn't surprise me in the least. I don't know if you've noticed how Monique has to remind everyone how sexy she is. She posts those stupid selfies constantly because she feeds off the attention."

"I've noticed."

"Good. Now, you just need to stop letting some insecure drama queen make you feel bad about the mistakes you've made. She's not one to talk either, by the way."

"Courtney!" I exclaimed "You're straight fire tonight! What's gotten into you?"

She laughed. "To be honest, I'm not sure. Monique

cornered me as soon as I got home from work, and I just got fed up with her drama and how she treats you. Carly, you're one of the few friends I have where I know you'll always have my back."

Tears smarted in my eyes, knowing that she meant every word.

"I am just ready to start a new chapter in my life," she said wistfully. "Things feel pretty serious with Mike too."

"Has he mentioned getting married?" I asked. "You guys have been together for over a year."

Courtney blushed. "It's definitely come up."

"So, why are you talking to me about getting our own place if you're just going to become Mrs. Yates anyway? You know I can't afford a place on my own."

"Well, he hasn't put a ring on my finger yet, so don't jump the gun. I would never want to leave you high and dry like that. I just don't know how much longer I can stand living here."

I glanced over to the bedside clock. "Well, it's almost eleven, and Monique's not home."

"Happy hour," we said at the same time and then laughed.

"Carly, I know you compare yourself to Monique a lot, but just remember that all of the boozing and sleeping around she's doing now will show up on her face. One day, you'll both be forty, and you'll still have that perfect, heart shaped face, and she's going to look like a dried up, leather wallet."

I burst into laughter at her vivid description.

"I'm not joking!" she said.

"Court, you act like I've led some perfect life. We both know that's not true."

"I know you feel bad about Dylan and the three toads, but Monique has an army of toads and an iron liver. I know you don't believe me, but I have a hard time believing your mother wouldn't look at our so-called friend and not cover her in an avalanche of abominations."

I snickered. "Mike is a good influence on you. It's nice seeing this feistier side of you, my friend."

She looked radiant and in love. "I know I swore I'd never attend a mega church, but going to First Baptist of Parkview was probably one of the best decisions I've ever made. I don't think I would have met Mike otherwise."

"I know," I said, smiling back at her.

"Oh! Did you know that Joe Trautweig goes there? Every time I see him at our Sunday morning Bible study, I think of you."

Immediately thinking of those jade eyes and what they'd done to my insides, I blushed.

Courtney raised an eyebrow.

"I'm just surprised," I said, hoping she didn't notice the tremble in my voice. "What makes you think of me when you see him?"

"You've mentioned the guy so many times that if I didn't know him from church, I'd feel like I knew him just from talking to you."

"Great," I said morosely. "Now I sound like a creeper and I stan the guy."

"I didn't say you were a stalker or anything, and he's got a fan club because of *Tikkun Olam*," she said, referring to Poppy's book. "You might have to take a number to get in line."

"That must be so hard for Joe." I pictured the man I'd met over frozen yogurt fending off a horde of women eager to be adored by him.

"He's got a good sense of humor about it," Courtney said, oblivious to my inner turmoil, "and he's actually a pretty funny guy. If I didn't think you already had a crush on him from the book, I think you could have one in real life too."

"Except that he's a born again Christian," I said, throwing ice water on myself, "and we both know I am far from that."

"Look, everybody has a past, and we only know the version Poppy put in her book. You might be surprised."

CHAPTER 4

MONIQUE MADE HERSELF SCARCE OVER THE NEXT FEW weeks, but she updated social media with pictures of herself and her latest boyfriend. This one was older with some money, so she made sure to flaunt bikini shots of herself on vacation across the Caribbean. Her absence brought some tranquility into our house, and Courtney seemed to lose interest in the apartment search as a result.

I didn't see Joe Trautweig after our initial meeting outside of Let it Fro-yo, and I avoided Zach Perkins as much as possible. He still acted interested, but I did my best to be as unfriendly as professionally possible. Poppy snickered to herself every time she caught Zach hovering around the office. Eventually, she made it a point to tell him I wasn't around before he even opened his mouth to ask.

About a month after the frozen yogurt incident, I walked back into my office from a lunch break and found Poppy and her husband, Jared, in low conversation in front of her desk. They had their heads huddled close together, laughing and talking amongst themselves.

"Hey guys," I said, greeting them and dropping my purse into a desk drawer.

"Carly, always a pleasure," Jared said, straightening up and smiling at me. "Thanks for being the answer to our prayers. You've taken so much stress off of Poppy, and it's been a blessing to our entire family."

I scoffed. "I don't think I'm the answer to anybody's prayers, but thanks anyway."

Poppy and Jared exchanged a knowing glance.

"I know you're not interested in the Sunday night Bible study," Poppy began, "but what about a traditional synagogue? Ryan's Sunday school class is helping to lead the liturgy this Shabbat, and I wanted to invite you to come."

"Synagogue?" I repeated in surprise.

She shrugged. "Why not? Rabbi Cohn is gone, and everybody likes the new rabbi they just hired."

"Oh yeah, the young guy," Jared said. Winking at me, he added, "According to my mother-in-law, he's also very single. You could do a lot worse, kid."

I had to laugh at the absurdity of his suggestion. "Last time I checked, I'm definitely not Jewish. Thanks for the thought, but I don't think so."

"Oh, did I tell you Joe was coming?" Poppy said, turning to Jared. "His niece is in the same class as Ryan."

Jared's jovial expression disappeared. "Is that right?"

Poppy rolled her eyes. "Jared, he told both of us last week at Bible study, remember?" Lowering her voice, she added, "You told me you had no problem with Joe being there. Has something changed since then?"

He responded in an equally hushed tone. "I didn't mind it

when Joe came with that girlfriend he had. I still don't like how he looks at you."

She exhaled a disgusted sigh probably the same way her fourteen-year-old daughter would. "It's ancient history. Everybody seems to have moved on except for you."

Unbidden, the words flew out of my mouth, "I could hang out with Joe. I mean, I know he's a hundred years older than me, but everyone around here seems to think he's a cool guy."

"A hundred years?" Poppy choked. "Carly, you're making us sound like dinosaurs. Forty-two isn't ancient."

"Then thirty-one should mean you guys can stop calling me a kid," I retorted.

Jared studied me, a tiny smile on his mouth. "You know what, Poppy, I don't think it's a bad idea at all. It could be one of those *beshert* moments like in all of your romance novels. Carly's single, Joe's single, and stranger things have happened."

She cracked up laughing at the suggestion, and I did my best to hide my irritation. I felt Jared watching me again.

"It was just an idea," I said, feigning nonchalance. "I've never actually been to a synagogue before. Can't be any worse than First United, right?"

"I forgot about that," Poppy said, sobering immediately. "You poor thing! Even with Rabbi Cohn and his high and mighty attitude, he was nothing like Rebecca's father. Rabbi Zendler is very down to earth, and it will probably be nice to hear someone give a sermon without breathing hell fire condemnation."

"Synagogue is very different than your standard church service," Jared added, trying to reassure me, "but there's no pressure at all here, Carly."

"No, I'm fine. I think it might be interesting to see the differences."

That tiny smirk reappeared on Jared Levine's face, but Poppy remained oblivious.

"Services start at seven thirty," she said. "Beth Tefillah isn't super fancy, but it's definitely not a jeans and flannel church."

"Got it," I said, plopping down into my chair.

"Do you want me to pick up something for dinner on the way home?" Jared asked Poppy before giving her forehead a kiss. "I doubt the kids would mind."

She grinned back. "Sure! We've been so slammed with all of our October 1 renewals. Ryan and Natalie have been complaining about those ready-made frozen meals."

Jared smiled down at his wife, and Poppy beamed back at him. Feeling a tug at my own heart, I wondered if I would ever get a second chance at love like the Levines. Lost in thought, I opened up a spreadsheet for one of our associates and began mindlessly plugging away edits. For the first time in over three years, I felt like I had hope and a future beyond Dylan Greene.

"Carly?" Poppy asked. "Did you hear what I said?"

I shook my head. "No, sorry. What's up?"

"I said that I appreciate you offering to hang with Joe and making things a little less awkward with him and Jared. For the record, I think you'll do just fine keeping up with him. You both are pretty quick witted, come to think of it."

"Do you think Joe is still hung up on you?" I asked, dreading her answer.

She shook her head vigorously. "Not at all. It's still a sore subject for Jared, but you already know why."

I nodded, opting to give less information than more. I had also committed most of Poppy's book to memory, especially the parts involving Joe Trautweig.

"I just want to see Joe happy," she continued. "I didn't really see things going anywhere with the last girlfriend, but I'm proud of him for putting himself out there. The first step is always the hardest."

"Did you have anybody else in mind for him? I mean, I know you've sworn off trying to play matchmaker, but I was just curious."

Poppy paused before answering, studying me instead. "Carly, you know that Joe is a flesh and blood person and not just a fictional character in a book, right?"

"Of course!" I said, somewhat offended.

She eyed me over the rim of her afternoon coffee. "Just checking. If I had known my book was going to make him First Baptist of Parkview's most eligible bachelor, I would have done a better job disguising his identity. The poor guy is fighting off these barracudas with a stick."

"Barracudas?" I repeated. "Is it really that bad?"

Poppy tossed her head back and laughed. "Are you kidding? These women are shameless. They also come up to him like they already know him, quoting my book instead of realizing that I might have changed some details to protect his privacy as well as his ex-wife's."

I cringed, replaying that embarrassing part of my conversation with Joe. It was no wonder he reacted the way he did. He probably assumed I was another groupie confusing fantasy with real life.

At my elongated pause, Poppy said, "I romanticized Joe's first marriage a little too much in my book. That's what I get for thirteen years of R.D. Hampton novels and courtly love. I'm sure most of these ladies probably mean well, but they all think they're the magic cure to mend Joe's broken heart."

"Aren't you the one who says it's nobody's job to fix what's broken inside of us other than ourselves?"

"Exactly," she said, waving her arm dramatically. "Joe knows this too, by the way. When he meets the right person, I have a feeling he's just going to know. And I, for one, will be the first out there leading the celebration parade."

I hid my smirk, wondering if Poppy might have to eat her own words. Exhaling a soft chuckle, I shook my head free of the ridiculous notion that Joe's perfect woman would be the *abomination* known as Hannah Miller's daughter.

As Friday night services approached, I stood in front of my floor length mirror trying to discover what Courtney claimed the rest of the world saw in me. Buxom was an understatement, and I had caught Zach Perkins staring at my chest far too much for my own comfort. I had jokingly lamented to Poppy that even in a turtleneck, I'd still be worried about showing too much cleavage. She just laughed it off and told me to be thankful my back was strong enough to carry my twin blessings.

"Blessings, huh?" I said, staring at myself in the mirror. "More like the perfect way to make sure no man ever actually looks me in the eyes."

For the rare sort like Dylan, my turquoise eyes seemed enough of a draw to something above my neckline. Dylan had complimented my eyes frequently as well as the rest of my cherubic features. When my ex-boyfriend said it, he probably meant my small nose and dark pink lips. For me, it meant the extra pounds of padding also seen on Valentine's Day cupids.

I sucked in my stomach and turned to the side, hoping for a weight loss miracle. I sighed as it only pushed my chest out even further. I tugged at the modest, scoop neckline of my blouse, hoping I wouldn't give Joe Trautweig a free show in the middle of all the Hebrew chanting. Adjusting the floral top over my pencil skirt, I noted that I did have nice legs even though they were short. The lift from my chunky heeled, ankle boots certainly helped.

"Hot date?" Kelsey asked, poking her head in my room. "Is it that guy from Burger Palace?"

"Nope. My coworker invited me to synagogue."

"Synagogue?" Kelsey said, blinking rapidly. "You won't set foot in a church, but you're going to a *synagogue?*"

"Looks like," I replied. "Do you have a problem with that?"

"It just feels like a step backward. You do know that Jews don't believe in Jesus, right?"

I turned to face my roommate. "Kel, I'm not even sure if *I* believe in Jesus anymore."

Carly!" she gasped.

I rolled my eyes. "You barely go to church yourself, and you're the one who's always telling us that you're a backslidden Christian. At least I'm not putting on a show to keep people off my back."

She pressed her lips into a flat line. "So, maybe I'm not exactly living right, but that's not the same as denying Christ. Do you want to go to hell?"

"Go ahead and call me an abomination too," I said coldly. "You're doing a great impression of my mother right now."

I could not have slung a more potent insult at Kelsey if I had tried. "Maybe you need to move out," she threatened. "You're always causing drama with Monique, and I don't want to hear you blaspheming Jesus in my house. I never said that me or Mon are perfect, but what you're saying is beyond extra."

Incensed, I replied, "What do you call the partying you and Monique do almost every weekend? You can look down your self-righteous nose at me all you want, but at least God knows I'm not a two-faced liar. I heard all the same youth group sermons that you did about sex before marriage."

Her nostrils flared. "That's not the same thing as recanting Jesus, and you know it! I don't know what you think you're going to find in that synagogue, Carly, but I hope you're happy. Once this month is over, I want you out. This is still my house, and I get to decide what kind of people I want renting space here."

"Fine with me," I shot back. "Maybe the next time I hear you or Monique screaming 'Oh, God!' you'll actually be praying."

Kelsey slammed my bedroom door, and I glanced up at heaven wondering what I'd just done.

CHAPTER 5

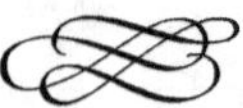

WHEN I ARRIVED IN THE BETH TEFILLAH PARKING lot, I took a moment to breathe and then ground myself using a five-step technique I'd read about online. I replayed the altercation with Kelsey all the way there, no less angry than I was standing in my bedroom twenty minutes earlier. I wobbled when I stepped out of my car, partly from my heeled boots and partly from the remaining adrenaline.

My eyes fell to the street display for the synagogue, and it reminded me of the guiding light that had brought me to Beth Tefillah that evening. I wondered if I had imagined a connection with Joe Trautweig over held hands, winks, and smiles. It felt ridiculous even entertaining the thought, but I couldn't shake Jared's words about the possibility of things being meant to be. I had to ask Poppy later what "beshert" meant after Jared left, and I nearly fell out of my chair when she told me.

"You can do this," I said, pulling my shoulders back. "Kelsey doesn't know what she's talking about." Contrary to my roommate's misguided beliefs, I didn't feel like I was betraying Jesus by being at Beth Tefillah. I had already betrayed Jesus more than two years earlier. In all likelihood, Jesus had forgotten about me and acted like he didn't know me. My mother had told me as much when she called me a rebellious goat who would be cast aside on the Day of Judgment.

I caught the eye of a small family walking toward the synagogue, and the wife smiled impassively while the husband ignored me.

"Just like church," I mumbled, exhaling a sarcastic laugh.

I followed the family toward the main building, walking past a row of knock-out rose bushes. Even with a mild drought, Beth Tefillah clearly kept their landscaping well-watered and healthy. I paused to admire the fuchsia blooms, impressed with how lush they looked. In comparison, the bushes at Kelsey's house were parched and overrun.

Noting that the family entered through a side door, I trailed behind them at a safe distance. I found myself at the end of a long dark corridor with light pouring in from the end of the hallway. The building was so different from First United or any other church I had visited, and I found myself disoriented.

Walking slowly and taking in my surroundings, I stopped in front of a glass window with Judaica displayed on the shelves. A lone light shone inside, illuminating the items.

"Oh," I breathed. My eyes feasted on stunning artwork for sale, toys, religious artifacts, and two more overflowing bookshelves.

"See something you like, dear?" an older woman said, approaching me.

"It's all so beautiful."

She smiled at me, dark eyes lit with amusement. "That's our

gift shop. It's not open on Shabbat, but you're free to come back any time during the week."

"Thank you," I said, eyeing a pewter menorah with golden pomegranate blooms on the branches and base.

"Is this your first time here, dear? I don't think I've seen you before."

"Yes," I said, smiling back in return. "My friend, Poppy, invited me. We're coworkers."

"Oh," the lady said with understanding and a hint of mischief. "Are you one of those Jews for Jesus too?"

I shook my head, chuckling softly. "No, I'm not much of anything. My mother is very religious, but I haven't been to church in a long time."

"I see," she said, appraising me with new eyes. "Well, you're certainly welcome here, my dear. My husband and I helped build this synagogue fifty years ago. Beth Tefillah holds a very special place in my heart."

"What does the name mean? I don't know any Hebrew."

The lady smiled, her face aglow. "It means 'House of Prayer.'"

"I think there's a Christian version," I said. "One of my roommates used to go there."

"Oh, the *goyim* have a copy for a lot of the things we do," she said tolerantly, "but the Bible belonged to the Jews before the Christians came along and played with it. My husband, Murray, loved to read the Bible. It's not such a common thing for many of the Reform Jews, but my Murray was special." Her eyes teared at the mention of her husband.

"He sounds like a wonderful man."

"He was," she sniffled. "I miss him terribly."

"How long ago did he pass?"

"Fourteen years ago, my dear, but it feels like yesterday."

I reached out to touch her arm in comfort. "I'm so sorry."

She placed her wrinkled hand on top of mine and smiled up at me. "It was a wonderful life. I wouldn't trade a minute of that happiness for anything."

I felt tears stinging my own eyes. "I wish I knew what that was like."

"I'm sure you will. You're still young. My name is Hannah," she said, patting my hand.

I blanched, startled that this kind lady shared anything in common with my mother.

"Are you okay, dear?"

I forced a smile on my face. "I'm fine. My name is Carly, by the way. Carly Miller."

"Miller?" she repeated, penciled eyebrows raised. "Are you related to Rick and Diana Miller on our trustee board?"

"No, just my mother," I said. "I've never met my father."

"Oh," Hannah said, looking sad.

"It's okay," I replied. "I know she did the best she could."

Hannah seamed her lips but nodded at me reassuringly. She looped her arm through mine. "You seemed a little lost when I saw you, so why don't I take you to the sanctuary? You said you're here to meet Poppy and her family, *nu*?"

"Yes," I said, smiling at Hannah. "Thank you for helping me."

"Always a pleasure to do a *mitzvah*," she said, guiding me and leaning on me at the same time.

From the corridor, we entered a tiled atrium with a raised ceiling. "Here you are," Hannah said, releasing me. "Marv and Walter are ushering, so they'll help you with anything you need. You can tell them you spoke with me."

"Thank you, Hannah. You were my guardian angel tonight."

She blushed but waved me off. *"Feh,* I'm just an old lady. Don't start with that Christian *mishigas."*

"Carly!" Poppy called, waving me over.

"Looks like your friends found you," Hannah said. "Maybe I'll see you at the *oneg* after the service."

"Sure," I replied, having no clue what an "oneg" was. I counted on Poppy explaining it to me later.

I walked over to the Levines, both of them dressed to the nines.

"Oh, I'm so glad you made it," Poppy said, pulling me into an embrace. Stepping back, she looked me up and down. "Good thing Zach isn't around to drool all over you. Carly, you look incredible! I want to know where you got those boots."

I laughed and blushed.

As Poppy shifted to her left, I locked eyes with Joe Trautweig just beyond her.

I watched his lips form a silent "wow," and it sent a rush of butterflies down to my toes.

"Hi again," I said shyly.

Joe gave me an incredible smile, one that had Poppy looking back and forth between us in confusion. Jared, meanwhile, was grinning ear to ear.

"Have you guys already met?" Poppy asked, her voice sounding squeaky.

"We share a fondness for taro frozen yogurt," Joe said, not breaking eye contact with me.

Poppy began to splutter. "When? How? Carly is this why...why didn't you say anything?"

"Poppy," Jared said sweetly, "since Joe and Carly have clearly been introduced already, why don't we give them some space to get to know each other better?"

"But how…?" her voice trailed off, her hand wagging back and forth between Joe and me.

Jared brushed an arm around his wife and led her away. I watched him speak close to her ear while Poppy glanced back at the two of us one more time. She did not look happy one bit. Jared grinned wider, looking like he'd won the carnival jackpot. He motioned toward his two daughters, Natalie and Madison, to join him and their mother inside the sanctuary.

"That's one way to make an entrance," Joe said. "I think it goes without saying that you look beautiful. Give me one second, and I might be able to find something less off putting to add to the conversation."

"How have you been?" I asked. "You missed out on BOGO fro-yo last week."

"I assume you already had your plus one to get the deal," he replied. "Unless Zach is lactose intolerant or something."

"I'm pretty sure I'm *Zach* intolerant."

Joe's green eyes glowed. "Is that right?"

I cocked my head to the side, catching something in his tone. "Do you know something I don't?"

"Ah," he said with a smirk. "Did Zach forget to tell you that he's your boyfriend? He asked us to pray for you at Bible study and gave us all the impression you were dating."

"Have you been deliberately avoiding me?" I asked, searching Joe's face.

"Guilty as charged."

"Because of Zach? Joe, he's a kid!"

"A kid?" he repeated, that troublesome eyebrow raised once again. "He's two years older than you are."

"How do you know how old I am?"

"Some discreet inquiries. You have a baby face. I didn't want to be accused of robbing the cradle."

"Who's accusing you of anything?"

"Your jealous boyfriend, Zach. He told me to back off, and I did."

I gaped. "Are you kidding? I can't believe I actually felt bad avoiding that toad at work. There has never been and never will be anything going on between me and Zach Perkins."

Joe watched me intently. "That's not what he said."

"That's because he's delusional!" I exclaimed, catching the attention of people around us. Lowering my voice, I said, "The date he claims we went on was a complete setup. He told me it was just a bunch of people meeting up. I had no idea it was a group date."

"I see."

"Look, I have no idea what kind of stories Zach is telling everyone at your Bible study, but it sounds like he's jealous of you."

"Does he have a reason to be?" Joe asked, riveting me with that jade green stare.

"Apparently not," I shot back, "but that was your choice, not mine."

"Carly, what are you saying?"

Not willing to take the bait, I retorted, "Joe, what are you *not* saying?"

"I don't know." He broke eye contact and stared at the patterned, tile floor. "I have absolutely no idea what I'm doing right now."

"I thought you were here to see your niece chant Hebrew," I said coolly.

His gaze came back up to mine. "That's why I'm at Beth Tefillah tonight. Poppy didn't mention you were coming until two minutes before we saw you. I have no ulterior motives for being here." Noticing the blush on my cheeks, he asked, "Why are you here tonight?"

"Poppy invited me."

"And that's it?"

"Would it make a difference?" I asked, the disparity between fantasy and reality colliding together. I quickly realized I preferred the iteration of Joe Trautweig in my head. That version, I could predict.

"Carly, you told me that you went through a bad break up. I've been in this position before, and I know you've read Poppy's version of it."

"I have," I said blandly. I didn't want to mention just how many times I'd read Poppy's memoirs or asked for more details beyond the pages.

"You have to understand why I'd be cautious," Joe said, unnerving me once again with that jade stare, "especially with Zach Perkins acting like I'm hitting on his girlfriend."

My own eyes widened in surprise. "Is that what you were doing?"

"Zach thought so."

"That's not what I asked."

"No, I wasn't hitting on you," Joe said, "but you definitely caught me by surprise. I'd be lying if I said otherwise."

"Meaning what?" I pressed.

"Guys," Jared called from the doorway, "they're starting the service."

I glanced up at Joe, feeling anxious, unsure, and like I'd just made a huge lapse in judgment. I teetered in my boots, suddenly nauseous and light-headed.

Without a word, Joe took me by the arm and led me toward the sanctuary. He handed me a blue prayer book as he stepped further inside. He then grabbed a velvet *yarmulke* from a container on a side table.

"Thanks," I whispered.

He looked at me encouragingly. "We'll figure things out later, Carly. For now, let's remember why we're here."

I nodded, terrified of the path I'd just set for myself and the cost of my own foolishness once again.

CHAPTER 6

I WAS THANKFUL FOR MY OWN PRAYER BOOK SO THAT I wouldn't have to share one with Joe. I could already imagine an accidental brushing of fingers over the pages of the *siddur*. After our embarrassing exchange in the synagogue lobby, I realized my own imagination had led me straight off a cliff. My mind raced with thoughts of how I could beg Kelsey's forgiveness or go back in time to fix the mess I'd created.

I followed Joe toward a row of chairs where the Levines awaited us. Poppy planted herself firmly on my right side with Joe on my left. Jared looked highly amused by the entire situation, and his daughters glanced over at their mother more than once in concern.

"You can follow along with me," Poppy whispered.

"Are you okay?"

"Fine," she huffed. "I just thought you might need some help with the Hebrew."

"I think Carly will be just fine," Jared said, leaning toward his wife, "and if not, she's got Joe to help her."

Poppy glared at her husband while Jared seemed ready to burst out laughing. He winked at me, then deliberately pulled Poppy closer to him.

"I knew this was going to get weird," Joe said low enough for my ears only. He exhaled a heavy sigh. "I'm sorry, Carly."

"Don't be," I said coolly. "She's got her husband sitting right next to her."

He gave me a sidelong glance and hid the smirk tickling at the corner of his mouth. "I knew I liked you," he whispered.

"Pay attention," Poppy hissed next to me. "They're starting on the *bima*."

Joe fought against laughter, pressing his lips together. I realized staring at Joe's mouth was a dangerous idea, and I shifted my attention to the synagogue stage.

"*Shabbat Shalom*," a large man in ceremonial robes said to the congregation.

They responded in kind.

"Is that the rabbi?" I asked Poppy.

She snickered, her dark mood lightening somewhat. "No, sweetie. That's Cantor Allen. He's the one who leads the singing for the congregation. He's practically an institution here."

"Ah," I said, glad to know that Jared Levine wasn't trying to pawn me off on someone twice my age and size.

The next ten minutes was a series of prayers that involved rising and sitting. It reminded me of the one time I had attended a Catholic wedding. After a short series of announcements, it was back to our holy exercise.

"Please rise for the *Sh'ma*," Cantor Allen said.

I glanced around the room, noting that half the people had covered their eyes with their right hand. I looked at Poppy who left her face uncovered, same as Jared and her children.

"They're doing it as a sign of respect for God," Joe whispered just as Cantor Allen began singing in his booming bass. "It's not required."

"*Sh'ma Yisrael Adonai Eloheinu. Adonai echad. Baruch shem, k'vod malchuto l'olam va'ed,*" the congregation chanted in unison. In English, they said, "Hear O Israel, the Lord is our God, the Lord is one. Blessed is the name of His glorious kingdom for ever and ever."

I looked around the room, awed by the words and the unity of people gathered there. I spotted Hannah near the front, her eyes covered. Her devotion to God and to her heritage was palpable. Unlike Hannah Miller, it was clear that the Hannah of Beth Tefillah came to worship God, not the man in the pulpit claiming to speak on His behalf.

I shivered at that revelation, wondering why the truth behind my mother's religious hypocrisy suddenly hit me so hard.

"Carly, are you all right?" Joe asked, turning his face toward me.

I shook my head, trying to stem the flow of tears. The next twenty minutes of the liturgical service passed by in a blur of beautifully chanted Hebrew. I had no idea what any of the words meant, but it touched my heart, nevertheless. Poppy had mellowed considerably once the service started, and it also eased my own tension. She and Jared both closed their eyes through much of the liturgy, clearly soaking in every word. When Ryan Levine came on the podium microphone to chant his portion of the Hebrew prayers, Poppy and Jared looked ready to burst with pride. Little Madison waved to her brother, and Natalie smiled in approval.

When Ryan finished, Jared whispered, "Well done, son."

Another unexpected lump of emotion formed in my throat. I

inhaled a painful breath, acknowledging that those simple words had never parted from my mother's lips. A sudden hunger to know the man who fathered me also welled up inside. My mother had never spoken the man's name, instead telling me that God had granted her a child like Hannah in the Bible. Having learned a long time ago how babies were made, I wondered what youthful indiscretion had transformed my mother into the uptight zealot who raised me.

This time, it was Poppy who leaned in to check on me. "How are you doing? This isn't triggering for you, is it?"

I shook my head and looked at her. "Not the way you think."

She studied my face. "If you need to get some air, I'm happy to go with you."

"I'm fine."

I shifted back in my seat, noting that Joe's arm sat on the armrest between us. The temptation to take his hand in search of comfort set my heart pounding in my chest once again. The anguish of fantasy versus reality, of desire versus fear waged war in my heart. I glanced down at my neckline, realizing that my heaving chest would heave right out of my blouse if I didn't get myself under control.

"Breathe," I whispered. "Breathe, Carly."

Without a word, Joe reached across the seat and took my hand in his. He squeezed it once, warming my ice cold fingers. Surprisingly, his touch helped calm my racing heart rather than excite it further.

"In through your nose, out through your mouth," he whispered, his gaze still focused on the bima in front of us.

Tears filled my eyes. "Thank you."

He pushed his mouth into a tight smile. "Any time."

I forced myself to look away from his handsome profile, inhaling another breath as deeply as my lungs would allow. I marveled at the strange sensation of peace and security I felt with my hand held firmly in Joe's.

The young rabbi Jared had mentioned came forward, and I couldn't argue with Jared's assessment. Studiously handsome would have been a better way to describe him, but he still paled in comparison to the man sitting to my left.

"Shabbat Shalom," Rabbi Zendler said, greeting the congregation in a soft spoken voice.

They responded with their own, "Shabbat Shalom."

He smiled, two dimples forming through his dark beard. His expression was both comforting and inviting.

I found myself smiling in response, immediately followed by the sensation of jade eyes lasering in on me.

Rabbi Zendler surveyed the smattering of congregants, his gaze suddenly stopping on me, narrowing for a moment, then continuing their sweeping motion across the room.

He cleared his throat. "I will be saving my *drash* for tomorrow morning's services, but I was so moved by our *Haftarah* portion that I felt compelled to share a little something with you all this evening."

"The *what*?" I asked Poppy.

"The 'drash' is the rabbi's spiel about the Bible reading and his interpretation of it," she said quickly. "The 'Haftarah' is another Old Testament reading that goes along with the weekly Torah portion."

"What's the Torah?" I whispered to her.

"First five books of the Bible," Jared said, overhearing our conversation. "The rest of the Old Testament is referred to as the Haftarah."

"I've never heard of any of this," I said. "How come they never teach about this in church?"

"Some do," Poppy said, "but most are completely ignorant or even antisemitic. Pastor Ivy falls into the latter camp."

"You're missing the message," Joe said, pulling my attention away from the Levines.

Gently, I tugged my hand free from his. "Thanks."

Reading from a Bible on stage, Rabbi Zendler said, "Sing, O barren, thou that didst not bear. Break forth into singing, and cry aloud, thou that didst not travail; For more are the children of the desolate than the children of the married wife, saith the LORD."

A shiver ran through me from head to foot. My chest constricted once again, and my breathing grew shallow.

"Carly?" Poppy asked, looking at me in concern.

My eyelids fluttered as I struggled to maintain consciousness.

"Carly!" Joe exclaimed, jumping from his seat.

The murmurs of the synagogue worshipers felt like whispered tendrils of smoke.

"Doctor Feldstein," Rabbi Zendler said into the microphone. "We need your help in the back."

"Breathe," Poppy said, holding my hand. "Breathe, Carly."

My heart pounded so loudly in my head, I thought it would burst from my chest. I wondered if this was God finally striking me down for what I had done.

"Stand back," I heard an authoritative male voice say. "She needs space, Poppy."

Some arguing went back and forth above me, and then I felt a hand of strength and comfort holding mine.

"Come back, Carly," I heard, though the voice didn't sound like Joe Trautweig. Instead, something around me broke. The darkness that had held me down for over two years spontaneously combusted. My mind captured the image of shattering glass.

Almost like rising from underwater, the sound level in the room returned to normal. I opened my eyes as if waking from a dream.

I looked up into the unfamiliar face of a Jewish man in his late fifties.

"Welcome back," he said, sitting on his heels in relief.

I glanced from side to side, realizing I had been moved from my seat into the aisle for more air.

"*Baruch Hashem,*" Rabbi Zendler said from just beyond me. I looked up into his blue eyes and saw recognition there. Something finally clicked into place, the reason why his dimpled smile had caused the impromptu reaction from me.

Wryly, he said, "This isn't how I would have planned our middle school reunion, Carly. I'm glad you're all right."

Doctor Feldstein leaned back down to check my breathing. Bringing a stethoscope onto my heart, he listened, his thick eyebrows drawn together in confusion, then wonder. "You sound perfectly fine. If I hadn't seen you collapse, I would never guess anything had happened."

"Can I sit up?" I asked.

"Slowly," Doctor Feldstein said, offering me his arm. As he helped me scoot against the back of a pew chair facing my friends, he turned to Rabbi Zendler and asked, "Rabbi, do you know our patient?"

"Arnold Vellum Middle School," he said, grinning at me.

I smiled back. "Nice to see you, Robbie."

"I go by Rob, now. Or Rabbi, if you prefer."

"Rabbi Rob?" I asked, chuckling. I paused, stunned that my lungs didn't hurt from the exertion.

"Speaking of beshert," Poppy said, looking meaningfully at Jared.

Her husband shrugged and held up his hands in surrender.

"I should go check on Emma," Joe said, referring to his niece. He left without sparing me a glance.

My mouth opened and shut, wanting to say something to the now vacant space in front of the Levine family. I frowned, wondering what had upset Joe and why he suddenly ignored my existence.

Cantor Allen approached Rabbi Zendler. "Do you want to continue the service?"

Rob looked around the room, realizing that our dramatic reunion had the congregation riveted by the wrong subject. "Good idea," he murmured. He nodded to Cantor Allen and followed him back on the stage.

Poppy helped me to my feet, and I joined her in my old seat, already missing Joe.

"That was certainly unexpected," she said, her face aglow with matchmaking delight.

"Everything has been unexpected lately." I wondered what had happened to me and why I wanted so badly to tell Joe Trautweig all about it.

CHAPTER 7

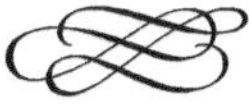

"Joe said he had to leave," Jared announced, joining Poppy and me in the synagogue meeting hall. A small table of refreshments had been set out for the attendees. Apparently, this was what Hannah meant by an *oneg*.

Not bothering to hide my disappointment, I simply said, "Oh."

"Come on, Carly," Poppy said with a cheshire grin. "You know nothing was ever going to happen with Joe anyway."

"Why not?" I demanded.

She looked at me like a child using some flimsy excuse to get out of chores.

"No, seriously," I said, beginning to get angry. "What makes you think I'm not good enough for your friend? What happened to leading a parade when Joe finds the right woman?"

Jared looked at Poppy in surprise. "Did you actually say that?"

"Yes," she said sheepishly, "but Carly, you can't really

believe that Joe's perfect woman is *you*, sweetie. I mean, that's crazy."

I seamed my lips, not wanting to create a scene or lose another close friend that evening.

She noted my sullen expression and tried to take a lighter tone. "Have you noticed that Rabbi Zendler hasn't been able to keep his eyes off of you since we walked in here?"

"Back off, Poppy," Jared said.

She glared at him. "Give me a break! Did you see how they were looking at each other?"

"This isn't one of your romance novels. You and I have had this conversation about Joe and his love life more than once."

"That is *not* what I'm doing," she insisted.

"Joe and Carly have been the ones eyeballing each other all night. You'd have to be blind to miss it." He gave her a quelling look.

Poppy harrumphed, clearly bothered by the idea.

Sensing a storm brewing between the Levines, I said, "I think I'm going to head out. Thank you for inviting me tonight."

"Carly," Poppy said in a pained voice. "I'm sorry I was meddling. Tell me what happened when you blacked out."

I waved her off. "Maybe another time."

I walked on unsteady feet, trying to remember which way led back to the corridor and to my parking space. From behind me, I could hear Poppy and Jared arguing.

"Hey, let me help you," Rob said, coming beside me. "I'll worry about the *yentas* later. Where are you parked? This place is like a maze until you get used to it."

I smiled. "Thanks."

"No problem," he said, returning my smile. "Where are we headed?"

"I parked somewhere near the gift shop. Hannah helped me find my way inside."

Rob smiled wider. "Hannah Birnbaum is an amazing woman. One of a kind. I'm glad you got to meet her. Her husband, Murray, helped build this place."

"That's what she told me."

He led me past the familiar atrium and back toward the darkened corridor. "Ugh, this is something out of a horror movie, hang on a second." He turned back about three feet, flipped on a light switch, and then waited for the fluorescent lighting to kick in.

"Better," I said. "Thanks for that."

"Come on," he said, looping my arm through his.

He opened the door for me, but I refused his arm a third time when he offered to retake it.

"I think I'm okay now." Strangely, I felt the need for distance.

"Are you sure?"

I nodded. "Yes, I promise."

"Can I walk you to your car?"

"Do you really feel like you need to? The parking lot isn't dangerous, is it?"

"No, but when a friend from Vellum drama club passes out in the middle of my sermon, I hope you can understand why I'd want to make sure she makes it to her car on two feet."

I grinned at the memory of our eighth grade school performance. The two of us had played an old married couple for a Mother Goose anthology.

"And don't forget the cream," Rob said, affecting the same wizened accent he'd used as a fourteen year-old.

I laughed. "I don't know how you still remember that."

"Obviously, you do too."

"Only because you brought it up! That feels like a lifetime ago."

"How have you been?" he asked, looking me over. "You're exactly how I remember you."

I didn't want to state the obvious about parts of me that had grown since those days in drama club. Instead, I gestured to Rob's beard. "I didn't recognize you with the facial fuzz."

"Part of the rabbi uniform," he quipped.

"They make you grow a beard?"

He laughed. "Just a little Jewish humor."

"Oh," I said, feeling self-conscious. I halted in front of my black sedan.

"Have we arrived safely at our destination?"

I nodded. "Yes, thank you."

"Carly, would it be okay if I got your number? I don't spend a lot of time on social media, and it's just really nice to see a familiar face. I spent eight years studying in Chicago to become a rabbi, and I just moved back to the area about a year ago."

"Where were you before that?"

"Training and interning at some of the larger synagogues in the Northeast. I did spend time down in South Florida, but that didn't last long. The old rabbi decided to unretire, and the congregation wanted him back."

"Oh," I said, thinking immediately of Taylor Horner and her family. "I know some people who live down there."

"Are they Reform too?"

I shrugged. "I have no idea. They're Jewish, if that's what you mean."

Rob smiled at me patiently. "There are three branches of Judaism: Orthodox, Conservative, and Reform."

"What about the ones who believe in Jesus?" I asked. "Like Poppy and her family?"

He frowned. "They're not considered Jewish anymore. Poppy and her family are tolerated because of her mother, but they're not allowed to proselytize the members here. Natalie Levine's bat mitzvah last year caused a dumpster fire that I'm still putting out."

My eyes widened in surprise. "Do you hate Jesus like the last rabbi?"

"No," he answered easily, "but there are many Christians who love Jesus and also hate Jews. I will never support a religion that embraces antisemitism."

"The Levines don't hate Jews," I argued. "They *are* Jews."

"They're Christians," Rob said, using the word as an insult. "They've turned their backs on Judaism to follow Jesus."

"What do you mean they've turned their backs on Judaism?" I asked, irritated. "Do you worship God, or do you worship your religion?"

Rob's mouth flattened into a straight line. "Jews don't believe in Jesus."

"Clearly, they do," I shot back. "The Levines may not be Jewish to you, but they were chanting all of that Hebrew along with everyone else in the synagogue tonight. Is the only requirement for being Jewish that you don't believe in Jesus? By your definition, that would make me Jewish too."

I expected Rob to respond with equal emotion, but his expression softened. "What happened, Carly? Every time I talked to you in middle school, you were always doing something at church. It seemed like you and your mother lived there."

"We basically did," I admitted, "but that was never my choice. My mother had us there any time the doors were open."

"So, what changed?" he asked, searching my eyes. "Did you realize the idea of God having a son was a ridiculous myth?"

"No," I said tersely. "My mother went to a church full of religious hypocrites. The pastor turned out to be the worst of all. He's a convicted felon now."

"Felon?" Rob gaped. Putting two and two together, he said, "Is he the sociopath that got caught molesting all of those kids?"

I shook my head. "No, my pastor was called 'the holy roller from hell' on the nightly news. One of my coworkers is married to his daughter."

"Wait, wait, wait," Rob said, holding up his hands. "Are you talking about the woman who wrote *Tabula Rasa*?"

"You know about that?"

"Everybody does. I'm friends with the conservative rabbi at Beth Emunah. He just got a ton of new members from Beth Shalom," he said, referring to the messianic synagogue where Jared used to attend. "Rebecca Margolin's book ticked off that entire denomination. It also upset a few pastor friends of mine who serve on our local ecumenical board."

"I'm sure Poppy's book made things even worse for Beth Shalom," I said. "How could you question her loyalty to Judaism or even Beth Tefillah after reading her book?"

"They're still clinging to their Christianity," he clipped.

"They worship Jesus, not Christianity. Believe me, I know the difference. I even saw some of that tonight during the service here."

"What do you mean? What did you see?"

"I watched Hannah cover her eyes during one of the prayers. She has the same name as my mother, but they couldn't be any more different. You could tell that Hannah Birnbaum meant every word that she said. All Hannah Miller does is quote Pastor Ivy or his interpretation of the Bible."

"I see," Rob said quietly.

"I had never heard that Bible passage you read before tonight. It just hit me in the gut. To be honest, I'm not even sure why."

"Why don't you come back for services tomorrow and hear the rest of the *drash*?"

I shook my head. "I think I've embarrassed myself enough for one day. Plus, I have to start looking for a new place to live. My roommate found out I was going to synagogue tonight and basically kicked me out."

"She kicked you out for coming here?" Rob asked incredulously. "Why? Is she one of those antisemitic Christians?"

I smirked. "No, she's one of those sanctimonious hypocrites who holds people to standards she doesn't keep herself. She said I was turning my back on Jesus by coming here."

"Well, we certainly don't worship Jesus," Rob said, mildly affronted. "She's not wrong about that."

"If Jesus is even real, he turned his back on me over two years ago. My mother calls what I did an abomination."

"Carly, what horrible sin could you have possibly committed?" he teased. "What, did you kill someone?"

"Yes," I whispered. I fought back tears at the thought of a child, now two-years-old, that I would never hold.

Rob looked momentarily stunned, then realization dawned. "Oh," he said softly. "I see. Why did you do it? Were you ashamed? Were you in trouble? Was your life at risk?"

"I don't even know why I'm telling you this," I said, sniffling and wiping away a tear. "Poppy and my roommate, Courtney, are the only other friends who know."

"I'm honored," he said, "and if you trust Poppy so much, I understand why you'd be so quick to defend her. That speaks very highly of you, Carly, even if I disagree with your theology."

I stuffed the pain back down and shifted my focus to the

matter at hand. "My mother always quoted this Bible verse about how we need to confess our sins so that God can set us free. I think she just used that verse to control me. She reported my every move to Pastor Ivy, and he would take me aside at church to tell me how I was breaking my mother's heart with my behavior."

Rob looked appalled. "Rest assured, I would never do that to a member of this synagogue. That's beyond disgusting!"

"I agree," I said. "I knew something wasn't right about First United for a long time, but my mother always blew me off. She said I didn't read the Bible enough to contradict her. She also told me that my job was to honor her as my mother."

Rob looked thoughtful for a moment. "The Hebrew word used for 'honor' in that verse is *kabbed*. It means to show weight or deference. In Judaism, we believe that honoring our parents means preserving their dignity."

"So, you're just proving her point," I said bitterly.

"Not exactly. It's more about how you handle yourself when you're confronting your parents, especially as an adult. Have you ever cursed at your mother?"

"No," I said. "Not once. And she has cursed me a million times. Maybe not with profanity, but in all the ways she's told me I'm going to hell, God hates me, Jesus won't forgive me, or everything I do is an abomination if she doesn't approve of it."

"Well, then she's violating the third commandment."

"How do you figure that? My mother thinks if she steps on a sidewalk incorrectly, God will strike her down with lightning."

Rob smiled tolerantly. "The third commandment reads, *Lo tissa et shem Adonai Eloheicha lashav.*"

I shrugged, having no idea what he meant.

"Most Christians translate the verse as 'take the name of

God in vain,' like using it as a curse word, but there's more to it than that."

"How so?"

"The root for the word *lashav* means vanity in the sense of emptiness, to make something worthless or into nothing."

"I'm not following," I said.

"When your mother tells you things about God that are patently false from what the Bible teaches, she's taking the Name of God in vain. When she uses God as her personal hitman, that's also taking the name of God in vain. Carly, you are not required to honor or obey someone who intentionally misuses the Name of God and demands you do the same. According to the Torah, she would have been taken out and stoned to death."

"Wow."

"So, rest assured," he said, placing his hand on my arm, "no matter what sins you've committed or think you've committed, there is no worse sin than misusing the Name of God. I think Christians call it 'blaspheming the Holy Spirit.'"

"Thank you," I said, feeling that familiar albatross of guilt losing its grip on me. "I need to get going, but I appreciate you making me feel so welcome tonight. I'm glad we ran into each other, Robbie."

He smiled at me. "Safe travels, Carly. I hope to see you again soon."

I smiled back. "You never know. If you can tolerate Poppy and her family coming here, you have nothing to worry about from me."

CHAPTER 8

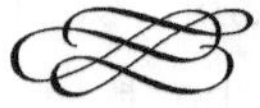

My apartment search was surprisingly less painful than I anticipated. I feared having to sublet another rental space with a gaggle of roommates, but I found an affordable, two bedroom space just off campus from a state university. Poppy insisted on helping me pack and move, offering to be a buffer between me and Kelsey as I vacated her house.

Thankfully, the buffer proved unnecessary since Kelsey went off on another weekend bender with Monique. Courtney had apologized profusely, feeling horrible about our botched apartment search. I told her the diamond on her newly engaged finger wound up being the best situation for both of us. Courtney promised to help decorate to make it up to me, and I intended to take her up on her offer.

Poppy recruited some mutual friends from the Margolin Bible study for the heavy lifting, including Kyle Goldstein and some other guys. I didn't bother to ask if Joe would be a part of their small moving party, and I knew Zach Perkins would not be invited either. Word got back about what he'd done to my reputation, and the mighty Margolin asked him to leave their Bible study group.

I stood inside of my new living space, looking over the couches I had found at my favorite thrift store. I didn't mind the few scratches on the burgundy leather sofa and loveseat as they were easily covered with throw pillows and a blanket. Kyle Goldstein and his wife gave me some end tables they no longer needed, and the Margolins donated a storage coffee table that lent an eclectic, shabby chic vibe to the entire living space.

"Do you need any artwork?" Poppy asked, looking over my family room filled with unopened boxes.

I glanced at the white walls. "Courtney is the one with the interior design degree, and she knows about all of these hole-in-the wall antique stores. I might buy some of those sticky hooks and see what I can find at Sally Sells Resales."

Poppy smiled. "I really liked meeting Courtney. She seems like a good friend."

"She is," I said, returning her smile. "I'm not happy about how the situation happened, but I think this is definitely the best thing for me. I hated living there, but I didn't think I could afford a way out."

"Nice job getting $75 off the rent, my friend."

I grinned. "Well, I'm definitely more stable than their university clientele, so there's that. I leave all the wild partying to those two hypocrites back at the house."

Poppy seemed to note the bitter tone in my voice and switched topics. "My mother said Hannah Birnbaum mentioned your name at their last women's meeting at synagogue. You made quite an impression."

"I'm shocked she remembered me. Maybe it was the fainting spell."

Poppy rolled her eyes. "No, Carly, it was you. Beth Tefillah isn't quite the happening, Jewish hotspot it was thirty years ago. Most of the people who attend now are related to the old guard who helped found the place. My mother hopes that bringing in Rabbi Zendler will attract a younger crowd to keep the synagogue going after they're all gone."

"What makes Rob so different from the last rabbi?"

Poppy raised a brow over my use of Rabbi Zendler's first name, but she kept her thoughts to herself. "He just comes with a different approach than Rabbi Cohn."

"To be honest, I don't think he likes your family much more than the last guy. I know Rabbi Cohn was really antagonistic toward you, but it seems like Rob is just tolerating you guys for your mother's sake."

Poppy exhaled a mirthless laugh. "Jared and I are well aware. Thank God for my mother," she said, shaking her head with a grin. "I can see God working on her heart, but her clout in the synagogue has been a bigger blessing than we could have imagined. I'm so thankful my kids are getting a Jewish education."

"Speaking of," I said, gesturing for Poppy to join me on the couch, "can you explain something to me? Rob, er Rabbi Zendler, mentioned it, but I wanted to get your take."

"What's up?"

"Well, he kept harping on you guys abandoning Judaism, which I don't see at all. It sounded more like you had defected to a different team, if that makes sense. I told him that if all it took to be Jewish was to *not* believe in Jesus, then that would make me Jewish too."

Poppy smirked. "It's a common accusation, and I used to throw it at Jared before I got saved two years ago."

I winced at the word "saved," reminded of my mother and a lifetime of Bible thumping.

"Can I share something interesting that I've discovered, Carly?"

Shaken from painful memories, I looked into Poppy's dark eyes. They held nothing but tender, motherly regard for me. I smiled back. "Sure."

"Some people think the hardest thing in the world is evangelizing to Jewish people. Martin Luther's antisemitic writings came from his frustration that he couldn't win the Jews over to Christianity."

"I didn't know he was antisemitic."

Poppy grimaced. "He helped inspire Hitler and the Nazis. Luther called Jews vermin who deserve to have our synagogues and Torahs burned. It just gets worse from there."

"That's horrible!" I gasped, immediately thinking of Beth Tefillah's beautiful sanctuary.

Poppy inhaled and exhaled deeply. "A lot of Christians aren't comfortable talking about the long history of antisemitism in the church, but it was a favorite topic of Rabbi Cohn. Like most anti-missionaries, he conflates the hypocrisy and antisemitism of Christians as being synonymous with Jesus."

"Is that why so many Jews don't want to hear about Jesus? I mean, it makes sense, if I'm being honest. Even Kelsey has this condescending attitude about Judaism, and she's about as heathen as they come."

Poppy frowned. "Christian hypocrisy and persecution has always been the biggest objection I've heard. But, I'll tell you what's even harder than trying to share the gospel with a Jewish person is trying to share it with people like you."

"You mean, because of what I did?" I said, hurt and betrayed. "I can't believe you're throwing that in my face!"

Her eyes went wide in horror. "No, no, no, don't misunderstand me! I'm talking about how you were raised."

"What do you mean?" I demanded, still feeling resentment.

"Carly, you know all the talking points already. You know the apologetics and terminology that Christians like to use. You've heard your mother and Pastor Ivy twist the Bible to beat you into submission. You were raised in a place that should have taught you about Christ and then helped you to grow and flourish in your faith. Instead, the hypocrisy turned you completely off from God. Your mother also showed zero forgiveness or grace for your mistakes. It's just condemnation with no love at all."

Tears filled my eyes.

She reached out a hand to my arm. "I know, sweetie. I know that as much as I may talk about what Jesus is doing in my life, you don't believe that He would ever do something like that for *you*. I watch you struggle wanting to believe it, but not being able to reconcile it with everything you've suffered from your mother and Pastor Ivy."

"What I did," I mumbled through tears. "It's unforgivable. I think about it every day. I can't stop thinking about it. It's one of my mother's abominations that I actually agree with."

Poppy remained silent for a moment before she answered, and instinctively, I knew she had been praying. "Carly, if you could go back in time and do it all over again, would you?"

"No!" I exclaimed.

"Sweetie, that right there already separates you from Pastor Ivy."

Caught off guard by her remark, my tears dried.

"What do you mean?"

"Pastor Ivy is still denying he did anything wrong, even with hard evidence corroborated by his elder, his daughters, his wife, and his victims. As far as we know, your mother still believes he's innocent, or she has all of these excuses to justify what he's done, right?"

"Yeah."

"But she disowned you when you confessed about the baby."

"Yes," I whispered.

Poppy whipped out her cellphone and opened her Bible app. "Carly, I want to read something to you. I think it will help explain where I'm coming from with this."

"Okay," I said warily, bracing myself for more judgment.

Reading from the screen, she said, "If we say that we have no sin, we are fooling ourselves, and the truth is not in us. But if we confess our sins, God will forgive us. We can trust God to do this. He always does what is right. He will make us clean from all the wrong things we have done. If we say that we have not sinned, we are saying that God is a liar and that we don't accept his true teaching."

My jaw fell open. "It really says that?" I asked.

She held out her phone for me to see.

My hands trembled, and I dropped her phone onto the couch.

"Carly, are you okay? Are you having another breathing attack?"

I inhaled slowly through my nose and out through my mouth. When the trembling continued, I tried my five-step technique to ground myself.

"Carly?" Poppy asked. "Do I need to call an ambulance? Can you hear me?"

With measured breaths, I said, "I'm okay. Just give me a second."

Her lips moved silently, praying for me once again.

I opened my eyes and met the dark gaze looking at me in concern.

"That verse," I finally said. "The one about confessing our sins. My mother quoted it all the time. She would repeat anything I told her to Pastor Ivy, and then I'd get another lecture from him about God hating what I was doing and how I was dishonoring my mother."

"I can only imagine how horrible that was," she said. "I've heard some of the stories Rebecca did not find fit for print."

"It just hit me, when you read it."

"What did?"

"How my mother used that verse to bully me for so long, but she won't apply it to Pastor Ivy...or herself."

"But there's more," Poppy said, "and this is what I want you to see, sweetie."

"What?"

"Do you see where it says that anyone who claims they are without sin is calling God a liar? That anyone who claims they are sinless can't possibly have God's true teaching?"

I re-read the verses on her phone. Looking up, I asked, "So, what are you saying?"

"What I'm saying is that based on your mother and Pastor Ivy's behavior, would the Bible say they have the true teaching of Christ? Based on what these verses say, are *they* forgiven of their sins? Carly, your mother won't even admit that she got pregnant outside of marriage. She still hasn't confessed *her* sin."

"That doesn't make what I did okay."

"You're right," she said gently, "but the fact you feel remorse about it shows that you are so much closer to God than those two will ever be."

"What?" I gasped.

"Read it again," Poppy said. "Carly, you're not going around pretending you're a victim of your own sin or calling yourself Hannah of the Bible," she added with an eye roll. "Your struggle with God is that you don't think He loves you because of your past. Meanwhile, your mother and Pastor Ivy are completely unrepentant about their own sins."

"Meaning what?"

"Meaning that their phony good works and abomination name calling don't erase their own denial. Despite appearances, I am telling you that you are closer to God than they are."

"How is that even possible?" I asked, dumbfounded. "My mother reads the Bible for hours a day. She's constantly listening to sermons or Christian music. She's conservative, pro-life, you name it. Yes, she made a mistake with whoever my birth father is, but I've never seen a man in her life since."

Poppy raised an eyebrow.

"What?"

"There's been *one* man in her life," she said. "One man that she worships above any other. One man she's been devoted to for over thirty years. One man who can do no wrong in her eyes, even when the wrong is as plain as the nose on her face."

"No way! That's crazy!"

"Look, I'm not trying to insinuate that anything happened between the two of them sexually, but it sounds like your mother was in love with Pastor Ivy."

"But he's married!"

"And?" Poppy said flippantly. "He was still married when he carried on all of his affairs and justified it to his head elder. Oh, what was it that Rebecca wrote? Do you remember?"

I thought back to Rebecca's memoirs, having memorized nearly as much of it as Poppy's. "It was something about one of the wives being loved the way a woman truly deserves," I said with revulsion. "My jaw fell on the floor when I read that in her book."

"Because it was so different from the man you saw in the pulpit?" she asked.

"No," I replied, "because I could hear his voice in my head and exactly how he would have said it."

"Wow."

"If my mother knew that I work with the husband of Pastor Ivy's daughter, she'd lose her mind. She never liked Rebecca and used to make fun of her when I was younger. She called her a little pig."

Poppy tsked in disgust. "Probably just following her boyfriend's lead."

I pursed my lips. "He wasn't her boyfriend, Poppy."

"I meant it figuratively," she retorted. "Rebecca is one of my closest friends. Her father is a monster."

"I was there. I remember."

"I know," she said, exhaling a weary sigh. "I won't bring it up again, Carly, but I just wanted you to see the difference between you and them."

"What difference does it make? Sin is still sin, right?"

"Your mother and Pastor Ivy won't come to Jesus because they don't believe they need to be forgiven. In their own eyes, they've done nothing wrong. It's other people who are wrong for pointing it out."

I nodded, amazed to hear someone else perfectly describe the situation.

"Carly, you're aware of your sin every single day. They *deny* their sin every day. Look at that verse one more time and tell me again which one of you is closer to God."

I read it, feeling hope flutter in my heart for the first time in so long.

"Yes," she said gently. "God is faithful. He's just. Not only can He forgive you, but He'll make you clean."

"It seems too good to be true. I know what I did."

"So does He," she replied. "He's waiting for you whenever you're ready."

CHAPTER 9

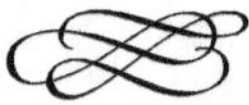

After my heartfelt conversation with Poppy, she let the matter rest. I wasn't sure if she'd go guns blazing back to work on Monday, but she simply smiled over the rim of her Vincenzo's cup and asked how the apartment setup was coming along.

"Good morning, ladies," Phil Robbins said, stopping by our office carrying doughnuts. "Apparently, I've been downgraded from CEO to delivery boy, but I thought I'd offer up these goodies before I leave it open for the vultures in the break room."

Poppy laughed and grabbed herself a powdered, cream-filled goodie.

"Carly?" he asked, lifting the box toward me.

I shook my head.

"New diet?" Phil asked. "I never know with the ladies around here, but I thought I'd at least offer."

I smiled. "Sort of."

"I think Carly prefers frozen yogurt," Poppy said, winking at me around a mouthful of her doughnut.

I blushed, wondering when and how Poppy had relented from her earlier disapproval of me and Joe Trautweig.

Phil looked back and forth between the two of us, clearly eager to be in on the joke. "Is that why our newest Benefits Producer has been stalking Let it Fro-yo? I thought maybe Zach was low on probiotics and needed the intestinal boost."

Poppy choked and nearly spit her coffee out through her nose. She swallowed quickly, then began a coughing fit.

"Occupational hazard," Phil said, handing her a tissue. "That filter people say you're supposed to have gets much smaller with age."

Hoarse, but fully recovered, Poppy said, "Like you ever had a filter to begin with, Phil."

Our CEO pretended to be affronted before he grinned. "Eh, guilty as charged. I guess I should be grateful Culver doesn't have to pay for a new set of monitors," he said, gesturing toward Poppy's desk. "That coffee had one destination in mind."

Poppy and I both laughed, and I suddenly realized how little I had done that in my life. One of my favorite things about Dylan was the goofball side of him and how fearless he was. He didn't care if a room full of people thought he was a complete idiot as long as he could make me laugh. Expecting to feel my old depression again, I was surprised when the memory didn't remove the smile from my lips.

"Carly?" Poppy asked, pulling me from my thoughts. "You went off to la-la land for a second there. Everything okay? The big bad CEO took his evil sweets to the break room, so the coast is clear."

I scanned the office quickly to verify. "Yeah," I said, surprised. "I'm okay."

She raised an eyebrow. "You definitely seem different. Usually, when I watch you go into your shell, you come back out with this haunted look in your eyes."

"Well, that's not humiliating at all," I deadpanned.

"Just an observation. You know there isn't any judgment from me. You just seem a lot lighter, and I don't mean the no doughnut policy."

I glanced down at my reduced stomach pooch. "Coping with sugar has always been a weakness of mine. Yesterday, I would have grabbed a doughnut and probably snuck a second one later. Today, I don't know. It feels different."

"Are you planning to get frozen yogurt?" she ventured.

"You mean, am I planning to stalk Joe Trautweig the way Zach is apparently stalking me?"

Poppy shrugged innocently, but her sparkling eyes said otherwise.

"What changed for you?" I asked, flipping the spotlight onto my coworker. "I thought you were totally against the idea."

She sighed. "My husband and I had a few words."

"Oh," I said, concerned. "Did you get in trouble?"

She laughed and waved me off. "No, not like that. I needed to be reminded that it's not my job to do God's job. And as much as I didn't want to see it, I have to admit to being a little jealous."

"Jealous?" I gaped. "Why? You and Jared are happily married now. Why in the world would you be jealous?"

Poppy glanced down at the half-eaten doughnut on her desk and sighed. "It was wrong of me, and I'm ashamed of myself."

"But why?" I pressed. "You have everything you ever wanted. Why do you need Joe too?"

"I don't! I am in love with my husband, don't misunderstand me. I just never considered the possibility of two people I consider friends no longer needing me as their connection. I also kind of liked being able to play matchmaker...and deciding who would be good enough for Joe," she added quietly.

"Gee, thanks."

She looked remorseful. "It was wrong, Carly. So wrong. The reasons why I thought the two of you didn't suit had nothing to do with you personally."

"Mmhmm," I said, not buying a word of it.

"The truth is that I liked pretending I was in control. I liked the idea of playing God and fashioning a woman of my own design. I didn't want to take my hands off the steering wheel or let God decide what was best for everyone. Just speaking it out loud, I can see how arrogant and ridiculous it was. I'm so sorry."

I watched Poppy, not sure if she had more to confess or if I could handle listening to it.

She looked down at the floor and then back up, her eyes moist with tears. "You have so much pain already, and I hate that I caused you more. If you want, I can talk to Joe and apologize."

I held up my hand. "I think you've done more than enough."

"I'm so sorry, Carly."

"I know," I replied. "I just need some air."

I left her with a grim smile before I found my way to the elevators. Let it Fro-yo wouldn't open for another hour, and my stomach felt too knotted for yogurt regardless. Needing to work off some steam, I marched over to Vincenzo's. Poppy and Jared had given me a gift card for Christmas, but I had procrastinated on finally trying their Italian roast coffee for myself.

I walked into the small storefront, hoping to discover why

the place engendered such loyalty from my coworkers. With travertine floors, terracotta paint, and mahogany tables and coffee bar, Vincenzo's had that "old world feel" Poppy always gushed about. At the same time, the modern world also existed inside the cafe. A large sign with the wifi password sat just inside the front door. Stuffed chairs alternating between brown leather and chartreuse colored velvet reminded the Vincenzo's faithful that they had entered an American coffee shop, not a *trattoria*.

Surveying the room, I noted a pretty brunette pushing a stroller back and forth. When her honey brown eyes briefly met mine, I smiled at the thought of finally encountering Jessica Goldstein, now Jessica Ballinger. Leaned in close to her was a man I assumed was her husband, Micah.

"Small world," I muttered.

"Indeed," I heard from my right.

I grinned before turning to face those jade eyes. "Fancy seeing you here," I said to Joe, "but to be fair, I can't get any frozen yogurt until ten."

He glanced at the oversized wall clock. "Shouldn't you be at the office right now?"

"I should, but I suddenly had a craving for..." my voice trailed off as I looked at the specials menu and purposefully mispronounced the name of the featured drink.

Joe laughed, his eyes crinkling on the sides. "Your Italian is impressive."

"*Grazi,*" I responded in actual Italian.

The barista took notice of the two of us, made quick eye contact with Joe, and then darted his gaze over to me.

"It's on me," Joe said to the barista. "This is Carly's first time here, Niccolo. Get her whatever she wants."

Niccolo grinned. "What would you like, *signorina?*"

I shrugged. "I honestly have no idea. I'm not a big coffee person."

"How about a cappuccino?" Joe suggested. "It won't be quite as strong as a regular coffee, but it's not a total milk bath like a latte."

"Sounds good," I said.

Joe stepped past me and pulled out some cash from his wallet. He dropped his remaining change and dollar bills in the tip jar. Niccolo nodded approvingly.

"Thank you," I said to Joe.

"My pleasure." He turned and waved at Jessica and her husband before ushering me toward a set of leather chairs.

"Joe!" Jessica called. She walked over and embraced him warmly. "Nice to see you."

"You look great," he said. His eyes quickly shifted to the baby stroller. "Motherhood suits you."

She smiled and then looked back at her husband. "That's Micah," she said with an incredible sparkle in her eyes. She glanced at me and then back at Joe. "Hi. Are you a niece of Joe's?"

Niccolo coughed from behind the bar, hiding a laugh while he placed my order on the pick-up shelf.

Joe made a quick escape to fetch my drink.

"I'm Carly," I said, extending my hand to her. "I work at Culver."

"Oh," she said, her expression falling. "Do I even need to ask?"

"I work with Poppy."

Some of the joy returned to Jessica's eyes. "I haven't seen her around much since I had Aria," she said, looking over her shoulder once again at Micah and her daughter. "Please, tell her I said hello, and that I'll text her soon to meet up."

I nodded, not trusting myself to say much else regarding my coworker.

"Your cappuccino," Joe said gallantly, handing me the to-go cup.

I smiled. "Thanks."

Jessica now watched the two of us more critically. Noting what Jared Levine claimed the world would be blind to miss, she hid a furtive grin of her own. "Good to see you, Joe," she said, clapping him lightly on the arm. "Carly, it was nice to meet you."

"Likewise," I said, genuinely smiling at her.

"Those books," Joe groaned. He took a long sip of his coffee before sighing heavily and sinking into one of the chairs.

"I don't think I would have met you without those books," I said, "so we can be thankful for that, right?" I sat down opposite him and smiled.

He watched me for a moment. "Are you really glad that you met me?"

"Why wouldn't I be?"

Our eyes met and locked, and my heart began that familiar cadence that seemed to beat only for Joe. "Breathe," I whispered.

Joe's eyes widened in alarm. "Carly, are you okay? Do you feel like you're going to pass out? Do you need to lie down?"

I shook my head, my eyes riveted to his. He knelt beside me and laid his hand on top of mine, and I felt the same peace and calm that had comforted me in the Beth Tefillah sanctuary. I glanced down at our connected hands and then back at Joe.

"I don't understand," he whispered, staring into my soul it seemed. "This doesn't make any sense."

I exhaled a short laugh and fought the urge to lean my face

forward just a few more inches. I wondered if a kiss with Joe would be different than Dylan or the three toads.

"How can you look at me like that?" he asked. "I'm old enough to be your—"

"Boyfriend?" I interrupted. "That's the only word that would be appropriate here, Joe. You're not half dead with a foot in the grave, and I graduated from high school a long time ago."

He smirked, releasing my hand, and getting up from the floor. He sat back down in his chair, releasing a shaky breath.

"This shouldn't be happening," he said.

"Why not?"

"Don't you have a rabbi ready to join your list of admirers?"

"Yes, but that doesn't mean I'm interested in the rabbi."

"I thought you were old friends," he said, watching me in that searching, intimate way of his. His eyes traced over every feature on my face as if physically touching them.

"Joe," I whispered.

"Don't say it."

"I'm not Poppy." I met his eyes and challenged him to stay in the moment with me. "I'm not sitting here with Robbie Zendler. I'm not thinking about Dylan Greene. I'm here with *you*. Nobody else."

CHAPTER 10

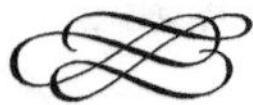

"WHAT DO YOU WANT FROM ME?" HE ASKED.

"For one, you could lighten up. I just want to get to know you. I'm not asking you to give me 'til death do us part.'" I paused to savor the delicious flavors in my coffee cup. "Joe, I think you may have started me down a very slippery slope with Vincenzo's. You're not going to be able to get rid of me now."

The break in tension gave him the moment of air he needed. He watched me, bemused. "I'm glad you're enjoying the cappuccino."

"Of all the things my mother didn't want me to try," I mumbled, shaking my head.

"Your mother? Why wouldn't she want you drinking coffee?"

"Because anything not approved by Bernard Ivy or First United of Hillcrest is an abomination," I said with an acerbic smile. I watched and waited for Joe to make the connection.

"Are you talking about Rebecca Margolin's father? How are you mixed up in all of that?"

"My mother took me to First United since infancy. She said Pastor Ivy was willing to welcome her into the church when she found out she was pregnant with me. I literally grew up there."

"Wow," Joe said, that familiar stare now seeing me anew. "Do you and Rebecca know each other?"

"Only through working with Ted. I'm actually closer in age to her little sister, Ada, but Rebecca and I weren't friends. My mother never liked her, but that was because she followed Pastor Ivy's lead. If the man had told her to drink poison, my mother probably would have done it."

"Back up for a second," he said, his green eyes bright. "You said your mother found out she was pregnant?"

"Yes."

"So, where was your father?"

I shrugged. "My mother pretends I was some miraculous conception. Her name is Hannah, so she goes around acting like she was Hannah of the Bible who prayed to have a child."

Joe frowned. "That's strange."

"I didn't know any better for a long time. My mother was so brainwashed by that church, and I had no choice about going until I was a teenager."

"Where is your mother now?"

"She still lives in the same trailer I grew up in. I haven't talked to her in a few years, but I can't imagine her ever leaving that place."

"Why haven't you talked to her?" he asked.

I waited for the albatross of shame to land firmly around my neck. I nearly welcomed that familiar enemy, so used to its presence in my life. Instead, I felt a strange sense of peace and resolution. Poppy was right. Something had definitely changed.

"Carly?" Joe prompted, eyeing me in concern.

"Long story," I said, not willing to ruin the moment or his opinion of me.

He nodded slowly. "So, where are you with God or religion in general?"

"Still figuring that out."

My cell phone chimed from my purse, and it shook me from the momentary fantasy that no world existed outside of Vincenzo's. I frowned, reading the message from Poppy. I didn't want to think about her jealousy when the object of her self-appointed matchmaking sat in front of me.

"Duty calls?" Joe asked, eyeing the wall clock once again.

"I needed a break. Looks like it's over. As usual, the mighty Margolin is keeping us up to our eyeballs in work."

Joe nodded in understanding, a former coworker of Ted's himself. "I need to get to the office too. Since Cooper & Jaye is next door, can I walk you back?"

I beamed at him, and those pale eyes reached into my soul and pulled out a piece of me with them. I fought the urge to leap out of my chair and wrap my arms around his neck.

Instead, Joe stood up and held out his hand. Smiling and taking it, I followed him out of the coffee shop. I felt the eyes of Jessica Ballinger and Niccolo trail us out the door.

I expected Joe to release my hand once we stepped outside, but he didn't. Instead, he pulled me closer to him, inspecting our joined hands together. He brushed his thumb lightly across my knuckles.

I felt lightheaded, but not from a panic attack.

"Carly," he breathed.

After a moment of locked eyes and shortened breath, Joe seemed to come back to his senses. He shook his head and released my hand.

"I don't know what I was thinking. I'm too old for this, and you're too young to know any better."

"Joe?" I asked, unable to hide the sob in my voice.

"I'm sorry. You shouldn't be here with me. Make a go of it with Rabbi Zendler or somebody your own age. I've got my own baggage and demons to deal with. You don't need any of this."

Summoning courage I didn't know I had, *chutzpah*, as I'd heard Poppy say on more than one occasion, I took a step closer toward Joe Trautweig. Wasting no time, I pulled his face down and proved I was no innocent school girl. What started as initial resistance on Joe's part melted into arms pressed around me and a low groan.

"Carly," he said against my mouth.

My fingers found their way into his hair, and senses long dead since the days of Dylan resurrected inside me. I didn't want the kiss to end. I also didn't want to think about the consequences of where kisses and caresses had led three years earlier. All I wanted to do was enjoy every second wrapped securely in Joe Trautweig's arms.

"Carly," Joe said again, this time with gravitas rather than passion. He pulled away from me. "We have to stop."

I looked up at him, his hair mussed, pupils dilated. "What are you scared of? Poppy? Anything that happens between us is absolutely none of her business."

"No," he said, gently removing my hands from his face. "I'm scared of history repeating itself."

"So, it *is* Poppy." My arms fell heavily to my sides.

"Carly, I haven't felt like this since I met Catherine," he said, surprising himself as much as me with that admission.

"Oh."

"I don't know how to process what's happening." He raked a

hand through hair that had been thoroughly tousled by me already.

I smiled, realizing it was a nervous habit of his.

"Why are you looking at me like that?" he asked.

"You're kind of adorable when you're flustered."

Joe paused, staring at me as if I was a ghost. "Is any of this real?"

"Do you want me to kiss you again to prove it?"

He held up his hands. "No, I shouldn't have let this happen."

"Stop acting like you're taking advantage of me. I'm the one who came onto *you*, and not because of Poppy's dumb book. I like you. I like how I feel when I'm around you. I like how your arms feel around *me*."

"You're bold," Joe said. "Face of an angel, kiss like—"

"The devil?" I finished for him, feeling shame but not because of my past. "I forgot that you believe in all of that Christian stuff."

"And you don't," he said with a note of sadness.

"Clearly," I said self-deprecatingly. "An abomination, just like my mother said."

"Stop! It was a kiss, not some abomination. You caught me by surprise, but nothing happened that I didn't want to happen. Nobody held a gun to my head."

"Why did you do it?" I asked. "If you're so convinced that this is all wrong, why did you let me kiss you? Why did you kiss me back?"

"Because I wanted to!" His soulful eyes eviscerated any pretense I might have used to protect myself. "I wanted to kiss you the first day we met."

"Then why did you abandon me at Beth Tefillah?"

"Because I saw you with Rabbi Zendler. I saw you smile at

him and the way he looked back at you. I felt like a dirty old man wanting something that belongs to someone else."

"I don't belong to anyone! You're scared, Joe. Do you think I'm going to lead you into temptation?"

"You're already a temptation." He leveled me with his jade eyes.

"But it's more than that," I replied, now giving Joe Trautweig a dose of his own medicine. I peered at him just as intently. "You had enough self control to stop just now. You had enough self control to walk away from Poppy when she threw herself at you before she got back together with Jared."

I expected Joe to look distressed at the reminder, but he continued to hold his gaze steady with mine.

"Keep going," he said tautly. "Apparently, you've got me all figured out."

"I'm not Catherine. I'm not going to go cuckoo and hurt myself."

He winced, and I hated myself at that moment.

"You're right that you're not Catherine," he said coolly, "and I'm not some twenty-one year-old head over heels in love."

"Then why did you kiss me back? You said you kissed me because you wanted to. *Why* did you want to kiss me, Joe?" I glanced down at my chest and then back at his eyes in silent accusation.

He looked angry. "I don't have an explanation that makes sense. I feel like an idiot. A forty-two-year-old idiot taking advantage of a young girl who thinks she's in love with a character in a book."

"Not anymore," I spat, disgusted with myself and with Joe's indecisiveness. "You need to figure out what you want instead of leading me on one second then running away the next. I can't keep up with the hot-cold routine you have going on."

"Nor should you," he replied morosely. "You can do a lot better than me, and I don't understand why you keep pursuing this."

"What do you want?" I asked, daring those jade eyes to unnerve me. "Not, what do you think is the right thing to do. Not, what are you afraid is going to happen. What do you actually want, Joe?"

"What do I want?" he repeated.

"Yeah. What do you actually want?"

He looked at me for a long minute, but I held my ground. "What I want, Carly, is what I shouldn't have."

"And what if you could have it?"

"Then, it would still be wrong. The mistake I almost made with Poppy was because I didn't know any better. Now, I do. I don't want to kiss you or any other woman like that unless I'm doing it as a husband."

"A husband?" I choked.

"And that is not a marriage proposal, by the way."

I waved him off. "I already told you I wasn't looking for any of that."

"Carly, I don't know what happened that caused you to turn your back on God, but I can't allow anything to happen between us unless I know we're walking on the same path."

I pursed my lips, the sound of Pastor Ivy in my head. I inwardly raged at the hypocrisy and corruption of a man who had chastised me for sexual impurity while he'd carried on affairs for decades. I wanted no part of the hypocritical Christian lifestyle. As much as I wanted to rail at Joe for rejecting me, part of me was thankful he wasn't like Kelsey or Monique.

"Why did you walk away from God?" he asked softly, watching me again.

"He walked away from *me*."

"I can't believe that, Carly. I tried to kill myself, and God raised me out of a coma to save my life. I don't think for one second that God ever abandoned you."

"I never walked with God," I admitted. "I faked it for my mother, but when I'd see her raise her hands in church then gossip behind those same hands an hour later, I couldn't believe any of it was real. I didn't want anything to do with Jesus if it meant being like her."

"I'm sorry, Carly."

"Don't be. I didn't become a bitter, dried up prune like her. I had fun. I had a life outside of that rotten corpse she calls a church. I hate that place. I hate everything it represents. I don't pretend to be perfect or some moral holy roller, but no one will ever accuse me of being a hypocrite."

"Are you happy?" Joe asked, searching my face. "You choose to live the opposite life as your mother, but you still have guilt about something in your past."

I pressed my lips together, unwilling to share what I knew he was asking.

"Look," he said, "I can't pretend there's not a connection between you and me that I don't fully understand. I also can't pretend there's not a distance that even one incredible kiss can't fix."

"It was incredible, wasn't it?" I murmured, lightly touching my mouth.

Joe's gaze followed my fingers then he exhaled a harsh breath. He ripped his eyes away from me. "Was that on purpose?"

I shook my head. "For the record, I've kissed quite a few toads."

He looked back at me, troubled and also disappointed. At that moment, I knew that closely guarding my secret was the best decision. I couldn't bear to see Joe look at me with the same disgust that Dylan had.

Gathering my last bit of dignity, I said, "None of them have ever kissed me like you just did. Whoever you wind up marrying, Joe Trautweig, is going to be a very lucky woman."

CHAPTER 11

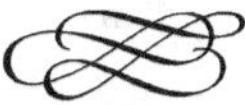

When I walked back into the office, Poppy took one look at me and knew something was amiss. I winced in anticipation of her questions, but the deluge of work requests kept the office quiet save for the clicking of computer buttons.

I felt haunted by that kiss from Joe, constantly fighting the urge to relive those few, precious moments in my mind. When Poppy disappeared into the break room to make her afternoon cup of coffee, I sighed and slumped into my chair.

"Why?" I groaned quietly.

"Carly?" Zach Perkins asked from the doorway. "Can I talk to you for a second?"

As if I needed to be reminded of another toad, I rolled my eyes. I was thankful this particular toad still remained unkissed. I swiveled around in my chair with a note of annoyance and long suffering.

"Hi, Zach," I said coolly. "Poppy should have that last round of edits for Geneva Group ready by EOB."

"That's not why I stopped by."

"You know, the mighty Margolin had HR update those Culver sexual harassment guidelines for a reason. You can stop canvassing Let it Fro-yo or telling people that we're dating. You're lucky I haven't reported you."

"I saw you and Joe outside of Vincenzo's," he said, stepping into the office and lowering his voice.

"Spare me the jealous boyfriend routine. You're out of line."

"Do you even know what you're doing, Carly?"

"Mind your own business." I turned my focus completely to my computer monitor.

"Didn't we have something special that night? I mean, I thought we did."

Exasperated, I stood up, glad that my boots made me slightly taller than my 5'4" frame. "Zach, what are you talking about? You tricked me into going to a Christian concert. You made it sound like a bunch of people hanging out, but it was a group date. I took the stupid selfie with your friends, and suddenly it's your new profile picture."

"Why were you trolling me on social media?" he asked, eyebrows raised as if I'd proven his point.

"Because you tagged me in the photo. I don't want to be mean, but I am not interested."

"You made that point pretty obvious with Trautweig," he said bitterly. "I didn't realize you were the kind of girl who sexually assaults a man in public."

"And the only reason why you're judging me for it is because you're jealous it wasn't you," I shot back. "You can get off your holier-than-thou pedestal. I'd know a Christian hypocrite a mile away."

"Takes one to know one," he sneered.

"No, you pompous toad, I don't claim to be any kind of Christian. You, on the other hand, are an opportunistic liar."

Before I could unload some saltier language, Poppy arrived with her coffee.

"Zach," she said, skirting around him toward her own desk, "I've tried to be polite, but it's obviously not working. Unless you're here to discuss a work project for Culver, you need to leave our office. I've already mentioned it to Phil."

"Why don't you ask Carly why she was slobbering all over your good buddy, Joe Trautweig, in the Vincenzo's parking lot? You should be protecting your friend from a Jezebel like that." He looked me over as if he suddenly couldn't stand the sight of me.

"Zach," the mighty Margolin called, entering the fray, "we need to have a chat in my office." He stood outside of our doorway, apparently having overheard the exchange.

"Oh, come on, Ted. You saw them too! You were more disgusted than I was."

"*Now,*" he growled with controlled anger.

Practically dragging him away, Ted disappeared with a disgruntled Zach still arguing with him as their voices faded. I slumped into my chair, not sure I could feel any more humiliated.

"I wondered what took you so long," Poppy mused over her styrofoam cup, "but whatever did or didn't happen is none of my business."

"Thank you," I said, finally working up the courage to look her in the eyes. "Zach made it sound like we were animals on the side of the road. He's disgusting."

"Agreed. He's also jealous, and that's not a good look for anybody. Present company included."

I waved her off. "There's no comparison. Zach is jealous because of his own imagination. Anything that happened between me and him took place in his head."

"And anything that happened between me and Joe," Poppy added, "is ancient history. It was holding hands and a kiss that never happened. That's it."

"He also tried to kill himself. That's not nothing."

She sighed wearily. "Has he talked to you about any of this?"

I shook my head. "We didn't get that far. I don't think we will anyway."

She raised an eyebrow but didn't say anything.

"Oh, come on," I laughed, "I know you're dying to know. I appreciate the restraint though."

"Carly, I screwed up big time. I'm not trying to manipulate information out of you, and I feel guilty even having this conversation right now. You don't owe me any explanation about what happened. You and Joe are both grown adults. Like Jared said, you'd have to be blind to miss the chemistry between the two of you. Based on what apparently happened at Vincenzo's, the feelings are mutual."

I scoffed. "Feelings and reality are two different things. Joe Trautweig from your book isn't the Joe Trautweig in real life."

"That's because Joe isn't the same man I wrote about anymore. He's changed, and that's my fault."

"No, it's a little less dramatic than all of that. I appreciate the self-sacrifice, Poppy, but you're flattering yourself too much."

She digested the new information. "I see."

"I'm not trying to be a jerk, but you just told me that what happens between Joe and me is none of your business. If it helps ease your conscience any, the kiss happened because it was something we both wanted. We're not pieces of bread around a Poppy sandwich."

"Touché," she said, holding out her cup. "Why don't we put the tales of romance aside and get back to work?"

Things felt tense in our tiny office after that, and I knew Poppy's curiosity battled against her self-control. I found myself unconsciously touching my lips then mentally rattling myself to focus on work. Poppy left to go pick up her kids from school, and I pushed through an extra couple of hours of work. I wanted to distract myself from the thought of Joe or what I knew he wanted from me.

Bleary eyed, I finally shut off my computer and made my way through the lamplit version of my office park. I paused to take in the landscape, utterly altered from its daytime persona. During the day, Parkview felt like an uptight executive with her hair firmly tied in place and impeccably dressed. At night, she let her hair down, put on something sparkly, and became the life of the party.

I smiled to myself, noting the new set of locals walking up and down the streets.

"I didn't expect to see you again so soon."

I whirled around. "Wh-what are you doing here?" I gaped.

Joe shrugged. "I had this feeling you'd still be around. I don't know. I couldn't shake it."

"That still doesn't explain why you're here. You told me nothing would happen unless I became a Christian."

"I said I wasn't asking you to marry me. That doesn't mean I don't care about you as a person."

I rolled my eyes. "You're not going to romance me into the Kingdom of Heaven," I said, quoting one of Pastor Ivy's famous evangelism phrases. "They used to call it missionary dating in youth group. Going out with someone who wasn't a Christian to try and get them saved."

"Excuse me?"

"Like you said, you aren't a character in some romance

novel. This isn't the noble hero converting his lady love to Christ by manipulating her emotions against her."

Joe took a step closer, his eyes resuming their caress of my face. "Is that what you think I'm doing? Playing around with your feelings? You're the one who kissed *me*, remember?"

"And you're the one who said you wanted to kiss me the first time we met," I retorted.

"All I told you was that I wouldn't kiss any woman like that unless I was married to her. I didn't say anything to you about salvation, Jesus, or treat you like you weren't good enough to be in my presence."

"Give me a break! You don't think I've heard a million sermons about being equally yoked? Meanwhile, Pastor Ivy treated the women in his congregation like his personal set of prostitutes."

"So, are you accusing me of being a hypocrite?" Joe asked. "Do you think I'm being disingenuous like Rebecca's father?"

"No, but I think you eat up every word of that garbage from the Bible. I'm just telling you that I don't."

Joe studied me, and I shifted uncomfortably. "I don't think you truly believe that," he said. "I can tell you're angry, and based on your upbringing, it sounds like you have reason to be."

"Don't act like you know me. One kiss doesn't mean you suddenly see into my soul."

As if to prove me wrong, there were those jade eyes peering into the depths of me. "I didn't need a kiss to see that you're in pain, Carly."

"Likewise," I shot back. "You're so busy trying to convince me that you're too old for me, but it's all a facade to hide the fact you think I'm not good enough."

"I never said that! Stupidly, I keep throwing you at guys your own age even though it's killing me to do it."

"And why would you do that unless you thought I wasn't moral enough for you? We know Rob doesn't believe in Jesus. Is that what makes him a perfect fit for a heathen like me?"

"Carly," Joe said, straining for patience. "You asked me what I want. I've been in denial about it from the moment we met. I've invented any excuse I can think of, yet you've challenged me every step of the way."

"So, what are you saying?" My heart resumed that familiar beat. Rather than hopeful, I felt anxious, fearing what would be asked of me next.

"What I want is you, Carly," he said, his eyes pinning me in place. "I can't explain it. The more I keep making excuses, the more God won't let me go about it."

"That's impossible. God wouldn't choose me for you. God wouldn't choose me at all. He hates me. I'm an abomination."

Joe stepped forward, his hands suddenly on my shoulders. "You are *not* an abomination! Whatever your mother told you or the garbage you heard from Pastor Ivy, that is not who you are!"

I sloughed off the comfort of his words. "You don't know what I've done."

"Then, why don't you tell me?"

I shook my head.

"Carly," he said, eyes pleading, "if you don't believe in God, if you don't believe that Jesus is real, then why are you so tormented with guilt?"

"I don't need Jesus to know what I did was wrong," I said, fighting off tears. "I don't need to believe in the Bible to regret what I've done. I know how you're going to look at me when I tell you what I did. You think I'm just making a big deal out of nothing right now, but I'm not. Rob understood, but I don't think you will."

He looked shell-shocked. "You told the rabbi? When? How?"

"It slipped out," I said, already feeling Joe withdraw from me. "I didn't confide in him on purpose. He walked me back to my car after services. He thought I was just exaggerating about my mother."

"How is that possible?" Joe asked, his voice tight. "You're intentionally withholding this information from me, but you were so comfortable with *Rob* that it just flew out of your mouth."

"Because I knew he wouldn't reject me!" I said, agitated by his persistence. "Robbie and I disagree about a lot of things, but I knew he wouldn't judge me for what I did. Christians pretend they're so much better than everybody else, but they're some of the most hypocritical and judgmental people I've ever met."

"Not everyone who calls themselves a Christian is your mother," Joe said quietly. "You work with quite a few of us. Are you going to tell me that Ted or Poppy or Miss Belle are just like every other member of that church you grew up in?"

"Miss Belle has no clue," I said, referring to Culver's mother hen. "She treats me like I'm five years-old."

Joe's grim expression softened. "I'm familiar."

"So, I read."

"Carly, you asked me what I want. I told you. I guess the next question is what do *you* want?"

CHAPTER 12

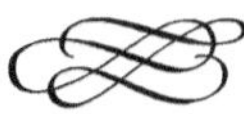

"I thought I made that obvious already," I said defensively.

"Is that all you're looking for? A physical relationship with some guy you read about in your friend's book?"

I stared at Joe petulantly, indignant at his mischaracterization but knowing exactly why he goaded me with it.

Inching closer to me, he said, "You told me to lighten up and that you weren't looking for marriage. Is that true, or were you just saying that for my benefit?"

"I'm too young to think about marriage," I said, lying through my teeth. "Maybe you were right about this age thing." I tried a nonchalant flick of the wrist but probably resembled a flightless bird vainly flapping its wings.

"You told me that you'd never been kissed like you had today. Was that true?"

I knew he saw the answer on my face before I attempted another lame denial. I closed my eyes, still feeling that jade stare deep in my soul.

"Carly," he said gently.

I breathed deeply through my nose and out through my mouth. I didn't tremble in fear of judgment for what I'd done almost three years ago. I realized that my shame had been removed. What I felt, though, was fear, and I knew exactly why.

"How do I know?" I whispered, finally meeting Joe's eyes.

The tenderness on his face nearly ripped the confession out of me. "How do you know what?"

I sniffled back tears, pressing my hands to my face. "How do I know you won't call me a Jezebel like Zach Perkins or an abomination like my mother?"

"Because I have my own demons," he said. "Whatever this heinous sin you've committed, I'm not without my own. I tried to take my own life, remember? If not for the grace of *Yeshua*, the name Jesus gave me when I was in that coma, I wouldn't be standing here right now."

"No," I said, bracing myself for the end of Joe Trautweig's interest in me, "you'd be in heaven with my baby, and I'm the one who sent her there."

Joe's momentary confusion was replaced with widened eyes and a convulsive swallow. I knew the two worst sins for Christians like my mother were homosexuality and abortion. I had never committed the first, but now my abomination lay open before the last person I wanted to reveal it.

"When did it happen?" he asked, his voice subdued.

"More than two-and-a-half years ago."

I watched Joe mentally track the chronology. "About the same time everything started with Poppy."

"While you guys were trying to rebuild your lives, I was busy destroying mine."

"Where was the baby's father?"

"He didn't know. I was ashamed, and I knew my

mother would freak out seeing me follow in her footsteps as a single parent. She was already in denial about me having sex even though she accused me of fornication constantly. I think she did it to reassure herself when I denied it."

"I'm sorry," Joe said.

"Why would you feel sorry for me? Nobody forced me to have an abortion. I chose to do it. Dylan probably would have married me or at least helped take care of the baby."

I was surprised when the name of my ex-boyfriend didn't produce the same longing and knives to the heart that I anticipated.

"Why didn't you tell him?" Joe asked.

"Because I tried to convince myself it was no big deal and that it was better for everyone that way. I kept rationalizing how he would understand."

Joe looked at me, with compassion in his eyes rather than the revulsion I feared.

"How?" I asked. "Why aren't you cursing at me like Dylan did? Like my mother did? She told me I murdered her grandchild and God would send me to hell for what I'd done. She said Jesus would never forgive me and neither would she."

Joe sucked in a breath as if reliving the pain with me. "Carly, I'm so sorry."

"But why?" I demanded. "Don't you understand what I did? What I willingly chose to do? I murdered my own child, and for what? Because I was afraid of my mother," I said bitterly. "You're free to go now, Joe. This is why I didn't want to tell you. I knew you'd freak out and leave."

Instead, Joe Trautweig remained firmly planted, watchful and searching.

"Carly," he said softly.

"I don't understand," I said through my tears. "Don't you hate me now?"

He looked aghast. "Why would I hate you? I'm only just getting to know you."

"I'm a murdering whore. A Jezebel. An abomination."

My voice broke on the last word, the pain of my mother's angry, contorted face before me. My mind flashed to Dylan, screaming how I had betrayed him and murdered our baby. I remembered the clinic, the cold staff, how I'd gone to sleep for what they called a "simple procedure," yet I'd woken up with an unimaginable emptiness.

"They told me it was nothing," I said in between sobs, "that I wouldn't feel any pain, that the *fetus* wouldn't feel anything."

Joe's eyes shed silent tears as he continued to stand with me. He made no effort to comfort me beyond the wounded look on his face, but that gaze may as well have been an embrace. Somehow, he sensed I needed physical space.

"I knew," I said, sobbing again. "I lied to myself over and over, Joe, but I *knew*. I knew it the second I woke up. There was this hollow ache that I couldn't fill, and believe me, I've tried."

"The toads?" he asked quietly.

I nodded. "Dylan wasn't my first boyfriend, but we were together for four years."

"That's a long time. Even if things had ended differently, I don't think anyone would recover quickly from that kind of a relationship."

"Dylan did," I spat. "He just got engaged to some college girl. If you want to accuse anybody of robbing the cradle, it's my ex."

Joe's somber expression softened. "And it's been a while since you graduated from high school, right?"

I exhaled a short laugh despite the watery mess I'd made of my face. "So, you don't hate me?"

He raked a hand through his hair. "I don't hate you, Carly. I know all too well what losing a child can do to someone." He raised his hand to cut me off, knowing my next objection. "No matter how you lost your child, Carly, you *lost* your baby. I understand why you didn't want to tell me, especially knowing what happened with my ex-wife."

"But she didn't want to lose that baby," I said. "She just went crazy from grief."

"And you're being eaten alive by guilt and from that monster who calls herself your mother. Hannah from the Bible, my foot!"

"Now, do you understand why God hates me? Why I would never call myself a Christian?"

His eyes no longer held me because his arms did. He didn't speak a word while I cried ugly tears. He simply rubbed my back and let me grieve for my child and what my own fear had wrought. "Selfish," I mumbled, "so selfish. I didn't want to become my mother, so I became something worse!"

Again, I appreciated how Joe didn't soothe me by white-washing what I'd done. He didn't shush me or help me place my grief carefully back on the shelf. At times, it felt like he mourned with me, his shoulders shaking.

I don't know how long we stood there, only that time stood with us.

"Do you remember what I said the first time we met?" he murmured against my hair.

I shook my head.

"I told you not to put a time limit on trauma."

I pulled back and looked into his eyes. "Trauma? Joe, this was all my fault. I did this to myself...and my baby."

"Trauma," he repeated. "The decision was yours, Carly. You're right about that. But you had no idea what it would do to you. You had no idea that your mother would disown you, that this boyfriend would betray you."

"Joe!" I gasped. "How can you say that? I actually agree with Dylan. You can't tell me that if you were put in the same position that you wouldn't have been just as upset."

"I was," he said slowly. "I told you that Poppy changed some of the details."

"What do you mean?"

"Catherine lost our first baby," he began, "but the miscarriage came after a horrible fight we had. There had been some flare ups with her personality disorder, but she hadn't been diagnosed yet. That night was the first time she had gotten violent, and she was horrified at what she'd done. Catherine didn't know she was pregnant, and she drank herself unconscious. When she started bleeding the next day, we went to the doctor. He said that anything could have caused a miscarriage so early, but neither of us believed him."

"Oh, Joe," I said, tears forming on his behalf instead of mine.

"Poppy omitted that from her story. Catherine blamed everyone and everything, especially when she lost two more babies after that. She stopped taking the medication for her bipolar disorder because she was convinced it was causing her to miscarry. That's when she blamed me for forcing her to get psychiatric treatment for the violent episodes."

I inhaled a sharp breath, seeing Joe's guilt and regret laid before me.

Haunted, he continued on, "It was either take the medicine to stay sane or keep losing babies and lose her mind anyway. There was no way to win. No hope for either of us."

Unable to resist, I reached up to wipe the tears from Joe's face. He held my hands in place as he held my heart with his eyes.

"I didn't try to take my life because of Poppy. I felt like a failure and an idiot for thinking I could ever get past what became of Catherine. I wanted to see her again to apologize. I wanted to see our children."

"Do you feel responsible?" I asked. "For Catherine taking her own life and for the babies she lost?"

"How could I not?" His voice was thick with emotion. "Carly, I live every day with the guilt of three dead babies."

"That wasn't your fault! You didn't make the *choice*," I spat, hating how unclean I felt. I slid my hands out from under Joe's. "I don't deserve to have a man like you be so kind to me."

"You don't think so?" he demanded, allowing a glimpse of his own pain beyond those jade eyes. "Every time I watched Catherine take a pill, I wondered if I was killing a child. Catherine was obsessed with having a baby after our first miscarriage, and every lost baby after just drove her even more crazy with grief."

"Why did you divorce her?" I asked quietly. "Why did you abandon her?"

Joe lifted a section of hair to reveal an inch long scar on his head. "I didn't have a choice, Carly. In her grief, Catherine attacked me on more than one occasion. One night, she became so violent, she hit me with a stone figurine I bought for her on our honeymoon."

I gasped.

He swallowed, reliving the memory before me. "I woke up on the floor, Catherine screaming over me that she would kill me. I remember the look in her eyes when she said it, Carly, and I knew she meant it. I don't know what happened to the woman

I had fallen in love with, but she was gone. Catherine's mother was a holy roller like yours and wanted to perform an exorcism."

"Are you serious?" I said, mouth open. "Did you do it?"

He shook his head. "I didn't believe in demons and all of that then. I certainly do now."

"Do you think she was possessed? Like in all of those movies?" I shuddered at the memories of films I wished I could go back and unsee.

"I don't know. This is still pretty new to me. What I do know is that I couldn't look Catherine in the eyes anymore. There was something there, something that made my stomach turn and my palms sweat. Looking back, I'd probably say it was a demon, but that's only a guess. It got to the point where I was experiencing panic attacks knowing she was in the room. I could feel her presence before I saw her."

I shivered, remembering when I had also felt the exact same way. "Pastor Ivy gave me the creeps like that."

"What do you mean?"

"He would smile and work the room, but there was something about him that had me on constant alert. The way he looked at me always scared me."

"Looked at you?" Joe repeated. "Like he had designs on you like every other woman there?"

"No," I said, shaking my head. "I just always felt like a bug under a microscope. Sometimes, I was afraid to breathe the wrong way."

Joe frowned. "That sounds like some of the stories I've heard from Rebecca."

"There was this one time he cornered me against a wall. He didn't touch me, but the way he got in my face terrified me. He had this evil smile too. I know that sounds corny, but I don't know how else to describe it. He would smile while he was telling me how horrible I was and how much my mother suffered because of me."

"How old were you?"

"Thirteen," I said. "It may have been the first time I finally put all the pieces together and realized my mother worshiped a monster. Sometimes I felt like she put him up to it."

"I wouldn't doubt it," Joe said, "but what's bothering me is why. Narcissists are opportunists, and I don't know what Bernard Ivy would stand to gain from your mother other than a physical relationship."

I shrugged. "I don't know. My mother was one of those worker bees who would do anything Pastor Ivy asked of her. I think she was just slave labor and an ego boost for him."

"Carly, I've been hesitant to go down this path, but there is another possibility here."

"What do you mean?"

"Did Pastor Ivy treat anybody else in that church the way he treated you?"

I shook my head. "Maybe Rebecca, based on her book, but what she went through was a million times worse than what Pastor Ivy did to me."

"We both know your mother wasn't Hannah from the Bible," he said with a smirk, "but do you think it's possible she stuck around the church to keep you close to your birth father? Do you think that Pastor Ivy treated you like his own daughter because you *are* his daughter?"

CHAPTER 13

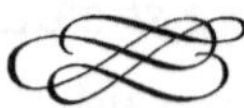

My world was spinning. I couldn't process any more information. Not Joe's confession. My own confession. Or the horrific possibility that the man who sired me could possibly be worse than the nameless phantom my mother refused to identify.

"Joe, I…" the words wouldn't come out.

He glanced at his watch and grimaced. "I had no idea it was so late. Are you okay getting home by yourself?"

I met his eyes for a long moment, and in that instant, we both knew. We knew exactly what would happen.

"Nevermind," he said, shaking his head. "Bad idea. Very bad idea."

"I think I'm okay to drive. "Thank you for confiding in me, Joe."

"Now, do you understand why I'm not condemning you to hell like your mother or some other self-righteous hypocrites?"

I nodded. "You'll never be able to convince me that we're guilty of the same sin, but I definitely understand the pain you feel. It's a nonstop agony, like you're bleeding out, but you never run out of blood to finally put you out of your misery."

His mouth was grim. "That's probably the best way I've ever heard it described. How do you make the pain go away?"

"You're asking *me*?" I said with a short laugh. "Aren't you the one with the Bible and all the answers for life's trials?"

He pulled a face. "The only people who really believe that are the ones faking it. Any true believer I know struggles with their own fears and doubts, regardless of how much they love the Lord. Struggle isn't the absence of faith."

I raised my eyebrows. "That's not what I was taught."

"And you really think that the lessons you learned from your mother or Pastor Ivy are the true teachings from God?"

Piercingly reminded of the Bible verse Poppy had shown me, the bottom dropped out of my stomach. "Wh-what did you say?"

"You look like you've seen a ghost. What's wrong?"

"Poppy," I said, struggling for breath. "She showed me a Bible verse. I can't remember where it was. Something about confessing our sins and if we don't, then we're calling God a liar."

"I think I know which one you mean." Joe whipped out his cellphone and opened a Bible app. After a quick, keyword search, he found the verses. "*1 John*," he said. "Yep, there it is. If we think we haven't sinned, then we don't have the true teachings of Christ."

"I feel like I'm seeing part of the puzzle, Joe, but not everything. All I know about God or the Bible I've learned from my mother or First United. I've tried reading the Bible, but all I ever hear is Pastor Ivy yelling from the pulpit or my mother shaming me for existing."

"You're not wrong," Joe said, studying me. "Your existence

does bring your mother shame, but not because there's something defective in you."

"What are you saying?"

Joe took a step closer, holding my hands and staring into my eyes. "Your mother knows good and well she's not Hannah of the Bible. She was a woman who got pregnant out of wedlock and raised her baby as a single mother. No matter what airs she put on for you, Pastor Ivy, or the church, your existence was proof that your mother has made at least one lapse in judgment. Your existence brought *her* shame because she couldn't maintain her hyper spiritual facade with a daughter who was conceived outside of marriage."

"I see."

"You were Hannah's reminder of her own sin. Instead of truly repenting, she makes you her scapegoat instead. She condemns you for *her* sin of fornication because she refuses to acknowledge what she did thirty-one years ago. She can't pretend she's perfect when her biggest 'mistake' is alive in the world."

"Mistake?" I repeated. "Is that what I am?"

"No!" Joe said, eyes wide. "That's not what I mean. To your mother, you're just proof that she isn't perfect. To God, you are fearfully and wonderfully made. He knew you before you were formed in your mother's womb. No matter the circumstances, God wanted you here in this world."

"What about my baby?" I asked. "What about all of yours? Are you saying God didn't want them alive?"

Joe inhaled a pained breath, and I watched him struggle to reconcile his own burdens with what he claimed to believe.

"Sorry, I shouldn't try to ruin your faith just because I don't have any of my own." I glanced away and released his hands. "Joe, I can't tell you God does or doesn't speak to people, but I can guarantee that He wouldn't tell you I'm the right one for you. Jared called it *beshert,* but I don't see how that's possible."

"There's no black and white formula for why God does the things He does. I know He uses suffering to bring us closer to Him. I've seen that in my own life and in the lives of my friends."

"Every sermon I heard was how God blesses us for obedience. Every Bible verse Pastor Ivy used was how God wants us to walk in victory, *from glory to glory,*" I said, mocking his pious tone.

"You don't think those two can coexist?" Joe asked. "Suffering and victory?"

"How could they? Doesn't God bless people who are good with answered prayer? Doesn't he curse everyone who disobeys Him? Why would he allow good people to suffer? If He did, then why would anybody want to worship a God like that?"

Joe smiled at me, his eyes shining.

"What?" I asked. "Why are you looking at me like that? I'm questioning everything you believe."

"No," he said, softly, "you're confirming it, believe it or not."

My own eyes went wide. "How?"

"Carly, when Jesus suffered and died on the cross, He won the ultimate victory."

"I've heard all this," I clipped, not wanting another salvation message.

"Bear with me," he said. "You asked me why anybody would love God if He allows innocent people to suffer. It seems impossible to the human mind, right?"

"Right."

"I would never wish what I've been through on anyone, but I would never be able to empathize with you and the decision you made if I hadn't suffered myself. Can you see that?"

"So, you're saying it's God's will that I got an abortion?" I scoffed. "Try telling that to my mother or any of these fire-breathing pro-lifers out there."

Joe shook his head. "You're intentionally being difficult right now, and I see right through it. You know that's not what I'm saying."

I pursed my lips.

"Listen, I'm not going to stand here and pretend like I know why God does the things He does. He's God, I'm not. There are things He allows where I have to step back and seek Him about why."

"Like Catherine," I said quietly.

"All the people I know have ugly in their stories. I know you've read the books, but even people like Miss Belle have suffering and pain in their lives. I was reading in the Bible a few days ago how believers in Christ overcome the world by the blood of the Lamb and the word of our testimony."

"Testimony," I said, quoting that familiar word. "You mean how you got saved."

"No," Joe said, his jade gaze stirring up embers of hope in my own heart. "Your testimony goes beyond that moment when you accept Christ in your heart as Lord."

"I don't understand."

He smiled encouragingly. "The testimony of any true believer in Christ isn't doctrine, worship, or serving in a church. Our testimony is what God is doing in our lives daily. It's all the ways we see ourselves growing closer into the image of Jesus. It's the way He unravels the tangled up messes in our lives and sets us free, one victory at a time. It's not your mother or Pastor Ivy pretending they're perfect. It's people like Poppy, Ted, or Kyle Goldstein who can openly admit when they're wrong, confess it to God, and then grow from the experience. It's admitting how much we need Christ and then allowing Him to change us."

"And you have those victories?" I asked skeptically. "Weren't you the one asking me to tell you how to conquer regret?"

"I never said I was perfect," he said with a small grin. "I just know that I wouldn't be alive without Jesus. I know He saved my life for something bigger than commercial insurance or walking in constant guilt about Catherine or our babies."

"Do you think that something bigger is me?"

"In part, I think. I mean, I don't know if God brought us together so that I could share a gospel message that's completely different from all the lies you heard growing up, but I know there's a reason. Beshert isn't always 'meant to be' in a romantic sense."

"But that kiss!" I protested.

"God didn't bring you into my life so we could sin," Joe said plainly. "I'm still making sense of what exactly my feelings are, but no matter how much my body may want something more with you, God's purpose is bigger."

"Are you talking about *marriage*?" I squeaked out the last word.

He shook his head. "No, I'm not talking about that either."

"Well, how does any of this physical stuff work if we don't follow your rules? You won't touch me without a ring on your finger. I can respect that, Joe, but I'm not going to stick around while you try to convert me."

"I won't lie and pretend there's not a physical attraction here. I won't even deny we have a connection beyond just a kiss. After hearing you share your story, it helped me gain some perspective into my own situation with Catherine. I could sit here and preach at you about forgiving yourself and God's mercy, but I need to say all of that to myself first."

My mouth opened and shut, stunned that Joe's reaction to my confession was self-reflection rather than self-righteousness.

"Carly, everything you've shared regarding your doubts and fears are all things I've struggled with too. It's hard to imagine a God who is so merciful and so loving that even if my worst fears are true, even if each of those babies my wife lost was completely my fault, He still loves me, still forgives me, and still wants me to draw close to Him."

Tears pricked my eyes, challenged to see God beyond the vengeful persona presented by my mother and Pastor Ivy. I liked Joe's version much better, and I no longer heard that heavy accusing voice in my head.

"Joe, can I share something with you? I haven't told anybody this, but I wanted to tell you the night I passed out in synagogue."

He gestured for me to join him on the same bench where we first met over frozen yogurt. "Sorry, tired feet," he said sheepishly.

I smiled back. "I didn't notice until you said something, but mine are a little sore too."

His eyes sparkled as he sat a foot away from me. "What's up?"

I inhaled, pausing to think about how I could articulate my experience. "Something happened to me when I was unconscious on the floor."

"What do you mean?"

"I heard someone say, 'Come back, Carly,' but I didn't recognize the voice. I felt someone holding my hand. At the time, I thought it was you, but this was different."

Joe's brow furrowed, mentally retracing the events of that night. "I don't remember anyone saying that. The doctor asked

Poppy to step aside so we could get you into the aisle, but nobody said what you're describing."

I frowned, scared to believe what I knew deep down in my gut.

He sensed my discomfort, but he didn't press for more details. "Is that what you wanted to share with me?"

I shook my head. "No, there's more. After I heard those words, I felt something break. I don't know how to describe it or even how I saw it with my eyes closed, but I *saw* it."

"Saw what?"

"It was almost like glass breaking. I've been carrying around this weight for more than two years about the abortion, but I watched it shatter all around me."

Joe's eyes filled with tears as his face glowed. He never looked more handsome to me than he did at that moment.

"What?" I asked.

He shook his head. "Keep going. What happened next?"

"I woke up. It felt like coming up out of water. Everything was muffled, but then it became clear."

He smiled at me, his eyes dancing in delight. My own heart responded in kind. Whatever unspeakable joy brought that look to his face, I suddenly wanted it for myself.

"God set you free," he said quietly. "Carly, God broke those chains of guilt and condemnation."

CHAPTER 14

"Impossible!" I said, jumping to my feet. "I told you God turned his back on me after my abortion."

"And I'm telling you He never abandoned you. It sounds like He's calling you back to Him."

"Why would God want me?" I asked bitterly. "Nobody does."

"That's not true!"

"Oh really? Tell that to my mother."

"I have a lot of things I'd like to tell your mother. Give me her address, and I'll give her a piece of my mind."

I rolled my eyes and waved him off.

"Do you think I'm bluffing?"

"Aren't you?"

"No!" he exclaimed. "I already told off Zach Perkins when he dropped by Cooper & Jaye this afternoon."

"What?" I gasped.

"Ted had him fired over something to do with you. Zach was livid and caused a huge scene at our front desk. The mighty

Margolin confirmed the details when I texted him afterward to tell him what happened."

My jaw dropped. "Are you serious? Why would Zach do that?"

"Apparently, he saw us outside of Vincenzo's."

"He sure did," I said, feeling the acrimony rise. "He accused me of assaulting you and called me a Jezebel."

"Then I don't regret the black eye I gave him before security escorted him out," Joe said with a satisfied smirk.

I blanched. "You did what?"

"I punched him, Carly. After he accused me of being a cradle robbing pervert, he started in on you. Jezebel was fairly tame compared to the words he used with me. I wonder if his pastor knows what a foul mouth that punk has on him."

I shook my head in disgust, fighting back tears. "People like Zach are exactly why I want nothing to do with religion."

"Do you think people like Zach truly represent Jesus?"

"I grew up with people just like him, Joe. I've spent the past five years living in a house with them. I think people like you or the Levines might be the exception, not the rule."

He sighed. "I can't argue with that. I've seen plenty of it myself."

"I don't understand. You're actually making my case."

"How much do you remember about the gospels growing up?" he asked.

"Not much beyond the basics. Jesus loves the little children blah blah."

My attempt to push away Joe's penetrating gaze failed miserably. He smiled instead. "Do you remember any of the stories about the women Jesus encountered? Women with bad reputations? Women who would be condemned even by our standards today? Do you know how Jesus treated them?"

My heart fluttered inside my chest. I waited for the hammer to fall.

"Jesus didn't condemn any of them."

"He didn't?" I breathed.

Joe shook his head. "No. He didn't judge any of them based on their pain or their sin. He accepted them. He blessed them. He healed them. He allowed them to touch Him when society expressly forbade it. He praised them for their hearts that turned away from their sin and turned toward Him instead."

"That seems too crazy to believe. That's not what I was taught."

Half of Joe's mouth lifted into a smile. "Are you really going to accept the word of a convicted felon with a rap sheet as long as his list of mistresses? I'd like to believe I'm a little more trustworthy than that," he said with a touch of feigned offense.

I chuckled softly. "You are, Joe. It just seems too good to be true."

"Forgiveness isn't something we earn or have to be good enough to receive. It's a free gift. God says He has mercy on whomever He wants."

The smile fell from my face. "How do you know he wants to show me any mercy, Joe? I killed my baby."

"If God can forgive me for everything I've done, including trying to take my own life, I know that your sin isn't too big for Him either."

"My mother told me shedding innocent blood is an abomination. She showed me in the Bible."

"So is calling evil 'good' and perverting justice," he replied. "So is intentionally turning people away from Christ because we think we get to decide who is worthy of Him. Do you think it's worse to take a life or to turn someone away from God and then have that person lead others to hell too?"

"I never thought of it that way."

"In Bible study last week, we were reading from *Romans 11*. It describes God's olive tree and Jews and Gentiles being grafted in together."

I shrugged, having no idea what he was talking about.

He smiled patiently. "Well, Jared and some others from Beth Shalom shared that they used to look down on Christians and other gentile believers in Christ because they weren't Jewish."

"Why?"

"Because it seems like no matter what flavor of believer you want to call yourself, a lot of people struggle with pride and self-righteousness. Ted's mother, Rose, calls it worshiping our worship."

"I've never heard of that. What does it mean?"

"Basically, instead of worshiping God, we worship our religion. God set His own standards in the Bible, but our human tendency is to do that with our own traditions and rules. We make ourselves the head, and we condemn anyone who doesn't believe or act just like us. It's a very cultic and narcissistic mind set."

My mind traveled immediately to Robbie Zendler and his snide attitude toward the Levines. I also thought of Pastor Ivy condemning Jewish people for their traditions. Kelsey flashed before me next with her hypocrisy regarding her backslidden lifestyle.

"It's all just pride and self-righteousness," Joe continued, "but there was something more I wanted to share with you."

"Go ahead, I'm following."

Joe smiled at my response. "Rebecca had us read a passage where it talks about how we are only grafted into Jesus because of our faith."

"Grafted in? Like in gardening?"

"Exactly!" he said, impressed with my agricultural know-how. "The analogy in Romans is that God has fused both wild and cultivated branches into His olive tree. It's a picture of Jews and gentiles coming together in faith to worship Jesus."

"Hmm," I murmured. "Interesting."

Joe's green eyes glowed. "The point Mrs. Margolin wanted us to see was how none of us have room to boast about ourselves. Whether we're Jewish or Christian, none of us are better than any other. Every single one of us is saved by our faith, not our bloodline, our identity, or the church where we belong."

I considered his words, once again seeing the disparity from everything I was raised to believe. Both Pastor Ivy and my mother presented First United as a cut above every other church. There was an arrogance and elitism among the members. I frowned, remembering the disparaging comments from members regarding mega churches, televangelists, and Jewish people "under the law." Naturally, the First United members and their cult-like messiah understood the Bible better than anyone.

"Did I lose you, Carly?"

I shook my head. "No, I'm just putting it all together. Thank you for sharing all of this with me and for your patience."

"My pleasure," he said, grinning with that same, winsome smile that made me forget how eleven years separated the two of us.

"Why does all of this sound so different when you say it, Joe? I mean, it's not like Poppy hasn't said a lot of the same things, but from you, it's just easier to hear."

"Probably that kiss," he teased.

I blushed. "No, I don't think so. I'm not listening to all of this because I'm hoping for another one."

He placed a theatrical hand over his heart as if mortally wounded. I laughed, grateful my tears had dried and I was sitting on that Parkview bench well past my bedtime.

"You have a beautiful smile," Joe said. "I don't know if you realize that your eyes change color too."

I shook my head. "Nobody's ever mentioned it."

"Well, they do," he said. "Normally, they are a very lovely shade of aquamarine. When you laugh, they turn to a darker blue. When you're sad, they become more green."

"And you've already noticed all of this in the short time we've gotten to know each other," I mused. "Joe, you have this way of looking at me. I don't know how to describe it. It's like I can't hide."

"You do that to me too, you know."

"Do I?"

"Yes," he said. His green eyes were luminous under the evening lights.

My heart began that familiar cadence, and I stood up. The temptation for a kiss and what it would require of me was too much to bear. "I need to get going. I have to be up in seven hours to start this work day all over."

Joe rose with me, offering me his arm to escort me to my car. Smiling, I took it, unashamed and less self conscious with nobody from Culver to see us.

After a quick elevator ride, we made it to the fifth floor of the parking deck.

He gave an overly elaborate bow. "Your chariot, my lady."

I giggled, not remembering the last time I had done that. "Thank you, good sir."

Joe grinned back, and there was the pull again. The humor fell from his face as desire took its place. He reached out to hold my hand. "What is it about you?"

I took my hand away. "I'm not ready yet. I'm not ready to talk to God. I appreciate everything you told me tonight, and I promise I will think more about it."

"He loves you, Carly. He never stopped."

Although I knew Joe was referring to Jesus, I couldn't help feeling a bit of Joe Trautweig in that declaration as well.

"Thank you," I said simply. "Thank you for not rejecting me. I've been so scared you would find out what I did and run away."

He held my gaze captive with his own. "No matter what you've done, you are not unworthy to be loved or to be shown grace and mercy. That's what I hope I was able to give to you tonight. I want you to see how Jesus would treat you."

"Don't make me cry again," I sniffled.

Impulsively, he pulled me into an embrace. "You *are* loved and worthy to be loved," he said into my ear. "Don't listen to any lie saying otherwise."

Unable to resist, I leaned back far enough to cup Joe's face and stare into his eyes.

"Carly," he said low. "We can't."

I shook my head, hoping to reassure both of us that I wouldn't repeat my behavior outside of Vincenzo's. "I just have to make sure you're real, Joe Trautweig. Nobody has ever shown so much kindness to me. I know Poppy feels bad for me, but you gave me something different tonight."

He gently pulled my hands from his face, though he continued to hold them. "Acceptance," he said, smiling at me. "Forgiveness. Hope."

"Yes."

He released my hands. "I hope you can see how Jesus called you on the floor of Beth Tefillah. He's the same One who has been speaking through me all night. As much as I like you,

Carly, I feel like God has given me a glimpse of the love He feels for you. It's overwhelming." He reached up to wipe tears from his own eyes.

"Jesus loves me?" I asked. "Me?" I repeated in disbelief.

"You," he said firmly.

For the first time, I noted something in Joe's eyes beyond the beautiful jade color. It was a light from within, a light warming my own heart. This wasn't lust, desire, or even the romantic love that had me swooning over Taylor Horner's memoirs.

"Yes," he said softly, sensing the change.

"How?" I asked. "How is this even possible?"

Joe grinned widely. "All things are possible with God."

CHAPTER 15

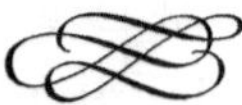

I woke up the following morning feeling lighter. I experienced a deep, dreamless sleep that left me more rested than I could remember. I discovered a text message from Joe, and I smiled just seeing his name on my phone.

I hope you don't mind, but the Lord reminded me of these verses. I wanted to share them with you. This is from 2 Corinthians 5:16-19 if you want to see for yourself or read it with the rest of the chapter.

Speaking the words aloud, I said, "So from now on we regard no one from a worldly point of view. Though we once regarded Christ in this way, we do so no longer. Therefore, if anyone is in Christ, the new creation has come: The old has gone, the new is here! All this is from God, who reconciled us to himself through Christ and gave us the ministry of reconciliation: that God was reconciling the world to himself in Christ, not counting people's sins against them. And he has committed to us the message of reconciliation."

My hands trembled reading the words, desperately wanting to believe they were true. My mother's angry diatribes still rang in my head, though not as loudly as before. Throwing caution to the wind, I worked up the courage to offer my first prayer to heaven in fifteen years.

"Are you even there?" I whispered shakily. "Are you sure you don't hate me?" After a few moments, I snickered at the idea I would hear an audible voice.

Refocusing my attention, I stared at myself in the bathroom mirror. I wondered what Joe would say about the vivid shade of aquamarine eyes peering back at me following my childlike prayer. I twisted my thick hair into a chignon, easily pinning the honey blonde strands in place. Satisfied with my makeup and outfit, I said, "Not too shabby, Carly. Even Hannah Miller couldn't pick this one apart."

There was a spring in my step entering the office, relieved that I wouldn't find Zach Perkins lurking around. Dreamily, I wondered if Joe would somehow find a way to stop by and see me.

I greeted Poppy with a large smile. "Morning!"

"Wow," she said, taking me in. "Carly, you look like a completely different person. What happened?"

"I'm still figuring that out," I said with a wistful tone.

"You and Joe?"

I raised my eyebrows. "I thought you weren't fishing for info."

"I wasn't planning on it, but you're glowing. I don't think I've ever seen you look so happy." Her expression fell, looking like she developed a sour taste in her mouth. "Did something happen with you two after work? You seemed a little disoriented after your kiss at Vincenzo's, but this looks like you woke up with a smile on your face."

Any shred of sunshine I'd brought into the office hid behind a cloud of offense. "Is that the only reason you think I could be in a good mood? Glad to know you think so highly of me."

Defensively, she replied, "In the two years we've been working together, I have never seen you look this happy. Yesterday, your kiss with Joe got Zach Perkins so riled up that he wound up getting fired. You can't blame me for assuming things went further than making out when you waltz in here walking on cloud nine."

"How about you stop assuming or butting your nose into my business?"

Poppy tsked. "You're the one who invited me into your love life within your first week of working here. It was one dating drama after another. I hope you can understand why I expected more of the same."

"No," I argued back. "You were disinterested, at best, when it came to the toads. With Joe, it's personal for you, and we both know why."

"How many times do I have to tell you I've moved on?"

"Then, butt out," I said, unwilling to clear up the misperception. "Like you said, whatever happens between me and Joe is none of your business. You have absolutely no idea what's going on, but you're still standing there judging me anyway."

"So, you're happy you made a man stumble?" she hissed, eyes narrowed. "You know what Joe believes about sex before marriage. How could you do that to him?"

I grabbed my purse and headed for the doorway. "This conversation is over."

"What about your own past?" she pressed. "What happens if you find yourself back in the same situation you were in with Dylan?"

I sucked in a breath, stunned by the accusation. "After two years of seeing my misery and regret about what I've done, you have the nerve to ask me that?" I snapped. "I'm leaving, Poppy."

Her self-righteous anger turned to dismay. "Wait, where are you going? Are you quitting?"

"I'm going to Vincenzo's," I said coolly. "If you press your face to the window long enough, you'll probably see me sinning with your ex-boyfriend. Enjoy the view."

I didn't spare a backward glance as I stormed out of the office. I knew good and well I'd gone for blood with that last remark, but I didn't care. I had been robbed of the peace and hope that I felt reading Joe's earlier text message, and I blamed Poppy for it.

"What gives her the right to judge me?" I muttered to myself. "Self-righteous hypocrite! How dare she act like she didn't try to sleep with Joe once upon a time. She's no better than Zach!"

I stomped along the sidewalk texting Joe as quickly as my fingers would allow. Distracted and upset, I nearly toppled over the mighty Margolin. His coffee splattered on the ground as we collided.

"Oh! I'm so sorry!" I exclaimed.

Ted stared down at the mess that had nearly baptized his shoes. "That was close. I can spare another coffee. The suit, however, has a meeting with Triple J in an hour." Noting my stricken appearance, Ted asked, "Is everything okay? Is this about Zach?"

"No, but Joe told me what happened at Cooper & Jaye after you fired him."

"Ah," he said, studying me. "I noticed you were working late yesterday. I didn't get out until close to seven myself. I'm guessing you talked to Joe after hours."

"Not that it's anybody's business, but yes, I did. Is that a problem for you too?"

"Carly, whatever is going on with you and Joe is none of my business."

"I've heard that before," I said, "and Zach said you hated the idea of me and Joe being together more than he did."

Ted considered my words before responding. "Are you heading to Vincenzo's? We can talk and walk while I go pick up another coffee."

I nodded. Ted jerked his chin and motioned for me to walk next to him.

"You and Joe are both adults," he began, leading me toward the crosswalk. "I can understand why some other people in our office are protective of Joe," he said, implicating Poppy without calling her by name, "but Zach's version of what we witnessed is very different from mine."

"Is that right?" I followed Ted as we traversed the busy intersection into the shopping plaza. We continued past several restaurants and retail stores.

The mighty Margolin stopped, meeting my eyes. "Carly, I don't know your history, but I do see a competent and caring individual who has been a tremendous asset to our marketing department. Joe is a little bit older than you, but that also means he's less likely to waste your time or his own if he doesn't think a relationship is possible."

"Zach said you were disgusted."

Ted sighed and rolled his eyes. "Zach said a lot of things yesterday, most of which were patently false. After I saw the text message from Joe about the altercation at Cooper & Jaye, I told him I would gladly back him up if Perkins tried to press any charges for battery."

"Oh," I said, surprised and relieved. "Thank you."

"For the record, my disgust was with Zach's reaction to the two of you kissing, not to the kiss itself. I didn't look for long. Zach acted like a sports commentator."

I smacked my hand to my forehead in embarrassment.

"Carly, Joe is a good friend and a brother in the Lord. I care about him."

"Meaning what?"

"Meaning that if the two of you are happy with one another —and from my brief look, it certainly seemed that way," he said with a grin, "then, I'm thrilled for both of you."

"I wasn't expecting that."

"What were you expecting?"

"Something a lot less supportive, to be honest. Poppy and I got into a huge fight this morning."

He grimaced. "I can't imagine this is easy for her."

"Why?" I asked. "What right does she have to Joe? She had her chance. She chose Jared."

"Did you know Kyle and I were with Joe in the hospital when they revived him from his coma?"

"I do," I said, recalling that portion of Poppy's book. "Joe gave me some more details last night."

"Then, you know that Joe's attempted suicide had very little to do with Poppy."

"Yes," I said. "He filled in some blanks regarding his ex-wife and their marriage problems."

Ted nodded. "I hesitated telling Poppy the full story because I knew she'd blame herself. She tends to take on unnecessary responsibility."

"She also thinks I'm not good enough for her friend. I've shared some of the bad decisions I've made, and now she's holding it against me."

"That's wrong," Ted said without hesitation. "No matter

your past sins, you deserve to be happy just like anybody else. Poppy gave me quite a lecture regarding Jessica Goldstein on this very topic."

"She needs to take her own advice."

Ted exhaled a soft chuckle. "So it would seem, but show her some grace. It sounds like Poppy isn't extending much of it at the moment, but she'll come around. She's always been quick to apologize when she's wrong."

"Thank you," I said, meaning it. "To be honest, I expected you to be overprotective of Joe."

"Why would the mighty Margolin need to protect me?" Joe asked, joining us as the door to Vincenzo's closed behind him. "I'm a big boy. I can handle myself just fine."

"Just ask Zach Perkins," Ted quipped, winking at Joe.

Sparkling jade eyes and an incredible smile greeted me. "Good morning," he said. "I saw you through the window."

"Hi," I replied. I couldn't keep the blush or matching smile off my face.

Ted looked back and forth between the two of us, amused. "Play nice, kids."

Joe rolled his eyes good naturedly. "Thanks, Dad."

Turning to me, Ted said, "Carly, I'll see you back at the office. I may even have a few words with our mutual friend."

"Don't talk to her on account of me. You don't need to stick yourself in the middle."

"Whatever I say is because I choose to do so," he reassured me. "We all have our weaknesses and blind spots. It's a real friend who can lovingly and tactfully hold up a mirror while still encouraging us."

Joe took Ted's vacated spot as he disappeared into Vincenzo's for his replacement coffee. "What's going on?" he asked. "I saw you texted me, but I didn't get to read anything yet."

"Poppy," I spat. "God forbid, I walk into our office with a smile on my face. She assumed we slept together."

He blanched. "Excuse me?"

"She threw the abortion in my face too. She accused me of making you stumble, then asked what I would do if I wound up getting pregnant again."

Joe looked appropriately appalled. "What? Why? Why would she do that? That doesn't sound like Poppy at all."

"She's jealous," I said. "She's constantly reminding me how she's so in love with Jared, but then she grills me for details about you."

He frowned, the sparkle dying in his eyes.

My rant wasn't over. "Poppy wants to be happy and move on, but I don't think she really wants that for you, Joe. She's only happy as long as you aren't."

"That's not true," he said, coming to her defense. "I'll admit things get a little awkward sometimes because of our history, but I'm not some knight agonized by his courtly love, and Poppy is no damsel in distress."

I smirked, reminded of Poppy's fondness for medieval themed romance novels and unrequited love. "Apparently, I'm the evil seductress trying to lure you away from Jesus with my feminine wiles." I batted my eyelashes for dramatic effect.

Joe laughed despite the serious turn of our conversation. "You're not evil, and it's not a seduction when I'm fighting the same feelings you are."

"Really?" I asked. "This isn't just some fantasy in my head?"

"No," he replied. "I'm real. This is real. Nothing I said last night has suddenly changed just because it's daylight."

CHAPTER 16

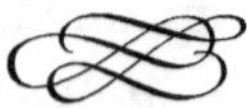

AFTER A TENSE MOMENT WHERE WE BATTLED AGAINST a repeat performance of our Vincenzo's kissing scene, Joe grabbed me by the hand and led me into the coffee shop.

"Can I get you a cappuccino?" he asked.

I smiled. "Sounds great."

Niccolo burst into a wide grin as we approached the counter. "Same as yesterday, *signorina*?"

"*Si*," Joe replied, "and her drink is on me."

Niccolo's wide grin spread wider. "Of course."

Joe chuckled softly into my ear. "The matchmakers are everywhere."

Niccolo shot Joe a conspiratorial smile as he handed me my drink a few minutes later.

"Our usual spot?" Joe asked, gesturing toward the leather chairs.

"I didn't know we already had a usual spot."

He shrugged. "Looks like."

Ted appeared to be hanging up a phone call as he stood up

from a corner table and walked over toward us. "Joe, are we still on for lunch today with Kyle, or do you have other plans?" He glanced at me in question.

"Lunch as usual," Joe replied. "I can't monopolize all of her time today."

Ted looked down at his watch. "Carly, can we expect you back in the marketing department by ten?"

I nodded. "Yeah, I'll just make this my lunch break. Thanks, Ted."

He gave a quick jerk of the chin, then clapped Joe on the shoulder. "High noon, Trautweig. We're on *Galatians 4.*"

He chuckled. "I'll be there."

Ted took one last look at the two of us, smiled encouragingly, then exited the front door with his new cup of coffee.

Joe leaned in toward me. "How did you wind up talking to the mighty Margolin outside? We ran into each other about fifteen minutes ago in line, so I was surprised to see him back here again. Ted is already pretty high strung without a second espresso shot."

I snickered. "We literally ran into each other while I was on my way here. I was texting you and not looking where I was going. Ted's coffee hit the sidewalk."

"Ah," he said, reaching for his cell phone. "Do you want me to read your messages, or did I get the whole story outside?"

I gestured toward his phone. "Go ahead and read them. I want to enjoy my cappuccino while it's hot."

Joe smiled at me, then his expression sobered as he pored through my litany of typo laden rants.

"Wow," he said, sighing and slumping back in his chair. "That's a lot to happen before 9 am."

I matched his sigh with one of my own. "I was so happy after I saw your text this morning. I even prayed to God for the first time since high school. Then, Poppy started in with all of her nasty little comments, and I feel like I'm right back where I started."

"You prayed?" he asked, immediately perking up.

I felt a bit of the dark cloud shift away. "Yeah," I said sheepishly. "I did."

"What happened after that?"

"Nothing. I mean, I don't know why I was expecting to hear a voice or something, but I tried to listen. Maybe God isn't ready to talk to me yet."

"I'm proud of you," he said, beaming at me.

"Why? I didn't really do anything and nothing happened."

"Because it was a huge first step, Carly."

"Yeah, I guess it was," I said. "Thank you. I've always been so scared that I wasn't doing it right or that God wouldn't listen."

"Well, I believe that God hears all of our prayers, the spoken and the unspoken ones."

"Then why doesn't He answer them?" I asked.

Joe looked thoughtful for a moment. "Because God doesn't serve us. We serve *Him*. He's not required to do anything for us."

"Then why pray at all?"

"Ted's mother has talked about prayer as a way to get our hearts right with God. It's a chance for us to make our requests known to God, and then we give God the space to answer how He sees fit. Sometimes, He'll challenge us to change our mindset, and other times, He'll encourage us to keep trusting Him even if it seems impossible."

I took a moment to digest Joe's explanation and compare it to my own upbringing. "Pastor Ivy always talked about God's promises as 'yes and amen.' It sounded like some kind of formula. You do xyz, and then God answers your prayers."

"That makes Jesus sound like a vending machine. Say the right prayers, believe the right doctrine, push a button, out pops a candy bar. It also sounds pretty arrogant."

"Arrogant?" I jerked in surprise. "His point was how we need to obey God if we want to receive His blessings. My mother liked to throw that in my face any time I asked for something. Of course, I was never obedient enough for her."

Joe reached out to hold my hand. "Carly, that's horrible. It's wrong on so many levels."

"Are we talking about me?" Poppy said icily from just beyond us.

Joe and I both stood up to see her standing a few feet away with her arms folded across her chest. Her eyes darted to our held hands and then narrowed at Joe.

"Don't you look at me like that, Poppy," he said, pulling me closer toward him. "You are so out of line, it's not even funny. I'm halfway tempted to call Jared myself."

"Do you know what you're doing?" she asked, her voice thin. "You've been through so much, and Carly isn't a Christian. I don't want to see you get hurt again."

"Wow," I mouthed, stunned by the woman I had mistakenly viewed as a loving mother figure. The betrayal felt like a punch to the gut.

Joe's expression grew more rigid. "Nothing happened between Carly and me that I didn't want or encourage myself. You have no right to interfere, and you're only hurting yourself by making assumptions without facts."

"So, what are the facts?" she snapped. "By all means, enlighten me."

"None of your business," I piped up next to Joe. "The facts

are that you're a self-righteous hypocrite sticking her nose where it doesn't belong."

Ignoring me, Poppy looked at Joe. "Is that how you feel?"

"What are you doing here?" he asked with strained patience.

"Trying to keep you from ruining your life." Charitably, she glanced over at me and tacked on, "And you too, Carly. You guys have no idea what you're doing."

"I don't recall the Holy Spirit taking a day off and putting you in charge," Joe said coolly. "Carly and I are both adults. We don't need your permission or approval to have a relationship."

"So, it's a *relationship* now?"

"It's none of your business," I repeated, taking a step closer to Joe. "I don't understand why you can't get it through your head. I knew you were full of it when you said you'd lead a parade when Joe found the right woman."

He glanced sharply at her, horrified.

"Carly, why would you share that?" she hissed, glaring daggers at me.

"Because it's completely inappropriate!" Joe said angrily. "Poppy, you're being ridiculous. I didn't assign you to be in charge of my love life just because something almost happened between us two and a half years ago. Whether you want to believe it or not, I *have* moved on. Supposedly, you did too."

"I just don't understand," she said, looking me up and down. "Why her?"

"What's wrong with *her*?" Joe demanded, answering Poppy before I could blast her into outer space. "Don't act like you don't have a past or that your husband doesn't either. You put that entire story to print for the world to read, so I'm struggling to understand why Carly's sins are somehow worse than Jared's."

"But she's my coworker," she blurted out, her eyes tearing.

My angry response died, realizing the truth.

"Is that what this is about?" Joe asked, his voice pitched higher in shock. "Do you think my interest in Carly is just some stunt to make you jealous? Like I'm secretly in love with you or something?"

Poppy's face had gone white, her own secrets exposed rather than ours.

Joe gently tugged me along with him as he drew closer to Poppy. Softly, he asked, "Do you think I'm still mooning over you and using Carly as revenge?"

"Aren't you?" she asked weakly.

"Poppy," he said in disbelief, "you've worked with Carly for almost two years. How did you miss how incredible she is? This woman is bright, funny, caring, compassionate, and persistent. I'd still be pushing her off on Rabbi Zendler if she hadn't challenged me to be honest with my own feelings about her."

Poppy and I both shared shocked expressions at Joe's declaration.

Continuing, he said, "Carly caught my attention the first time I met her. I hadn't felt that way about anyone since Catherine."

I winced, knowing what that confession cost Joe and what it would do to Poppy. Despite my frustration with her, I knew Joe had painfully deflated her ego. I realized how she had romanticized Joe's interest in her, perhaps rewriting history as the heroine of her own tale of courtly love.

"I...I don't know what to say," she murmured. "Carly, I did think Joe was just using you to get back at me."

He sucked in a breath, stunned to hear Poppy actually confirm his suspicions.

"And since I'm not a Christian, you blamed *me* instead of Joe," I said, putting the puzzle pieces together. "Poppy, you knew you'd be out of line confronting Joe, but heathen Carly was fair game, right?"

Joe's expression was a mixture of outrage and disappointment.

"I'm sorry," she said numbly, her head bowed.

I shook my head in disgust. "And you wonder why I want nothing to do with Jesus when there are Christians like you."

"Carly," Joe said, squeezing my hand. "This is Poppy at her worst."

"And yet she's judged me for what I did at *my* worst," I spat.

"You're right," she said contritely. "I don't even know what to say, guys. I've made a huge error in judgment."

"Judgment would definitely be the appropriate word to use," I bit.

"I think I'm going to take the rest of the day off," she mumbled. "Carly, I don't mean to dump all the work on you, but I think that might be best for everyone. I'll leave as soon as you get back."

I nodded stiffly. "Probably for the best. I'm not sure I can stand to be working in the same office with you right now."

Braving a glance into my eyes, I saw the pain and regret in Poppy's gaze. My heart softened at her obvious remorse, but the anger remained.

"I'm so embarrassed!" she said, touching her hands to her cheeks. "I don't know how I got things so horribly wrong. Joe, can you ever forgive me?"

He frowned. "The apology you owe is to Carly, and quite frankly, to your husband. As for me, I don't need anything from you other than a clear understanding of boundaries."

She swallowed audibly. "I understand." Glancing back over at me, she said, "Carly, I'm sorry. I violated your confidence and threw it in your face. I'm ashamed of myself and how I've behaved. I hope you can forgive me one day."

I acknowledged her apology with a slight nod. "Thanks."

Wiping tears from her face, she turned and slipped through the Vincenzo's glass door.

"You okay?" Joe asked, studying me.

"Did that really just happen?" I breathed. "I mean, all of it? This woman with the gall to lecture me about torturing myself just threw my past in my face without a moment's hesitation. And for what? Her own stupid pride. She didn't care how she hurt me at all. It was about keeping her claws all over *you*."

Joe shook his head sadly. "Not that it's any consolation, but her attempt to humiliate you exploded in her own face."

"No, it's not any consolation. I don't need or want revenge. I just want to meet a Christian who isn't a judgmental hypocrite."

Joe's mouth turned into a small smile. "You'd be hard-pressed to find any human on this planet who isn't guilty of being a hypocrite."

I held up a hand to stop him. "Don't do that, Joe. Pastor Ivy had this glib, condescending attitude about people who'd left First United. He'd tell the members how *every* church had hypocrites. He'd smirk and say there was always room for one more in the pews. He made it sound like people who left were just being petty and ridiculous."

"I see," he said, studying me with that penetrating, jade gaze. "Carly, you know that's not what I meant though, don't you?"

"No," I answered honestly. "Part of me knows you're different from any other man I've known, and part of me keeps waiting for you to act just like everybody else."

CHAPTER 17

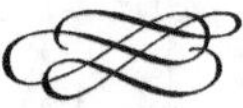

"THERE'S NO PRESSURE FROM ME," HE SAID, STARING intently into my eyes.

I glanced down at our held hands. "Is that right?"

He pulled his hand away. "I'm not manipulating you, Carly.

"You told Poppy we were in a relationship."

"I did," he admitted, "but that's also because I don't quite know what to call this thing going on between us. Clearly, we're more than friends, but we also have some barriers keeping us from moving beyond a platonic relationship."

"I can't do the hot-cold thing," I said, staring back into his eyes. "You said you know what you want."

"I did. I also asked what *you* want."

"What I want comes with strings, and it puts us right back where we were last night in the parking deck."

"I understand," he said. "If and when you give your heart to Christ, it needs to be a decision you make for yourself, I don't want you to fake it or do it to placate me."

I sighed, plopping into the leather chair I'd vacated.

Joe sat back down next to me, watchful.

"Can I ask you a favor?" I said.

His eyes brightened. "Sure."

"Something happened to me when we were at Beth Tefillah. I have to go back and see if it was a one off or if the God they worship in that synagogue is real."

Joe's brows drew together in question. "It's not two separate gods, Carly."

"Robbie seems to think so."

He pulled a face. "That's not much of a surprise. He's a Reform rabbi."

"But the experience I had in that synagogue was *real*. I've never felt anything like that in a church."

Joe studied me. "How many churches have you been to other than First United?"

"A few," I hedged. "Different events, but nothing as often as First United."

"So, what are you saying?"

I swallowed before speaking. "What if Jewish people are worshiping the *real* God, and Christians got it all wrong, like Robbie, er Rabbi Zendler said?"

Rather than dismissing me as I suspected Poppy might, Joe considered my question. "When I was in that coma, I had a vision of Yeshua. He told me He loves me and He has a purpose for my life."

"Is Yeshua different than Jesus?" I asked.

Joe shook his head. "No, Yeshua is the Hebrew name for Jesus. It's the name they called him living as a rabbi in first century Israel."

"Jesus is Jewish?"

"Yes," Joe said, smiling encouragingly. "I'm sure it was something Pastor Ivy would have intentionally ignored."

I nodded. "He always talked about Jesus starting a new religion. He said the Law was nailed to the cross and only someone who wanted to be enslaved to man-made rules would follow it."

Joe held up a hand to object. "The Torah is God's Law that He gave to Moses. That's what they read at synagogue."

"I remember."

"So, it doesn't make any sense that Pastor Ivy would call the Torah 'man-made' when it's very clear that it's the word of *God*."

"Well, don't Jewish people have a bunch of extra rules they follow? Traditions and all of that? Pastor Ivy talked about it a lot."

"We do," Joe said, "but if you ask a Jew from New York or Israel or Morocco which traditions they observe, they're all going to have a different answer. There's no ubiquitous, gold standard for practicing Judaism."

"Meaning what?"

"Meaning that it's not the tradition in and of itself that makes someone Jewish."

"Then, what does?" I asked, genuinely curious. "Rabbi Zendler said that the Levines aren't Jewish because they believe in Jesus."

"Most rabbis believe the same," Joe said, "but my mother is still a Schwartz whether I believe in Jesus or not. I still had a *bris* as a baby. Faith in Jesus didn't change any of that."

"I read about the bris in Taylor's book," I replied. "I never knew there was an actual ceremony for circumcision. Seems kind of cool, actually."

"It's been going on for four thousand years. It all started with Abraham and was a physical sign of God's covenant with the Jewish people."

"So, then what's the right answer?" I asked. "Are you

supposed to be Jewish, or are you supposed to be a Christian? I mean, I don't agree with everything Robbie said, but I know he would never act like Pastor Ivy. Is the Jewish God the real God, or is it Jesus?"

"Yes," Joe said with a smile.

I pursed my lips. "I'm being serious."

"So am I! Jesus is God's son. Above the cross, they wrote the words 'King of the Jews.' He was called *rabbi* by his disciples, and everything He did fulfilled the Jewish Scripture. No matter what Pastor Ivy or anyone else says, Jesus didn't come to start a new religion. He came to reform the version of Judaism being practiced two thousand years ago."

I shook my head. "How am I supposed to keep all of this straight? I feel like I need a theology degree to keep up."

Joe chuckled. "Then, let me simplify it. God set up His laws and His way of being made clean when we inevitably fall short. They used to sacrifice animals in the Temple."

"What?" I gasped. "People actually did that?"

"Animal sacrifice might offend our modern sensibilities, but it was common practice in ancient culture. Pagans performed all sorts of animal sacrifice rituals themselves, some of which God expressly forbade in the Torah."

I leaned my cheek into my fist, absorbing every word from Joe. "Keep going."

He grinned. "Now keep in mind, I didn't know all of what I'm sharing when I prayed with Kyle and Ted to believe in Jesus. I just knew that I was dead, and God allowed me to wake up. I asked Ted if he knew who Yeshua was and that I'd seen him while I was unconscious. I've never seen the mighty Margolin cry before or after, but he wept. Kyle started shaking."

"Wow."

"When they told me that I had seen a vision of Jesus, I felt this sense of peace that I couldn't explain. I knew down in my bones it was the truth."

"How?" I asked. "How could you possibly know something like that?"

Joe shrugged. "I just did. When I prayed with the guys, I felt these chains come off of me. I didn't feel so heavy anymore."

"Oh," I breathed, immediately thinking of my own experience. "Is that what happened to me at Beth Tefillah?"

He smiled brilliantly. "That's what it sounded like when you told me. It shocked me how similar it was to the vision I had."

"But why would a Christian God talk to me in a Jewish synagogue?"

"That's what I'm trying to tell you," Joe said. "Jesus isn't a *Christian* God. He's the Jewish Messiah, Son of the Living God. He is worshiped by Christians, but He wasn't created by Christians. Before the beginning of Creation, He *was*. Jesus created the cosmos."

"Wait, what?" I said, confused.

"Here," Joe said, pulling out his phone to read from *John 1*. "In the beginning was the Word, and the Word was with God, and the Word was God. He was with God in the beginning. Through him all things were made; without him nothing was made that has been made. In him was life, and that life was the light of all mankind."

"Then why don't Jews believe in Jesus?" I asked. "If Jesus was with God in the beginning, why do Jewish people act like Christians started some new religion?"

"Because they did start a new religion," Joe said, "but not because Jesus did. Pastor Ivy might have purposefully misrepresented verses about the Law being nailed to the cross, but there are so many other verses in the New Testament that uphold the importance of the Law. Jesus died to take away the punishment we should have for not keeping God's commands. He didn't put an end to the Law itself, and He said that pretty plainly. *Matthew 5:17-19* comes up in Bible study quite a bit."

"So, then why aren't Christians keeping the Law?" I asked. "If what you're saying is true, and Jesus didn't throw the Law away, then why do Christians have their own holidays and seem to know nothing about the Jewish ones?"

"Not all Christians do," Joe said. "In fact, many of them embrace the feasts of the Bible. Unfortunately, even that can get taken too far. Jared came out of the messianic synagogue thinking that part of being right with God meant he was required to keep every word of the Torah."

"I'm so confused," I said, taking a sip of cappuccino that had grown lukewarm. "It sounds like you're contradicting yourself. Are Christians supposed to keep the Law or not? If Jesus didn't get rid of it, then what was the point of Him dying on the cross?"

Joe smiled broadly at me, that jade sparkle causing my heart to skip a beat.

"What?" I asked, blushing. "Why are you looking at me like that?"

"You ask amazing questions, Carly. If someone were faking their faith, they'd never get it past you. No wonder your mother and Pastor Ivy worked so hard to gaslight and control you. Nothing they believed in was real. They worshiped that church and Pastor Ivy."

"Pastor Ivy worshiped himself?"

Joe raised that wonderfully expressive brow. "You even have to ask?"

I exhaled a soft chuckle. "No, I guess not. I can't tell you how many times they called me rebellious, or they just shut me down."

"I'm sure they did," Joe said grimly, his expression falling. "Like I said last night, your questions aren't making me doubt my faith. It's forcing me to really think about what I believe. Having to defend and explain it just confirms why I gave my life to Christ."

"So, are you going to answer my question about keeping the Law?" I asked with a note of teasing.

That winsome smile reappeared as did the familiar heartbeat dedicated to Joe Trautweig. "You're helping me with my Bible study, believe it or not."

"I am?"

Joe pulled open his Bible app again. "The guys and I have been reading the book of *Galatians*, specifically because we want to understand how we're supposed to live as Jews and believers in Jesus. Having to explain it to you has helped solidify my own feelings about it."

"Interesting," I murmured, now returning Joe's intense scrutiny with my own. "Nobody ever took the time to explain this to me. I think I've learned more in the last twenty minutes than I did in eighteen years going to church with my mother."

Joe reached over to hold my hand again. "Carly, I'm sorry you've met such empty, soulless people calling themselves believers."

"It's not all of them," I said quickly. "My old roommate, Courtney, was one of the good ones. She just doesn't understand all of this Bible stuff like you do. Is that because you're Jewish?"

Joe laughed, a deep baritone that brought a smile to my own face. "Carly, do you think being Jewish automatically makes me an expert on all things related to Judaism or the Old Testament? I assure you, it doesn't."

"Oh," I said, feeling embarrassed. "Poppy and Jared both seem so knowledgeable. I guess I assumed it was all of you."

That irresistible smile appeared again, and I wondered how much longer I would be able to drag my heels hashing things out with Jesus. I didn't want to go another day without seeing that smile on Joe's face. I realized I didn't want to spend another day not seeing or talking to Joe Trautweig.

"Carly?" he asked, noting I had slipped from the conversation.

I stood up too quickly, wobbling as the blood rushed to my feet. Joe rose to steady me.

"What's wrong?" he asked, searching my face. "What happened? Are you okay? You disappeared for a minute, and then you looked like you'd seen a ghost."

I shook my head. "Not a ghost, Joe, but I do need to get back to work. I don't want to push Ted's kindness this morning. He's still Culver's biggest moneymaker, and I've got a project of his sitting on my desk."

"Let me walk you back," he said, gathering his own empty cup of coffee.

I shook my head. "No, don't worry about it. I'll be fine."

"Carly," he said warily, "you're starting to scare me. I thought we were having a great discussion. What happened?"

"I promise I was enjoying our conversation as much as you," I said. "I just realized there are some things I need to take care of, and I'm losing my morning."

"And that's it?"

I couldn't stand one more lie, so I simply nodded.

It was way too soon to tell Joe Trautweig I had fallen in love with him.

CHAPTER 18

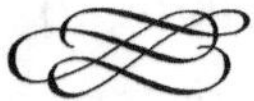

D ESPITE A FEW MORE PROTESTS, I FINALLY RELENTED and allowed Joe to escort me back to the office. Truth to be told, I didn't want to relinquish my hand on his arm, the butterflies in my stomach, or the near surge of tears that it was possible to be in love after Dylan.

Secretly, I spied on Joe any time his gaze was pulled from mine, drinking in the sight of him as if I needed to commit the moment to memory.

"What?" he asked, turning toward me.

"What?" I repeated, feigning ignorance.

He stopped and began the onslaught of those jade eyes. "You keep staring at me. Why?"

"What do you mean I'm staring at you?"

He pulled a face. "Carly, you've almost tripped half a dozen times. You're not wearing those red boots of yours, so you tell me what's got you so distracted."

"You have to ask after everything that's already happened this morning?"

"Okay, I'm just going to have to be more direct, aren't I?"

I gulped, my heart pounding.

"Carly, the way you're looking at me has nothing to do with Poppy Levine. The way it makes *me* feel has nothing to do with Poppy either."

"Joe," I whispered, absolutely drowning in his eyes.

He cupped my face, then rested his forehead against mine. I sighed, thankful for a respite from that soulful stare further connecting my heart to his.

"How did this happen?" he asked, chuckling softly. "How in the world did this happen so fast, so soon?"

I shrugged. "I am done trying to figure it out. I'm tired of fighting it."

He peeled his forehead off of mine, delving deeply into my eyes once again. "Against all odds, hmm?"

"I'm not saying it first," I blurted out.

"Good," he said, smiling at me, "because I need more time to process all of it and make sure I'm not getting caught up in feelings and pheromones."

I laughed. "Pheromones?"

He winked at me. "You're an irresistible force, Carly Miller."

I grinned back.

"Come on," he said, gently tugging me forward. "I need to get you back before curfew. The warden likes to crack the whip at Culver."

Joe's cellphone buzzed as we entered tornado alley, and with a frown, he said he had to take the call. I nodded in understanding, thankful I wouldn't have to fight against the goodbye kiss I wanted to receive. I waved briefly at Joe as he walked toward the adjoining high-rise housing Cooper & Jaye.

True to her word, Poppy cleared out of the office as soon as I returned. Phil stopped by to check on a project, surprised to discover Poppy had left. I kept my excuse vague, deciding she could explain her hasty departure for herself. When Ted arrived for an update on his latest RFP, he was stunned to learn Poppy had stormed down to Vincenzo's.

"Did you speak to her?" I asked.

He shook his head. "No, I wound up on an unexpected conference call. Is Poppy planning to come back to the office?"

I shrugged. "No clue."

"Can I ask what happened, or is it none of my business?"

"It might affect the business if she decides to quit."

Ted's eyebrows raised in alarm. "Quit? Why? What happened?"

I exhaled a heavy sigh. "The short version is that Poppy embarrassed herself by confronting me and Joe. This was after already sticking her foot in her mouth before you and I ran into each other this morning."

Ted took a step closer and lowered his voice. "What do you mean by confronting you and Joe? Why didn't she stop by to apologize? Forgive me, but I'm actually shocked. This doesn't sound like Poppy at all."

I frowned, not liking the same response from Ted that I had earlier received from Joe. It meant that sentimentality wasn't clouding his judgment. It also meant I couldn't write off Poppy as easily as I wanted. "She read us the riot act like God's self-appointed messenger."

"Ah," he said, computing the information. "Knowing Joe, I doubt things went the way Poppy anticipated."

"No, they did not. He removed her from her self-made pedestal."

The mighty Margolin winced. "I have a feeling I'll be hearing some version of this from my wife later. She and Poppy are best friends."

"Speaking of," I said, not wanting to discuss my coworker anymore, "do you remember saying Rebecca would be willing to meet me for lunch?"

"I do," Ted said, cocking his head to the side. "Did you want to set up a time?"

"Yes," I said. "Talking to Joe has forced me to reconsider a lot of the stuff I learned from Pastor Ivy and from my mother. Sometimes, you don't know you're believing a lie until someone speaks the truth."

He assessed me for a moment before a smile appeared. "I'd be glad to reach out to my wife and see when she's available. The girls have a music class two days a week, so I'll ask Rebecca what will work with her schedule. Do you ever eat at The Soaring Scone? It's her favorite restaurant in Parkview and where she likes to meet her friends for brunch."

"Other than the occasional trip for frozen yogurt, I bring my lunch," I said. "Money got a lot tighter when I moved into my own apartment."

"Not a problem. We'd love to treat you anyway, Carly."

I gaped. "No, I couldn't ask that! I'm the one asking for a lunch date anyway."

"It's our pleasure," Ted said in a tone that let me know arguing would be fruitless. "Rebecca is always happy to help any abuse survivor and answer questions."

"Didn't she go on a book tour for *Tabula Rasa*?" I asked.

That infamous golden sparkle lit the mighty Margolin's eyes. "My wife is an extraordinary woman, and she deserves every bit of her success with the book. She's certainly earned it after all the hell she's been through with her father and that sociopath."

"I witnessed some of it," I said, surprising him. "I was closer in age to her baby sister, but I did see Pastor or Mrs. Ivy scold Rebecca on more than one occasion. One time, I saw Pastor Ivy slap Rebecca. I told my mother about it because I wanted her to see how Pastor Ivy wasn't some angel of light. She grabbed me by the arm and beat me at home."

"What?" Ted said, appalled.

I swallowed. "My mother was Pastor Ivy's biggest fan other than his wife."

"So, she was one of the adoring legion," he said derisively.

"It's possible," I hedged, "but my mother acts more like a Puritan than the characters in Poppy's romance novels. What I know for sure is that my mother protects Pastor Ivy at all costs. I was beaten with books or shoes for pointing out weird things happening in the church."

"Carly, I am so sorry," Ted said with emotion in his voice. "I'd wind up in jail for what I'd do to anyone who ever laid a finger on Rebecca or the kids."

I smiled, comforted by his protectiveness over his family. "Congratulations, by the way," I said, remembering their recent announcement. "How is Rebecca feeling?"

Ted's somber expression gave way easily to a large grin. "She's doing great. And, as it turns out, we're going to be calling Rabbi Peretz."

"Rabbi Peretz?" I asked. "Didn't he perform Poppy and Jared's vow renewal ceremony?"

"That too," Ted replied. "He also performed the bris for Ian and Taylor's first son."

"Oh!" I gasped, having momentarily forgotten the connection. "*Mazel tov!* Did I say that right? I'm still working on all of the Jewish lingo I've picked up around Poppy."

"Perfect pronunciation, Carly. You said it like you've been using Hebrew your entire life. My wife and I are obviously thrilled, although Rebecca was a bit shell shocked after the sonogram. She says she has no idea how to shop for a little boy."

I laughed. "I'm sure she'll figure it out. Every time I see your girls, they're always beautifully dressed."

Ted chuckled. "Rebecca will tell you my mother and her Nana have more to do with those cute outfits than she does. Her tastes aren't quite as fancy as theirs, but I suppose that's a grandmother's prerogative to shower her granddaughters with frilly dresses."

I pushed back thoughts of my own child, reminding myself that I *would* find a way to move past what I'd done.

"Carly?" Ted asked. "You all right?"

"Fine," I said, sniffing back the sadness that continued to dull since the floor of Beth Tefillah. "I appreciate the offer from you and your wife."

"Absolutely our pleasure," he replied. Glancing over the messy piles on my desk, he asked, "Will you be okay with Poppy out? Do you know if and when she's coming back?"

"I don't, but corporate finally beefed up their after hours help desk, so I can send some of the smaller projects out to headquarters."

"That's something," he said. "Poppy doesn't typically use corporate if she can help it."

"Well," I said with a fake smile, "I'm also not as controlling as other people around here. If a document doesn't come back as perfectly as I would do it, I don't lose my head about it."

Ted frowned, but he couldn't fault the bitterness in my tone after such an abysmal morning. Later in the day, he sent me an email offering a few dates Rebecca would be available. Poppy, meanwhile, sent an email copying me, Ted, and Phil that she had a "family emergency" that would be taking her out of the office for the rest of the week.

"Family emergency," I muttered, "probably Jared ripping your head off for being so stupid."

I felt a twinge of guilt at my less than charitable musings, but I couldn't shake the look of betrayal in Poppy's eyes when she'd asked Joe, "Why her?" like I was inherently defective.

I stayed an extra hour to get caught up on all of the documents now dumped on me from Poppy. I texted Joe that I was finally leaving the office.

Can you meet? I asked him.

Already took off, sorry. Early flight to Cleveland in the AM.

"Probably for the best," I muttered, knowing I wanted Joe to console me with more than just words. Texting back, I wrote, *How did your Bible study go?*

Very interesting conversation. I mentioned several of the things we discussed this morning.

Sounds good.

Carly, how are you doing with everything?

Everything being you and me, or everything being the disaster with Poppy this morning? I asked.

Yes.

I chuckled at his dry sense of humor. *I'm okay, I guess. I don't know how I'm ever going to look at her the same way. She took off the rest of the week. Not sure if she's coming back...or if I want her to.*

I don't blame you. Sunday at the Goldsteins' will be pretty awkward if the Levines show up. Jared wasn't exactly my biggest fan before all of this morning's festivities.

I smirked. *Well, I know he was a fan of you and me being together, so he might be further in your corner than you think. When do you get back into town?*

Late Saturday, he replied.

Too bad. I would have invited you over for dinner. I make a mean chili.

I felt and noted Joe's hesitation before he responded to my text message. The unspoken connection made the prospect of time together in close quarters a greater temptation.

Or we could go out, I finally wrote back.

Probably better that way. I'll text you when I get back into town. I've got an early flight and need to run some errands before I call it a night.

I felt the sting of rejection, but only because of my own disappointment in wanting to see Joe. Forcing a smile on my face even though I knew he couldn't see it, I sent a lighthearted text and then pressed my head back into the driver seat of my car.

"Stop it, Carly," I muttered to myself. "It takes two people to actually be in love. Otherwise, it's just infatuation."

I sighed again, hardly convinced by my own ice bucket to the face. Instead, I contemplated doing something I had been ruminating over the last few days. Rather than using Joe Trautweig as my guiding force, I decided to make another trip to Beth Tefillah to see if Jesus was in the building or if I had discovered an entirely new faith.

CHAPTER 19

I DECIDED TO TRY A PARKING SPOT TOWARD THE front of Beth Tefillah, not wanting another dark hallway escort from Robbie Zendler. The thought of seeing him filled me with a strange disquiet. Even though Robbie was no temptation with my heart firmly tethered to Joe, something about the idea of more than friendly interest from him made me queasy.

Hoping to calm my misgivings, I read over a text message from Joe. He had sent another Bible verse about God's love, letting me infer what I wanted about his own feelings toward me.

Texting Joe, I wrote, *Crazy as it seems, I feel like I'm being romanced by Jesus through you. Does that sound weird?*

Not at all. It's actually a huge encouragement for me that I'm doing a good job in sharing the gospel.

Sharing the gospel? Do you mean Jesus died for my sins and all of that?

No, Carly. The gospel that God so LOVED the world, and that includes YOU. He loves you. Nothing you have done or could ever do will separate you from His love.

I blinked back tears, my heart so desperate to hear that God truly saw me as anything other than the abomination of Hannah Miller's creation.

Carly? You still there?

Still here. Don't make me cry off my makeup before I go into the synagogue.

Wouldn't want that, he wrote, adding some silly faced emojis. *Let me know how it goes, okay? I'm bored out of my mind in this hotel, and I miss seeing your smile.*

I blushed, halfway tempted to send Joe a selfie of me in my synagogue apparel. I wore black slacks and a simple top, not wanting to draw undue attention to a figure that already called for it. I left my hair loose around my shoulders, hoping to present just well enough to blend in.

Throwing caution to the wind, I took a picture sticking out my tongue and looking cross-eyed into the camera. Taking a second selfie, I gave a genuine smile. I sent both to Joe and waited.

I could almost hear his baritone laugh as he sent the corresponding emojis. *Gorgeous as usual,* he wrote back. *Thanks for that. I hope you enjoy the service tonight and that you get the answers you're looking for. I'll be praying for you.*

My smile grew, and I thanked Joe quickly before packing up my cell phone and heading inside the synagogue. This time, I walked directly into the atrium, feeling a bit out of place without a posse of friends to help insulate me. I was both relieved and disappointed that no one made it a point to introduce themselves, but I reminded myself that had been my intent.

Familiar enough with the layout, I easily made my way toward the sanctuary.

"*Güt Shabbos,*" one of the ushers said, handing me a paper program. I walked past a bookshelf full of blue prayer books and grabbed a siddur. Pushing away anxious thoughts of navigating the Jewish book without any of my synagogue tour guides to help me, I remembered that Hebrew read right to left, as did the prayer book. I just hoped I'd be able to follow along.

The synagogue seemed emptier than when I'd attended services with the Levines. I found a seat closer to the back and wondered if anyone would join me. Instead, I remained an island. I realized the smattering of congregants probably represented the usual weekly turn out.

"No wonder they hired Robbie," I said, glancing around the room. Hannah Birnbaum was missing from the front row seat she'd occupied last time, but Dr. Feldstein sat in the second row with his wife. I didn't see Poppy's mother or father in attendance, just a few silver-haired members and the same young couple I'd crossed paths with the first time I'd attended Beth Tefillah.

Cantor Allen began the service with the booming voice I remembered from before. I smiled, hoping to feel the same reverence and awe. Keeping my head lowered throughout all of the liturgy, I read the words on the page of the prayer book and avoided Robbie's gaze from the stage. Not long into the service, I frowned, wondering why this night felt so different.

The recitation was exactly how it had been months earlier, only it felt lifeless. Much like flat soda, the novelty of that previously unopened bottle had worn off. In its place were beautiful words chanted with little enthusiasm. I wondered if it had been the devotion of the Levines or even Hannah Birnbaum that had touched my heart. Back then, the words seemed to have meaning for all of them, and hence, for me. This group felt like they were bored and going through the motions.

Doctor Feldstein seemed distracted by something on his phone, and the other members recited the Hebrew in monotone unison. I glanced up at Cantor Allen leading the liturgy from the bima, and he at least, seemed reverent in the prayers he chanted. I smiled slightly, hoping to siphon off some of that joy for myself, but the gnawing emptiness persisted.

I made the mistake of letting my gaze drift over to the side of the bima, and I caught Robbie's eye. His face brightened immediately, and I felt a lead ball in my stomach. I looked away, wishing I had Joe Trautweig standing beside me.

Although Robbie didn't linger long on the Torah reading or the drash, the Scripture recitation did nothing for me. There was no heart pounding, moment of clarity, no sudden discovery of Bible verses never heard before. Instead, I felt more hollow and confused than I did before entering the building. With everything in me, I wanted to escape and run back to my car. I couldn't shake the overwhelming waves of panic, and I didn't know what had triggered my fight or flight response.

When Robbie dismissed the congregation, I bolted for the door. All I wanted to do was flee to my home, text Joe, and maybe even attempt to talk to Jesus again. I wanted to know what exactly happened the last time I had attended Beth Tefillah and why it didn't happen again.

"Carly!" Rob called, just as I opened my car door.

He puffed out a few breaths as he met me, jogging up to me in the parking lot.

"Hi," I said sheepishly.

"Leaving so soon? I don't think I've ever seen anyone leave the sanctuary so fast. Was it that bad?" he teased.

I shook my head. "No, it just wasn't what I was expecting."

He raised an eyebrow. I noted he had glasses on this time, looking even more studious than before. "I'm curious what expectations you had, Carly. We didn't do anything differently than we do any other week."

"I think that's the part I wasn't expecting."

"What do you mean?"

"Don't you guys ever get bored? I mean, it's the same prayers done the same way week after week. Last time was different for me, but maybe that's because it was the first time I'd ever heard any of the liturgy."

"Our prayers and our traditions are part of who we are," Robbie said. "Any Jew across the globe will be saying some version of these same prayers. It's what connects us together in Judaism."

"But what about God?" I asked. "How do you connect with God when you just go through the motions of saying the same thing every time?"

Robbie's frown grew more pronounced. "What are you saying? That we should just make up prayers *ad hoc?* Give up who we are? People take comfort in these prayers. It gives them a sense of belonging."

"But they're just words," I argued. "Is God real to you, or is it all about religious performance?"

"Why do you keep asking me about this?" he said, annoyed. "You're insinuating that practicing Judaism is somehow separate from God. It might not look like what you're used to in a Christian church, but the people here are devoted to God and to Judaism. We practice our Judaism to honor *Hashem,*" he added.

"But is God real to *you,* Robbie?"

"Real?" he asked, raising an eyebrow. "I believe God exists if that's what you mean."

I shook my head, hoping I could get him to understand.

"Something happened to me when I was here last time. I don't know how to describe it other than I think God spoke to me when I was passed out on the floor."

He scoffed. "God spoke to you? Like an audible voice?"

"Yes!" I said, growing irritated. "I thought if I came back to Beth Tefillah, it might happen again. I need to know which God is real. Robbie, you guys have all of these incredible prayers in the siddur, but do they mean anything to you other than identifying with other Jews? I understand wanting to connect as a community, but have you thought about the stuff you're saying? Do you believe any of it?"

"Who are you to question what I believe?" he asked imperiously. "What do you know anyway? You were raised in a church. I don't owe you an answer."

Unfazed, especially since his response reminded me of something my mother would say, I dug in my heels. "Are you saying it's impossible for God to speak to a lowly gentile? He couldn't possibly speak to an uneducated idiot like me, right?"

"I never said you were an idiot!"

"May as well have," I shot back. "I don't understand why you're so defensive about this. Don't the people in synagogue ask questions too? Last time, you told me you were putting out a dumpster fire because of Natalie Levine's bat mitzvah. Are people asking questions about God and about Jesus? What do you even tell them? 'Hey guys, take comfort in these prayers, but don't actually *believe* anything that we recite each week.'"

"Slow down," he said, agitated. "You're putting words in my mouth."

"And you're implying that my head has nothing in it."

Ignoring my retort, he said, "Natalie Levine's public declaration of Jesus caused several members to leave or threaten to do so. Some of them wanted Harriet Berman removed from the synagogue board for supporting her granddaughter. There's been concern that Beth Tefillah would turn into a church or that Natalie's behavior would encourage others to misuse the bima as a platform for Jesus."

"Jesus was a rabbi, wasn't he?" I asked. "Didn't it say King of the Jews above the cross?"

Robbie squirmed. "I am not discussing Christian apologetics with you. Besides, I thought you didn't believe in any of this Jesus *mishigas* yourself."

"I'm not sure what I believe anymore. I had an encounter with God on the floor of your synagogue. It seemed like a crazy idea that Jesus would speak to me in a Reform synagogue, but I'm running out of ways to explain what happened."

Robbie's expression turned dismissive. "You were unconscious, Carly. It was probably your imagination."

I studied my old friend, saddened and disappointed to realize the truth before me. Quietly, I said, "Would you even know if God spoke to you, Robbie? Do you believe that's possible, or is it just going through the motions of Jewish prayers and then telling yourself God is happy with it? Don't you want to be able to ask Him for yourself?"

"That's Christian doctrine talking," he smirked. "I've heard all of the 'personal relationship' stuff and pretending that God actually speaks to people like He did in the Bible. Things are a little different than they were three thousand years ago."

Offput but not undaunted, I asked, "Why do you assume that your understanding of God or the Bible has to be the only correct one? What makes you so convinced you're infallible?"

He seemed offended by my question. "Your Christian theologians have misunderstood Scripture and twisted it for their own antisemitic agenda since day one. Go read what they did at the Council of Nicea when they enacted Christianity as the state religion of the Roman Empire. Read about the antisemitism going back as early as 50 BCE with Justin Martyr. Whatever Jesus may have intended in traditional Judaism, all you have to do is start reading the heresy of Paul's books to see how anti-Torah and anti-Jewish these Christians were. It's why I can't wrap my head around the Levines or anyone else claiming that they're Jews, yet they follow these antisemitic men."

"I hear what you're saying, Robbie, and I don't know enough about church history to debate all of this with you."

He crossed his arms over his chest as if that settled the argument.

"But have you ever thought about your own attitude toward Christians? As someone who came to Beth Tefillah searching for answers, what makes you think that I would reject Christianity when I get the same nasty, arrogant attitude that I experienced from the narcissist who led my mother's church? Do you know that every argument you've made about Christians not under-standing the Bible are the same arguments I've heard about Jews, only in reverse? All of you act like you have a monopoly on understanding the Bible and everyone else is stupid and wrong. You sound exactly like all the other self-righteous hypocrites I know who look down their noses at anyone who doesn't interpret the Bible exactly like they do."

His mouth opened and shut, his eyes burning bright.

I continued, "You can keep treating me like I'm ignorant and uneducated, but you're just proving my point."

He puffed out his chest. "So, you've spent eight years studying the Bible at a Hebrew university, Carly? Eight years reading the Bible in its original language and studying thou-sands of years of commentary by the brightest minds in Judaism?"

I sighed wearily. "Every time I asked my mother or Pastor

Ivy any questions, they gave me the same condescending attitude you are. Instead of admitting they don't have all the answers, they just shut me down and insulted me. You can't tell me any you're different when you act exactly the same."

"Well, it *is* different," he huffed, still glaring at me.

"Prove it," I replied. "I didn't come here tonight looking for tradition. I came here looking for God. Is He here? Would you know it if He was."

"You're confusing Judaism with Christianity. I'm sure your relationship with the Levines hasn't helped," he said with a sour expression.

"You're probably right," I said, stepping into my car, "but the fact you refuse to answer my questions speaks volumes. You can hide behind offense all you want, but if you can't answer what I'm asking, then there's nothing more I need from you or Beth Tefillah."

"I see," he said coldly.

"Look, this is a beautiful building, and there are some wonderful people who come here. I missed seeing Hannah tonight."

His expression softened. "She's been a little under the weather. Some of the ladies brought her chicken soup earlier today."

I smiled. "And that's the kind of community I think we all want. We want a congregation that actually takes care of one another."

"But it's not enough for you," he said, meeting my eyes.

I shook my head. "I need to know if God is real. I need to know if all of those prayers in the siddur or any other prayer book are true, or if people are just making up poems and words that are simply meant for comfort. If you can't tell me based on your own experience if God is real, then there's really nothing you can offer me."

"I suppose you think you can get that from the Levines."

"From Joe Trautweig," I replied, feeling a smile at the mention of his name.

"Joe?" he repeated, stunned. "Are you two dating?"

"I'm not sure what we are, but when he talks about God, I feel Him. God isn't some faraway cosmic being who hates me. He's *real*. He's accessible, and He might even love me. How do you say no to something like that?"

CHAPTER 20

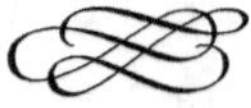

"Am I really here?" I asked myself, standing in the driveway of Kyle and Abigail Goldstein's house.

"Yes, you are," Joe smiled down at me, "and you'll be fine, Carly."

"Does anybody know?" I whispered. I searched that jade stare for reassurance.

"Oh," he said, realizing what I meant. "The only people who know about your past are me and Poppy, and neither one of us would share personal information like that. If and when you want to talk about it, it's completely up to you. Nobody here will judge you, but if you don't feel comfortable speaking at all, that's fine too."

"Are you sure? I feel like a scared little girl on her first day of school."

He smiled reassuringly. "I'm just impressed you're here."

"I have to know," I said. "I have to know the truth."

"I understand," he said, having been fully apprised of my

experience at Beth Tefillah two days earlier. "People here aren't like Rabbi Zendler or Pastor Ivy. Everyone in this room has struggles, good days and bad days. Nobody pretends to be perfect or acts like they have all the answers. We just read the Bible together and discuss how we think we can apply it to our lives."

"Seems simple enough." I forced a brave smile I didn't feel.

Joe reached down and held my hand. Giving it a gentle squeeze, he said, "The first step is always the hardest, Carly, but you're here."

He knocked on the front door of the Goldsteins' two-story, traditional home. He was greeted with a hearty handshake from the man whose dating reputation had once made him the talk of Culver Incorporated.

"Hi," Kyle Goldstein said warmly, quickly noting my hand still firmly held in Joe's. "I'm Kyle."

"Carly," I said.

He assessed our joined hands once again, then looked over at Joe in question. "Looks like you left out a couple of details at lunch, Mr. Trautweig."

Joe grinned back. "Well, we weren't there to discuss my love life, were we?"

Kyle stepped aside so Joe could usher me inside the foyer and toward the hum of conversation happening in the next room. I took in my surroundings, noting the modern country decorating style. The entry walls featured large, black and white photos from the Goldsteins' wedding and also of their newborn son.

"Your house is beautiful," I murmured.

Kyle smiled back at me, gauging me with new eyes. "How did you and Joe meet?"

"I work at Culver," I said. "A coworker had some stories he apparently shared about me with the group. None of them were true, by the way."

His face made a silent "oh," quickly piecing the information together. His wife, Abigail, joined his side, baby Isaac sleeping in a sling wrapped around her middle.

"Abigail, this is Carly," Kyle said, gesturing toward me.

"Pleasure to meet you." She extended her hand for a quick shake and then turned to her husband. "Hon, can you grab the dip I made? I can't bend over to get it out of the fridge."

Kyle smiled at his wife before excusing himself.

"Gotta keep the baby in the sling," she said, tossing red hair over her shoulder.

"Understood," Joe said, still holding my hand. "Are the Margolins or the Levines here yet?"

Abigail shook her head. "Rebecca sent me a text that they're running behind. Potty training drama apparently," she said, rolling her eyes with a smile. "I haven't heard from Poppy, but Jared told Kyle they needed to take some time off. Not sure what's going on, but I hope everything is okay."

Joe glanced over at me, his expression holding both concern and relief.

"Do you know either of the families?" she asked, turning her blue eyes to me.

"I work with Poppy and Ted," I said.

"Oh," Abigail responded in surprise. "When did you and Joe get together?" She eyed our held hands.

"Still ironing that out," Joe said with a strained smile. "Do you mind if I take Carly to meet everyone else? Poppy recruited a few of the guys to help Carly move this summer."

"Oh, that's right! Carly, you'll probably remember Jackson

and Aaron. Poppy said they did a great job with all of the heavy lifting. Sorry that it took me a minute to realize where I'd heard your name before."

I genuinely smiled, some of the tension leaving my shoulders. "Not a problem. The guys were a huge help. I'll be glad to see them again."

Abigail returned my smile. "I'll catch up with you in a few minutes. I need to help Kyle finish setting up the snacks." She excused herself, and Joe led me toward the family room.

"We survived," he whispered. "Ready to meet everyone else?"

I nodded. "I think so."

Joe released my hand, probably to avoid more uncomfortable questions, and I greeted both Jackson and Aaron with quick side hugs. Jackson introduced me to his girlfriend Leila, and Aaron seemed to note how closely and somewhat possessively Joe stood near me.

I felt someone watching me, and I looked over to see a silver haired woman with hazel eyes looking in my direction. Knowing her instantly, I left Joe and walked over to her.

"Hi, I'm Carly. I've heard a lot about you, and I wanted to introduce myself."

"Rose Margolin," she said, standing up. "Pleasure to meet you, honey. I see you've arrived with our dear friend, Joe."

"Yes," I said, glancing back briefly at him. "I also work with your son."

Her smile widened. Are you in the marketing department as well?"

"Yes."

"So, you work with Poppy?"

My smile dimmed.

Rose raised her eyebrows but didn't ask any further questions on the subject.

"I, um, used to go to First United of Hillcrest," I said, gauging her for a response. "I actually grew up there. I remember Rebecca from when I was a child."

"Oh, honey!" She immediately grabbed both of my hands. "I can only imagine what kind of torture that must have been."

"Thank you," I said, blinking back tears. "Not everybody understands."

She smiled encouragingly. "Well, I want you to know our group is nothing like that awful place. No kings of the castle around here. We all come just as we are to worship Jesus." She gestured for me to sit next to her in a dining room chair, and I sat. "I imagine you probably have a lot of questions."

"I do," I admitted. "The way Joe talks about Jesus is so different from anything I grew up hearing from Pastor Ivy or from my mother. He's been really nice about answering my nine million questions."

"Joe is a very sweet man," Rose said, her gaze sweeping over my face. "My goodness, you are so beautiful, honey. I apologize for staring, but you have the face of an angel."

I blushed. "I've heard that before."

"Ah," she said, grinning as her gaze drifted to Joe. He looked over at the two of us in silent question, and I smiled back.

"He's checking up on you," Rose said with a note of approval in her voice.

"Yes, he's very good about that."

"It bodes well for the future. Not that I'm trying to meddle, of course."

"Of course," I replied, neither of us fooled.

Rose chuckled ruefully. "Matchmaking is an unfortunate

hobby of mine. Please, forgive me. I don't want to make your first visit with us uncomfortable."

I waved her off. "It was bound to be awkward, regardless. A former coworker of mine used to attend your Bible study and told everyone he and I were dating. I have no idea what Zach said about me, only that Ted asked him to leave."

"Ah, I remember," Rose said. "There was something about that young man I never really liked. Couldn't quite put my finger on it. Thank you for providing confirmation. Ted didn't say much about the situation."

"Sounds like your instincts were spot on," I said absently, wanting to ask the question of the hour but not sure how to broach the subject.

"What's wrong, honey? You seem nervous."

"I am. I went to synagogue on Friday night looking for answers, but I didn't find any."

"Really?" Rose asked, her voice coming out noticeably higher. "How did you wind up there? Did you go to Beth Tefillah?"

"I did," I said. "I visited a few months ago with the Levines and with Joe, and something happened to me there. I passed out, and I think God talked to me while I was on the floor."

Tears filled Rose's eyes. "Go on, honey."

I smiled back. "Well, I still don't know what exactly happened, only that something changed. I'd been carrying around guilt over something I'd done, but it was like the burden was lifted. I went back to the synagogue wondering if it would happen again, but it didn't."

"I see," she said, her eyes searching mine. "You were hoping to recreate the experience again."

"Yes! I've tried talking to the rabbi, but he just blows me off every time I ask if God is real. My mother and Pastor Ivy did the same thing whenever I would ask them questions. Joe is the only one who has ever sat and talked with me about any of this. I just want to know what's real. Does that make sense?"

"Perfectly," she said, taking hold of my hands again. "I think you've come to the right place tonight. When my son and daughter get here, you can talk to Rebecca about some of this in more detail as well."

"I already have plans to meet her for brunch this week."

Rose smiled wide. "I'm so glad, honey. That girl has been the best thing that ever happened to my family second only to Jesus. I consider her a daughter just as much as my own two girls."

Tears stung my eyes, seeing again that my mother's version of loving me paled in comparison to the real thing.

"Perfect timing," Rose murmured as Ted and Rebecca entered the room with their young daughters.

"Gramma!" the oldest said, running toward Rose. She leapt into Rose's arms, her curly pigtails bouncing along with her.

"Carly," Ted said in surprise. "I'm so glad you made it." He glanced over at Joe, grinning at him. He clapped him on the shoulder and whispered something in his ear. Joe responded with that devastating smile that made me fall in love with him all over again.

"Hi," Mrs. Margolin said, approaching me. "I'm Rebecca."

I stood up and shook her hand. "It's nice to finally meet you. I'm Carly Miller. You might remember my mother, Hannah, from First United."

Rebecca frowned for a moment before her eyes went wide. "Oh! I remember you! I remember your mother too." She hesitated before asking, "Is she, um, still the same?"

"I haven't spoken to her in more than two years, but yes," I replied. "I've always wondered if anyone saw the same behavior that I did at home."

Mrs. Margolin nodded, sitting down gingerly on a dining room chair.

"Oh, honey!" Rose exclaimed. "Take the recliner. You've got my grandson in there. I'll go sit on the couch with Tabby. Come on, sweetheart," she said, scooping up the four year-old in her arms.

Rebecca stood up, waddled over to the recliner, then sat down with a sigh. Rubbing her belly, she said, "I don't think I remember being this tired with either of the girls."

"That's because you're chasing two preschoolers," I said with a smile.

Rebecca smiled back, that infamous, megawatt grin truly lighting up the room. "Wouldn't trade it for the world, but being thirty-nine and pregnant with baby number three is definitely taking its toll."

"Congratulations," I said. "Ted told me you would be needing Rabbi Peretz for the bris."

"Oh, he mentioned that?" she asked, surprised. "Do you know Rabbi Peretz too? I'm a little surprised since I know you grew up at First United."

I blushed. "I read about it in Taylor's book first."

"I'm assuming you've read all of our books then," Rebecca said, referring to her memoirs as well as Taylor's and Poppy's.

"I have. It's how I met Joe," I said, ripping off the band aid. I watched and waited to see how much Poppy had already shared about the situation.

"I've gotten some texts from our mutual friends," she began, watching me with equal wariness. "It's a very touchy situation to say the least."

"I'm not asking you to get in the middle, and I told Ted the same thing. I wanted to meet with you to talk about First United, not about Poppy."

"Understood." Her expression brightened immediately.

Speaking loudly to the room, Kyle announced, "Hey guys, we're about to get started. Snacks are on the dining room table. Grab some food, and then we'll start digging into the Word."

CHAPTER 21

I sat next to Joe on the sofa, balancing a small plate of cut veggies, spinach dip, and grapes on my lap. He had his Bible opened to the book of *Romans*, and I leaned in to follow along.

In a resounding voice, Ted read from chapter twelve, "Do not repay anyone evil for evil. Be careful to do what is right in the eyes of everyone. If it is possible, as far as it depends on you, live at peace with everyone."

Several murmurs went throughout the room, and I wondered at the meaning of those verses. Despite a lifetime of sermons at First United, something about hearing the Bible from someone who wasn't a complete fraud cut straight to my heart.

"So," Ted said, eyeing the room at large, "what do you think it means when it says *as far as it depends on you* to live in peace with others? What happens if we can't live in peace at all?"

Rose grinned at her son, beaming with pride. It reminded me of Jared watching his son on the bima, and I realized I did miss Poppy after all. I frowned, ruminating over the Vincenzo's fiasco and considering how I could have handled things differently.

Rebecca cracked her knuckles over her baby bump. "I think we all know how I will answer that question."

The room let out a soft chuckle.

"Okay," Aaron said, leaning back in one of the dining room chairs, "where do you draw the line? How do you know what's actually within your power and what's manipulation? How do you know if it's pride keeping you from reconciling with someone or if you have a legitimate reason to cut off a relationship?"

"That's a great question," Ted said, glancing at his wife and then at his mother. "How do we check ourselves against pride versus throwing pearls to pigs? The easy answer is pray and ask God, but what happens when our emotions are confused? Does anyone have any signs or practical steps to look out for?"

"Well," Rose interjected, "the easiest litmus test for me is confusion. Confusion comes from the enemy, not from God. Even when the Lord tells me something I don't necessarily want to hear, I will always have peace. When I have confusion, I can guarantee that either my heart isn't right, or there is some sort of lie or manipulation going on with the other person."

"Interesting," Ted said. "Can you give an example, Mom?"

"Of course, dear." She patted his knee. "When you're dealing with a toxic individual, confusion is a way of life. Their actions and words never match. They can use some of the most beautiful prose, tell you whatever you want to hear, but the behavior is manipulative or unreliable at best. They may profess how much they love you, but they ignore you, neglect you, or even purposefully hurt you. When confronted, they aren't ashamed of their behavior or remorseful. Instead, they blame shift or simply ignore your complaint altogether."

The bottom fell out of my stomach, hearing a virtual stranger perfectly describe life with Hannah Miller. Joe's green gaze crashed into mine, concern in his eyes.

"Breathe," he whispered, noting the sudden rise and fall of my chest.

"Carly?" Ted asked. "Are you all right?"

I closed my eyes and focused on one inhalation of air at a time. "Just give me a minute."

"In and out," Joe said, my hand held securely in his once again. "You're okay, Carly. Breathe."

I nodded while keeping my eyes shut.

"Can we pray for you?" Rose asked.

I waved her off. "I just need to breathe."

"Give her a minute," Joe said to the room. "Carly, are you still with us?"

I squeezed his hand in response.

It seemed like the room held their collective breath while I tried to recover mine. Finally, I opened my eyes and beheld the concerned stares of eight new acquaintances. The ninth member of the study had volunteered to watch the Margolin girls in another room.

"You gave us a bit of a scare," Ted said, smiling at me. "Is everything better now?"

I shook my head. "I keep having these breathing episodes every time something triggers me about my mother. I don't understand what's going on."

"Panic attack from PTSD," Rebecca said immediately, holding my gaze. "They happened to me a lot when I began healing from my family and from SBC. I wrote about some of it in my book, but they are very real and very scary when they're happening."

I nodded, seeing compassion in her dark brown eyes. "Yes," I whispered.

"I know it doesn't feel like a good thing, Carly, but your body is trying to get rid of the pain and help you heal. All of that toxic garbage that was poured in is coming to the surface so that it can be scooped out."

"Really?" I asked.

"Yes," she replied emphatically. "I remember your mother well from First United, and I can only imagine what she was like at home. Please, hear me when I say that whatever she told you were lies. Even if Hannah was one hundred percent convinced herself, I can assure you none of it was true."

"How would you know that?" Jackson asked Rebecca. "I mean, it's obvious Carly got triggered, but how could you possibly know something like that?"

Rebecca held up a hand as Ted looked ready to pounce on Jackson. "It's a fair question. Carly, are you okay if I share some details about my father's church, or would you prefer to discuss them privately?"

"Privately," Joe and I answered in unison.

I glanced over at him and smiled. "Thanks," I whispered.

He smiled and pulled me in for a side hug. I sighed into his embrace and finally felt my heart rate calm back to normal.

Rebecca turned her attention to Jackson. "In the interest of protecting Carly's privacy, I'll just say that I have been made aware of some details regarding her mother as a member of my father's church. She also taught in the children's ministry for a long time at First United. I got to witness her behavior first-hand as a student and later as an adult. The trauma Carly's experiencing is very real. I will absolutely vouch for her."

Jackson looked wide eyed at me. "Sorry," he said contritely. "I didn't know."

Rebecca quickly reassured him. "It's always a fine line between wanting to believe people are telling the truth but also using your discernment and asking questions. I didn't take any offense, Jackson. Carly, is your breathing back to normal?"

I nodded.

Ted looked at Joe and then shifted his gaze to me. "Is it all right if my mom finishes what she was saying, or should we move on?"

Wishing for the spotlight to be anywhere else, especially with the pitying gazes from Abigail and Kyle Goldstein, I offered a tight smile. "I'll be fine. Go ahead."

Ted and Rose exchanged nervous glances, but then he lifted his chin as a sign for her to continue.

Rose appeared to be silently praying. Pierced again with memories of Poppy, I resolved in that instant to truly forgive her.

"We've talked about some warning signs to look out for in others," Rose said as she made eye contact with several people in the circle, "so let's talk about ways we can check our own hearts. What do you think would be some red flags to watch out for?"

"Motivation," Abigail said, nursing Isaac with a blanket draped over her shoulder. "One of the things I ask myself is if I am trying to control something, am I afraid of something, or am I anxious? My tendency is to blame myself before assuming the other person has an agenda."

"Which can be a double edged sword," Rebecca said. "A toxic person will count on you blaming yourself since they'll never own up if they did anything wrong."

"And it's always possible to fool yourself," Rose added,

"especially when you'd rather take the blame in a situation instead of see someone fall off their pedestal or truly believe they had selfish motives."

"But how do you know?" Aaron asked. "Isn't it possible to deceive yourself?"

"Absolutely!" Rose replied. "Our human tendency is to see what we want to see and ignore warning signs that challenge us. *Cognitive dissonance* keeps us in unhealthy relationships and situations."

"I've heard of that," Jackson said, "but I'm not really sure what it is."

Ted inclined his head, letting his mother know he would answer the question. "The simplest definition is being at war with yourself. It's when your beliefs or perception don't match reality, and you're torn between what you're actually seeing versus what you've always believed to be true."

Kyle piped up and said, "I had been taught my entire life that you can't be Jewish and believe in Jesus. Rebecca and I have known each other for a long time," he said, smiling at Mrs. Margolin, "and she had this knack for saying things that would just cut me to the heart. Every time I wondered if maybe there was something to her faith, those old thoughts would creep in. No matter how sincere she was about Jesus, I believed it would be impossible for me to accept it as a Jew."

Aaron nodded, his brows drawn together. "I think I get it."

Quietly, I said, "I struggle with it now."

The eyes of the room fell on me, and I wondered why the words had tumbled out of my mouth.

"You don't have to do this," Joe whispered.

I offered him a tiny smile. "I'm okay. I think this will be good for me."

"Carly, whenever you're ready," Ted said, giving me the floor.

"Like Rebecca said, I grew up going to her father's church." I looked down at the empty plate in my lap, needing a respite from the curious eyes. "You weren't allowed to disagree or even question what Pastor Ivy said. My mother made sure of that."

Rose sucked in a breath from across the room.

"She's not wrong," Rebecca added. "I was abused horribly for asking questions. My parents and their minions called me every Biblical insult under the sun for disagreeing with my father. He was a tyrant who tolerated no dissension."

I inhaled and exhaled slowly. "Sorry, everyone, I just get nervous talking about this. I don't have the best experience when it comes to sharing my questions or doubts."

"Perfectly understandable," Kyle said, studying me. "It's your first time here, Carly, and we're not asking you to bare your soul."

"Thanks," I said with a slight nod. "I tried talking to the Reform rabbi at Beth Tefillah a few days ago, but he shut me down pretty quickly."

Rebecca and Ted both raised their eyebrows.

"Are you Jewish?" Ted asked, surprised.

"Not that I know of. My mother isn't Jewish, and I've never met my father."

"So, what brought you to the synagogue?" Rebecca asked. "I'm intrigued by your story." Her megawatt smile buoyed my confidence.

I smiled back. "Well, Joe has been sharing a lot with me about Judaism and the Bible, and I've been wrestling with everything I've heard growing up from my mother and Pastor Ivy. He talks a lot about God's love and grace. I didn't hear any of that at First United."

Joe planted a kiss on top of my head. "You *are* loved," he said close to my ear.

Staring up into those jade eyes, I saw the reflection of my own feelings beyond Bible verses. Joe didn't need to say the three little words because I could see it in how he looked at me. Not wanting to make a spectacle of myself more than I already had, I swallowed down the lump in my throat and forced a smile on my face.

Rebecca watched us carefully, her dark eyes aglow. "Joe, I'm glad you're speaking the truth to Carly. She needs to hear it. Most of my father's sermons were guilt trips about members needing to give more money or serve in the church. He'd invent these ridiculous stories about people taking second jobs just to support his latest fundraiser, and then he'd lie about how much he and my mother gave. Once, I remember him telling everyone that if they had a savings account, they should be donating at least $1,000 for the building fund. Then, he twisted the Bible verses from Matthew about storing up treasures in Heaven."

"That's disgusting!" Rose said, hand on her chest.

"I remember that," I said, the sound of Pastor Ivy's righteous indignation still ringing in my ears. "He claimed he and Mrs. Ivy had already donated $5,000 toward the building project."

Rebecca rolled her eyes and pulled a face. "My father had some sort of building drive going on every year. He bragged about all of the new members joining the church while conveniently ignoring the revolving door of people who'd wised up and left. Then, he'd talk about these grand plans to expand the narthex and a special wing just for the children's ministry. Before they finally closed the church, they were still using the portable trailers from when I was growing up. Twenty years of empty promises, yet people kept giving money."

"How did he fool people for so long?" Leila asked. "Didn't

folks eventually catch on? What happened when they asked questions about where the money went?"

Replying first, I said, "My mother was one of the members who believed every word from Pastor Ivy. She'd have me wearing clothes that were too small or falling apart, shoes that cut my feet, and we lived in a single wide trailer. She didn't hoard much money for herself, so I can't even imagine how much she gave to First United. I started working as soon as I was old enough just to buy myself things that fit properly. My mother didn't ask where they came from, and she believed I should be paying for it myself anyway."

Abigail and Rebecca both inhaled a sharp breath while Ted and Kyle looked horrified.

Rose Margolin's hazel eyes burned bright in holy anger. "You deserved so much better than the mother you had," she said, staring into my soul. "Do you understand that neglecting your needs and putting that church above taking care of her own daughter was child abuse?"

"It was?" I whispered, shocked.

"Yes!" The Margolins and Goldsteins said in unison along with Joe.

"I never realized that." Tears stung my eyes. "My mother talked about serving the Lord and not wanting God's curses on us for being stingy about giving to the local storehouse. Pastor Ivy always quoted those tithing Bible verses from *Malachi* when they took up the offering."

"Ah yes," Rebecca said, her expression hardening, "and let's not forget his weekly admonition to people just like your mother." Taking on his holier-than-thou tone, she said, "You can't *afford* to tithe? You can't afford *not* to tithe!'"

Jackson and Leila shook their heads while Aaron stared at me sympathetically. I shifted my gaze, not wanting anyone's pity. I didn't feel like a victim, and I didn't want to be seen or treated like one.

"So, Carly, where's your cognitive dissonance?" Aaron asked, still watching me. "How could you believe anything that Pastor Ivy or your mother said with the way they treated you? I don't mean to be rude, but isn't it kind of obvious that everything they said was wrong?"

"Obvious to *you*," Joe said tersely. "You're on the outside looking in. You weren't raised in this cult without an outside voice of reason. You didn't have that psycho yelling at you from the pulpit or your mother beating the hell out of you if you dared to disagree."

I squeezed Joe's hand and then released it. "I can talk for myself."

His jade eyes held an apology. "Just trying to help."

I smiled back. "I know, and I appreciate it." Looking at Aaron, I said, "My mother has called me an abomination for as long as I can remember. She talked about Jesus as if he agreed with everything Pastor Ivy said. She had me convinced that Jesus hated me because I didn't honor her or love her enough. Any time I brought up how Pastor Ivy treated people he saw as beneath him—including my mother—she always had a million excuses for it. If I ever tried to use those same excuses for my own mistakes, she would beat me with shoes or books. Loving my mother meant letting her control every aspect of my life without complaint. No matter how hard I tried, she made sure nothing was good enough or worthy of her approval. Her devotion to God, to the Bible, and to First United made me want to do the exact opposite. I wanted to be nothing like her."

"Makes perfect sense," Abigail said. "Why embrace Jesus or anything else your mother loved when she used it to justify how she treated you?"

"Exactly," I said, turning to Kyle's wife, "but then Joe talks to me about God's mercy and forgiveness, and it just seems too good to be true. I still hear Pastor Ivy or my mother in my head when I try to read the Bible. It's hard. Part of the reason I came tonight was to find out if any of this Jesus stuff is real."

Rose looked at me with admiration. "That takes so much courage, honey. If no one else has told you this evening, I'm proud of you."

The others nodded in agreement, and Ted Margolin beamed like a proud papa. Embarrassed, I stared back down at my empty plate.

"You're a survivor," Rebecca said, "and don't let anyone tell you otherwise."

CHAPTER 22

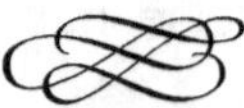

I FELT AWKWARD AFTER MY EMOTIONAL STORY, BUT Abigail, Rebecca, and Rose huddled around me like mother hens nursing a wounded chick. Rose and Rebecca lavished on praise for my bravery and fortitude while Abigail called me inspiring. I didn't know how to handle such a deluge of affirmation and acceptance, so I let them talk around me.

I glanced over my shoulder to see Joe in heavy conversation with Kyle and Ted. Joe seemed troubled, and I wondered if I was the cause.

"Carly, you are incredible," Rose said. She placed her hand on my arm and pulled my attention back to the small circle of women. "I've always been so impressed with Rebecca's testimony, but yours is equally as impressive."

"You don't know all of it," I said quietly. "I haven't always made the best choices."

"As if any of us have," she scoffed, still smiling. "Just because someone claims faith in Jesus doesn't mean we're impervious to deception, mistakes, or life-altering blunders."

I wanted to argue, but I didn't want to expose my long-held secret. I didn't have the emotional capacity to open up that wound again.

Rebecca watched me closely. "There's no pressure to share, so please don't feel like you have to. Also, whenever you and Joe are ready, I can talk to you about Bud Riley's confessional. He had a few things to say about your mother."

"I appreciate that," I said, meeting her eyes. "I have a lot of questions."

"No doubt," she replied, "but fair warning, it's not pretty."

"Why don't we let you two talk before it gets any later?" Rose said, glancing down at her watch. "Rebecca, you'll need to get the girls to bed soon anyway."

Her daughter-in-law winked back. "Thanks, Mom. Abigail, I'll text you later."

Mrs. Goldstein nodded. "No problem. Let me find my husband and get started on cleaning up."

"Oh," Rose said, looking beyond our small circle, "they're praying for Joe."

All of us turned, and I saw Joe surrounded by the men of the Bible study, each with a hand on him and their heads bowed. Joe's shoulders shook in silent tears.

"Come on, Carly," Rebecca said. "We can fill Joe in later. It looks like he's exactly where he needs to be right now."

The sight of Joe in pain constricted my own heart, but I knew Mrs. Margolin was right. I had one burning question to ask her above all others. Following her into the Goldsteins' kitchen, we sat down at their breakfast table.

"Where would you like to begin?" Rebecca asked.

"Are we related? Everyone keeps telling me the reason my mother worshiped Pastor Ivy is because he's secretly my biological father. Is that true?"

Rebecca shook her head. "No, we're not related as far as I know. Your mother was already pregnant when she came to First United, and my father seemed to enjoy throwing that in her face."

"How would you know something like that?" I asked.

"Bud Riley detailed as much as he could before he passed away. He talked about my father's relationship with any person in leadership and comments he made about them. Bud covered the thirty years he served at First United."

"How could he possibly remember all of those people? Wasn't he close to death when he wrote it all down?"

"Bud battled with stomach pains for fifteen years. He began documenting things once he realized the cause. When Ted and I met with him before he passed, he told us that he wanted to help bring closure to as many of my father's victims as possible."

"How could my mother possibly support Pastor Ivy? I know she's read the confession. If what you're saying is true and Pastor Ivy manipulated her for three decades, why is she still listening to cassette tapes of his old sermons? Why was she protesting his arrest and sentencing outside of the courthouse?"

"Because she assumes Bud is lying. I saw how Hannah idolized my father, Carly. My mother knew it too. All she had to do was tell Hannah that Pastor Ivy specifically requested her help with something, and your mother would jump. Half the time, my father didn't even know what my mother claimed he wanted from Hannah."

"How did you find out about that?"

"I overheard my parents on more than one occasion talking about her," Rebecca said with palpable disgust. "If they were discussing something that needed to happen at church, one of them would flippantly say, 'Just ask Hannah to do it.' They knew she would never say no to my father. There was no care or concern for Hannah, let alone the neglect of you as her child. She was just a pawn to be used, and you were the collateral damage."

I shook my head, remembering countless nights alone in our trailer, my mother working at the church long after she'd gotten off her secretarial job. "I just accepted it, Rebecca. I don't think I realized before tonight that neglect truly *is* abuse. My mother would abandon me at the drop of a hat if First United needed something."

"Did you have a babysitter or any other relative to watch you?"

"When I was little, she brought me to the church with her. I remember falling asleep on the pews a lot. When I was in second or third grade, she just left me at home."

"That's horrible!" Rebecca gasped.

I shrugged. "I didn't know any better. I learned how to take care of myself early on. I learned not to depend on anyone or need anybody else."

"You never got to be a child, Carly. Hannah stole that from you."

I inhaled deeply, allowing the weight of her words to wash over me. "I just grew up knowing that nothing was more important to my mother than First United and Pastor Ivy. She'd tell me that she loved me, but I stopped believing her a long time ago. I never felt loved. Loving my mother meant being her obedient slave."

"Which is exactly how she was treated by my parents," Rebecca said. "You felt abandoned and rejected and rightfully so. Your mother put on quite a show of loving the children she taught on Sundays. My father loved to parade Hannah to the congregation. What I remember is seeing you sit by yourself in the back pew, scared to death to do anything other than breathe."

"You saw that?" I asked, stunned. "I didn't think anybody noticed me other than Pastor Ivy. I feel like my mother asked him to keep an eye on me."

"I wouldn't doubt it, but I don't know the reason why he'd take such an interest in you or in helping Hannah when he had such little regard for her otherwise."

My shoulders slumped, frustrated how I was no closer to solving the biggest mystery of my existence.

Rebecca smiled sympathetically. "Carly, I wish I could help."

"Well, what else did Bud have to say about my mother or about her relationship with your father? Are you sure there was nothing going on between them?"

Mrs. Margolin shook her head. "According to Bud, my father called your mom a *useful servant*."

"What does that mean?"

"Pretty much what I told you earlier. He and my mother viewed Hannah as free labor for First United. From what I gathered, it sounds like your mother felt she owed some sort of unpayable debt to the church, or more specifically, my father."

"And it has something to do with me," I said, trying to fill in the missing pieces.

"That's what it looks like."

"But this still doesn't make any sense. You said Pastor Ivy liked throwing my mother's out of wedlock pregnancy in her face. Why would he take any interest in me if I were just a way to shame my mother?"

"Maybe he used the phony concern to keep her in line. You have to remember that Hannah had no idea my father was manipulating her. My father could read people very well. He knew what they needed, what motivated them, and what buttons to push to gain loyalty or compliance. He played on your mother's shame in getting pregnant, but showing an interest in you as her daughter would be vicarious attention for her. It would make your mother feel special."

"But she hated me, Rebecca. I was an abomination."

"But you were also a source of narcissistic supply for her. Whether your mother ever told you she was proud of you or not, whether she even noticed you while she was so busy trying to impress my father, any interest he demonstrated in you would have been used as praise for herself. Likewise, anything you did that didn't meet my father's approval would have been shame for her. To a narcissistic parent, their child is just an extension of themselves. You don't exist outside of your relationship to them and how they think you reflect on them."

"I see what you're saying, but what does any of that have to do with Pastor Ivy's extra concern for me or the guilt trips about my mother?" I asked.

"Anything less than perfection meant that *she* was a failure as your mother. My father knew how to shame Hannah into working harder or dangle out the carrot of praise from the pulpit. He'd use either method to manipulate her into the next ridiculous task. My father also enjoyed the power he had to make people jump to do his bidding. He's sadistic and a sociopath at best."

"Wow," I murmured, thinking of all the times my mother had beaten me following a "bad report" from Pastor Ivy or one of his leadership lemmings.

"Carly, my father knew your mother was hypersensitive about the daughter she had with no father. It wouldn't surprise me if he manufactured complaints when she ever showed resistance to a request."

"That's so heartless!" I cried. "Pastor Ivy really seemed to care about me, even if it was in a super controlling way."

Rebecca shook her head. "My father cares about no one other than himself. Any line he may have fed you about being concerned for your welfare or life decisions had an ulterior motive. He needed to keep your mother on a tight leash so he could use her for the church. If he feigned an interest in you, your mother took it as a sign of my father being pleased with *her*. To both of them, you were nothing more than a tool to be used or collateral damage if my father needed to tighten the screws on your mother."

Tears filled my eyes. "I never liked Pastor Ivy, but the idea of any person being that calloused toward an innocent child is just so hard to believe."

"There's that cognitive dissonance again," she said gently. "It's a very ugly reality to accept. One of the hallmark traits of any narcissist is their total lack of empathy. They feel nothing. Love is an emotion they fake in order to manipulate and control others. The only genuine emotion I experienced from either of my parents was anger or disgust. As the child of a narcissistic parent, you learn to walk on eggshells very quickly. You fear their wrath and disapproval. Conversely, you'll do anything just to earn a crumb of acceptance from them."

"Yes," I said, suddenly seeing my mother's pathologies clear as day. This time, the piercing revelation was not met with shortened breath. Instead, I realized I was truly accepting the difficult truth before me.

Continuing on, Rebecca said, "These narcissistic parents know what they're doing and what they're deliberately withholding from their children. In their mind, you don't deserve the *privilege* of their attention or concern. They cling to offenses against you, whether real or imaginary, to justify why they intentionally abuse and neglect the ones they're supposed to nurture. As long as they can convince you that you're unworthy to receive what should be a natural thing for a parent to give, they'll keep you on that performance hamster wheel trying to earn it."

"So, my mother did to me what Pastor Ivy and your mother did to her," I said, echoing Rebecca's earlier words. "She just perpetuated that same, sick cycle of abuse. She bullied me because she was bullied by them."

"Yes, she mimicked their example."

"Do you think my mother ever realized nothing she did was going to be good enough for them? I had that moment when I was eleven or twelve. I stopped trying beyond the bare minimum. Eventually, I rebelled."

Rebecca sighed heavily. "Having seen your mother in action often enough, I'd say that Hannah conflated serving God with serving my parents and First United. I don't know if she was trying to be good enough to earn God's love and acceptance, but it's clear my father kept her brainwashed and compliant. According to Bud, my father would laugh about how much money he could squeeze from your mother knowing that the two of you lived in poverty."

"What!" I gasped. "That monster! Just thinking about all the things I went without..." my voice trailed off. As much as I wanted to blame my mother, I also saw the puppet strings being pulled by the holy roller from hell.

"Oh!" Rebecca exclaimed, looking like she'd seen a ghost. "Oh my!" She placed her hand over her mouth.

"What?"

"Oh!" she said for a third time, her hands fluttering. "That just makes too much sense."

"What does?" Joe asked, entering the kitchen.

I looked up as the seeming other half of my heart approached. Joe's tears had dried, but his eyes still looked red. I raised an eyebrow in question, and he shook his head with a small smile. He placed a hand on my shoulder and stood behind me.

"I was just telling Carly about the relationship between my father and her mother," Rebecca said.

I turned and glanced at Joe. "We're not related. Pastor Ivy used my mother like a slave. He basically did to her exactly what she did to me."

His mouth thinned. "I see."

"What was the big revelation you seemed to have?" I asked Rebecca.

"It's about your father."

"*My* father? I thought you didn't know who he was."

"I don't," she said, "but I think *my* father does. I think that's what he held over Hannah's head all those years."

"How?" Joe asked.

"I know for sure Hannah showed up at First United already pregnant. That's how I know my father isn't responsible. How old was she when she had you, Carly?"

"Twenty-two," I replied.

Joe sat down next to me at the table. "Okay, so she was young, naive, and too trusting of Pastor Ivy."

"And alone," I added. "She hated my grandmother, but I have no idea why. I never met any extended family. It was always just me and my mother."

Rebecca nodded, seeming to have her suspicions confirmed. "Whoever your biological father is, I think my father knows exactly who it is and the circumstances of how Hannah got pregnant. That's how he's kept your mother on his hook for the past thirty years."

CHAPTER 23

Joe reached for my hand and held it. Turning to me, he said, "Rebecca's theory makes a lot of sense. We both know your mother isn't Hannah of the Bible."

Mrs. Margolin added, "That would explain why my father feigned interest in you, Carly. I can easily see him playing off any fear Hannah had of you becoming like your biological father or even finding out who he is."

"She had John Doe put on my birth certificate," I said. "My mother clearly didn't want anybody to know, including my birth father."

"What about your grandmother?" Joe asked. "Do you know her name? Maybe we could find some other relatives and contact them for information."

"Could we try to find your mother's birth certificate?" Rebecca asked. "Even though there's probably a thousand women with the same name, we could narrow it down by her birthday."

"My mother didn't believe in celebrating birthdays," I said, suddenly understanding her bizarre superstition about it. The pain and horror left me winded like a punch to the gut.

"Carly?" Joe asked, noting my labored breathing. "What's going on?"

"My mother," I said, gulping for air. "It makes so much sense now."

"Breathe," Joe said. "In and out, Carly."

I gripped his hand tighter as I strove to inhale a full sip of air. Slowly, my heart calmed its thunderous beats. I looked over at Joe and his eyes found the truth in mine. "It's not hard to believe, Joe. Just so hard to accept."

"I know, Carly. It's horrific."

Rebecca frowned. "Obviously, I'm missing something. Can you guys fill me in?"

Joe answered for me. "The birthday thing. Hannah needed some hyper spiritual reason to avoid celebrating anything about Carly's existence."

"Ah," Rebecca said, a pained look on her face. "There's also the possibility she didn't want to draw suspicion to when and how you were conceived."

Tears filled my eyes. "Do you know, I didn't have one birthday cake as a kid? Not one cupcake? I wasn't allowed to attend parties either."

Rebecca looked confused. "What about the birthday cake we had every month at First United?" Explaining to Joe, she said, "My father would have all the members stand up at the beginning of the month and then sing this cringey birthday song. It was to the tune of one of the older praise hymns, but they changed out the words."

I rolled my eyes. "Another positive to First United closing is that no one will ever have to hear that stupid song again."

Rebecca smirked. "My father made the members pay for a birthday cake too. Whoever was on kitchen duty that week had to purchase enough sheet cake for at least one hundred people. Every other week, the church had these gourmet muffins and doughnuts because they got day-old bakery goods for free from Georgie's. All the members raved about how my parents must have spent a fortune feeding the parishioners and visitors. My father didn't dissuade anyone from believing it either."

"Wow," I said, stunned. "There truly was nothing real about First United, was there?"

Rebecca shook her head. "Narcissists will always allow someone else to do the work while they make sure to take all of the credit. To your face, they'll ignore or minimize your accomplishments. When you're not around, they'll rave about how amazing you are, but only so they can steal the glory because you aren't around to receive it directly. They funnel the praise for themselves instead."

"To my knowledge, my mother never praised me to anyone."

"Oh," Rebecca said sadly. "When I came home with straight A's, my father would ask why my 97 wasn't a 100. Then, I'd overhear him bragging to a leadership minion how his daughter excelled in school. They'd fawn all over their beloved Pastor Ivy saying how I took after my father."

"He never said any of this to your face?" Joe asked Rebecca. "Not one word of appreciation or approval?"

She shook her head. "There is not one ounce of truth in that man. Even when Edie Riley would make her famous carrot cake, my father found some way to make it all about himself. He'd say that's why he put her in charge of the kitchen committee. People would praise my father for utilizing her talents rather than praising Edie for her *actual* talents. It was insane to watch. Some of the women complained or purposefully made excuses to avoid kitchen duty if they knew they also had to provide the birthday cake that week."

"That's crazy!" Joe said. "Why didn't the church just pay for it themselves? Considering all the money your parents used to keep themselves in the lap of luxury, how hard would it have been to buy twelve cakes a year?"

"Why pay for anything when you can strong arm your members into footing the bill?" Rebecca said with disdain. "Some of the ladies brought scratch made or even boxed cakes, but my father hated those other than Edie's food. He liked nothing that looked less than professional. Eventually, he made up some song and dance about why the cakes needed to come from Georgie's or a regular grocery store. My father was all about appearances, not substance."

A memory resurfaced of a beautiful floral sheet cake my mother had purchased just after my eighth birthday. "Rebecca, I remember asking my mother why she bought a birthday cake for the church but not for me." Surprised, I wiped away tears. "While she was busy serving coffee, I snuck a piece in a corner. I even sang *Happy Birthday* to myself."

"Oh, Carly!" Rebecca exclaimed, reaching out to touch the hand not held by Joe. "I am so sorry. How did your mother reconcile her own ridiculous rule with the church birthday cele-brations?"

"She said Pastor Ivy was indulging the congregation and their secular traditions," I quoted with heavy sarcasm.

Joe raked a hand through his hair, that familiar, nervous habit reappearing.

"What's wrong?" I said, turning toward him.

"You have to ask?"

"Well, you came in here after crying with all the guys. Yeah, I have to ask," I said, harsher than I intended.

He squeezed my hand. "Sorry, I'm just upset about your mother. She treated you horribly to cover for her own sin. You didn't deserve any of it, Carly. *She* does. I'm buying you whatever cake you want as soon as we get out of here."

I laughed through my tears. "Thank you."

"Not that this is any consolation," Rebecca said, leaning back in her chair, "but Hannah is reaping the consequences of her decisions now. First United has been closed for over two years, and your mother has no one to care for her or even pretend to care. She's alone."

"Good," Joe spat. "It's no less than the witch deserves."

My knee jerk reaction was to defend my mother, but the protest died in my throat. My mother had never protected me a day in her life outside of not having an abortion. The immediate comparison between us stood in accusation, but I refused to own that shame anymore. I carried regret and remorse for what I had done to my child. I knew it was wrong, and I would have done anything to go back in time and make it right. Conversely, I knew my mother would never relent from her lifelong abuse. She'd simply demand I "honor" her by putting up with it.

"I think I've had about all I can handle," I finally said. "Rebecca, maybe we can talk about this some more when we meet for brunch this week."

"I'd like that," she said, her somber expression giving way to the megawatt smile on her face. "I know this conversation wasn't easy, Carly, but you're handling it like a champ."

"And she's also not alone," Joe said, smiling at me. "Not anymore."

Rebecca's eyes grew wide, but she said nothing. Instead, she seemed to be contemplating something as she took in the sight of Joe and me together. Yawning, she put a hand over her mouth and sighed. "I guess that's my cue to get my babies to bed. No rest for the weary when your toddlers arise with the sun. Little Man's got me pretty exhausted too." She smiled down at her baby bump.

"Congratulations!" Joe said in surprise. "I didn't realize you guys found out the gender."

Rebecca rubbed her belly. "It should be fun to see how Ted handles the bris. He barely survived when Taylor and Ian had their first one."

Joe laughed, apparently familiar with the story beyond Taylor's memoirs.

Rebecca eased herself out of the chair, playfully complaining about being old and pregnant. She called out to her daughters as she exited the room.

I looked up at Joe. "You okay? You seemed really upset when all of the guys were praying for you."

He smiled. "I was about to ask you the same question."

"You first," I said, smiling back.

He sighed, searching for the right words. "I asked for prayer about Catherine. I told them that I wanted to get past the pain and regret and bury it."

"Did you?"

"Not in one night, but I do feel different. Lighter."

"Hmm," I murmured. "I felt the same way when I woke up at Beth Tefillah."

His jade eyes sparkled. "We're quite a pair, aren't we?"

"Depends on who you ask," I deadpanned.

Joe laughed fully, that wonderful baritone sound warming my soul. "We can ignore the less than enthusiastic reactions of a few people. Putting them aside, when I look at my past and yours, Carly, I am just in awe of God."

I felt my heart flutter, and I gauged him for a moment. "Why?"

"Because both of us have been so broken by our choices and also by what we've suffered. As much as anyone would look at the two of us and wonder how a relationship could work, God sees how well all of our jagged edges fit together."

"Do you see our relationship going somewhere?" I asked. "I remember what you told me after we kissed at Vincenzo's. I also remember what you told me in the parking deck. Jagged edges or not, I don't have the Christian walk with Jesus that I know you'd want in a wife. I love you too much to let you compromise your standards."

I gasped, realizing my unintentional confession. I vainly hoped Joe had missed it, but that jade gaze plumbed the depths of my heart. "You do?" he asked.

"Don't make me say it again," I begged. "I don't want to hear how you're flattered by my feelings."

"I'm not flattered," he said. "I'm honored."

I frowned. "That's not much better."

"Carly, I've told you over and over how much Jesus loves you. I told you He showed me just a small taste of His love for you."

"You have," I said warily.

"How could I possibly experience God's love for you and not feel that myself? I do love you, Carly. I love so many things about you. I love the questions you ask, the way your eyes change color, the passion you have for right and wrong."

I swallowed, still not hearing what I was hoping for.

"What's wrong?" he asked.

"When I said I love you, Joe, I meant it as more than just a friend. Is that the kind of love you feel for me too? I can see you admire me as a person, but what about as a woman?"

I had no idea Joe's eyes could become even more intense, that gaze more intimate and searching than what had already set my heart beating just for him. I inhaled a shallow breath, mesmerized.

That unspoken connection gripped both of us, irrepressible and magnetic. Before I knew it, Joe's hands were cupping my face, his passionate kiss wiping away the pain of Dylan and the tormenting lies that I would never love or be loved again. I wound my arms around his neck, wanting to be worthy of the man who insisted he would only kiss his wife that way.

Joe pulled away first, tracing my hairline with his fingertips. "You are so beautiful," he murmured. He kissed my forehead then rested his head against it.

I closed my eyes and sighed into his touch, amazed that I wasn't swimming in a fantasy of my own design. "You're real, aren't you, Joe?"

He answered with another kiss that drove me to prayers of thanksgiving to Jesus. To be simultaneously desired and loved had Bible verses pinging in my brain without hearing the voice of Pastor Ivy reciting them. I heard declarations of an "everlasting love" and a love that could not be separated by height, depth, angel, nor demon. The love I felt from Joe's touch had me longing for something more from God that I never believed was truly accessible. I broke away from the kiss as something shattered and loosened within me.

"He's real," I said, looking up at Joe through my tears. "He's really *real.*"

His green eyes were full of awe and delight. "Yes."

"Jesus loves me," I repeated, stunned to hear the words come out of my own lips. "He really loves *me.*"

Tears fell down Joe's cheeks, and there was a light in his eyes I instinctively knew was Jesus.

"Even after everything," I whispered.

"Nothing will separate us from the love of God. No sin is too big for Him to forgive. You aren't beyond hope or redemption, no matter what anyone has told you. You, Carly Miller, are greatly loved."

CHAPTER 24

Joe smiled across the table as our Parkview Diner server placed my dessert before me. When we first entered the restaurant, I'd stood before the glass display case of cakes as if I'd died and gone to Pastry Paradise. It took a bit of coaxing and encouragement from Joe, but I pushed through my initial embarrassment of wanting the cake that screamed childhood wish fulfillment. From the tiers of vanilla cake and frosting to the whipped cream and maraschino cherries on top, that cake symbolized every bit of celebrating I had missed growing up. It could not have been a more precious slice of heaven, second only to the man determined to give it to me.

"Happy Birthday!" Joe said grandly, handing me a fork to dig in.

I blushed. "You don't need to make all this fuss."

He grinned at me, his expression boyish and utterly adorable. "I have thirty-one birthdays to cover here. I hope this is the exact piece of cake you want and the most delicious dessert you've ever eaten. If it's not, we'll just have to get you another one."

"Are you serious? If I don't like this piece, you'll just get me more?"

"Why, are you having second thoughts?" He eyed my chosen dessert with a more critical eye. "Would you rather try the death by chocolate or the tiramisu?"

"No," I said, pulling the confetti cake slice closer to me. "If I was eight years-old, this would be the exact piece I would have picked. It's perfect. If you're nice, I might even let you try a bite."

Joe jutted his lower lip in a comedic pout. "Not even a teensy taste?" He waved his own fork in the air.

I laughed. "Oh, fine!" I pushed the plate toward the center of the table. "I can't eat all of this anyway. I don't think anybody could."

"I think a very hungry eight year-old could tackle this."

"Well, I'm not eight years-old, and neither is my metabolism," I quipped. "If I share the cake, I share the calories. Everybody wins."

"Spoken like a grown up," he retorted with a dramatic eye roll. "Forget the calories for one night. We're celebrating. Calories don't count."

"Oh really?"

"Absolutely. You can even check the nutrition label. The waitress showed me." Pretending to read off an imaginary box, he said, "Calories become null and void when cake is consumed for celebration. It's all right there."

I shook my head, "You are incorrigible."

"I didn't think anybody under thirty-five used that word anymore," he said.

"Meh, I like big words. I might also be one of the rare

members of my generation who doesn't use the word 'like' as a comma."

Repeating one of my favorite Joe-isms, he replied, "I knew I liked you."

I grinned back. "The feeling is mutual."

After a moment of locked eyes and unspoken words, he said "Do you want me to sing for you? I've been told I can carry a tune. Also, it gets me one step closer to putting my fork in that cake."

I chuckled at his enthusiasm. "No, I think the candle is enough. Thank you, Joe," I said, smiling and losing myself in those wonderful jade eyes.

"Make a wish," he said playfully.

"Don't need to. It already came true."

"I'm flattered," he said, his eyes dancing.

I stuck out my tongue at him and laughed. "Believe it or not, I actually wasn't talking about you."

He raised an eyebrow. "You've got me curious, Miss Miller. Was it really just the birthday cake the entire time? I think I might be genuinely hurt."

I laughed and shook my head. "No, silly. My deepest wish has always been for God to think I'm good enough. I never wanted my mother's hyper faith, but something in me still wanted to know Jesus. I wanted to know if He was real, and I wanted Him to love me."

"Perfectly understandable," Joe said, his expression turning serious. "There are many people in your shoes, I think. Some of the millennials in our Bible study have struggled with wanting their own walk with Jesus instead of riding on their parents' coattails."

"When I read Rebecca's book after First United closed, it shook me to my core."

"Why? All of the scandals and abuse?"

"No, it was seeing Rebecca's faith even with everything I know she's suffered. I've sat through those sermons her father gave. My mother drilled them into me at home. Rebecca had to live with Pastor Ivy 24/7, but she was nothing like him. When she talked about Jesus in her book, she described it like a conversation. I'd never seen anything like that. I knew it didn't come from any of Pastor Ivy's teachings, and it was the first time in so long that I really considered a version of Jesus different from what I'd learned from First United or my mother."

"Wow, I can't imagine what that must be like. You're having to unlearn everything you were taught."

"Courtney helped too," I said. "She's not as Bible savvy or spiritual as you all, but I know her relationship with God is real. She treats people the same in public and in private. You're never walking on eggshells wondering which version of Courtney you're going to be dealing with."

"Which was hardly the case with your other roommates," Joe said, having heard tales of life in Kelsey's house.

"I eventually came to believe that what Rebecca and Courtney have is real. I even wanted it for myself. I just never believed God would forgive me for what I'd done. I told myself that it was different because they had never sinned like I had."

"But God *has* forgiven you," Joe said, holding my gaze. "You know that now, don't you?"

"I do." Pausing, I smiled as I realized my heart's deepest desire at that moment beyond mountains of birthday cake. "Can I tell you something crazy?"

"Sure," he said.

"I can't shake this feeling of wanting to lock myself in my bedroom and just start reading the Bible. Weird, huh?"

"Not at all," he said, his eyes bright. "In fact, it reminds me of *Song of Solomon*."

I shrugged. "I've never heard of it."

"It's a book in the Bible. Come to think of it, maybe we should hold off on talking about it right now," he said, suddenly blushing.

I raised an amused eyebrow, perplexed by his response. "It's the Bible, Joe. What would be wrong about us reading it?"

His embarrassment gave way to incredulity and a small smile. "You really don't know, do you?"

"Know what?"

He cleared his throat and laughed self-consciously. "It's a book about a husband and a wife in love. It describes their passion for one another in poetic, and um, semi explicit detail."

"Shut up!" I exclaimed in disbelief. "There's no way my mother would read the Bible with something like that in it! With all of the Bible verses that woman has tried to shove down my throat about sexual purity, I can assure you this book was never mentioned."

Joe laughed more genuinely this time. "Absolutely factual, my dear. God gave us a picture of what marriage and desire are supposed to look like. In the right context, it's a holy, pleasurable, and wonderful thing."

"Then why did me spending time with Jesus make you think of it?" Misunderstanding his meaning, my smile fell. "Oh. So, all of this stuff is suddenly kosher between us?"

Joe shook his head emphatically. "No, Carly! I wasn't going there at all."

"Then, help me understand, because I'm lost."

He smiled patiently. "In case you haven't figured this out by now, you'll never see me tossing out breadcrumbs or forcing you to fish information out of me."

"And yet here we are," I said, bringing my first forkful of cake to my mouth. "What do you need to tell me?"

"First," he said, "how's your dessert?"

I smiled around a mouthful of sugary sweet goodness.

Grinning at my response, he said, "Your comment about wanting to run off to spend time with God reminded me of some verses in Song of Solomon. The book is written almost like a song or a play. There's a bride, a groom, and then a background choir of women who all take turns speaking."

"Wow," I said, swallowing another bite of cake. "I never knew any of this."

Joe finally took his fork to the dessert. As the cake hit his taste buds, he winced. "That's a sugar bomb!"

"A very delicious sugar bomb," I amended, savoring yet another mouthful.

His eyes sparkled. "I'm glad you're enjoying it."

"I am," I said. "This definitely tastes like thirty-one birthdays rolled into one. Good work, Mr. Trautweig."

His amused smile softened to one of adoration. "This is a good look for you, Carly."

"What is?"

"Happiness."

"I think this cake would make anybody happy. Except for maybe you and your grandpa taste buds," I teased.

Joe tried another bite of cake before placing his fork down once he swallowed the bite. "Way too sweet for me."

I shrugged. "More for me. Plus, I want to hear the rest of what you were saying. You talk. I'll eat."

He winked at me and continued. "There's a section where the groom calls out to his bride. He says, 'Rise up, my love, my fair one, and come away,' When you mentioned wanting to run away to spend time with God, that's where my mind went. The

Bible talks about every believer being a part of the Bride of Christ and Jesus as our bridegroom."

"It really says that?" I asked.

That winsome smile appeared, answering my question.

I grew thoughtful for a moment, recalling what I had texted Joe that Friday. "Wow," I breathed, piecing it all together. Tears filled my eyes as a feeling of love overwhelmed me from within.

"You're glowing," Joe said, marveling at me. "What's going on?"

"Do you remember what I told you on Friday? You sent me all of those Bible verses, and I told you it felt like God was romancing me."

Understanding lit those jade eyes. Joe's hand came across the table to take mine. "Carly, Jesus truly is the lover of your soul. More than I ever could, His love for you will never fail, never quit, and never let you go."

The tears now escaped down my cheeks. I didn't have to question what Joe was saying because I felt that invisible embrace around my heart. "How could my mother know all of this but still act the way she does? I don't understand."

"Because whatever version she believes about Jesus is a distortion. God's love is meant to transform us. It's supposed to be shared with the world. It was never meant to punish or abuse others. That's not love. It's control."

"What about Poppy?" I asked quietly. "She was trying to control things between you and me. Are you saying she doesn't know God's love? I thought she was one of the *real* ones, but now I'm not so sure."

He sighed and released my hand, running it through his hair. "This is part of God's love too."

"What is?"

"Forgiveness and reconciliation with one another. If

anything, Poppy knows that better than anyone. Her story is the perfect picture of God's love covering many and *any* sin."

I frowned. "Help me understand, Joe. I'm not connecting all the dots."

"The Bible talks about us being transformed and changed daily."

"Okay," I drawled.

"Meaning, that it's a continuous, ongoing process. We don't come to faith in Jesus and then wake up magically perfected. Poppy is still a human and still capable of making mistakes. That didn't change because she got saved. She's still battling her old tendencies the same way any of us do."

"So, what does that have to do with God's love? Her behavior wasn't loving at Vincenzo's at all. It was self-righteous and thoughtless."

"You choosing to forgive Poppy would be you demonstrating God's love to *her*," he said, leveling me with an intense stare.

"I've been thinking about it a lot, actually."

He reached for my hand again and squeezed it encouragingly. "You've gone to Poppy for comfort and strength for most of your friendship. The tables have turned now. She's the one who needs help and forgiveness. And don't forget that she's already apologized and shown remorse. I wouldn't suggest forgiveness if she hadn't yet."

"True," I murmured.

"I have no idea what's going on with her and Jared, but this is an opportunity for us to put Christ's love in action. We recognize that our friend has made a mistake, we love her anyway, we forgive her, and we move on from it."

I sat with his words, confirmation of what I had already resolved to do earlier that evening. I nodded and exhaled a heavy breath. Glancing up at Joe, I asked, "Do you think their marriage is in trouble?"

"None of my business."

I winced. "Is this still a sore subject for you?"

"No," he answered equally as fast. "Poppy's relationship with Jared has nothing to do with me, and it hasn't for a long time. Whatever issues they have because of Poppy's meddling is for the two of them to sort out. It also has no bearing on my relationship with you. As a friend and a sister in Christ, I want to see Poppy's friendship with you reconciled, but that's as far as my interest goes."

I mulled over his words and wondered if I would see Poppy the following day at work. Lost in thought, I startled when Joe tapped my plate with his fork.

"You gonna eat your cake?" he asked, his tone significantly more light hearted than a moment earlier.

"Why? You want some sugar after all?"

"No, but I want to make sure you get to savor every single bite. You deserve no less."

I beamed at him. "Thank you."

"I love you, Carly," he said, his searching gaze finding my heart and grabbing hold of it.

I responded by reaching for his hand across the table. "I love you too."

CHAPTER 25

"This was a big night for you," Joe said, walking me to the front door of my terrace level apartment.

I grinned back. "Sort of surreal, actually. God really loves me. *Me.*"

His infamous smile sent my heart beating in cadence for him.

"You are so beautiful," he said.

I blushed. "You say that a lot."

"That's because it's true."

I shook my head and exhaled a self deprecating laugh. "I wish I saw what you do."

He took a step closer, taking hold of my hands with his own and my soul with his eyes. "Has no one ever told you that before?"

I shrugged. "I never really believed Dylan when he said it, and the toads only wanted sex."

His expression hardened.

"Joe, you know I have a past even beyond the abortion," I said warily.

"That's not what I'm upset about."

I raised my eyebrows. "Then what?"

"I hate that you were used like that."

"Joe, I used *them*! At the very least, it was mutual. I knew what I was doing."

"Or," he countered, "they saw you were in pain and took advantage of you."

I waved him off. "I don't want to argue about this. It's in the past."

"Is it?" he asked. "You said Dylan called you beautiful, but you didn't believe him. I'm standing with you three years after all of that, and you're still having trouble believing that your reflection would take any man's breath away."

I scoffed and released his hands.

"That's what I mean!" he said with a flourish. "You think it's all romantic hyperbole. Carly, I promise you that objectively, you are gorgeous."

"I guess," I mumbled, unsure how to process Joe's compliment or his passionate delivery.

"Where is all of this coming from?" He lifted my downcast face to meet his eyes. "Is this about your mother?"

Giving a moment to ponder his question, I thought back to any instance where Hannah Miller had commented on my looks or appearance. I frowned.

"What lies did she say to you?" Joe asked gruffly. "I don't understand how she could look at this perfect, cherubic face and not see an angel."

I smiled, touched by his sincerity. "Thank you."

He smiled back. "Any time."

He waited patiently for me to gather my thoughts and

process through the painful words spoken over and again.

"With my mother, everything was backhanded," I began. "She would never tell me that I looked pretty. It was always an accusation that I was dressing for attention, or she caught someone staring at me at church. By default, that meant I was attractive enough to be noticed, but she made it sound dirty and shameful."

Joe's mouth was grim. "So, she was jealous."

"Jealous?"

"Yes. Your mother was alone and unloved. Meanwhile, her gorgeous daughter, Hannah's proof of abandonment, was garnering male attention she couldn't gain for herself."

My eyes went wide as a memory stirred. "Joe!" I cried, suddenly straining for air.

"Give me your keys."

Handing them over, I continued to suck in as much breath as my lungs could contain.

He led me inside my apartment, pushing the door shut with one arm as he held me in the other. Gingerly, we sat together on my burgundy sofa. Joe pulled me into his chest, allowing me to rest my ear against the steadier rhythm of his own heartbeat. As my breathing normalized, I melted into him, sliding my hand from atop my own pounding heart to join the other around his waist.

I savored the embrace, snuggling closer and realizing how much I had missed the feeling of intimacy and contentment. After several quiet moments, the temptation for something more tugged at me. I turned my face upward and glanced from his eyes to his mouth. His heart rate accelerated beneath my ear, and I knew it was time to pull away.

"Thank you," he said, his jade gaze revealing both relief and tightly wound desire.

"Joe," I said, testing out my breath. "I want to tell you, but I know you're not going to like it."

"What happened? What did you remember?"

"It was the comment you made about my mom being jealous."

"What about it?"

I paused and inhaled a deeper gulp of air.

He reached his hand over to cover mine. "Carly, I don't want you to black out again. You don't have to tell me now."

As my mind replayed the entire traumatic episode and subsequent events, my hand flew out from under Joe's to cover my mouth in disbelief.

"Ohhhh," I murmured, dragging out the vowel sound. My eyes flew to Joe's. "She knew!" I gasped. "Joe, she *knew!*"

"She knew what? You're scaring me."

My brain worked feverishly through multiple encounters with Pastor Ivy and then all the brainwashing and gaslighting from my mother. "I told you about the time Pastor Ivy cornered me in middle school. It wasn't the only time."

His jaw clenched. "Did he touch you?"

I shook my head. "Nothing more than a brief side hug or pat on the back. It was how he looked at me, Joe, and apparently how he looked at me when he thought people weren't watching."

"What do you mean?"

"My mother," I said. "All of those shaming comments about my appearance. I don't think it was about jealousy. I mentioned to her a few times about catching Pastor Ivy watching me or complimenting my outfit. Sometimes, he would look me up and down. When I told my mother, she said that's just how he was. One time, I argued with her, and she slapped me for suggesting Pastor Ivy looked at me inappropriately."

Joe shook his head in disgust, too horrified for words.

"This time was different though. I think my mother was protecting me from Pastor Ivy, but she had to do it in a way that still covered what he really was."

Joe looked aghast. "But she beat you with shoes and books, Carly! She denied you a single birthday celebration."

"I know, and I'm not excusing it. But the incident that I remember happened after my last service at First United. I was wearing a new dress I had purchased for myself, and to be fair, the neckline was a little low."

Joe blew a raspberry. "Doesn't mean it's okay to stare."

"You're right, and I did catch Pastor Ivy staring repeatedly during another one of his tithing sermons. At first, I thought I'd imagined it, but it happened so often that I eventually kept my head bowed so I wouldn't see his eyes on me even though I felt them. My mother seemed oblivious at the time."

Joe's eyes flashed dangerously.

"Pastor Ivy is already in prison," I said to reassure both of us. "He never touched me, I promise."

"I'd still kill him for what he did to you as a child."

I smiled sadly. "I believe you."

Joe swallowed convulsively. Inhaling his own calming breath, he asked, "So, what's the rest of the story?"

I inhaled, seeing the confusing scenario much clearer at thirty-one than I had with eighteen-year-old eyes. "Mrs. Ivy noticed her husband ogling me, and she chewed my mother out. I witnessed part of it in Pastor Ivy's office because we were the last ones to leave that day. My mother screamed at me all the way home in the car, calling me every version of whore and insult you can imagine."

"I can imagine," he muttered.

"So, we got home, and that's when the beating began. She

was grabbing anything she could find."

Joe's eyes welled with tears. "How can you say she was trying to *protect* you, Carly? That woman was more of a monster than she ever was a parent."

Ignoring his question because it hurt to name my mother what I knew she was, I continued. "I finally locked myself in the bathroom. My mother had pulled at my hair and literally ripped the dress off my body. She told me I had been cursed with the same breasts that had made her easy prey."

"Easy prey?" he repeated. "Was she raped? Is that why she's been so secretive about your birth father?"

I shrugged. "I know as much as you do. I couldn't see my mother's face at that point, but when it came out of her mouth, she stopped raging."

"Then what?" he asked.

"She forbade me from ever going to First United again."

Joe raised both eyebrows. "You told me she had dragged you there since infancy. Why would she ban you from attending?"

"This is why I think banishing me was her backhanded way of protecting me. I don't see how she could have been oblivious to Pastor Ivy's cheating since she spent so much time at the church. This was the only way to keep me away from him without implicating herself for covering it up."

"Carly," Joe said imploringly, "please tell me you don't think her behavior was justified. It was abuse. Period. I don't think this was about protecting you from Pastor Ivy but protecting Pastor Ivy from himself. I also wonder if maybe she wasn't jealous that he turned his eyes to your chest instead of hers."

"You know, you guys keep saying that about my mother and Pastor Ivy, but I don't see it. Obviously, I'm not impartial here, but my mother didn't seem like she was in love with him. She was scared to death of displeasing him."

Joe considered my words and then raked a hand through his hair. "So, what are you saying?"

I sighed. "I agree with Rebecca's theory that Pastor Ivy knows about my birth father. I also think he used that to keep my mother enslaved to the church."

Joe seamed his lips. "I think you're giving Hannah Miller too much credit here. The woman still listens to his sermons. She kept attending long after you were an adult. She covered for him long after you would have been old enough to handle the truth."

I conceded his point. "You're right," I said, "but my mother was so crazy and out of control that night—even for her. I was shocked she was forcing me out of First United but obviously grateful too. I hated going, and I hated Pastor Ivy."

"Understandably."

"My mother just kept accusing me of being a Jezebel and trying to ruin Pastor Ivy's marriage by tempting and tormenting him."

"Tormenting?" Joe repeated in disgust. "That just proves he'd been making eyes at you for more than just one sermon, and your mother knew it."

I shuddered. "Why did she lie to me then? Why did she go out of her way to convince me that I couldn't trust my own eyes or intuition?"

"Because as long as she could convince you to believe the lie, she could keep pretending the lie was the truth."

"So, what was different about that night?"

He looked nonplussed. "I don't know what snapped in your mother. Maybe it was embarrassment. Maybe it was jealousy. Who knows? But I will never agree that Hannah Miller has a protective bone in her body as a mother. I can't think of one instance you've shared where she showed an ounce of concern for your wellbeing. She denied you love, even basic necessities! So no, Carly, don't you dare tell me this woman was trying to protect you while ripping your clothes to shreds and forcing you to lock yourself behind a door."

"Does it dishonor my mother to think of her this way?" I whispered. "Will God be mad at me for thinking she was a horrible parent?"

"God isn't a liar, and He would never ask you to do it either."

"What do you mean?"

"Meaning that to call your mother anything other than a self-serving, hypocritical lowlife would be a lie. You're not dishonoring your mother by calling her behavior exactly what it is. However, you would be dishonoring God if you continued to lie and make excuses for your mother's abuse the same way she did for Pastor Ivy."

My stomach dropped, seeing the truth of his words.

"Carly, you have to end the cycle now. No more enabling and explaining it away because you're afraid of the bully abusing you. Your mother treated you the same way Pastor Ivy treated *her*. You're the only one who can make it stop."

"Haven't I already done that Joe? I don't treat people the way my mother does."

He shook his head and then beamed at me with a smile so dazzling, my breath caught from something other than panic.

"Your children," he said.

"My children?" I gaped, feeling the loss of the little girl I imagined. "Joe, I don't understand."

He took hold of my hand. "Let me rephrase. *Our* children."

"Ours?" I repeated, barely above a whisper.

The next question Joe asked me was followed by a kiss reserved only for the future Mrs. Trautweig.

CHAPTER 26

WHEN MONDAY MORNING ROLLED AROUND, IT FELT like a lifetime of events had transpired since the previous week of work. I wasn't sure whether to expect Poppy back in the office or not, and I walked into the building simultaneously dreading and hoping she'd be there. Though I had no ring on my finger to boast of the promises Joe and I had made to one another, I felt like the entire world could see the answer on my face.

I stopped short as I approached the doorway, locating Poppy through the glass window of our office space. On the surface, nothing seemed different as she clicked the mouse and stared at her dual computer monitors.

I took a deep breath and thanked God for the Bible verse Joe had texted me that morning about courage. As I entered the office, Poppy's head lifted immediately.

"Hi," she said. She lifted her cup of Vincenzo's coffee and nearly hid behind it.

"Hi," I replied, raising my own cup in salute.

"When did that happen?" She glanced at my matching coffee counterpart. "I thought you didn't drink coffee."

"Apparently, I like cappuccino," I said with a smile, "or at least the way Niccolo makes it."

Poppy allowed herself a tiny grin of her own. "Niccolo is a genius and very good at what he does."

"He is. I don't know what I'm going to do when the gift card from you and Jared runs out." Even as I said it, I felt guilty for the half-truth. Joe would never let me purchase my own coffee anyway. When I had tried to pay for my cappuccino that morning, Niccolo insisted it was taken care of already. I realized Joe had instructed him to put it on his own tab.

"Are you enjoying the coffee?" Poppy said blandly.

The awkwardness and tension stretched, begging to be released. Unable to endure any more small talk with the pink elephant still sitting in the room, I said, "Are we gonna talk about last Tuesday, or what?"

"Which part?" she asked. "The mess I made at Vincenzo's or the one I created at home?"

"Are things with you and Jared okay?"

Poppy glanced up in surprise. "To be honest, I wasn't sure if I would even say something or not."

"Why?"

"I thought you might be telling me I got what I deserved."

I pulled a face as I sat down at my work station opposite Poppy. "I was mad at you for what happened, but I'm not vindictive like that. I don't wish marriage problems on you or Jared."

"Sorry," she muttered. "It was a dumb thought anyway. I just meant that I wouldn't blame you for thinking that."

"So, are you guys okay?" I repeated.

"Honestly, no," she said, "but I have nobody to blame but myself."

"He's not holding you to some crazy double standard, is he?" I said, offended. "I mean, anybody who's read your book knows exactly what Jared's sins are."

Poppy smirked at my impassioned response. "So, now you're on my side?"

"No, I just hate hypocrisy."

"Well, it's not quite that simple," she said with a heavy sigh. "Yes, Jared had an affair, but I can't throw that in his face every time I make my own mistakes."

"Well, isn't this just about Jared's jealousy anyway? He should understand better than anybody how it feels, right?"

She shook her head. "I forgave my husband for what he did. I'm not going to keep holding his affair over his head when I know he's genuinely sorry and we've both moved on. It's not fair, and it doesn't change any of my own stupid choices."

I conceded the point, impressed she hadn't chosen the easy way out. "So, what's going on? Is he having trouble forgiving you for it?"

"The fight wasn't about forgiveness, Carly."

"I'm confused. What are you guys fighting about? You told Jared what you did, and it's obvious you regret it. What's the problem?"

"First of all, I appreciate you saying that," she said, her smile brightening. "You're showing me a lot more grace than I deserve or even expected to receive. And to be clear, my expectations weren't based on your character but on how badly I know I messed up."

"Okay," I drawled.

Continuing she said, "With all of the history between me and Jared, you'd think it'd be my husband struggling with thoughts of temptation outside of our marriage. It turns out it was me."

I mulled over Poppy's confession and willingness to reveal her own vulnerability. "You've been telling me you love Jared. You've denied any interest in Joe a million times. Was it a lie?"

Poppy sighed again. "It was about me letting my thought life run amok. Was I going to throw myself at Joe again? Absolutely not! But the situation wasn't like Jared cheating on me with Leah. Yes, he chose to cheat, but he also had my former best friend encouraging him every step of the way. When Jared and I were definite about reconciling, Joe backed off. The only person keeping the fantasy alive was me, and Jared had every right to call me out on it."

"Wow," I murmured.

"Wow what?"

"I'm impressed, Poppy."

"Impressed?" she gaped. "I don't understand. There's nothing impressive about any of this. It's humiliating how stupidly I behaved and how much I hurt my husband and two friends I care about very much. I *do* care about you, Carly," she said, meeting my eyes. "I know I didn't act like it last week, and for that, all I can do is keep apologizing."

I was tempted to tell her right then that I had already forgiven her, but there was something else needing to be said. "I believe you," I murmured.

She stared at me dumbfounded. "Really? I figured you'd tell me off or that I should get a job somewhere else."

I shook my head. "No, I don't think I've ever had anyone actually apologize to me like this before, or for that matter, own their behavior and feel bad about it. It's taking me a second to process all of it."

"Ah," she said. "I guess we can add me to the list of jerks, right?"

I paused, not sure if she was fishing for sympathy or truly giving way to self pity. Instead, I answered a question with a question. "Do you think that what you did to me compares to Pastor Ivy or my mother?"

"Oh, I uh..." she stammered.

"Because what you did was wrong. I'm not going to sugar-coat it," I said, "but it's not the same thing as abusing and brainwashing me my entire life. In all fairness, though, you did give the same basic message they did."

"I know," she said, hanging her head. "I know how much pain you have, Carly, and I hate that I added to it."

"Are you trying to make me feel sorry for you?" I asked.

Her head jerked up. "What? No! I feel horrible about what I did. Scum of the earth. I've sat with you in this office while you cried on my shoulder. I'm disgusted with myself, and my husband is too."

"Because of your feelings for Joe?" My heart immediately squeezed at the thought of any other woman longing for the man I loved.

"No, because of what I did to *you*," she said, her voice anguished. "Jared was irritated about the Joe thing. He was livid about how I treated you."

"Me?" I squeaked. "Why?"

"Because he's heard bits and pieces of our conversations. I haven't told him any personal details," she said, holding up a hand in innocence, "but he was furious that I had treated you almost like another daughter and then stabbed you in the back. He asked how you were going to think any Christian was different than Hannah Miller."

My eyes widened in shock. "I...I never thought Jared would defend me like that."

"That's why I came back," Poppy said meekly. "My husband told me I need to make things right with you, and God has said the same thing. Carly, from the bottom of my heart, I am so sorry. I wronged you, and I did it with an exponent."

I chuckled softly. "Thank you."

"Do you forgive me?" she asked, her face hopeful.

"I forgave you this weekend already."

"Wow."

"It happened at the Margolin Bible study."

"Oh!" she exclaimed, her eyes wide. "You went? I had no idea! Jared said we weren't going until I talked to you first."

"Why?"

"He didn't want me near Joe."

"Because of your old feelings?" I asked.

Poppy shook her head and took a sip of her coffee. Her posture was already more relaxed than when I had initially arrived. "He said that if Joe felt as strongly about you as it seemed, he'd probably rip my head off for how I'd treated you. Jared didn't want to fight with Joe out of obligation to defend me, or worse, split the group."

"Wow," I said, once again impressed with Jared Levine. I smiled, thinking of how much Poppy's husband had changed since the early pages of her book and from my first few months at Culver. They had only just begun the process of reconciliation back then. I still remembered her complaints about their marriage counselors.

"What's got you tickled over there?" she asked, taking another sip. "I didn't think any part of this situation was particularly funny."

"Just thinking about where you and Jared were when I

started working here," I said, drinking from my own coffee cup. "It's hard to believe he's the same person."

"That's because he isn't," Poppy said, a twinkle returning to her dark eyes. "For all the years I endured and put up with that man, he's now having to deal and put up with *me*."

I smiled genuinely at Poppy, and she took note, studying me.

"Something is definitely different about you."

"God loves me," I said.

Her eyes widened larger than I thought possible before she burst into tears. "Oh, sweetie!" she exclaimed. She jumped to her feet and pulled me into a grappling bear hug. "I'm so happy for you," she said into my hair.

Helpless to do anything other than hug her back, I leaned into the embrace, briefly imagining it was my own mother hugging me. Poppy leaned back and held me at shoulder length.

"When? How?" she asked.

"This weekend."

"Was it the Bible study?"

I shook my head. "I talked to Rebecca for a while about my mother and Pastor Ivy. Joe stopped by later. He told me he loves me," I added, gauging her reaction.

Instead of pain, I saw her eyes dance in delight. "He did?"

I nodded.

Her eyes filled with tears. "It's not what you think," she said, waving me off. "Even with my mountain of screw ups, I've only ever wanted Joe to be happy. I truly mean that."

"I believe you," I said again.

"Oh, Carly, I don't even need to ask if you love him too. I saw it the night we all went to synagogue."

I exhaled a short laugh. "You probably did."

"Did Joe lead you to Christ?" she asked.

"No, I think Jesus led me to Jesus," I said, feeling a beautiful smile on my face. "Joe told me that God has shown him how much He loves me. He's been trying to show that same love to me. He sends me Bible verses during the day."

Poppy's hand fluttered to her heart, savoring every word as if it were one of her inspirational romance novels. "Go on. This is so beautiful!"

I beamed at her. "Joe kissed me, and somehow in the midst of that, I felt how much God loves me. I don't know how else to describe it, Poppy. It was like he used Joe to show me that I am worthy to be loved."

"Oh, sweetie," she murmured, tears wetting her cheeks. "I'm so happy for you. Happy for you and Joe, but even happier you know how much Jesus loves you."

"You helped too," I said. "I want you to know how grateful I am for all of the conversations we had where you didn't judge me or condemn me. You just listened."

"Until last week," she said, her happy expression falling.

"Poppy, you've already apologized, and I promise that I've really forgiven you."

She stared at me for a long moment. "Joe Trautweig better know what kind of a blessing he has in his life."

"Oh, he does," Joe said from the open doorway.

CHAPTER 27

"Hey!" I exclaimed, running into Joe's arms. "What are you doing here?"

"Just making sure everything is copacetic," he said, glancing at Poppy.

She acknowledged him with a deep bow of the chin. "Congratulations," she said, noting Joe's arm around me and my own arm around his waist. "I just got done apologizing to Carly."

"Good," he said, still eyeing her warily. "I don't need any more apologies. I just need to know it won't ever happen again."

Her eyes widened at his protectiveness. "It won't," she vowed. "I'm happy for you guys. Truly."

"All of this in just one week?" he asked. "I'm impressed, Poppy."

"Well, don't be," she said, flicking a wrist. "I screwed up. I'm still ashamed of myself, but I appreciate both of you not tearing my head off. Not that I don't deserve it."

The next question Joe wanted to ask lingered in the air,

unasked and unanswered. Instead, he ventured a simple, "You okay?"

She smiled back tears and said, "I think I'm on my way to getting there. Do you guys mind if I make a phone call?"

Knowing exactly who the recipient of that call would be, Joe and I nodded while Poppy hurried past us into the hallway. I heard her breath catch on a sob as she exited through a side door.

Joe tugged me gently into the office and wrapped both arms around my waist. I laid my head against his heart while he rested his cheek on the top of my head.

"Ooh, child, is Poppy all right?" Miss Belle asked, bursting into our shared office. "I saw her crying, and after last week I—" She stopped short as she caught sight of Joe and me. "Oh, Lord, not more of this soap opera drama!"

I felt and heard Joe's chuckle against my ear.

"You can put down the pearls," Joe said, seeing Miss Belle with her trademark necklace clutched in hand. "Yes, Poppy already knows, and that's not why she's upset." Releasing me to greet his former coworker, Joe hugged Culver's mother hen.

"Oh," she murmured, patting his bearded cheek, "you look so happy." Glancing past him over to me, she clucked, "and you too, Little Miss! Cuddling and canoodling in the office! You know how the gossips can't wait to get their hands on something like this."

Joe stepped back and reached for my hand as we faced Miss Belle. "I doubt anybody in this office remembers me," he said. "I left more than two years ago."

"But you've gone and punched the guy who had your old job and wanted your girl, Joe Trautweig. You know how the gossiping tongues love to wag around this place," she said with a long suffering sigh.

Joe looked surprised. "How did you find out about that?"

Miss Belle rolled her eyes. "Because Zach Perkins has a big mouth, and the mighty Margolin had to threaten him with a restraining order if he ever set foot within ninety feet of Culver or Carly."

"What?" Joe and I exclaimed.

Miss Belle covered her mouth with her hand. "Lord, now I've gone and done it again!"

"Who has Perkins been talking to?" Joe demanded, pulling me closer toward him.

"Some of the girls in Benefits," Miss Belle said, jerking her head toward a set of cubicles outside of my corner office. "Kacie and Wanda got an earful about it a little while ago. They went to the mighty Margolin to find out what happened."

"So, how did you find out about it?" I asked. "You're over in CID."

"Avatron, baby girl."

"Ah," Joe said. "I brought that client to Culver almost five years ago. It was a joint deal with commercial and benefits. Margolin and I were both producers for that account. Zach must have taken over for Avatron when I left for Cooper & Jaye."

Miss Belle confirmed Joe's theory with a swift nod. "They already knew about Zach getting in trouble for buzzing around Carly's office too much. They took everything to Ted to manage."

"And he did," I said, "because I didn't even know about any of this."

"Baby girl, you know how hard it is to keep anyone in this department," Miss Belle said, glancing around the room. "All of you ladies come in here single, meet the man of your dreams, and then we have to start all over finding a body who can handle all the work y'all do."

Joe chuckled softly. "I'd hate to break the streak."

Miss Belle did a double take, raising her penciled eyebrows high. "How long has this been going on?" she asked, waving her hand in our direction.

"Does it matter?" Joe said. "End result is the same."

Her neck and shoulders rolled back as if hit with a sudden burst of wind. "Well, okay then! I like hearing a man who knows what he wants. Go on and get your girl!"

Half expecting a church choir to materialize and shout a resounding amen, Joe and I laughed at her enthusiasm. He kissed the top of my head.

"You gonna invite me to the wedding, right?" With her tone smooth as butter, she fluttered her lashes and then winked at us.

Right on time, Phil Robbins must have heard the "w" word and poked his head in the office. "Wedding? What wedding? Poppy already had hers last year. Oh," he said, stopping short next to Miss Belle. "What do we have here?"

"Office gossip if you don't lower your voice, Phil Robbins!" Miss Belle admonished.

Phil chuckled as his blue eyes sparkled in mischief. "This is an unexpected development, but I promise to keep my lips sealed."

"Good," Joe said, "and I have to get back to work in my own office."

He approached us with a fatherly smile and clapped Joe on the shoulder. "I'm happy for you, Trautweig. You deserve it."

"Thank you, Phil."

My CEO turned his attention to me. "You are just full of surprises, aren't you, my dear?"

"I'll never tell," I said with a saucy grin.

Phil guffawed loudly, and I saw Miss Belle eyeing Joe and me with a gleam and a smile.

"Hey, I'm back," Poppy said, entering the fray. "Wow, we have a whole congregation today." She edged around Miss Belle to sneak behind her desk. Seeing Joe and I in the relatively same position as when she had left, Poppy picked up her cold coffee and smirked behind her cup.

"Ah, so you already knew about this," Phil said, watching her.

Poppy's eyes flashed brief panic as they darted to me and Joe, but she hid it moments later. "Yes, I did. I'm very happy for Joe and Carly."

Miss Belle watched Poppy carefully, her lips pursed, but she kept her thoughts to herself.

"See you tonight?" Joe said close to my ear.

I grinned back. "Of course."

He leaned in to kiss me, hesitated with our audience, and instead, squeezed my hand. He angled himself between Phil and Miss Belle before tossing one last sidelong glance in my direction. My heart knew the words his eyes spoke.

Joe took his leave, and I migrated back to my desk.

"Ooh Lord!" Miss Belle said, fanning herself. "Carly, child, when you find a man who looks at you like that, you hang onto him, ya hear? I don't know if Mr. Vickers ever gave me such a smolder," she said, referencing her late husband.

Poppy held back a laugh as she sipped on her latte.

"Never a dull moment, is it, my dear?" Phil said to our beloved mother hen.

"You know, I might just be getting too old for this kind of excitement. Most of us aren't coming to the office to make a love match and write a book about it," she said, leveling her gaze at my coworker. "First Rebecca, then Taylor, now Poppy. You gonna be next, child?" she asked, turning to me.

I shrugged innocently. I didn't want to mention I had already begun to journal the past few months.

Phil chuckled and said, "Miss Belle, you know you love it."

She demurred, mild offense on her face.

Grinning, Phil said, "Tell the truth, and shame the devil!"

"Oh, you're so bad!" she squealed, swatting him in the arm. "You just can't help stirring the pot, can you?"

"Guilty as charged, but at least I admit it."

Miss Belle pursed those infamous lips at our CEO.

"Don't make me say it again," he teased.

Relenting, she shook her head and laughed softly. "I have a good mind to sic my Mama on you, Phil."

"You leave Mama Jenkins out of this. I wasn't asking for that kind of trouble."

This time, Miss Belle gave a full smile. Looking once more at Poppy and me, she said, "You see what I've been putting up with the last ten years at this company?"

Phil slung his arm around Miss Belle's shoulders and led her out of our office. "Didn't you receive a *very* expensive watch at our annual meeting a few months ago? Not too shabby for a ten year anniversary gift from Culver, was it?"

"Don't try my patience," she shot back, "you know I earned every teensy diamond on that thing."

Snickering quietly as their voices trailed off, I glanced at Poppy. Her earlier mirth had been replaced with a more pensive expression.

"How did it go?" I asked.

She sighed. "We didn't talk long, but Jared is very happy for both of you."

I offered a tiny smile. "I'd like to move forward, Poppy. You can tell Jared I'm not mad at you anymore. He doesn't need to be upset on my behalf."

"It just triggered an avalanche of old baggage," she replied, "and none of that was your fault. Jared and I will get through it, but if you don't see us for a little while at Bible study, that's why. There are some issues we still need to iron out."

"Are you guys going to be okay?"

I watched Poppy catch herself from snapping back at me. She inhaled a deep breath and closed her eyes. "Sorry, Carly. None of this was your fault, but I'm struggling."

"With what?"

"Just seeing how horribly I messed up. Seeing how easy it was to slip right back into the person I used to be. Seeing how my own selfishness hurt so many people."

"Poppy," I said gently, "you were the one who told me for the last two years that Jesus could forgive any sin, even mine. You told me He would take away my shame and that He loves me."

"I did," she said quietly.

"Don't you think that applies to you too?"

"But I *knew* better!" she cried.

"You think I didn't?"

"You weren't a Christian," she argued.

"I knew it was wrong when I went into the clinic, and I felt how wrong it was every day since I did it."

"So, what are you saying?"

"Didn't Jesus forgive the men who put the nails into His hands and feet? Courtney has told me that a hundred times. You're the one who told me that the disciples who also 'knew better' abandoned Him."

She sniffled back tears as understanding illuminated her

dark eyes. Exhaling a chuckle, she said, "Look at you preaching the gospel back to me. Thank you."

"I had a good teacher."

She stood up from her desk. "Can I give you a hug?"

"Of course!" I said, rising to meet her in the middle of the four feet separating her desk from mine.

From just beyond us, my cell phone buzzed. Poppy glanced over my shoulder to the upturned phone on my desk. "Looks like Mr. Trautweig has a message for you."

Laughing, I released my coworker and checked to see what he'd sent.

Carly, what do you think about meeting my parents?

Stunned, I took a moment before replying.

"Everything all right?" Poppy asked, now seated back at her own desk.

"Yeah," I said absently. "No worries."

Nodding, she turned to her computer monitor and began edits on an employee benefits guide.

My cell phone buzzed again. *You still there?* Joe asked me.

Yes. Processing.

My mother called and left me a voicemail. After the big virus scare with my dad, she's been on this YOLO kick. She asked me if I was seeing anyone the last time we spoke, and I mentioned you.

My heart fluttered in my chest. *You already told your mom about me?*

Of course!

I could envision the smile on his face and in his voice reading the text to myself. *Was this before or after our conversation last night?*

I mentioned you about a month ago. My mother's been harping on it ever since.

Will they care that I'm not Jewish?

They've already accepted the fact I believe in Jesus, so it won't be much of a surprise. Catherine wasn't Jewish either, so they're used to it.

Biting the bullet, I asked, *Is she anything like my mother?*

Joe's reply was swift. *Not at all. If she was remotely like Hannah Miller, I never would have suggested it.*

Inhaling a sigh of relief, I asked, *When were you thinking?*

How about this weekend?

CHAPTER 28

"Carly, if you aren't okay with this, you can tell me," Joe said as I climbed into his car.

"I'd be lying if I said I wasn't nervous."

He paused to take me in, a soft smile on his mouth. "You look beautiful. As always."

I smiled back. "Thank you. I wasn't sure how fancy to get for the occasion."

His eyes roamed over my chevron striped maxi dress. "Is that new? It looks great on you."

"It is. Rose Margolin emailed me some coupons from Mercer's she wasn't going to use."

"Oh," Joe said, turning out of my apartment complex. "I didn't know you guys had become such fast friends."

"Rebecca met me for lunch at the Soaring Scone on Thursday, and Rose tagged along."

"How was it?"

I grinned. "Really nice. They were both very supportive of me."

His eyes crinkled as he smiled. "I'm so glad. They're both amazing women."

"Yes, they are. To be honest, I didn't know what to expect last Sunday, but they answered a lot of questions for me."

"What kind of questions? More information about Pastor Ivy?"

I shook my head. "No, questions about my mother actually."

"What answers did you think they would have for you?" he asked, glancing over his shoulder to merge onto the highway.

"Well, it wasn't so much about First United as it was trying to get a better understanding of how my mother treated me."

"In what way?"

"Just trying to understand what was normal and what wasn't. I had a lot of questions about Bible verses she's used my entire life. They helped me understand what the verses meant and how my mother used them to control me."

"Ah," he said, stealing a glance over at me. "Did it help?"

"Yes and no."

"What do you mean?"

"Well," I said, taking advantage of my position in the passenger seat to study his profile, "it helped me see how my mother has twisted Jesus into her personal bully, but I didn't feel much better after hearing it."

"Why not? I thought it would be some validation for you."

"I guess because I'm praying to Jesus myself now. I don't feel all the shame and condemnation my mother put on me. When I talk to Him, I just feel peace and comfort. It makes me sad realizing how many years I thought God didn't love me or He hated me because of some lie my mother spewed. It hurts that someone could talk about God that way when it's the complete opposite of what it's been like for me."

Joe's smile, even in profile, was breathtaking.

"Like what you see?" he teased, feeling my gaze without needing to confirm it.

"Handsomest man I know."

"We gotta get you out more," he said before hitting me with a blast of that jade stare.

"Watch the road," I said, laughing.

His smile widened to my favorite winsome grin. "I think I get what you're saying, Carly, and it says a lot that you aren't frothing at the mouth about your mother."

"I'm disgusted, don't get me wrong. I'm slowly seeing how much she's stolen from me. It's a lot to digest."

"Of course," he said, "and healing from the continuous abuse she and Pastor Ivy gave isn't going to happen overnight either. Like I told you the first day we met, we can't set a time limit on how long it takes to process through trauma."

Changing the subject, I asked, "Did you say your brother was going to be there today too?"

Joe nodded in the affirmative. "Yes, it was a surprise visit. He lives in Cordele."

"And his kids are grown?"

"Yes, two are in college, and my oldest niece, Samantha, is working for a marketing firm not too far from us in Parkview. Darren is the oldest of the three of us."

"What about your niece who is in the same bar mitzvah class as Ryan Levine?"

"Ah, my little Emma," he said with a smile. "That's my sister's kid."

"Tell me the ages again, Joe."

"My sister, Rena, has two kids, Emma and Caden. She got a later start on family life, so her kids are twelve and eight. She turned forty-seven earlier this year."

"And your other brother?" I asked.

"Darren is fifty-three."

"Wow," I said. "That's a big age gap between the three of you."

"I was a surprise," Joe said, "and my mother had a tough time getting pregnant after Darren. Rena was a miracle baby, and I don't even know what I was."

"My miracle," I said, beaming at him.

Joe inhaled a ragged breath. "I'm halfway tempted to pull this car over and kiss you for saying that."

"I wouldn't stop you, but then you'd have to explain to your mother why we're running late."

"Still worth it," he said, wiggling his eyebrows for effect.

"Do they know about our age difference? Your big brother is the same age as my mother. It's kind of freaky."

A strange look crossed over Joe's face.

"What?" I asked.

"Nothing," he said, shaking his head. "Just something odd that came to mind, but it's crazy."

I raised my eyebrows. "What are you thinking?"

"Tell you later," he said, pulling off the highway to the second exit in Danbury. "My parents live off Sycamore not too far from here."

"Pretty close to Poppy's parents, if I remember correctly," I said, referencing *Tikkun Olam* once again.

Joe chuckled. "Did you memorize these books? How do you remember all of these tiny little details?"

Blushing, I replied, "Because I live here too. Everything that Rebecca, Taylor, or Poppy wrote all happened in my backyard. When they're referencing specific towns or streets, I know exactly what they're talking about."

"Have you ever lived in Danbury? I thought you and your mother lived across town in Hillcrest."

"We lived in a trailer park further north of Hillcrest. Maybe fifteen minutes from Cordele, actually. My mother drove forty-five minutes each way to be at Pastor Ivy's beck and call."

Joe whistled as he continued to navigate the side streets off the highway. "And how many days a week were you guys at that church?"

"Anywhere from three to seven. It depended on what was going on. During the summer, my mother was responsible for the Vacation Bible School, so it was weeks of setup beforehand and then the actual week of camp."

He frowned. "How did she manage all of that plus hold down a fulltime job?"

"She used her vacation time from work to run the VBS at First United. The other week of vacation she used for all of the Christmas festivities."

"So, she never took any time off for just the two of you? Not even for herself just to rest?"

I laughed bitterly. "Rest? You've clearly never met my mother. Anything less than serving to the point of exhaustion was considered laziness to her."

"I have a feeling that day will come soon enough."

"What day?"

"When I meet your mother face to face."

"What? Why?" I said, alarmed.

Joe pulled into his parents' driveway. "Because I want to look that woman in the face and tell her how horribly she's treated you. I want to tell Hannah Miller that *her* behavior as a so-called Christian is the real abomination."

"Oh, Joe," I said, placing my hand on his arm. "You don't need to do that."

"I do," he said, shutting off the engine and staring into my eyes intently. "You deserve no less. You also deserve to know who your father is."

Before I could respond, a woman in her late seventies tapped on Joe's window.

"Joseph Michael Trautweig, you open that door and let me meet her!" his mother demanded imperiously.

Snickering, I glanced at Joe who also held in a laugh. He turned toward his mother who ventured her first glance inside the car window to better see me. Her eyebrows raised in surprise.

Joe opened the door gently, giving his mother time to step away.

"You said she was young," she murmured, "but she can't be older than Samantha can she?"

"Samantha is only twenty-six. Carly is thirty-one," he said quietly.

"Oh," she replied, her brown eyes resting on my face. "She looks like a baby."

"Well, *she's* not," I said good naturedly. I stepped out of the car and walked over to formally greet Joe's mother. "I'm Carly," I said, extending my hand to her.

His mother looked me up and down, her eyes resting briefly on my bosom, then back to my face. "She's lovely."

"And she's standing right in front of you," Joe said with some irritation. He moved away from his mother's side to stand next to mine. "Carly works at Culver."

"She doesn't work with um...?" his mother asked, her hand gesturing where her words trailed off.

Joe's tight smile disappeared. "How awkward are we going to make this visit, Mom? Yes, Carly works with Poppy. They're friends."

Seeming to catch herself in the faux pas, his mother shuddered and finally extended her hand out to me. "I'm Miriam Trautweig. My husband, Paul, is inside."

"Are Darren and Rena here?" Joe asked.

Miriam turned her focus to Joe. "No, Rena had to cancel at the last minute. Caden cracked a tooth during little league, and they're at the ER."

"Oh no!" I gasped.

Miriam assessed me to gauge the sincerity of my reaction. With an approving nod, she continued. "I'm not sure there's much they can do, but she said it was a bloody mess."

"I can believe it," Joe said.

"Your brother is in the family room. He's also in a bit of a mood. Just got into another fight with Susan."

"His ex-wife," Joe explained to me. "They got divorced after thirty years together."

"Wow," I said. "That's so sad."

"She cheated on him with his best friend, so it's gotten pretty ugly. The kids won't talk to Susan, and she's blaming all of that on Darren."

"I am so sorry to hear that," I said, glancing at both Joe and his mother sympathetically. "That must be incredibly difficult for everyone."

Miriam nodded, blinking back tears. "That's very sweet of you to say, Carly. Why don't the two of you come inside? Hopefully, Darren will cheer up."

I held Joe's hand as he led me into his parents' ranch style home. After traversing a narrow, tiled foyer, we entered a great room with Joe's brother sitting on the couch.

"Hey," Joe called.

Darren seemed engrossed with his cellphone, his features looking both pained and angry. "Unbelievable!" he fumed.

"Darren?" Joe said with some hesitation.

Shaking off the anger almost like a stupor, Joe's older brother tossed his phone aside in disgust and finally glanced up at the two of us.

"Sorry," Darren said sheepishly. "The witch is at it again."

"Block her number," Joe suggested.

"Can't yet, but hopefully soon."

Joe nodded, his smile pained. Brightening some, he said, "I'd like you to meet Carly."

As Joe's older brother finally turned his eyes to me, his face lost all its color.

"Darren?" Joe asked warily. "What's wrong?"

He blinked rapidly, staring at me as if trying to place me.

The bottom dropped from my stomach. "You knew my mother, didn't you?" I whispered.

Joe glanced back and forth between me and Darren. "What's going on?"

Darren raked a hand through his salt and pepper hair, sharing the same nervous habit as his baby brother. "This is insane. I mean, I'm suddenly back in college."

"Darren," Joe said, his tone almost a growl, "why do you keep looking at Carly like that?"

Asking my question again, I said, "Do you know my mother? Hannah Miller?"

He nodded, swallowing convulsively.

"The better question," Joe said, "is do you know Carly's father?"

CHAPTER 29

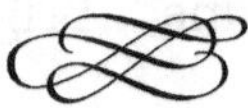

"WHAT IS ALL OF THIS *mishigas?*" MIRIAM TRAUTWEIG said, joining us in the family room. "Darren, what's the matter with you? Is that no good *shiksa* causing trouble again?" Her gaze shifted between Darren and me.

"Mom, can you give us a few minutes?" Darren asked.

Miriam scoffed. "In my own home, you're asking me to leave, Darren Mark?"

He rolled his eyes. "Spare me the Jewish guilt. I'm too old to fall for it."

"It's important," Joe said, watching his brother stare at me in both fascination and horror. "Where's Dad?"

"Probably asleep somewhere, but I can go look." She harrumphed but respected our wishes. Joe watched her leave the room while Darren kept his gaze fixed on me.

"Tell me," I said, staring back at Darren Trautweig with equal intensity. "I've waited my entire life to know who my father is."

"She never told you?"

"First, how did you know Carly's mother?" Joe asked.

"The same way I know Susan's boyfriend," he responded cryptically.

"Meaning what?" Joe asked. "What does Hannah Miller have to do with Adam Zendler?"

I took a step backward as if punched in the stomach. "No, no, no," I murmured.

"Carly!" Joe said, rushing to my side. "Breathe, honey."

I fought hard to maintain consciousness. The blow of Darren's words made me want to curl up in a ball on the floor.

"What's going on?" Darren asked, eyes wide. "Is she okay?"

"Breathe," Joe said again, leading me to a leather loveseat. He sat down next to me, one arm around me, the other holding my hand.

My heart continued to pound heavily, my thoughts returning to the blue eyed rabbi who might be in for a horrible surprise.

"Joe, how did you find this girl?" Darren asked.

"First of all, Carly's not a girl. She's a thirty-one-year-old woman."

"She's young enough to be my daughter," he said.

"Well, she's not young enough to be *mine*," Joe said tersely, "so let's move on."

Darren sighed, once again performing the Trautweig agitated gesture of running his hand through his hair. "Sorry, I'm just still in shock. I haven't seen Hannah in thirty years, and I feel like I'm staring at her."

"How did you know her?" I asked, sucking in wind but needing to ask the question.

"Breathe," Joe commanded again.

"What's going on with her?" Darren asked Joe.

"It's a panic attack," he said to his brother. Turning back to me, Joe said, "Listen to my heartbeat." He snuggled me closer to his chest.

Eager to calm my heart rate, I obeyed.

Darren continued to watch me. "Carly, I never knew your mother was pregnant, only that she dropped out of college. I guess you're the reason why."

"What does this have to do with your ex-wife's new boyfriend?" Joe asked.

Darren sat down on a large, circular ottoman in front of us. "Adam Zendler, Susan, Hannah, and I all hung out together in college. This was before Adam met his ex-wife, Barbara."

Finding my breath and my voice I asked, "What was my mother like?"

"What do you mean?" Darren said.

"After my mother had me, she joined First United of Hillcrest. She became a religious nut. Their pastor, Bernard Ivy, was arrested a few years ago on multiple felony counts."

"The holy roller from hell?" Darren asked incredulously. "Hannah was a part of that?"

I nodded. "She raised me there. She sacrificed my childhood to be at Pastor Ivy's beck and call. I've never understood why."

Darren rubbed the back of his neck, lost in thought. "That's so wild! I'm having a hard time picturing Hannah as some kind of Christian zealot."

Angrily, Joe said, "She's called Carly an abomination her entire life. She abused her and treated her like dirt. Any insight you can give would help Carly make peace with the past."

Darren grimaced. "I'm so sorry. That wasn't the Hannah I knew at all."

"Which version of my mother did you know?" I asked.

Darren exhaled a deep sigh. "Hannah was fun, loved to laugh, and Adam wasn't her first boyfriend."

I gasped at the revelation.

"Breathe," Joe commanded once again.

I patted his hand still holding mine. "I'm okay, I promise."

"Are you sure?" he said, glancing down into my eyes. "I thought you were going to pass out again like you did at Beth Tefillah."

"Beth Tefillah?" Darren said, stunned.

Lightbulb going off, Joe realized the connection between the past and the present. "Darren, there's a Rabbi Zendler at Beth Tefillah. He's a young guy and just took over the synagogue. Any relation?"

"Adam's nephew. The kid's a *macher* too. People were so upset with how he ran things at his last place in South Florida, they begged the old rabbi to come out of retirement. Adam said he pulled a few strings to get his nephew on the short list of candidates after Rabbi Cohn quit."

"Oh," I murmured, recalling Rob's version of events. "How did you learn about any of this?"

"Adam and I were still friends up until nine months ago."

"What happened nine months ago?" I asked.

"I found out my wife was sleeping with him."

"I'm so sorry," I said, meeting his brown eyes.

"Do you think that Adam could be Carly's father?" Joe asked Darren. "Hannah put 'John Doe' on the birth certificate."

He frowned. "Look, all I know is that Hannah and Adam were dating, and then she disappeared. When I asked Adam what happened, he didn't want to talk about it. He seemed angry and upset."

"Do you remember when this happened?" Joe asked.

Darren threw his hands in the air. "No idea, Joe. It was over thirty years ago."

"You said my mother had a lot of boyfriends?" I asked.

Darren nodded. "Yeah. I mean, I don't think she would have cheated on Adam, but Hannah had a reputation for being pretty easy."

I blanched. "Unreal."

Joe gazed back down at me again. "Are you able to breathe?"

I nodded against his heart. "My chest is still a little tight, but I feel better."

"We don't have to do this now," he said.

"I promise, I'm strong enough." I reached a hand to the side of his face. "I've got this."

I felt Darren watching the two of us. From the corner of my eye, I saw him shake his head and run another hand through his hair.

"This is just bizarre, I'm sorry," he said standing up. "Joe, it's like seeing you sit there with a thirty-year-old memory."

"I'm not my mother," I said, meeting Darren's eyes. "I haven't spoken to her in more than two years, and as far as Hannah's concerned, I'm already dead to her."

"I'm sorry to hear that. I never would have imagined Hannah turning out the way you described."

"For the sake of this entire story not becoming a Greek tragedy," Joe said to his brother, "did you ever sleep with Hannah?"

"What?" he exclaimed. "Why would you even ask me that?"

"Because I want to make sure I didn't just ask my niece to marry me," Joe said tautly.

Darren looked horrified.

I studied Joe's brother, searching for any shreds of familiarity beyond the man holding me in his arms.

Darren shook his head in disgust. "Both of you can stop staring at me like I'm going to ruin your lives. I never touched Hannah. I was in love with Susan."

Joe and I heaved a sigh of relief at the same time as well as a slight laugh.

Darren's expression brightened. "Well, I suppose there's one glimmer of good news today."

"I don't want to press on a raw wound," Joe began, "but if there's any chance that Carly is Adam's daughter, she has a right to know. Frankly, so does he."

"I can't," Darren said. "Joe, I'm sorry, but I can't."

He nodded. "I understand. I'll find a way to reach out."

"Honestly, I think Carly's got a better shot of getting through. Joe, if you contact Adam, he'll just assume you're doing it for me."

At the thought of possibly meeting my long lost father, I felt my breath slip away once again.

"Carly!" Joe exclaimed. "Keep breathing. You're safe."

I fought to stay awake and listened to the beat of Joe's heart to calm my own. Instead, I was lulled to sleep, heavy and so weary from carrying a thirty-one-year-old burden.

"Joe," I whispered.

He rocked me gently in his arms, and I closed my eyes, focusing on my breathing. I don't know how long I remained asleep, only that I woke up still in Joe's arms. We were alone in the Trautweig family room, and I could see the sun had shifted to late afternoon.

"Welcome back," he said gently.

I yawned and stretched my arms. "How long was I out?"

"Two and a half hours."

I blanched. "What!"

"I guess you were tired."

"Oh, Joe, I'm so embarrassed!"

"Don't be," he said, taking my hand to reassure me. "Darren

needed the time to process, and Mom and I just talked while you were sleeping."

"She must think I'm a baby," I moaned.

Joe's winsome smile appeared. "Actually, she said you looked like an angel and that you belonged in my arms."

"Really?"

"Mom can be a little rough around the edges, but she's a hopeless romantic. Her romance novel collection rivals Poppy's, and Mom is not reading the Amish ones either."

I chuckled. "Oh, is she a fan of R.D. Hampton and all of that medieval, courtly love too? Poppy was still reading all of those books up until a year ago. She said Natalie found one of her bodice rippers, and she was embarrassed."

"My mom isn't as squeamish as Poppy when it comes to all of that. The Trautweig kids got the birds and bees talk pretty early in life."

This time, my chuckle turned into a full laugh. "So, basically the opposite of my experience with *my* mother."

Joe shook his head. "I'm still trying to wrap my head around the connection between your mother and Darren."

"I'm just glad he's not my father. As soon as your brother saw me, I had this bad feeling in the pit of my stomach."

"You and me both."

Darren entered the room, glancing between Joe and me. "Mom said she's going to order pizza if you guys are planning to stick around."

"It's up to you," Joe said to me. "I know this was a lot to take in, Carly."

"Pizza sounds good."

"Also, there's one other thing," Darren said, studying me again.

"What?" I asked.

"I sent Susan a text about your mother."

"You did?" Joe gaped. "Darren, why?"

"Because this is the happiest I've seen you in ten years, and you deserve it."

A sheen of tears covered his beautiful green eyes. "Thank you, Darren. That means a lot. I know how hard it was for you."

"Don't worry about it," he said, waving him off. "It was the most civil conversation Susan and I have had in over a year."

Joe's eyebrows raised in surprise. "How did you convince her to help?"

"Don't forget that we were all friends. Hannah fell out of touch with everyone. I asked Susan if she remembered Hannah Miller. She asked me why. I said because my brother is dating her daughter."

"Nice," Joe said. "Thanks for sugarcoating it."

Darren smirked. "Susan loves her gossip, so I had to make it interesting."

"What did she say?" I asked, finding my breath coming in short again.

"She thinks she might have information that will help you."

CHAPTER 30

"Are you going to leave us hanging?" Joe demanded.

Darren ran a hand through his hair. "No, but Susan is. She offered to meet with Carly to talk about it."

"Why me?" I asked. "Why didn't she just tell you?"

Darren rolled his eyes. "Why does Susan do anything? She loves dangling out little carrots. Joe, I texted you her new number. Send it to Carly, and she can reach out to Susan whenever she's ready."

"Thank you," I said to Darren. "I can't imagine how hard that was for you."

He shrugged. "I see the way my brother takes care of you. I also see the way you let him. It's sweet."

I peeked at Joe and exchanged a smile.

Three days later, I met with Susan Brown, formerly Trautweig, outside of Let it Fro-yo. Her response to seeing me was not dissimilar to her ex-husband's reaction.

She touched her own face in wonder. "It's like looking in a

time machine," she murmured. "You look just like your mother."

I stood up to greet Darren's ex-wife, noting that she kept herself in great shape. Susan hadn't succumbed to the temptation to alter her face with plastic surgery, but she showed off her toned arms in a sleeveless dress.

"I'm Carly," I said.

There was an awkward pause as we both knew our meeting was not a happy occasion. I offered a smile and gestured for her to join me on the same bench where I had first met Joe Trautweig face to face.

"So, Darren says you're dating Joe," Susan said.

"Yes, he brought me to meet his family this past weekend."

She raised her brows over pale blue eyes. "Sounds like things are pretty serious. I didn't think Joe would ever get over what happened with Catherine."

Unwilling to divulge personal information, I offered a bland smile.

"Oh, give me a little something," she said with an artificial laugh. "We both know why I'm here."

"Are you going to help me or not? I don't have time for games."

Susan looked taken aback.

"I'm not interested in what did or didn't happen in your relationship with Darren. It's none of my business. I just need to know if Adam Zendler is my father, and if he's not, then who is."

"There's the Hannah I remember," Susan said. "Your mother could be a lot of fun, but there was nothing stopping her when she wanted something."

I felt my patience growing thin. "Who is my father?"

Susan was not done toying with her prey. "Don't you have a birth certificate?"

"My mother listed 'John Doe' as the father. To my knowledge, Bernard Ivy is the only other person who might know who my biological father is."

At the mention of the holy roller from hell, Susan turned ashen.

"How is Pastor Ivy connected to all of this?" I asked, reading her expression immediately. "Did you know him thirty years ago?"

She nodded, her hands nervously grasping her gold pendant.

"Susan, what's wrong? You look like you've seen a ghost."

"I...I haven't heard that name in a long time."

"Didn't you watch the news the past few years? He was a featured story for almost a year."

She shook her head. "I knew it was some pastor in Hillcrest. I never bothered paying attention to who. I didn't want to know."

Catching the time on my cell phone, I said, "I have to get back to work. Are you going to help me or not? And why are you acting so weird about Pastor Ivy?"

"Weird?" she repeated, her voice sounding higher.

A memory stirred from Rebecca's memoirs as well as Pastor Ivy's notorious, roving eye. "Bud Riley mentioned how Pastor Ivy had affairs with a few college girls. Was my mother one of them? Is he really my father?"

Whispering, Susan said, "I was."

"What?"

"Your mother was already pregnant when we visited First United. She wasn't showing yet, but she didn't want to tell her parents. She was planning to have an abortion."

I felt the weight of her words like a punch to the gut. I

sucked in air, praying fervently for my airways to open. From just behind us, Joe bolted over, rushing to my side.

"Joe!" Susan exclaimed. "I didn't know you were here."

Ignoring her, he pulled me into his chest. "Listen to my heart," he said, establishing our grounding pattern once again.

Susan watched us closely. Lifting her chin in the air, she said, "I assume you came to spy for your brother."

"Don't flatter yourself. Carly's been suffering from PTSD breathing attacks. I stuck around to make sure she'd be okay. What did you say to her?"

"I'm shocked you didn't already overhear it," she said coolly.

"Like I said, my concern is for Carly. Breathe, honey," he said, kissing my temple.

I focused on calming my galloping pulse, willing my heartbeat into submission.

Susan continued to watch us. Her expression softened, and she said, "Joe, what did you mean when you said Carly has PTSD attacks?"

"Exactly that. Hannah became a religious nut, enslaved herself to First United and Pastor Ivy, and she made Carly the sacrificial lamb. Carly's been battling PTSD as she's been reliving all of it."

"What?" she gasped.

"Hannah ate, slept, and breathed every word that deviant spewed. She abused Carly in every way and was no kind of mother at all."

"Oh," Susan said quietly. "That's so sad. That's not the Hannah Miller I remember at all. Something must have changed."

"Who is my father?" I rasped. "No more games. Please."

"It's not Adam," Susan said, sitting back down.

"How do you know?" Joe asked.

"Because I was there when Hannah confessed to Adam that she was pregnant...and that he wasn't the father. Adam was devastated."

"Then, who is?" Joe asked. "Was it Pastor Ivy?"

Susan shook her head. "No. He was never interested in Hannah like that." Her gaze shifted away.

I saw Joe studying her, his jade eyes widening as he correctly discerned the source of Susan's guilt. Thinking better of commenting on it, he instead asked, "Why did Pastor Ivy help Hannah? What did he do that made her give up her entire life and her own child for that man?"

"Pastor Ivy talked Hannah out of having an abortion. Hannah told me he offered to be a father figure for her child, but she would need to serve in the church as if she was a member of the Ivy family—that she was as good as dead to her parents. He got Hannah a job working as a receptionist for a dental office. He gave her money when Hannah dropped out of school. The church bought an extra trailer for their kid's program, and he let her take it and pay him rent to live there."

"But why abuse Carly?" Joe asked.

"Oh Joe," I murmured, my breathing normalized. "Oh, it makes so much more sense."

"What does?" he said.

"Every bit of security my mother had in life came from Pastor Ivy. He isolated her from anyone who could save her. If he ever got angry at my mother, he could have ripped away her job and our home. She had to jump at his command, or we would have been homeless and penniless. She was trapped."

"I see," he said.

Processing through the new information, I said, "My mother hated and resented me because she gave up her life and her freedom to have me. It was *never* about covering her sin. That was just the excuse she used."

"Couldn't she get away later on?" Susan asked. "Hannah got good grades in school, even with all the partying we did. Why not make a better life for you, or even just herself?"

"I don't know," I said. "Everything Pastor Ivy did to abuse her, my mother did to me in revenge. She probably blamed me for ruining her life."

"Carly," Joe said, pulling me into his arms as I began to weep. "This was the real abomination, not you."

"Abomination?" Susan repeated. "Hannah used that word?"

I pulled away from Joe's chest, my eyes a watery mess. "That's what she always called me. Every mistake I made, every move that Pastor Ivy didn't like, my mother called an abomination. She would beat me with books or anything else she could find."

Susan gasped. "Carly, I am so sorry. I never should have brought her to First United. That was my fault."

"How did you get there?" Joe asked.

Susan's guilty expression returned. "I met Pastor Ivy during a campus crusade event. This was *before* Darren and I began dating," she said pointedly. "He was charming, and I was stupid. It didn't last long, and I felt so guilty after I brought Hannah to the church. Pastor Ivy made motherhood sound so wonderful and noble, and Hannah bought into it."

Joe's expression was grim. "So, he talked Hannah into becoming a mother, but he also made her a martyr and his personal lackey in the process."

"That's what he held over her head," I said, glancing back at Joe. "My mother *did* have an image to maintain, but it had nothing to do with being religious at all. It was about protecting Pastor Ivy, or he'd expose what she almost did to me."

"And condemned you for doing," Joe said before thinking better of it.

I froze, half expecting Susan to jump on that salacious bit of gossip. Instead, her eyes filled with tears.

"What's going on?" Joe asked her.

"You're not the only one who's had an abortion," she said quietly. "Pastor Ivy gave me a very different sermon when I told him I was pregnant."

Without thinking, I reached out and took Susan's hand. "I'm so sorry."

She pulled away. "Why are you feeling sorry for me? Look at the life Hannah gave you. Do you think I would have been able to do any better for that baby? Pastor Ivy told Hannah he'd be a father to *you*, but he didn't want his own child."

"He was no kind of father," I said angrily. "He was a monster."

"With a public image to protect," Susan said bitterly. "I had no idea Hannah helped play a part of it for so long. I don't know which is worse."

"Any deal with the devil is going to be a miserable bargain," Joe said. "Susan, you still have three children who love you."

"Love me?" she repeated incredulously. "They hate me, and it's all your brother's fault!"

"Darren didn't force you to cheat with Adam Zendler."

"You don't think so?" she fumed. "You have no idea what kind of a husband Darren was to me."

"Try telling me he was anything like my ex-wife," Joe said, meeting the challenge in her eyes. "I know my brother loved you, Susan, and he still does. The kids are mad at you for breaking up your family to be with Adam. That's not Darren's fault. Those were your choices."

"I don't owe you any explanations," she sniffed haughtily.

"You're right," Joe conceded, "but that's not why we're here right now. Who is Carly's father?"

"All I know is that it's not Adam."

Joe looked nearly apoplectic. "Then why force Carly to meet you at all if you had nothing to share?"

"It wasn't nothing," I said, laying a calming hand on his knee. I looked over to Joe's former sister-in-law. "Susan, you helped solve one of the biggest mysteries of my life other than who my father is. None of the other reasons made sense. This one does. Thank you."

The offense left Susan's stiff shoulders. She looked at me pityingly. "I *am* sorry for you. It sounds like Hannah made your life hell."

"She did," I said, "because she made her own life hell first. I was the cause for all of it."

"No," Joe said sternly. "Carly, you were an innocent victim. You didn't ask to be there. These were all Hannah's selfish choices. She needed a scapegoat to blame."

Susan shook her head. "Tell me she finally got out of there."

"As far as I know, she's still listening to Pastor Ivy's old sermons on tape and CD."

"But why?" Susan asked. "You said he's in prison, right? Can he still hurt her?"

I shrugged. "I have no idea."

"What about Adam?" Joe asked. "Will he meet with Carly?"

Susan's expression turned hard again. "What's the point? He knows as much about who Carly's father is as I do. She never told either of us who he was. You'd be better off asking Hannah yourself."

"You don't think I have?" I asked. "All my mother ever told me was that God put me in her stomach as an answer to prayer, just like Hannah from the Bible."

"Answer to prayer?" Susan scoffed. "No offense, but your mother wasn't praying when she got pregnant."

"I know," I said flatly.

"And she never mentioned any other guys in her life?" Joe pressed.

"She and Adam dated exclusively for six months. That's why we were both so shocked when she said she was pregnant by some other guy."

Inhaling a sharp breath, I said, "What if she lied?"

CHAPTER 31

"Was my mother planning to have the abortion before or after she told Adam?"

"Oh," Joe said, following my line of thinking. "You think she told Adam a lie so he wouldn't pressure her into keeping you?"

"Is it possible?" I asked Susan, searching her eyes. "Is there any resemblance between me and Adam?"

The former Mrs. Trautweig shook her head as if clearing away cobwebs. "This is crazy, guys. If this is some stunt Darren is trying to pull, I'm not interested. Even if Adam *is* your father, Carly, that won't make me go back to Darren. That ship has sailed."

"Do you think we want it to be true?" Joe demanded. "Carly and I are getting married. That makes your boyfriend my future father-in-law. You'd be Carly's stepmother."

Susan's eyes went wide. "I can't be your mother-in-law," she said to Joe. "That's insane!"

"It might be insane," he said, "but it's still true. Technically, my nieces and nephew would also be Carly's stepsiblings."

Susan jumped to her feet. "I can't take any more!"

"Will you please talk to Adam?" I asked.

She shook her head. "There's no way...just *no* way. Adam will never go for this."

I stood up and reached for Susan's hand, but she jerked it away. Undeterred, I said, "Don't you think I deserve to know the truth?"

"I can't be Joe's mother-in-law. It's ridiculous."

"So, be my father's girlfriend," I said. "Look, I'm not here to judge what you did with Adam or to ask you to have any role in my life. You'll always be the mother to the children you share with Darren. They're going to become my nieces and nephew too, and Samantha is only five years younger than me. We can't escape the weirdness here."

"You would also have a half brother and sister," she said, "and cousins."

"I've already met my rabbi cousin, so there's one we can cross off the list."

"You know Rob?" she asked.

"She did. Rob and I went to middle school together, but we met up again when I visited Beth Tefillah. He wanted to get my number. I'm glad I said no."

"Me too," Joe chimed in from just beyond me.

Susan inhaled a weary breath. "I don't even know what to tell Adam. I'm not sure he'll believe me."

"Does he know you're meeting me today? Does he work close by?"

"His office is in midtown. He's a partner at his law firm, Schwartz, Zendler & Hoffer."

"Why does that name sound familiar?" Joe said, joining my side.

"Everyone's heard of Halpern Industries," Susan said, "and it was the firm's biggest client until one of their junior partners got caught screwing the CEO's daughter. I think they had a kid together, but I don't know. The daughter wound up in a mental hospital, and then, the whole affair was mentioned in someone's book. Adam said the author goes to Beth Tefillah."

Joe's hand found its way back into his hair at the same time my own hand traveled to my racing heart.

"Unbelievable," Joe said. "Carly, are you okay?"

I inhaled deeply. "Just when I think this day could not get any crazier." I reached for Joe's free hand and squeezed it. "Can you walk me back to the office?"

He nodded.

"What am I missing?" Susan asked.

"We know the author," Joe said.

"You do? How?"

"I work with her," I replied. "I was there when Poppy found out about Leah Halpern's baby."

"Hold on," Susan said, extending out her hand. "Joe, is this the same woman who broke your heart a couple years ago?"

"Ancient history," he said tautly. "Come on, Carly."

"How on earth did you manage to fall in love with the one person who has more connections to everything and everyone in your life who has caused you pain? The odds have to be a million to one."

Not missing a beat, he replied, "The same way God brought someone to help heal all of the wounds caused by everything and everyone in my life."

Susan rolled her eyes. "How can you even talk about God

after everything Carly has been through? You don't believe in any of this Jesus stuff, do you?" she asked, looking at me.

"I didn't for a long time, but I also didn't believe that God could ever love me." Smiling, I added, "I'm glad I was wrong."

"I think you're both crazy, but I'm glad you're happy. Joe, I know you probably hate me because of what happened with Darren, but I *am* genuinely happy for you."

"I don't hate you, Susan," he said. "I just don't understand what happened. But like you said, you don't owe me any explanations."

"Why aren't you judging me?" she asked. "I mean, it's not like cheating isn't frowned on in Judaism, but I know how you evangelicals feel about it."

"Why would we?" I asked her. "You know what I did. Who am I to look down on anybody when I've made so many of my own stupid decisions?"

"What about you?" she said to Joe. "I broke your brother's heart, right? Ruined my own family. Don't you have some Bible verse you want to throw at me?"

Joe's expression held compassion. "I'd be no better than Pastor Ivy if I did."

Susan winced again at that name.

"You know what happened to me a year and a half ago, Susan. I tried to take my own life."

"But it's not the same as adultery," she said, somehow wanting to hear us condemn her.

"No, it's murder," Joe said. "I had a vision of Jesus when I was in a coma. He told me He loved me and had a purpose for my life."

"And I suppose you think Jesus has one for me too?" she said mockingly.

"Why not?" I asked. "For almost three years, I thought my

life was defined by my mistakes. I didn't think I was good enough for God, and I'd heard it all of my life from my mother. I thought God hated me just like she did. Turns out, my mother was wrong."

Susan closed her eyes and sighed. Opening them, she said, "I'm glad this religious thing is working out for both of you. It's not the life for me, but I can appreciate that you both seem sincere about it." To Joe, she said, "I wasn't expecting any kindness after what happened with Darren. Thank you."

"Susan, you've been a part of my life since I was eleven years-old. You made me an uncle at seventeen. I don't understand what happened with you and Darren, but you and I have always had our own relationship."

"True," she said.

"Come on," Joe said, nudging me back toward the Culver high-rise.

"I'll talk to Adam," she called after us.

Joe and I turned back around.

"I'll talk to him," Susan said. "Carly, if he turns out to be your biological father, what do you want from him? You're marrying Joe, so I know you don't need any money."

He exhaled a mirthless laugh. "Thanks."

"Just a chance to meet him," I said, "and to find out more about his family and my mother's."

Susan swallowed and nodded. "I'm not making any promises, but I'll see what I can do. This is beyond awkward with you marrying Darren's brother."

"Like I said, the weirdness is unavoidable," I replied.

She smirked. "Fair enough."

Turning away from Susan as the sound of her platform pumps moved in the opposite direction, I leaned on Joe for support.

"You were amazing," he said, pulling me in for a quick kiss. "Carly, it has been one shock after another since Sunday, but you're handling it all beautifully."

"I don't feel very beautiful at the moment."

Joe stopped our forward progress and looked down into my eyes. "Are you okay? Do you need to go home?"

I shook him off. "No, Poppy is there, and she'll start mothering me as soon as you go. She'll call in the cavalry if necessary."

He chuckled. "Yes, there's always Miss Belle. She has no shortage of hugs or sage advice, does she?"

I smiled back. "Or opinions."

Joe and I laughed. We took our time heading toward the Culver office suite, Joe checking on my breathing any time it seemed labored.

As we stopped short of my office door, I noticed Poppy had a visitor. I saw the pink car seat stroller and had to laugh at God's sense of timing.

"Jessica," Joe said warmly. "What brings you here?"

She smiled. "Poppy keeps promising me she's going to meet me for coffee, but then something comes up. I decided to visit her at the office instead."

"And she's letting me hold the baby," Poppy said, cooing over the little one in her arms. "Oh, savor it, Jessica, because they grow up so fast. Natalie went on her first group date over the weekend, and now Maddie wants to know all about 'the bees and birds,'" she quoted with a martyred eye roll. "The look on Jared's face was worth it, though."

"Maddie's not even seven yet, is she?" I asked, tossing my purse into my desk. I plunked down in my office chair, and Joe sat on the edge of my desk facing Poppy and Jessica.

"Why is your first grader asking about all of that?" Jessica said, amused.

"Because Jared and I have been more selective about the songs we let the kids listen to," Poppy replied. "Apparently, just calling the song *inappropriate* wasn't enough of an explanation for Little Miss Precocious."

Jessica laughed. "Sounds like fun."

Poppy shook her head as she held the sleeping princess in her arms. "I forget they start off so little. This will probably be you two soon enough," she said, glancing at me and Joe.

He glanced sharply at me, and I knew it came out of concern for my reaction.

"Sorry," Poppy said, immediately realizing her mistake.

"It's fine," I said, waving her off. I met Joe's gaze once again, his eyes mirroring what I felt.

"When's the wedding?" Jessica said, watching the two of us. "Good grief, you guys are making *me* uncomfortable."

"I think it's sweet," Poppy said.

"You would," Jessica teased. "You and your love for romance novels and longing glances."

Poppy handed sleeping little Aria back to her mother. "Spoken by the same woman who can't spend more than one sentence without gushing about the most perfect husband in the entire world. It's amazing Micah doesn't have an ego the size of Texas with the way you talk about him."

Joe smiled at their playful banter. "I'm happy for you, Jessica."

"And I'm happy for you guys too," she said, placing the baby carefully back into the car seat. "Have you set a date yet?"

"I need to get this beautiful woman a ring first," Joe said, his eyes once again communicating the message my heart understood without spoken words.

Poppy watched us with an approving eye. "You both have been through so much. I'm glad you know what you want and you're not wasting time."

Joe reached across the desk to take my hand. "Speaking of," he said, turning his focus to Jessica, "we have sort of an odd question for you."

"For me?" she asked, placing a pink diaper bag into the bottom of her stroller.

"Well, it's about your old job," I said.

Her happy expression fell considerably. "What about it?"

Poppy looked ready to intervene until I said, "Is there anything you can tell me about Adam Zendler?"

"Zendler?" Jessica repeated, stunned. "He was one of the partners. Why?"

"Because I think he might be my biological father."

CHAPTER 32

"Your what?" Poppy gaped. "Carly, how in the world did you find out about any of this?"

"Zendler's got a son and daughter with his ex," Jessica said, "and last I heard, his girlfriend just moved in. Carly, how do you fit into all of this?"

"Because Adam Zendler's girlfriend is my brother's ex-wife," Joe said.

"What?" Jessica gasped. "Does everybody know each other in this town? How would that even be possible?"

"Joe, are you sure?" Poppy asked.

"I've known Susan since I was in sixth grade. Yeah, I'd say I'm pretty sure."

"I don't understand," Jessica said to me. "Zendler was married for over twenty years before he got a divorce. I know you're older than you look, but how could you possibly be his daughter? He would have been in his early twenties when you were born."

Poppy's eyes went wide, piecing together the information

with what she'd already heard from me. "How did you figure out it was Jessica's old boss?" she asked. "What possible connection could a member of Bernard Ivy's church have with a secular Jew? I can't imagine Adam is religious, is he?"

Jessica shook her head. "Zendler's definitely not religious."

"So, how in the world did he meet your mother?" Poppy asked me.

"Apparently, they knew each other in college," I said, "and my mother lived quite a different lifestyle than the one she pretends to live now."

"But how?" Poppy asked again. "How would you guys even know this? Carly's mother wouldn't have told her."

"She didn't," Joe answered for me. "When I took Carly to meet my family, my brother stared at her like he was hallucinating. It freaked both of us out."

"I'm sure," Poppy said.

"Apparently, I look more like my mother than I realized," I added.

"Oh, so Darren already knew Hannah," Poppy said before dread suddenly filled her face.

Reading her thoughts, I said, "We've covered that already."

"Are you sure Darren wasn't just covering his own tracks? Is there any possibility this relationship isn't kosher?" she asked, waving a hand at me and Joe.

Jessica looked simultaneously fascinated and horrified.

Joe gave a humorless chuckle as he replied to Poppy. "Carly and I aren't breaking any laws of consanguinity by being together. My brother said Hannah and Adam were dating at the same time she would have gotten pregnant with Carly. Susan, my brother's ex-wife, was best friends with Hannah at the time, and she confirmed Adam is most likely the father."

"Unfortunately," I said, "my mother told Adam the baby

wasn't his, so we don't know for sure, but Darren is definitely not my father."

Jessica's jaw gaped open at all of our revelations. "And so Zendler has no idea, does he?"

I shook my head. "If Adam Zendler is my father, my mother deliberately lied to him. At least, that's what Susan said downstairs."

Jessica heaved a deep sigh as she double checked the straps on Aria's car seat. "Wow. I didn't work too closely with Zendler, but I promise, he's not all bad."

"How did he handle the situation after Patrick left?" Poppy asked, referencing Jessica's office affair and the subsequent fallout. "You told me the partners looked the other way when you were getting sexually harassed by the other lawyers."

"Zendler was in the middle of his own messy divorce. I'm not sure how much he knew of any of it."

"Do you think he would have reacted like the other two partners?" Poppy pressed.

Jessica shrugged. "Honestly, I don't know. Zendler is pretty tough to read. He wasn't arrogant like the other two partners, just aloof."

I considered her words, hoping that maybe he wasn't as evil a villain as my mother.

"Have you tried reaching out to him already?" Jessica asked.

Joe replied first. "Susan, my ex sister-in-law, said she would."

"And there's no way to confirm any of this with your mother, is there?" Poppy asked me.

"Not sure I need to anymore. Also, it turns out that I may have a cousin you already know."

"Oh yeah?" she asked. "Is he a member of...*ohhhh*," she said, her hand flying to her mouth. "Oh Carly!" she exclaimed.

"Good thing your matchmaking efforts didn't work," I said with a wry smile.

"Matchmaking?" Jessica asked, looking back and forth between us.

"You haven't been to Beth Tefillah in a while, have you?" Poppy asked her.

Jessica blew a raspberry. "And probably won't, if I'm being honest. My ex turned me off to organized religion after what he did to me. If people get something out of it, then great, but I think all religions are basically the same. Sorry, if that offends you," she said, glancing at Poppy and then at Joe.

"No offense taken," Joe said. "Everyone in this room has had their own struggles with it."

I confirmed Joe's statement with my own nod. "I don't know if you know, but I grew up going to First United."

"First United?" Jessica repeated, stunned. "As in Rebecca's parents' church?"

"Yes."

"Oh," she murmured, assessing me with new eyes. "You've been through so much, haven't you?"

I nodded.

"I'm so sorry," she said, and I could tell she meant it. "I'm glad you're with Joe," she said, glancing at him. "I know he's going to treat you right. He's played knight in shining armor a few times."

I smiled, remembering Poppy's memoirs once again. When I had read about Joe rescuing Jessica from a public scene with her ex-boyfriend, I had gasped and swooned, half hoping they'd wind up together. Instead, I was never happier that things had turned out differently.

I peered into Joe's intimate, jade gaze pulling at my heart. His smile touched my soul.

"Okay, I'm definitely out of here," Jessica said as Aria began to stir. "Even the baby can't stay asleep with this much tension. You guys better get married *soon*, or something's going to combust."

Poppy laughed while Joe and I simply smiled wider at one another.

Jessica chuckled as she pretended to fan herself. "If I remember anything else about Zendler, I'll let you know. In the meantime, get married and get a room."

"Hopefully sooner than later," Joe said, reaching for my left hand and eyeing my ring finger.

Looking back over at Jessica, I realized my request would cause her to revisit some painful memories. "Thank you," I said, my smile dimming. "I'm sure that can't be easy for you."

"I got my happy ending," she said, glancing down into the car seat. "I don't begrudge that to anybody anymore."

"Are you ever going to call her?" Poppy asked Jessica.

Mrs. Ballinger sighed. "I don't think Rebecca wants anything to do with me. I know I wouldn't if I was her."

"Look, you and Taylor managed to make peace with one another for the sake of her brother and your husband, so anything's possible," Poppy said.

"Wow," I said, remembering their epic fight detailed in Taylor's memoirs.

Jessica glanced over at me in surprise. "Ugh, I forget that the whole world knows my business now. How do I know anything I say around you guys won't be put into a book? Micah's not exactly thrilled about it, but he says he doesn't care."

Joe offered his winsome smile, "I guess that's the risk we all take living near Parkview."

"And it's not like you came out unscathed either," she said, turning to Joe, "but at least you gave Poppy permission to write about *your* past."

"Jessica, you did have an impact on Rebecca's and Taylor's stories whether you like it or not," Poppy said gently. "And if not for them, you may have never met Micah either. Like you said, you've got your happy ending. The road it takes for most of us to get there is usually pretty messy."

Mrs. Ballinger gave a long-suffering sigh. "Fine. I'll think about it, okay?

"That's all I ask," Poppy said, holding up her hands in innocence.

After Jessica took her leave, Joe pressed a kiss to my mouth and made his own exit. Poppy grabbed her afternoon coffee and swiveled in her chair to face me.

"How are you holding up, sweetie?"

"Longest week of my life."

"Do you really think Rabbi Zendler could be related to you?"

"Only one way to find out," I said, "and I might need you and Jared for moral support when I go back to synagogue."

She frowned. "I'll have to ask Jared and see what he thinks about that."

"I understand."

"Don't you think you should confirm with Adam before you tell Rabbi Zendler you guys might be related? What about contacting your mother?"

"I don't trust her, Poppy. She's lied to me my entire life and worse than I ever thought possible."

"Just a thought," she said. Taking a sip of her coffee, she winced. "Oof! It's cold."

I chuckled as she left to brew a new cup. My phone buzzed with a new text message.

Hi, it's Susan. Just talked to Adam. He wants to meet you. Tonight.

Tonight? I asked, my fingers already typing while my brain struggled to keep up.

Yes, tonight. I'm assuming you want Joe there.

Thank you, yes. Will you be there too?

Too awkward. I think I've had all the weirdness I can take for one day. Going from Joe's sister-in-law to his potential mother-in-law is about all I can handle.

Valid, I typed back. *Can I contact Adam directly, or did he have somewhere he wants to meet?*

Do you and Joe ever eat at Los Bravos?

I snickered to myself, wondering what it was about the Mexican Cantina that made it such a hotspot for drama and shocking revelations.

Carly? Susan asked when I didn't respond.

Los Bravos sounds great. Meet at 6?

Adam won't be off work til closer to 7 if that works for you guys.

Done and done, I replied, firing off a text to Joe as soon as I replied to Susan.

I'll text Adam and let him know. Thanks for doing this on such short notice.

Thank you for everything, I wrote back, *I know today wasn't easy, but I hope this brings everybody some closure.*

She sent over a kissy face emoji and wrote, *I wish it were under better circumstances, but you and Joe are going to be great for each other. You didn't have any reason to show me kindness today, but you did. It means a lot.*

I smiled back at my phone, tears smarting in my eyes. The peace of the Lord surrounded me, almost as if patting me on the back for a job well done. *Like I said, Susan, we've all made mistakes.*

Darren will probably despise you for not hating me. My kids already do.

Feeling the sense of being played for sympathy, I wrote back,

I don't need to know about what happened with your marriage. I never would have known Adam could be my father without either one of you, and that's all that matters to me right now.

Fair, she wrote back.

Joe sent me a text in the interim, and Susan didn't comment any further. I was on pins and needles for the rest of the afternoon, and Joe showed up at the office around six. He sat with me and prayed while I alternated between nervous energy, all out panic, and fledgling faith that God knew what he was doing.

At 6:45, we began our walk to Los Bravos. We greeted Carlos, our favorite server and recently promoted assistant manager, at the host stand. Joe asked if a man named Adam had already arrived.

"Not yet," he replied in accented English. "Did you bring me some *novela* drama today? It's been so quiet since everyone got married. *Tan aburrido,*" he added in Spanish.

"No comment," Joe said, winking at him.

The mischievous waiter grinned and led us to a booth.

"Can you tell Mr. Zendler we already have a table?" I asked.

"*Sí,* of course." His gaze drifted back to the host stand, and I saw a silver haired man enter wearing an expensive, black suit. "*Momentito, mis amigos,*" he said.

The man chatted with Carlos for a few seconds, glanced over in our direction, and then headed toward us. As he stopped just short of the table where Joe and I sat next to one another, I ventured my first glance at the man who might be my father.

Sure enough, I was greeted with a pair of aquamarine eyes I would know anywhere. It was the one feature that differed on my face from my mother's.

Adam simply stared at me, his blue-green eyes searching mine.

"My God," he breathed, "you look just like her."

"She lied to both of us," I said. "She had John Doe put on my birth certificate. I never knew you existed until Sunday."

Adam finally noticed the man seated to my right. "Joe!" he said in surprise. "How did you get mixed up in all of this?" Before he could answer, Adam's eyes narrowed. "Did Darren send you?"

"Joe and I are getting married," I said to Adam. "That's why he's here."

Adam blanched, and I watched him quickly ascertain the age difference. "You don't seem young enough to be my son-in-law," he said to Joe.

"But Carly *is* young enough to be your daughter," Joe replied. "Why don't you sit down, and we can try to untangle this mess?"

CHAPTER 33

"I'VE NEVER SEEN A PICTURE OF MY MOTHER FROM when she was young," I said, "but based on the reaction from you, Susan, and Darren, I'll have to take your word for it," I said to Adam.

"How long have you known?" he asked me.

"I'm still not sure," I said. "I thought I was meeting Joe's family this past Sunday. I had no idea about all the connections his brother had to you or my mother."

"What can you tell us about your time together?" Joe asked.

Adam frowned, clearly not willing to part with any information in front of his girlfriend's former brother-in-law.

Hoping to thaw some of the ice, I asked Adam, "What has Susan already told you?"

He inhaled and exhaled, still studying me. "She said Darren contacted her about Hannah Miller's daughter. She told me she just wanted to see what you looked like, but after your meeting, she seemed shaken up. Susan insisted that I meet with you."

"Oh," I said. "Based on her text messages, it sounded like you were the one pushing for this meeting."

Adam shook his head. "Do you mind if I read the texts?"

Joe began to object, but I shrugged. "I don't mind." I handed over my phone, and Adam scrolled through my communication with Susan.

"Hmm," he said.

"What does that mean?" Joe asked.

Adam turned cold, aquamarine eyes on him. "I wasn't told you would be here."

"Well, that's news to us," I said, gesturing to my phone. "You can see for yourself what Susan told me."

The frown lines in Adam Zendler's forehead grooved deeper. "This feels like a set up."

"By whom?" I asked. "I don't want or need anything from you other than answers and maybe a DNA test, if you're willing."

"Not a chance!"

My eyes widened, shocked at his vehemence.

"Adam," Joe entreated, "look, I know the circumstances for you and Carly meeting are less than ideal. She just wants answers about her mother and potentially, her paternal side of the family. This has nothing to do with money, my brother, or anything other than Carly."

"I promise," I said, staring intently into Adam Zendler's eyes. I dared him to find a shred of dishonesty in them.

He expelled a harsh breath. "I haven't thought about Hannah in so long."

Noting a brief flicker of pain before he brought the wall back down, I said, "I haven't spoken to my mother in over two years. We had a falling out, and it's probably better for everyone this way."

"I had no idea she kept you," Adam said quietly.

"I don't think she had any plans to keep me either," I said, fighting back emotion at the thought, "but whenever I asked who my father was, she told me God gave her a baby like Hannah in the Bible."

Adam scoffed. "That sounds nothing like the Hannah Miller I knew."

"It's the Hannah Miller she became. She was one of the most devoted members of First United of Hillcrest other than Mrs. Ivy."

All the color from Adam's face disappeared.

"Susan already told us what happened with Pastor Ivy," Joe said. "We have no plans to tell anyone else, including my brother."

"I don't understand," Adam said, showing more emotion than I'd seen since the moment he sat down. "Why would Hannah go there knowing what he made Susan do?"

"Because Pastor Ivy owned my mother."

"Owned her?" Adam cocked his head as if he'd misheard me.

"Susan said he paid for the trailer I grew up in, and he got my mother the job she's been at for more than thirty years. According to Susan, Pastor Ivy forced her to cut off ties with my grandparents. He said she was as good as dead to them. Maybe she was scared of how they'd react to the pregnancy."

"That's not true," Adam said.

"What isn't?"

"I know Hannah's parents."

"What?" I breathed.

"They're on the trustee board of the synagogue where my nephew is the rabbi."

The air fled from my lungs and did not return.

"Carly!" Joe exclaimed. "Breathe, honey. Oh, Jesus," he murmured, praying for me once again. "Breathe."

I struggled and gasped while involuntary tears closed down my throat.

I heard Adam jerk to his feet. "Do something!" His voice was panicked but seemed far away.

"Carly," Joe called. His voice sounded like an echo deep inside a tunnel.

My head felt as though it was bobbing along the surface of water, up and down, above and below the waves. "Joe," I whispered on a slight exhalation of breath.

"Call 911!" Adam shouted as my world went black.

I woke up in a hospital room. Joe was sitting on a chair next to my bed, and Adam Zendler stood close to my heart monitor, pensive and agitated.

"What happened?" I asked, my chest tight.

"Thank God!" Joe said, reaching for my hand. "Carly, you gave us all a scare. Carlos got the drama he wanted and maybe a little more than he bargained for."

Gaining my bearings, I realized I had an oxygen mask on my face.

Adam glanced down at me, perhaps finally seeing me as a person independent of my mother. "Joe filled me in while you were unconscious."

I nodded. "The panic attacks started late last year."

"The first attack was at Beth Tefillah," Joe said. "Doctor Feldstein helped revive her."

"Nobody helped revive me," I said. "That was Jesus."

"Jesus?" Adam said skeptically. "Joe said you wanted nothing to do with your mother or her crazy, religious beliefs."

"Her beliefs *are* crazy," I said. "Jesus is not."

Adam's frown lines returned. "Regardless of whether you're my daughter or not, you *are* Jewish."

I looked over at Joe. "Is it true?"

He nodded. "I sent a text to Ted, Kyle, and Jared once we got to the ER. Poppy sent me a text back wanting more information. Initially, I just asked her to pray."

"Oh," I murmured. "What did she say?"

Joe offered a small, encouraging smile. "When I asked her how much she knew about the Millers at Beth Tefillah, she put two and two together."

"She's not going to say anything to them, is she?"

Joe shook his head. "She said she would pray with Jared and maybe do some careful digging with her mother."

"Poppy?" Adam repeated with a questioning gaze to Joe. "Why does that name sound familiar?"

"Has your nephew, Rob, ever talked to you about Natalie Levine's bat mitzvah or her family?" Joe asked.

"Yes, how did you know about that? I thought your family attended Beth Emunah. That's what Susan told me."

"She's partially correct," Joe said. "My parents switched to the conservative synagogue after Rabbi Epstein was fired at Beth Tefillah. Rena and her family prefer the Reform synagogue, and so they stayed. Their oldest, Emma, is in the bat mitzvah program. Carly and I were there a few months ago when they had the kids leading the liturgy."

"So, how do you know this troublemaker family?"

"Troublemaker?" I said. "Is that what Robbie called them?"

Adam now wore the look of surprise. "Robbie? I don't think anyone has called him that in years."

"We went to the same middle school," I said. "He recognized me the first time I visited Beth Tefillah. He wanted to get my phone number, but I wasn't interested." I glanced over at Joe. "I already had my eyes on somebody else."

"Thank God," Adam exhaled. "I don't think Beth Tefillah would have recovered from another scandal like that."

"So, are you saying you think Carly is your daughter?" Joe asked.

"I'm not saying anything," he replied coolly, "but on the off chance it's true, it sounds like you averted a disaster of Biblical proportions."

"No pun intended," I quipped. "And Robbie likes to remind me how much he knows the Bible—or specifically the Torah— much better than me."

"So, you've talked to him?"

"A few times."

"Pompous little *macher*, isn't he?" Adam said, showing a bit of humor.

I exhaled a short laugh, then winced at the pain in my chest.

"Carly!" Joe exclaimed, reaching for my hand.

Adam glanced over at the heart monitor, noting the sudden spike in my pulse.

A large nurse entered the room. She took a quick look at Adam and Joe, then down at me in bed. "Which one of the handsome fellas is giving you a hard time, sugar?"

I couldn't help but wheeze out a laugh, and it sent my heart monitor soaring again.

"Nevermind," she said, "sorry about that, Miss Miller." She checked my vitals while Adam and Joe watched on nervously. "Visiting hours are over gentlemen. You'll have to see Miss Miller tomorrow."

"When do you think she'll be released?" Joe asked.

"You'll have to ask the on-call doctor," she replied. "In the meantime, your daughter needs some rest."

"She's not my daughter," he said quickly.

"Oh," the nurse replied, surprised. She looked over at Adam. "Is she yours?"

It felt like an eternity waiting for Adam to reply, but he gave a simple, "No."

His response sent the nurse's eyebrows even higher on her face. "Don't tell me you've got two sugar daddies fighting over you," she said, eyeing me with a sidelong glance. She picked up my chart to confirm my age. "Oh, well that makes more sense, I guess. Such a baby face."

"If you're done commenting on Carly's love life," Adam clipped, "is there anything else we can help you with?"

Like a shark who knew how to put a mouthy barracuda back in its place, the nurse said, "I *work* here. It's my job to be in the room. What are *you* doing here? Visiting hours are over. And I don't see how you can't be this baby girl's father when you have the same eyes, chin, and forehead, but I guess that's none of my business." Rolling her eyes, she put my chart back down at the foot of my bed.

Joe looked like he was holding in a laugh. His jade eyes sparkled as they met mine.

"Two more minutes and then you both need to leave," the nurse said as she exited the room.

"Poppy said she'd call in to HR for you," Joe said, leaning down to kiss my forehead. "Get some rest, sweetheart."

I felt Adam's aquamarine eyes on us. I looked over at him in question.

"It shouldn't be possible," he said.

"You're right," I replied, "but there's nothing we can do to change it now."

CHAPTER 34

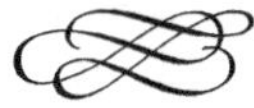

Resting comfortably at home a few days later, Joe sat with me on the sofa as we watched the final minutes of my favorite singing competition show.

Nestled in the crook of his arm, I said, "Think you're gonna vote?"

He smirked and planted a kiss on the top of my head. "Not likely. How are you doing?" he asked, flipping off the television.

I sighed. "My chest doesn't hurt anymore."

"The doctors were stunned when they couldn't find anything wrong on the EKG."

"Scary what stress can do to the body, isn't it?" I said.

"Have you heard anything from Adam?"

"He sent me a very strange text this morning, but I'm not sure what it means."

"Can I see?"

I handed him my phone, and he read, *I don't know what's true or what isn't, but I intend to find out.*

"Does this mean he's taking a paternity test?" Joe asked.

I shrugged. "Your guess is as good as mine."

"Darren said he heard from Susan."

"Really?" I said, surprised. "What did she want?"

"Apparently to talk. Darren asked how your meeting went with her. He was less than happy we also met with Adam, but he said he understood."

"What a mess," I said, sitting up to face Joe.

His hands immediately came up to cradle my face. "You're so beautiful."

I smiled. "You say that a lot."

"Why? Are you tired of hearing it?" he asked, jade eyes twinkling.

"Never!" I laughed. "Feel free to pour on the compliments."

He grinned back, and I inhaled a shaky breath.

"How do you want to do this, Carly?"

"Do what?"

"I see how you're looking at me, and believe me, my thoughts are right there with you. What kind of a wedding do you want?"

"You still haven't bought me a ring."

"Is that so?" He reached into his pocket and pulled out a small velvet box. "This thing has been digging into me all night."

"Can I see it?" I whispered.

"I've got to ask you first, sweetheart."

I rolled my eyes good naturedly and smiled. "You already know the answer is yes."

"Yeah, but you're probably going to put this in your book one day, and I want it immortalized as an epic proposal."

"Joe, *you* are epic."

Tears filled his eyes. "I had no idea I could ever feel this happy."

"Do you mean happy *again*?" I asked.

"No, I mean *this* happy. You and me. Now."

"Wow," I breathed.

Shifting from his seat on the couch, Joe got down on one knee before me. He opened the jewelry box to reveal a stunning, platinum ring with a baguette diamond and two smaller baguettes on either side.

"Now, remember," he said, "you're marrying *me*, not the ring."

I laughed. "No one has ever given me anything so beautiful."

"Well, it's not yours yet," he teased. "I still have to ask my question."

I laughed and cried simultaneously feeling like I was living in a dream.

"You actually have to look at *me*, Carly. Not just the ring."

"Party pooper," I said, sticking out my tongue.

His expression growing more serious, Joe said, "Carly Danielle Miller, I think I fell in love with you the moment we met. I've never known anyone like you, and I don't think the world will ever see a woman as special as you."

"Oh, Joe," I whispered.

"You refused to let fear steal what I really wanted, and I will always be grateful to you for that. You didn't give up on me even when I gave up on myself."

I beamed at him through my tears.

"Carly, you've suffered so much, and you deserve to be loved and cherished for the amazing woman you are. I'm asking for the honor of making you laugh and smile every day for the rest of your life. Will you marry me?"

"Yes! Yes! Yes!" I exclaimed. I wrapped my arms around his neck and kissed him as he said only a wife should. He pulled me down from the couch and onto his lap on the floor. Cradled in his arms, he held me against his chest.

"I love you, Carly."

"I love you, Joe," I said, snuggling closer to him.

After a tender, silent moment, he exhaled a sigh. "It's official now. When and how do you want to make it legal?"

"I just moved here!" I laughed.

Joe chuckled, and his chest rumbled under my ear. "Do you really want to wait another nine months to get married? I don't think either of us will make it."

I closed my eyes, knowing he spoke the truth. Despite my growing faith, I knew neither of us were immune from temptation. "I can't afford to break my lease," I said, pulling away to look into his eyes. "What do we do?"

"Have you considered subletting?"

"I don't know anyone who needs the space."

"I do," he said.

"You do?"

"Aaron mentioned a former member of Beth Shalom who needs a place. It's sort of short notice, but it may be an answer to prayer for everyone concerned."

"Anybody I know?"

"Lauren Fein."

My eyebrows knit together. "The name sounds really familiar, but I don't think I know who she is."

Joe feigned surprise. "I thought you had Poppy's book memorized."

"Only the parts about you," I teased.

"Lauren married Nathan Fein, Jesssica's former fiancé," he said, watching me and anticipating my reaction.

"Oh," I gasped. "That poor girl! Jessica went through hell and back after Nathan broke her heart. I can't imagine how much more devastating this has been for Lauren. She had no idea she married such a disgusting slime!"

Joe frowned. "And I'm sure we're only scratching the surface of what happened. Aaron made it sound like their entire marriage was a set up between Nathan, his parents, and the Beth Shalom leadership."

"Set up? You mean like an arranged marriage?"

He nodded gravely. "Yes, except Nathan led Lauren to believe he was in love with her when they got married. Aaron thinks they duped her into marrying Nathan to cover for his porn addiction...among other issues."

I gasped. "That's horrible! How did Aaron find out such personal information?"

"He said Lauren reached out for help. They both grew up at the messianic synagogue and attended youth conferences together. I don't know if you remember this, but Nathan got arrested for downloading underage porn while Jared was still a member at Beth Shalom. When the synagogue hid the crime, it opened his eyes to the corruption in that place."

"And his own demons," I said, recalling that part of Poppy's book perfectly. "So, Jared can vouch for what happened to Lauren?"

Joe nodded again in the affirmative. "Aaron said the entire synagogue has shunned her for speaking up. Nathan is back on leadership like nothing happened, and they're accusing Lauren of spreading slander about a man struggling with his *ongoing issues*."

"That's disgusting! Of course, I'll help her!

"Good," Joe said, "because her parents have been helping, but Nathan is harassing her at their house. Lauren got a temporary restraining order, but Aaron says Nathan skates by with barely legal behavior or gets others to spy on her. Lauren needs a safe place her ex and his minions don't know about."

"But how?" I said, horrified. "Why is that monster even allowed anywhere near Lauren or their son. He's a pedophile!"

Joe sighed. "According to Aaron, the pornography Nathan downloaded is of underage girls, but not small children. High school age, but minors nevertheless."

I shook my head in disgust. "I'm just glad I can help."

"I think this could be a great place for a single mom and her child," Joe said as he scanned the open kitchen and great room leading to the hallway and back two bedrooms "You'd be doing a *mitzvah* for someone in the same position as your mother thirty-one years ago."

"Only my offer wouldn't come with strings or lifelong indentured servitude."

"See, already a win for everyone." He gave me a bright smile.

I smiled back, then sighed as my focus shifted from helping Lauren to what it would mean for Joe and me. "If Lauren needs a place right away, that means we'd be getting married quickly so that I could move in with you. Are you sure we're ready to do that? We haven't been dating that long, and we still have a lot to learn about each other."

His eyebrows lifted in surprise. "This is what you want, isn't it?"

"Wanting it and reality are two very different things."

"That's still my ring on your finger."

I smiled as I stared up into those stunning jade eyes. "How did this happen so fast, Joe? What if everything is happening too fast?"

"What are you saying?"

"Look, we need a better reason to get married other than a legal and spiritual reason to sleep together."

Any shred of a smile on Joe's handsome face disappeared. "Is that all you think I want?"

"No, Joe. I believe you love me."

"Then what's wrong? I don't understand."

"Are we ready? I mean, truly? When we first met, you told me if I ever figured out how to deal with regret to let you know."

"I remember," he said.

"So, the answer for me was Jesus. It's how I made peace with what happened to Harper."

"Harper?" he asked.

"I always felt like I lost a baby girl. I wanted to give her a name so I could honor her memory."

He smiled sadly. "I like that."

"I've already apologized to Harper and to Jesus for what I did. It helped."

"Do you think I need to apologize to the babies Catherine lost?" he asked.

I thought for a moment before answering. "No, I think the only person you still need forgiveness from is yourself."

"Myself?"

"Yeah. You're still blaming yourself for what happened to Catherine even though she had a chemical imbalance."

"I made her take the medicine, Carly."

"What other choice did you have? She was volatile and violent. You were trying to *help* the woman you loved, not harm her. You had no way of knowing how the drugs would affect her or any babies. We also don't know for sure if the drugs caused her to miscarry or if maybe there were underlying reproductive issues."

He contemplated my words. "You know, that never even occurred to me as a possibility. Catherine was so adamant it must be the medication. I didn't think there could be any other reason for the back-to-back miscarriages."

I reached up and rested my hand on Joe's bearded cheek. "You did your best. You didn't divorce Catherine because you wanted to, and I know that. I just want you to have peace about what happened."

"What about you?" he asked gently. "If Dylan Greene were to suddenly break up with his fiancée and beg you to give him another chance, would you?"

"I'm with the right man," I said, beaming at him.

"I do have one other question, and it's been weighing on me."

"What?" Anxiety welled up at his pained expression.

"Have you given any thought to children?"

"Of course!" I said, surprised by his initial question. "I definitely want kids."

"What happens, God forbid, if we can't conceive, or worse? I don't know if I can handle that again, Carly. I don't want to see you blame yourself for a miscarriage either."

"I see."

"I don't want to hyper spiritualize this or pretend everything's going to be sunshine and rainbows because we love each other and we love Jesus. Suffering is a part of life whether we love Jesus or not."

"But trusting God doesn't mean we're burying our heads in the sand, does it? I feel like we're both walking this tightrope of wanting to be wiser than our past decisions but not giving into fear that history will just repeat itself if we take the risk."

His clenched jaw relaxed, and his expression softened into one of adoration. "Thank you," he said, pressing a soft kiss to my lips.

"What did I do?"

"You solved the riddle."

"I did?"

"You did," he said. "We conquer regret by facing our fears, not avoiding them. We take what we've learned from the past and dare to put ourselves out there again. It's not trusting God with a blind faith, but one that believes He can do *all* things."

"Yes," I whispered.

"Marry me," he said fervently, cupping my face in his hands. "We can figure out the logistics once you talk to Lauren, but tell me that this is what you want, Carly."

"You know it is."

"Then, we'll take the time we need. I shouldn't have pushed. God will provide for Lauren, and He'll provide for us too. You're right. We shouldn't rush things as an excuse for sex. We're not teenagers, and we both have more self control than that."

"We're also human," I said, smiling tenderly at Joe. "I never imagined myself getting married with the big white dress and all of that. I don't need to spend a million dollars, but I want our wedding to be special."

"Of course," he said, pushing back a honey blonde hair from my face.

"I also want to find out if we should have a Jewish wedding."

"Jewish?" he repeated.

"Yes. And we'll see what Robbie has to say when I tell him my grandparents are on the Beth Tefillah trustee board. He'll have a tough time telling me I'm not Jewish anymore."

Joe chuckled. "Especially if you turn out to be cousins."

CHAPTER 35

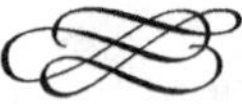

THREE DAYS LATER OVER TEXT, I RECEIVED A CURIOUS message from Adam. *Can you meet me at Los Bravos for lunch today? If you want Joe there, I understand, but I would rather speak with you privately.*

I frowned. *Joe's out of town, but I think I can meet you. What time?*

Can you be there at 1?

I assessed my stack of work requests. I had wrapped up a huge presentation earlier that morning, and only light admin work remained for the afternoon. Flicking my gaze to Poppy, she plunked away on her keyboard while making edits from a marked up Insurance Proposal in her document stand.

Pushing through the uneasy feeling in the pit of my stomach, I replied, *Yeah, I think so. Everything ok?*

We can talk about that at lunch. See you there.

My frown increased.

"What's wrong?" Poppy asked, turning toward me.

"Strange text message from Adam," I said.

"Do you think it has to do with your mother?"

"Only one way to find out."

I headed to Los Bravos fifteen minutes early, texting Joe along the way. He responded with a slew of Bible verses, all of them reminding me of God's protection and control over the universe. I hoped the extra minutes would give me time to pray and calm down.

Instead, I greeted Carlos at the host stand, and he pointed me to where Adam Zendler sat in a booth close to the bar.

I inhaled a deep breath and walked over to the table. Adam put his phone away once he saw me.

"Have a seat," he said, his tone pleasant but nothing more.

"What's going on?"

"Do you want to eat first?"

I shook my head. "I won't be able to focus on anything other than what you're waiting to tell me."

A waitress stopped by to place chips and salsa on our table. Adam informed her we would wait a few minutes to order, and my apprehension grew. I willed my lungs to inhale and exhale the air I needed while he took a sip of his diet soda. An uncomfortable silence stretched my patience to its utter limit.

"Well?" I finally said. I met the same aquamarine eyes that stared at me in the mirror. "Why am I here, Adam?"

He breathed in deeply through his nose, but his lips remained sealed.

"It's true, isn't it?"

"I spoke with Hannah," he said in a pained voice.

"How is she?"

His expression remained stoic. "It's been so long, Carly. I barely recognized her."

"You saw her? Face to face?"

He swallowed as if tasting something bitter. "I don't know

what happened to the Hannah Miller I knew. It wasn't the woman I met two days ago."

My heart grew heavy with disappointment. "I guess it was silly to hope she might have changed."

Adam's mouth thinned even further. "Apparently, I haven't changed quite as much as she has since college."

"Oh," I said, studying his nearly silver head of hair. "She recognized you?"

He nodded. "Immediately. She also deduced rather quickly why I had come to see her."

"Did she deny it?" I asked.

"No," he said wearily. "She just went on the most disgusting, vitriolic rant I have ever heard in my entire life."

The lead weight in my gut persisted. "About me, I'm guessing."

He looked angry. "No, about me, actually."

"You?" I said, stunned.

He inhaled another heavy breath. "She accused me of ruining her life among other things. Your name did come up, Carly, but it's nothing that bears repeating."

"I'm sure. She's called me an abomination my entire life."

"Ah," Adam said. "Your mother seems rather fond of that word."

"So, what now?" I asked, searching his eyes. "You know the truth."

"What are you looking for?" His posture stiffened.

"I don't need you to announce you're my father or anything like that. I mean, if you want to get to know me, you can, but I don't have any expectations here."

"What about money?" he asked.

I shook my head. "I don't want or need a dime. That's not why I reached out to Susan or to you."

"I saw the hovel where you grew up. That trailer should be condemned."

"Probably," I agreed.

"Why didn't your mother ever reach out to your grandparents. The Millers live in Garden Brook Country Club. They would have been able to help you, Carly."

I choked back a sob at the thought of tattered clothes and how easily my mother could have eased our poverty and suffering. "I don't know. There are so many things in my life that have never made sense. Susan helped me to understand a lot of it."

Adam grimaced.

"What's wrong?"

"Susan said she wants to reconcile with Darren."

"What?" I breathed.

"Apparently, the two of them bonded over *you*. She moved out this past weekend, and she and Darren have started marriage counseling."

"I...I don't know what to say," I stammered. "Darren is going to be my brother-in-law, so while I'm happy for him, I'm sure this isn't easy for you."

My father stared at me for a long moment. "You look like her, Carly, but you're nothing like what Hannah's become. Don't tell me it's Jesus because your mother made you sound like a demon from hell. You *are* Jewish, by the way," he added. "Both sides."

I couldn't help but smile at that revelation. "I have no idea where the blonde hair came from, but maybe my grandparents know. Do you think they'd want to meet me?" I asked eagerly. "Did my mother have any other siblings? Do I have cousins? Aunts and uncles?"

"Hannah was an only child," Adam answered. "I don't know

your grandparents very well, but I imagine they'd be very happy to know you."

I blinked back tears. "Thank you."

He swallowed again and then sighed heavily.

"Do *you* want to get to know me?" I asked. "I heard you have a son and daughter, and I already know Robbie."

"Under no circumstances are they to find out!" he barked.

Shocked at his vehemence, I shrunk back in the booth.

"I won't take a paternity test," he said. "As far as the rest of the world is concerned, we are the same strangers two weeks ago before we met."

"Okay," I said quietly. "I understand."

Adam's anger melted somewhat. "I'm sorry, Carly. I can't give you what you want."

"I don't want *anything*," I shot back, my own tone hardening. "I already told you that. I guess it was a stupid idea to think I had one parent on this planet who doesn't hate me or resent my existence, but I'm done believing it's my fault."

"It's not that simple."

I exhaled a harsh breath. "You've been a ghost my entire life, Adam, and I managed to survive just fine without you. I'll be fine now too."

"Carly, I had no idea about you," he said. "I've spent the last thirty-one years not even knowing you existed."

"Likewise," I replied tersely. "Here I was, offering myself to you as a daughter and hoping you'd find somebody worthy of your time and attention. It never occurred to me that you wouldn't be worthy of *mine*." Standing up I said, "You don't have to worry about hearing from me again. I don't plan to tell your kids or your nephew that we're related, but you're the one who'll be missing out, not me. You and my mother really are two peas in a pod."

I left the booth, tears falling freely down my face as I stalked back to the office. As my vision blurred, I stopped just outside of the high-rise lobby. I sunk down on a bench and wept.

"Carly?" I heard a tentative voice approach.

I gasped, stunned to see my ex-boyfriend standing beside me. "Dylan? What are you doing here?"

He scanned over my appearance before his brown eyes met mine again. "Rehearsal dinner," he said, almost wincing as he anticipated my reaction.

Strangely calm, I said, "Okay."

"I'm supposed to be meeting everyone at *Le Petit Versailles* at five. I came to pick up my tux and meet everyone at the Parkview Suites for the wedding rehearsal in thirty minutes."

"Pretty expensive dinner," I said, sniffling and wiping my nose. "You found someone with money, huh?"

His expression hardened. "That's not why you and I broke up."

"As if I could forget."

His gaze landed on my engagement ring. "Looks like you found someone else with money too."

"Joe could be dirt poor for all I care. He's the most amazing man I've ever met."

Dylan swallowed, his eyes searching mine for any hint of a lie. "Are you happy, Carly?"

My tears dried as I thought of those beautiful jade eyes that would be returning to Parkview later that evening. "I am. I hope you are too."

"Why are you crying?" he asked, still standing over me.

It was then I noticed my ex-boyfriend's navy suit jacket, khaki pants, and gingham shirt. Dylan looked so different than the scruffy guy I had dated. "I never thought I'd see you out of those black boots. You clean up well."

A bit of humor touched around the sides of his mouth and eyes. "Thanks. Tessa's a good influence."

At the mention of her name, I didn't feel my insides recoil. Instead, I finally felt peace about that painful part of my past. "I'm happy for you, Dylan. Truly."

"Thanks," he said, his gaze returning to my engagement ring again. "When are you getting married?"

I beamed at him. "We're still working on logistics. I have to sublet my apartment, but probably within the next couple of months."

"Apartment?" he asked. "So, you're not living with Kelsey and Monique anymore?"

I shook my head. "Courtney just got engaged too. It was definitely time to move out."

"I'm glad," he said, and I could tell he meant it. "Monique was never a friend to you."

"I'm seeing that now. She never forgave me for the crime of having you like me instead of her."

He smirked. "There wasn't anything to like below the surface."

I stood up, realizing Dylan needed to go to his wedding rehearsal, and I didn't want to drag out the conversation. Meeting his eyes, I said, "I just want you to know how sorry I am. I've thought about Harper every single day since it happened, and I'm finally making peace with what I've done. I wish I had talked to you about it first. I know we can't go back in the past and change things, but I sincerely hope you and Tessa will be happy with your own family."

"Harper," he said quietly. "You always liked that name for a girl."

"I've prayed for forgiveness from her and from God. I'm glad I got to see you today and do the same."

Dylan's eyes locked with mine, and a sheen of moisture covered them. "I would have married you, Carly. I had planned to ask you anyway."

"I know," I said, breaking eye contact, "and I ruined that. I'm glad you were able to move on. I've needed to heal from so much more than just the abortion."

"And you've done that with this Joe guy?" he asked.

It felt strange hearing Joe's name come out of my ex-boyfriend's mouth. It was like two foreign worlds becoming aware of each other's existence. "The healing came from Jesus," I said, "and not the messed up version my mother tried selling me. I don't think I've met a better representation of Jesus here on earth than Joe Trautweig."

"Joe Trautweig?" he repeated, his color fading noticeably.

"What's wrong?" I asked.

"You did say *Trautweig*, right?"

"Dylan? What's going on?"

"Trautweig?" he said again, his expression panicked. "This is too crazy."

"How do you know Joe?" I asked, my chest tightening.

"I don't know him, Carly, but I've definitely heard that name before. It's too unusual to forget. Tessa was ticked at her dad for shacking up with his best friend's wife. Her mom got remarried last year, and suddenly, her dad is living with someone like it's a competition. Everything's just been super awkward with the wedding coming up, and Tessa lost her maid of honor because it's the girlfriend's daughter."

Heart pounding, I said, "Dylan, what is Tessa's last name?"

"Zendler," he replied.

CHAPTER 36

"Carly, what's wrong?" Dylan said as I sucked air. I stumbled backward toward the bench.

"She can't breathe." Adam appeared, rushing past his future son-in-law and helping me sit down. I wanted to brush off my father's attention, but I needed the physical support more than I needed to salvage my pride.

"Adam?" Dylan said, stunned. "What are you doing here? I thought we were meeting at the hotel." Seeming to note our familiarity with one another he asked, "Do you know Carly?"

Adam and I both glanced sideways at Dylan, and his face went whiter than it had a moment earlier.

"No way," he drawled, his eyes darting between the two of us.

"Breathe," my father said to me, mimicking the same tone he'd heard from Joe. As I still struggled for air, Adam gave a resigned sigh and pulled me into his chest. Despite my misgivings, I listened to his heartbeat and worked on grounding myself.

"Adam, what's going on?" Dylan said harshly. "Why are you holding Carly like that?"

"Like what?" he demanded.

"Like a...well, it's not a boyfriend," he said. The jealous edge slipped from his posture.

"Like a father?" Adam asked, the sound of defeat in his voice.

I found myself at war with how much I both hated and loved his protection. It felt like a stolen moment belonging to Dylan's fiancée rather than the daughter he never knew he had. Nevertheless, the abandoned little girl in me flipped cartwheels of joy.

I peered up at Adam, my breathing slowly normalizing. A tiny smile moved his mouth, and it was the first time I had seen any happy emotion from my father. His expression looked almost tender.

"It's been a while since my daughter has let me hold her like this," he murmured.

"Daughter?" Dylan croaked.

"I mean, Tessa," Adam said, straightening his spine and hiding behind his indifferent mask once again. "Are you all right, Carly?"

I nodded, catching his meaning. "I think so. Thank you." I pulled away from him and placed my hand over my heart to help further steady its cadence.

"Call Joe," Adam said, standing from the bench. "I have to get to a wedding rehearsal and dinner for my daughter and future son-in-law, but I hope you're feeling better now."

I nodded. "I'm okay, thank you."

Adam glanced at Dylan and saw the way my ex-boyfriend gaped at the two of us. He frowned. "How do you two know each other?"

"Old friends," I said, recovering first. "I wanted to offer my congratulations to Dylan...and Tessa," I added. "*Mazel tov* to you too, by the way."

Adam's eyes held a brief twinkle of approval until he noted the slack jawed expression on Dylan's face. Putting the pieces together of my relationship to Dylan, he pressed his lips together tightly and swallowed. At the same time, I knew the question Dylan wanted answered. I felt his gaze burning into me. I looked away and feigned interest in finding my cell phone.

"Come on," Adam said, putting his arm around his future son-in-law. "Whatever got Carly so riled up seems to have passed. Why don't we walk over to the hotel?" He turned Dylan away from me and toward the Parkview Suites across the street.

I heard the suspicion in Dylan's voice decrease as Adam artfully distracted him. Their conversation faded, and I sunk onto the bench, emotionally and physically exhausted.

I decided to meet Joe at the airport terminal rather than waiting for him to get home. I purchased a mystery novel in a nearby gift shop and read absently until I saw that his flight had arrived. I waited just beyond the terminal barricade at baggage claim, scanning his face among the crowd coming up the escalator from the boarding gates.

"Joe," I called, waving to him.

His face lit up in surprise and delight, and he rushed toward me for a kiss and a long embrace.

Stepping back, he saw my expression, and his smile dropped immediately. "What happened?"

Mumbling, I wrapped my arms around his neck and cried.

Joe held the back of my head with one hand and the other rubbed small circles on my back. I wasn't sure if he computed the story beyond the words "father," "Dylan," and "sister," but his hand slowed with each revelation.

"Carly, I think I'm following everything, but I'm also not

functioning on a whole lot of sleep right now. That's a lot to take in."

I pulled my damp face from his chest. "Did you drive, or did you get a ride to the airport? I can take you home."

"A ride would be great, thanks."

Joe's Parkview condo was only twenty minutes away from the airport, and we rode up the elevator to his tenth floor unit.

"Come on in," he said, wheeling his carry-on suitcase behind him.

While Joe's overall square footage was not much larger than my apartment, I easily saw the difference between a Parkview luxury hi-rise unit and a Danbury college apartment home.

"Wow," I said, taking in the hardwood floors and wall of windows in his family room. The lights of the Parkview Pavilion twinkled from beyond the glass doors in the distance.

Joe smiled as he watched me. "Glad you like it."

"It's gorgeous! I don't think I've ever been in a place so fancy."

He chuckled at my word choice. "Goldstein and Margolin aren't doing too shabby with their homes out in the burbs."

I waved him off. "But look at this view," I said in a near swoon. I rushed to the sliding glass doors. "Can I go outside?" I looked beyond his patio furniture and out toward the Parkview city skyline.

"Be my guest," he replied. "I'm going to drop off my suitcase in my room. Be right back."

Smiling, I slipped onto the patio and then leaned my elbows on the concrete balcony wall. The twinkling stars overhead created an idyllic atmosphere. I inhaled deeply, seeking a moment's respite from the day's heavy revelations.

"Feeling better?" Joe asked, coming to stand next to me.

I heaved a sigh. "What a mess."

"So, your ex-boyfriend is marrying your half-sister who has no idea you're related. And your ex may have just realized the connection."

Mocking a daytime tabloid show, I quipped, "Adam Zendler, you *are* the father."

Joe chuckled. "Who would have guessed you have such an affinity for Jewish men? I guess now we know why. You've never mentioned Dylan is Jewish."

I shrugged. "It wasn't a big deal to either of us. Dylan is pretty much Jewish in name only, and from what I've gathered, Adam and his family don't practice much anyway."

"Who's performing the cere—?" Joe cut himself off, already knowing the answer. "Geez, that's so awkward. Carly, how did you manage to be connected to everyone without even knowing it?"

I shook my head ruefully. "Well, I don't know if Adam will ever acknowledge me as his daughter, but Robbie will be in for enough of a shock if the Millers decide they want me in their lives."

"I don't see why they wouldn't. They're not in the same boat as Adam. You wouldn't be a disruption to their lives the way you are to him."

Sarcastically, I faked a mock conversation with Tessa Zendler. "Oh hey, little sis, I used to date your husband. Not weird at all. Oh, and your dad hooked up with my fiancé's former sister-in-law."

Joe laughed and slung his arm around my shoulders. He pulled me in for a hug, and I gladly accepted.

Snuggling against his chest, I said, "I didn't think things could get more awkward after Susan found out she would be your future mother-in-law."

He chuckled. "Darren called to tell me about him and Susan. I wanted to tell you face to face, but Adam beat me to it."

"He's so hard to read, Joe. It seems like he's been hurt, but he hides behind this wall that feels impenetrable."

"Seems like you've been able to find a few holes in the armor," Joe said, turning his jade gaze on me. "You're hard to resist, Carly."

I rolled my eyes. "Yeah, nothing like a fainting damsel in distress."

"He didn't have to help you today. I mean, I have plenty of feelings about how Adam betrayed my brother, but you also didn't see how he looked at you while you were in the hospital."

I raised an eyebrow in question.

"I think he cares about you, certainly more than he wants to admit. It makes me wonder how badly your mother messed him up."

"It was over thirty years ago!"

"There's something about a first love, especially when you have your heart ripped out like Adam did. And then to find out that there's a piece of the woman he loved living in you."

"But I'm *not* her."

"No, you're not," Joe said, "but you represent happy memories. You're also a daughter who wants him to be a part of her life. Susan and Adam both hurt their children with their affair. The kids grew up playing together. Samantha was supposed to be one of Tessa's bridesmaids until Susan left Darren for Adam."

"Oh," I breathed. "Dylan mentioned that today too. Why didn't this come up when I met your family?"

"You and I were busy slaying our own demons. It didn't seem worth mentioning at the time."

"I also had no idea Adam Zendler was my father."

"How do you feel about that?" Joe asked. "I don't know if him rescuing you was a one-off or the start of an actual father-daughter relationship, but are you open to one?"

"I already told Susan we can't escape the awkward," I said dryly.

"And that's on her and Adam anyway, not you. Darren really likes you, by the way. Susan does too."

I smiled. "Thanks for telling me that."

"And based on what you've told me, it sounds like Adam may have a growing respect for you as well. I wouldn't put it past God to use you to bring healing to more than just my own heart, Carly."

Tears smarted in my eyes. "So, I'm not an abomination, am I?"

"Never were," he said, smiling down at me. "You are a *blessing*, and your mother is the one missing out. I was listening to the Hebrew version of an old Christian song, and it made me think of you."

"A Christian song in Hebrew? How did you find it?"

"Because the Bible was written in Hebrew first," Joe said, "and there are more Jewish people who believe in Jesus than you think. I found an Israeli congregation who posts their worship music online. Their cover of the song comes from *Psalms 51*. Do you want to hear the words?"

I nodded.

Quoting in Hebrew first, Joe said, *"Lev tahor b'ra li, Elohim. V'ruach nidibah tis'micheni.* Create in me a clean heart, O God, and renew a steadfast spirit within me."

"So beautiful," I breathed.

"Do you know the history of that psalm?"

I shook my head.

"Are you familiar with the story of David and Bathsheba?"

"Generally," I said. "They had an affair. That much I know. He caught her bathing or something."

"Well, the short version is that David took Bathsheba as his mistress while she was still married to another man. He had her husband, Uriah, murdered during wartime to make it look like an accident when he found out Bathsheba was pregnant with his illegitimate child. Before that, David tried to trick Uriah into sleeping with his wife to hide the paternity, but every plan failed."

"Wow."

"So, after Bathsheba's husband died, David took her into his house to join the rest of his wives. She gave birth to a son, but the baby died."

"Oh," I said softly.

"It was during the time that Nathan the prophet came to visit David. God had revealed to Nathan what David had done, and Nathan used a parable when he addressed the king. While David was raging at the thought of someone else committing his own sin, Nathan called him out for his behavior with Bathsheba. He also said that David's son would die because of his sin."

I gasped.

"Don't go there," Joe said, leveling me with that jade stare. "That's not why I brought it up. For you or for me."

"Okay," I drawled, blinking back the tears in my eyes.

"So, David fasted and prayed for the son. He refused to eat for seven days. Before they would have circumcised the boy, he died."

"How sad," I said. "That innocent baby."

Joe's eyes filled with compassion. "Children don't bear the sins of their parents."

"Then why did God take the baby?" I shot back. "Harper didn't deserve what I did to her, and neither did David's baby. Why would God do that?"

"Carly, I can only guess why He allowed it to happen. But I do know that all of our babies are safe with Him. I have no doubt about that. Bathsheba was the woman wronged in all of this, tossed around from man to man, and then she lost her firstborn son too."

"People don't talk much about her, do they?" I said.

Joe shook his head. "The Bible goes on to say that David comforted her over the loss of her first son, and she gave birth to another son named Solomon. He's the one everybody knows as the wisest man to live and the one who built the first Temple in Jerusalem."

"Oh," I breathed.

"So, God redeemed the evil that had been done," Joe said, "and he also blessed Bathsheba with more sons to love and raise. David wrote *Psalm 51* on the heels of having his sin uncovered and recognizing he had sinned. God called him a man with blood on his hands from all of the wars he fought, but He also referred to David as a man after His own heart."

"How is that possible?" I asked. "How can you be guilty of murder and still...?"

Tears flooded my vision.

Joe's eyes silently pleaded with mine to see beyond the pain of my sin. "David never pretended to be a perfect man, Carly. He didn't have to be. If you read the *Psalms* attributed to him, you'll see emotion, grief, anger, elation, and everything in between. I think what made him a man after God's heart was that no matter what emotions he experienced, He brought it before God."

"That's beautiful."

"You were *never* an abomination," he said, his words and his eyes speaking directly to my soul, "and whatever your sins have been, Carly, it's God who gives you a clean heart. It's not something you need to earn, and it's not something you repay being enslaved to a man like Bernard Ivy. It's a gift freely given and paid for by Jesus."

"He's already given me that clean heart," I said in awe, blanketed in peace and reassurance from the Holy Spirit. "I don't feel that gnawing guilt anymore."

"And He's also given you a willing spirit to help you remember that," Joe said, embracing me under the star filled sky.

CHAPTER 37

"Joe, will you go with me to synagogue this weekend?" I asked, snuggled in his arms on his couch.

"Why? I thought you weren't planning to tell Robbie you're related."

"No, I'm not. I gave Adam my word. I'm just wondering if my grandparents will be there. Maybe we've crossed paths already, and I didn't know it."

"It's possible," Joe said, "but I think they'd recognize you if you'd had. Darren, Adam, and Susan all looked at you like a ghost. That doesn't mean the Millers will be at services, though. All we can do is hope."

I prayed silently for a moment. Opening my eyes to the jade gaze peering into my soul, I said, "God knows what He's doing. He's shown me over and over how much He loves me. He's taken me step by step with every revelation about my mother and my father. It's been more of a whirlwind the last few weeks, but I'm still standing."

"You are," Joe said, beaming at me, "and I heard from Aaron today."

"About my apartment?" I asked.

He nodded. "Lauren is ready to move in as soon as you are ready to move out."

"Oh," I said, my eyes sweeping over the skyline through his sliding glass doors. "The timeline is really on us, isn't it?"

"Lauren isn't looking to pressure us, and Aaron said she's incredibly grateful."

I smiled. "I'm glad I can help."

"So, what do you think?" he asked. "Are we doing a Jewish wedding? Do you want a civil ceremony and then a Jewish one down the road? Rabbi Peretz certainly has no shortage of business from our little home group, does he?"

I chuckled. "I'll say. I wouldn't be surprised if he somehow knew my mother too. Apparently, everybody does."

"Which is probably why she hid from all of them. She couldn't risk anyone putting the puzzle together."

"It still makes no sense," I said. "Why hide from her parents? Did Pastor Ivy really brainwash her that badly? Why wouldn't they have supported their own daughter? Was she scared of them?"

"We have no idea what the Millers are like," Joe said. "They might turn out to be wonderful people like Rebecca's grandparents, or they might be just like Bernard and Deborah Ivy."

"I guess there's only one way to find out."

Four days later, Joe and I entered Beth Tefillah. The synagogue had finally reopened following the initial pandemic scare, and we noted the crowds seemed more sparse than usual. Some of the elderly still wore face masks. I received a few dirty looks for going mask-free, but I needed my grandparents to recognize me.

"Do you think they'll be here?" I asked, looking at Joe.

His jade gaze scanned the room. I saw his jaw tighten, and I glanced over at what caught his attention.

Poppy, Jared, and their family stood just outside the doors of the sanctuary.

"Let's bite the bullet," I said to Joe, pulling him forward. "Everything is fine at work with Poppy and me. She said she told Jared the same thing."

Poppy noticed us first and walked over to embrace me. "You look beautiful," she said, taking in my floral dress. With a more reserved tone, she added, "Joe, good to see you."

He gave a tight smile.

"Hi," Jared said, approaching us. "Always good to see you, Carly."

Joe and Jared eye one another warily.

"Carly, show Jared the ring," Poppy said, taking a step back and putting her arm around her husband. I inclined my head in thanks, proud of her for making her loyalties clear.

Jared shook his head as if snapping out of a daze. Pushing a half smile on his face, he said, "Let's see it."

I held out my hand as Jared eyed the glittering diamonds on my finger. "Good work," he said, jerking his chin toward Joe. "I'm happy for you both."

"Thanks," Joe replied.

I exhaled a chuckle. "I just can't seem to escape the awkwardness anywhere, can I?"

Joe pulled me to his side with a short laugh. "I guess not."

Jared's expression relaxed as he took in the sight of Joe and me. "Have you guys set a date yet?"

I met the adoring jade gaze that held a sparkle just for me.

"Apparently, not soon enough," Poppy said with a laugh.

"You can always call Rabbi Peretz if you decide to go that route."

"Rabbi Peretz?" Jared asked, turning his attention to his wife. "Does he do interfaith marriages now?"

Answering for her, I said, "I don't know how much Poppy has told you, but it turns out I'm Jewish after all."

Jared's eyes darted to Joe before he looked at his wife in question.

"It wasn't my place," she said. "Carly also wanted to meet with her birth father before she made any information public domain."

"It's true," I added. "Poppy wasn't deliberately withholding information from you. My father is very squeamish about any information leaking about us being related."

"But I'm her husband," Jared protested. "Carly, that's not right. If it was information my wife couldn't share with me, then you probably should have found a different confidant. We don't need any more secrets."

Joe's arm tightened around me protectively.

I sighed, weary of the animosity and misunderstanding between the two men. "I'm sorry that I put Poppy in that position. I wasn't trying to cause trouble, and I realize I did."

"You don't need to apologize," Joe growled.

Jared's eyes flashed in challenge.

"Apology accepted," Poppy jumped in, reining in her husband. "So much of this happened at work, honey. Carly needed somebody to confide in who already knew the details. She's waited her entire life to meet her father. Please, don't begrudge either of them their privacy. It had nothing to do with you and me."

I watched the offense melt away from Jared's face and posture. Joe's grip around my waist loosened.

"There's more," I said quietly. "I also found out my mother's parents attend this synagogue." I gazed around the sparsely populated atrium. "Poppy, do you know if the Millers are here tonight?"

"The Millers?" Jared asked, his eyes widening. "Do you mean Rick and Diana Miller? Poppy, she's been one of your mom's friends for years."

"Which is why I didn't want her to say anything," I said, looking directly at Jared. "I don't believe anyone would share my secrets on purpose, but I couldn't risk any slips either. Poppy wasn't violating your trust, but I understand why you're upset. The fault is mine, not hers."

"Let's keep the past in the past," Poppy said.

"No warning needed," Joe said, eager to change the subject, "and I hope this eventually gets less awkward for all of us." He extended his hand to Jared. "There are no hard feelings from me. I'm with the woman I'm supposed to be with, and I know you are too."

The tension finally broke as Jared offered a genuine smile in return. "I'm very happy for both of you. I'm sure you'll take good care of Carly."

"And vice versa," I said with an adoring gaze at Joe.

Jared chuckled as he sighed into Poppy's arm anchored around him. "You weren't exaggerating about the lovey dovey stuff."

Poppy shook her head and laughed. "Not a word. Set a date already, you two, and end the nausea for everyone else."

I stuck my tongue out at her.

"Have you seen the Millers?" Joe asked the Levines.

Poppy shook her head. "They usually only come for High Holidays and special occasions."

Confused, I said, "I thought they were on the trustee board."

"It's more of an administrative role than a spiritual one," Poppy said. "I'm sorry, sweetie. I can ask my mom if she's talked to them lately. Maybe we can arrange a run-in."

"Not necessary," Joe muttered. His gaze was fixed on something near the sanctuary doors. "Carly, I think the Millers just discovered they have a granddaughter."

"What?" I said, my heart rate accelerating. I gasped for air.

"Carly!" Poppy exclaimed.

God, not again! Please, not right now! My mind cried. *Please, let me meet them. Please!*

I let Joe guide me on feather light feet toward a nearby bench. Situated just outside of the women's bathrooms, he sat down with me and tucked me into his side. My head rested against his heart.

"Excuse me," an elderly woman said, approaching us. "I don't mean to stare, but this young lady…" her voice trailed off as emotion filled her throat.

"We lost our daughter many years ago," her husband said. "The resemblance between you and our daughter is uncanny."

My eyes flooded with tears as I willed myself to breathe.

"I know it seems silly," Diana Miller said, shaking her head self consciously. "I'm so sorry to bother you."

Joe held up a hand to halt her departure. "It's no bother. Carly suffers from panic attacks, but she'll be okay. I know she wants to talk to you."

"She does?" Rick Miller asked, surprised.

I dared a glance upward from Joe's chest, searching for my mother in both of their faces.

Diana gasped as she got a closer view of me.

"Yes," Joe said. "This is Hannah's daughter. You have a granddaughter."

Diana Miller now looked ready to faint. Rick helped her to a spot next to me on the bench. He stood next to his wife with his hand on her shoulder. She reached up and clasped his hand against her.

"It's true," I said looking into my grandmother's face. "Hannah Miller is my mother."

"How?" she whispered.

"She got pregnant with me in college. I found out she planned to have an abortion, but she was talked out of it. Unfortunately, she raised me in a horrible church."

"Hannah wrote a suicide note," Rick said shakily. "We thought our daughter killed herself thirty-years ago."

I gasped. Joe looked at me in alarm, but I patted his knee. "I'm okay."

"Did you know about us?" Diana asked, searching my face.

I shook my head. "I grew up isolated from anyone who might know my mother. She joined First United of Hillcrest while she was still pregnant and became a slave to Pastor Ivy." As I saw my grandparents' reaction, I added, "If the name sounds familiar, it's because he's the holy roller from hell that you've heard about on the news. That's where my mother raised me."

Rick inhaled a weary breath. "Why a church? I don't understand. Why put us through all of that grief? Is Hannah still alive?"

Tears fell from my eyes, mourning for my grandparents and for myself. "Yes, she's alive, but she wants nothing to do with me. I've also met my birth father," I said, going for broke. "He confirmed most of the details, but he doesn't want to be a part of my life."

Diana looked at me pityingly.

"My mother lied to him about being the father, so it's been a shock for him. He has his own family, so I can't begrudge him wanting to protect his other children. He said he confronted my mother and confirmed the details, but she's not the same person he remembers from college."

Diana reached out a tentative hand to me. Smiling through my tears, I met her hand with my own and held it. She gasped in delight and then pulled me toward her. I wept against her shoulder as she wept against mine. Rick patted my back.

Once the tears subsided, Diana cupped my face in her palms. Her eyes glowed. "I know you aren't Hannah, but it's like having a piece of our daughter back."

"No, I'm not Hannah," I said carefully, "and she is not the daughter you remember. My father confirmed that. But I'm here. I'd like to get to know you, if that's all right."

"Of course!" Diana exclaimed before glancing back at Rick. He nodded his approval, his lower lip quivering.

Reminded of the jade gaze I could feel without seeing, I turned toward Joe. "This is my fiancé, Joe Trautweig."

"I'm Rena Pinsky's brother," he said, referring to his sister by her married name.

Diana's gaze darted between the two of us, and she smiled. "When's the wedding?"

CHAPTER 38

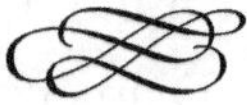

JOE AND I OPTED FOR A SMALL JEWISH CEREMONY JUST
outside the Parkview Pavilion. Rabbi Peretz graciously offici-
ated, thrilled to see me embracing my Jewish heritage.
Although he did not embrace my faith in Jesus, Rabbi Peretz
said I could email him with any questions about the Torah,
Judaism, or Jewish holidays. The warmth of the Orthodox rabbi
certainly made up for the arrogant condescension I'd received
from his more liberal counterpart.

My grandparents insisted on paying for a wedding reception,
and I was happy to give them that blessing. It was a day Rick
and Diana Miller never thought they'd see as parents, let alone
grandparents. Due to social distancing laws still in effect, we
met as a small party in the Parkview Suites dining room.

"I wish we could invite all of your friends," Diana said,
clinging to my arm as we entered the two-story restaurant.

I smiled at her. "This room is stunning. I can't ask for
anything more. The chandeliers look like something out of a
fairytale."

Diana grinned at my enthusiasm. "Well, I still wish we could have invited your friends from work. We've known Poppy's family for fifty years. I used to play Mahjong with Harriet Berman, Hannah Birnbaum, and Mindy Friedman when our kids were little," she said, referring to some of the synagogue matriarchs.

"I'm sure we'll find another way to celebrate," I said. "The most important part was that Joe and I got married today."

"Yes, you did," Diana said, her eyes glistening with tears. "Beautiful bride. *Sheyna meydeleh*," she said in Yiddish. The term of endearment matched the love in her voice.

"There's my bride," Joe said grandly, joining my grandmother and me. "Honeymoon suite is in order," he said with a wink.

I beamed at my handsome husband of two hours, still awed that the man from my coworker's memoirs was truly mine. I dove into that jade gaze and momentarily forgot anyone else was in the room. Joe gifted me with that heart-stopping, winsome smile of his, and he cupped my face to kiss me.

"Oy, save it for later," Diana said, laughing and swatting Joe on the arm. "Under the *chuppah* was enough of a scene. I wondered if you two would ever come up for air!"

Joe and I laughed as he slid his arm around my shoulders and hugged me to his side.

"Are you really complaining about your front row seat?" Joe asked, turning on the charm for my grandmother.

She rolled her eyes and laughed. "I'm still wondering why you asked a seventy-eight-year-old woman to hold up your wedding canopy."

I pulled away from Joe to kiss my grandmother's cheek. "Because you deserve the honor, and I couldn't be happier you're a part of my life."

Diana's eyes filled with tears once again, and she reached her hand to the side of my face. I knew at that moment she was seeing her own daughter rather than me. A bittersweet smile touched her mouth. "So beautiful," she said with a sigh. "You'll let me see a great grandchild before I meet my Maker, won't you?"

I pushed away guilty thoughts of Harper and smiled back. "I can promise we'll certainly try." As my grandmother's eyes widened, I laughed and said, "That's *not* what I meant!"

She chuckled good naturedly. "I'm sure we'll be hearing the pitter patter of little feet soon enough."

I glanced back at Joe, and his tight smile held the same fears I felt.

"All in God's timing," he said, rejoining my side.

Miriam and Paul Trautweig joined us along with my grandfather at the maître d' podium.

"You look so happy," Miriam cooed, her eyes aglow. "Joe, I never thought I'd see you like this again."

"Speaking of," I said, glancing at Susan and Darren who joined our small party.

"Carly, you're a beautiful bride," Susan said, leaning to press her cheek to mine in an air kiss. She held my eyes for a moment. "I would have done things differently if I had known," she whispered. "I wish Adam could have walked you down the aisle."

"I know," I said, squeezing her hands, "but I'm glad that you and Darren are together. I enjoyed meeting your kids at our engagement dinner."

Susan smiled and then stepped back closer to her ex-husband. "Isn't Carly beautiful?"

Darren nodded and clapped his brother on the arm. "I'm

happy for you, Joe. And you," he said, inclining his head toward me.

While Darren and Susan eschewed any traditional labels for the reconciled relationship, the rest of us jokingly referred to them as boyfriend and girlfriend. Their children seemed skeptical of welcoming their mother back in their lives, but they claimed they were happy to see their parents happy.

I half hoped that Adam would make an appearance in the hotel, but I realized it would probably cause more harm than good. The little girl in me wanted the daddy-daughter moment my half-sister, Tessa, had experienced two months earlier with Dylan. At the same time, I could offer nothing but prayers of thanks for the small contingent of people I now called my family. My eyes drifted from my grandparents to all of my in-laws and then to Joe. Paul and Miriam *kvelled* at every tender gesture from my new husband, and their joy at Joe's happiness brought more joy to my own heart.

After a week at the Parkview Suites enjoying our staycation honeymoon, I officially moved into Joe's condo. He insisted on carrying me over the threshold once my final box had made it inside of his home. I forgave him, of course, when he accidentally knocked my head into the doorframe.

I left most of my belongings in my apartment for Lauren Fein to use, and I met with her three weeks after my wedding. Seeing her face to face, I realized she carried enough pain in her eyes for someone far beyond her twenty-nine years.

"Thank you," she whispered, wiping away tears as she balanced her son on her hip.

"I'm just glad I could help. We cleaned out all of the closets and drawers, and the spare room is basically empty."

"You don't know what an answer to prayer this is. Nathan had his friends stalking my parents' place since I moved in with them. I've got a temporary restraining order now, but I can't stop the friends. Thank you for giving a safe place for me and Ari to stay," she said.

I reached out a hand to her tiny arm. "You deserve to be happy."

"Please, don't make me cry."

I pulled her into a hug anyway, surprised that I felt such motherly concern for someone less than three years my junior.

"Everything okay?" her friend Aaron asked, entering the apartment. His arms were laden with baby supplies and furniture.

"Fine," Lauren replied. "Are you sure you're okay carrying all of that? I can help too."

"Hang onto the baby," he said, jerking his chin toward Ari on her hip.

I noted the momentary, unguarded look of affection Aaron cast toward Lauren. Several times that day, I'd noticed how Aaron shielded his looks of concern unless Lauren was otherwise occupied. He'd turned away quickly when I caught him staring.

"What?" Lauren asked, her light brown eyes studying me as Aaron lugged all of Ari's belongings into the spare room.

"Nothing."

She pursed her lips. "Not you too!"

"Not me what?" I said, facing her.

"Why can't people accept the fact that Aaron and I are just friends? We've been friends since we were teenagers."

"Do you want an honest answer, or do you want me to pretend I don't see him eyeing you like a store window that's not open for business yet?"

Lauren gasped but swallowed her denial. "I know he's in love with me, Carly. I just...I don't feel the same way. Aaron's always been my friend. Sometimes, I wish I could see him the way he sees me, but I've just never had those feelings. Besides, I'm not single, and I have no idea how long the proceedings will take. My lawyer is saying divorces can take up to two years in our county. Nathan will fight me tooth and nail out of spite."

"How are you going to pay for an attorney?" I asked, changing the subject as Lauren clearly did not want to discuss her not so secret admirer. "If you need help, my friends might have some connections."

She gave me a grateful smile, exposing a dimple on either cheek. "I have money in savings I'm using right now. Everyone at the Goldsteins' home group has been so kind to me. Ted mentioned a friend who's a divorce attorney. I never had this kind of support at my old synagogue."

"Of course," I said. "We survivors need to stick together."

"Toddler bed is set up," Aaron announced as he joined us in my family room.

"Thank you," Lauren replied. She sighed, and some of the weight of the world slipped from her slim shoulders.

As she moved to take the baby toward the back room, Aaron held up a hand to stop her. "I've got him, Laur. You've been lugging around a thirty-pound kid all day."

"And you've been carrying furniture and boxes that weigh a lot more," she protested.

Aaron looked down imperiously at his childhood friend. "You're not going to win."

"Are you sure?" she asked.

Without a word, he slipped the sleeping preschooler from Lauren's hip and carried him to the bedroom.

"He's a natural," I said, eyeing her for a reaction.

She blushed and sighed. "This sucks. Why can't Ari's father act like that? The guy makes six figures a year, but he pretends he's too stupid to change a diaper or put his own son to bed. It's ridiculous. All of it is. I wish..."

Her shoulders shook in silent sobs, and my heart ached for her. Aaron seemed to sense Lauren's distress from the other room. He returned before I could offer her any comfort, and he pulled Lauren into his arms. Despite the earlier protests, I wondered if Lauren was in denial about her own feelings.

"Guys," I said, "I have to get back home. I know the baby's asleep in the next room, but it might not be the best idea for you two to be alone together."

Aaron's countenance looked heated, but Lauren dropped her arms immediately. Looking up at Aaron, she said, "She's not insulting my character or yours. Nathan will use anything he can against me."

"Who's here to see?" he growled.

She retreated further. "Aaron," she pleaded. "He has spies everywhere." Her gaze darted around the room with a hunted look on her face. I could only imagine the horrors she'd endured being married to a monster like Nathan Fein.

"I don't care what people think about me," he said, "but I don't want to hear anybody say a word about your character. You deserved so much better than what that pig has done to you."

"Carly, are you coming?" Joe asked, entering through the front door. "I thought you said it would just be a minute." His green gaze traveled from the close proximity of Lauren and Aaron to the bemused smile on my face. "This is totally going into the book, isn't it?"

Lauren's face paled. "What book?"

"Sort of a Culver tradition," I said, making my way to my husband's side. "Apparently, everyone in the marketing department publishes a version of their memoirs. It's my turn."

"Oh," she said.

"Don't worry, I'll get your permission before I talk about you," I assured her, "and if necessary, I can keep the same code names Poppy and Rebecca used in their own books too. Gotta keep the continuity."

Lauren did not look mollified.

"Nothing's gone to print, and I'm still in the early stages," I added quickly.

"Don't do anything to hurt Lauren in the divorce," Aaron warned.

Joe stiffened at Aaron's fearsome tone and expression. "Carly is not an exploitative person. You can take my word for it."

"Just wait until the divorce is finalized," Lauren said. "After that, you've got my permission to run with it. Please, make me taller and with a figure like yours," she quipped.

"There's nothing wrong with how you look," Aaron said gruffly.

I stifled back a grin. "You have my word. Also, I agree with Aaron. I wouldn't change a thing about you."

His look of admiration flashed briefly before he turned his attention to the front door. "I'm gonna get going. Text me if you need anything," he said to Lauren.

She smiled at him, and Aaron brushed past Joe and me as he exited the apartment.

My husband chuckled. "Yeah, it's totally going in the book."

CHAPTER 39

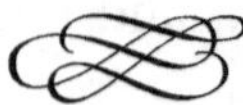

AFTER SIX MONTHS OF MARRIAGE AND NO POSITIVE pregnancy test, my faith wavered. Joe did his best to reassure me, but I knew he wrestled with his own doubts. I struggled to pray and read the Bible, my mind consumed with the hollow ache of an empty womb. Heaven seemed silent.

"Poppy, what if Harper was my only chance?" I asked over coffee at Vincenzo's.

She leveled me with her dark eyes. "Stop. You're going to drive yourself crazy with this, and you know it's a PTSD trigger for Joe too."

"I'm not Catherine!"

"I didn't say you were," she shot back. "Look, baby fever can make any rational woman act crazy. It's this constant anxiety and heartbreak of wanting something you can't control, no matter how much you try."

I sighed. "Thank you for not telling me to look on the bright side or all the other well-intentioned advice I got at Bible study on Sunday."

"Everybody means well," Poppy said, "and I know it's hard to see when you're in the thick of it. I just don't want you to look back with regret on this newlywed season of your marriage. Once you're a parent, you never stop being one. You won't get this time back with Joe, sweetie. Don't wish it away, no matter how much you both want to have a baby."

I exhaled wearily. "I know."

She pushed her mouth into a half smile. "God's not punishing you either. I hope you know that."

"Then why?" I asked, sniffling back tears.

"I could only guess. Have you heard any answers when you pray or read the Word?"

I shook my head. "My heart is such a mess. I don't have the patience for it. I don't want to hear God tell me to wait or trust Him."

"You just want what you want," she said softly. "I get it, Carly. I've thrown a tantrum or two with God for the same reason."

"You also wanted an affair," I said, "with Joe."

Her mouth tightened. "That was three years ago. I actually had a few other examples in mind."

"I'm sorry," I said contritely. "I just don't know how to let go of this anxiety. Everyone wants to tell me to lay it down and 'trust God.' I don't understand why I'm having such a hard time doing it."

"Well, what's holding you back?" she asked.

"What do you mean?"

Her eyes lit as if an idea had just presented itself. "Carly, this is more than just baby fever. I think there's an underlying fear keeping your death grip on this."

"Fear of what?" I asked.

Poppy looked thoughtful for a moment. "Do you think that

having another baby equates to forgiveness for the abortion? Like some sort of reassurance?"

The color left my face, and my stomach dropped.

She reached over to touch my hand. "God has already forgiven you. Don't let all of this doubt and fear creep in. Your husband loves you, and he needs you. You need him too. I'm wondering if maybe you both thought the battle was over the moment you said, 'I do.' Trust me, it's not."

I felt the peace of the Lord as my mind flashed to every private thought proving her point. "You're right," I said, ruefully shaking my head. "You're absolutely right. Wow."

"Talk to God about your fears. He can handle it. Talk to Joe too. I think it will probably help both of you."

I looked up and studied the former object of Joe's affection. I was glad to see Poppy's heart was in the right place. "Thank you," I said.

She nodded and stood up. "I'm going to head to the office and get cracking on the mighty Margolin's latest updates. See you in a few?"

"Yeah," I said, already reaching for my phone to text my husband.

Poppy took her leave, and I began typing a novel-length text to Joe.

"Carly?" a familiar voice called from just beyond me.

"Hi," I said, surprised. "I didn't know you got coffee here."

My father's expression remained impassive. "May I join you?"

"Sure. I have to leave for work soon, but I can chat for a minute."

Adam sat in Poppy's vacated chair. "How have you been?"

I raised my eyebrows. "Everything okay? I thought you wanted to pretend we were just strangers."

"I had a long talk with my son-in-law," he said. At my look of confusion, he added, "I mean Dylan."

"Oh."

"I asked him directly about his relationship with you. Things between him and Tessa have been rocky. My daughter came to me looking for legal advice."

"Oh no," I murmured. "I hope they can work it out."

Adam looked relieved. "So, you're not still pining for your ex?"

I shook my head vehemently. "Absolutely not. I love my husband."

"Dylan told me about the baby," he said, lowering his voice.

"Does Tessa know?" I asked. "Not about my connection to you or to Dylan, but about what happened?"

Agitated, Adam said, "I just can't seem to escape this, Carly. Your mother. You. Even Susan. All of you are connected by the pain you have from an abortion—or not having one."

I swallowed. "Do you wish my mother had aborted me? Do you think you would have married her and been happy with her if I'd never existed?"

His eyes widened in horror. "Not at all! Whatever became of your mother was her own doing, not yours. You've been innocent in all of this."

"Except for my *abomination*," I said bitterly.

"Your mother has no room to judge," Adam clipped.

"Why? Because she *almost* aborted me?"

"No," he said, "because she'd already had two abortions before you ever came along."

"What?" I breathed. "How do you know?"

"Hannah told me in college. After she raged about you 'murdering our grandchild,' I reminded her of her own choices."

I felt my mouth working, wanting to speak, yet no words came out.

"Obviously, you had no idea," Adam surmised.

Gasping and wondering aloud, I said, "Was that what kept her at First United?"

"You mean, besides the holy roller from hell?" he asked bitterly. "How long is the list of lives that monster has ruined?"

"Pastor Ivy knew exactly how to push people's buttons, especially my mother's. She probably struggled with the same guilt that ate me alive for years. I was the reminder of the other babies."

"Doubtful," Adam said, polishing off his coffee.

His icy words jarred me out of the compassion I began to feel for Hannah Miller. "What makes you say that?"

"I don't think your mother has felt a moment's guilt for what she's done. She tried to use your abortion to make me hate you. All it did was highlight her own hypocrisy."

"I don't understand, Adam. What are you saying?"

"Your mother hates you because she *didn't* abort you. She's furious about the abortion you had because she wishes she could have had another one thirty-two years ago. All of the Christian religious lingo was just to reinforce the brainwashing you got at that church."

My father's words landed like a physical blow. "How?" I croaked. "How could she feel no shame for what she did? How could she say all of those horrible things to me if she didn't believe them about herself?"

"There's an old adage that goes, 'accuse your enemy of that which you are guilty.' Your mother is no exception."

"I'm her enemy?" I asked, sniffling back tears. "It makes sense, but it still hurts. All I ever wanted was for her to love me. How do you hate your own child?"

Adam met and held my gaze. For a moment, I saw his guilt. I knew he didn't want me in his life, but he wasn't above pity on my behalf.

"It's okay," I told him. "You didn't know."

"Is that how you really feel, Carly?"

I shrugged, wiping the tears from my cheeks. "It doesn't matter what I feel. I gave you the option to be a part of my life, and you didn't want it. You have your own daughter already. You don't need me too."

Adam's jaw clenched, and his impassive mask slipped. "None of this is your fault. It's my own pride," he said, dragging a hand through his hair. "I don't want my kids thinking any worse of me than they already do. Please, forgive me."

I pursed my lips, not sure how to respond.

"There's more," he said with a heavy sigh, "and I'm sorry to cause you any more pain. I had planned to text you anyway because it's the one thing that would cause my children more hurt than discovering they have a long lost sister."

"What did I do this time?" I snapped.

Adam winced but pressed on. "Dylan figured out your connection to me, and he hasn't looked at me the same way since. Frankly, I think he's still in love with you."

Angry, I said, "I am done taking responsibility for everyone else's pain. I didn't force you to sleep with my mother. I didn't force her to lie about you being my father. I've already apologized to Dylan for what I did to our baby. He moved on with Tessa two years ago. I gave him my blessing. What else do you want from me?"

"Nobody is blaming you," he said gruffly. "You've made your choices, and you've suffered the consequences. We all have. There's no way you could have known about any of this. Dylan's responsible for his feelings, not you. I'm not holding you responsible, but I do have concerns for my daugh—for Tessa."

"Dylan's been with Tessa for two years. I just assumed he'd forgotten all about me."

"He hasn't, I assure you, which is why I needed to speak with you."

I swallowed the bitter pill of information. "Does Tessa love him?" I asked.

"She does. She's also hurting. She doesn't understand why her husband won't talk to her about it, and Dylan has sworn me to secrecy. He'll keep my secrets as long as I keep his."

"Which is a horrible position to put you in," I said, frowning. "So many secrets, and all they're doing is hurting everyone. I speak from experience when I say that hiding things from your children is much worse than just being honest. Look at what it has cost both of us."

My father studied me, his expression inscrutable. "Wise beyond your years."

"I've been told suffering will do that."

That brief expression of pain and regret flickered on Adam Zendler's face.

Seizing the moment, I said, "Don't repeat my mother's mistakes. Stop the cycle. We can't change the past. It's done. Believe me, I know that better than anyone. I've been tormenting myself for the past six months because I want to have a baby. It's hard not to wonder if this is some sort of punishment for what I did."

"I'm sure that's been very difficult," he said.

"Before you showed up, I was talking to my coworker about it. She said I need to face my fears head on. All I can do is encourage you to do the same. Like I told Susan the first time we met, there's no way to escape the awkwardness here. Tessa deserves to know the truth about me. From you and also from Dylan. What she does with the information is up to her, but if she loves both of you the way you tell me she does, she'll find a way to forgive you and move forward."

"It's not that simple," he argued.

"Tell her I'm happily married and suggest a marriage counselor for her and Dylan," I snapped. "I don't understand what you want from me, Adam. I won't give you my blessing to keep lying to your daughter. I told you I'll respect your decision not to be a part of my life, but if that's what you really want, then don't talk to me about your family problems anymore. It's ridiculously unfair and hypocritical."

I watched him open and close his mouth to speak, but he ultimately said nothing. The silence stretched uncomfortably.

I stood up from my chair and glared down at my father. "You need to figure out if your pride is worth everything it's costing you right now. Susan is working hard to make amends with her kids and with Darren. It's hard, but they all see she's trying."

"Just like that?" he scoffed, snapping his fingers.

"You can't condemn my mother in one breath while justifying the same selfish choices in the next. What you're doing to your own children isn't any better than my mother deceiving me all these years."

He remained silent.

"Goodbye, Adam," I said and walked out of the cafe.

CHAPTER 40

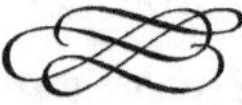

"HOW ARE YOU DOING?" JOE ASKED OVER FROZEN yogurt after work.

I sighed. "I wish the taro helped. It doesn't."

He glanced at me and smiled.

"What?" I asked.

"Just thinking about the first time we met. Hard to believe it's been over a year."

The black cloud sitting on my back lifted. "A lot has happened, that's for sure."

"Are you excited about the Goldstein Hanukkah party this weekend? It'll be your first time celebrating."

"I guess."

"Carly," he said, taking my hand, "it'll happen when it's supposed to. Breathe, honey."

"Do you really believe that, or are you just saying that to reassure yourself too?" The familiar sting of tears tormented me again. "Why, Joe? I don't understand. God forgave me, didn't He?"

My husband set down his cup of yogurt to pull me into his arms. I sighed into his embrace, and he kissed the top of my head. "You know I don't have any more answers than you do, sweetheart. Believe me, God knows how much you want a baby. He knows how much I want one too."

I looked into his pale eyes. "Then, why isn't He giving us one?"

"We didn't get married just to have children," he said, reaching into my heart with his jade gaze. "I love you. I want to spend the rest of my life with you whether we have biological children, adopted children, or even fur babies," he added, just to make me smile.

"So, I'm not a failure as a wife if I can't have any more children? You're not afraid I'll become another Catherine if we never get pregnant?"

Joe's anguished eyes tore at my heart. His hands came up to frame the sides of my face. "Carly, you are the woman I want. I *chose* you, and I didn't do it to replace anyone else. I'm not asking you to measure up to any standards here."

"Promise?"

He kissed me soundly. "Promise," he said, resting his forehead against mine.

As much as I continued to pray and ask the Lord to help me release the burden of wanting a child, I just couldn't seem to shake free from the gnawing ache. I'd have moments, even a few hours of peace, but then the thoughts would rage at me again. The tormenting voices attacked relentlessly. The night before the Hanukkah party, I caught Joe watching me, pain and distress on his face. I saved my tears for the bathroom so he wouldn't take on any more guilt on my behalf.

When we arrived at the Goldsteins' festively decorated home, I tried to distract myself by taking in all the sights and sounds. They'd decorated their front yard with hanging bulbs on the front porch and white lights wrapped around the trees. A massive, inflatable dreidel with a blue capped polar bear sat on their front lawn. Even from outside, I could hear the happy hum of the crowd within the house.

Joe put his arm around my shoulders and hugged me to his side. Tipping my chin up with his forefinger, he kissed me softly on the lips. "I love you, Carly."

I stared back into his eyes and understood the silent message also communicated. Joe's love didn't come with strings or pressures of performance. He brushed my cheek with his thumb as if wiping away old tears. Placing my hand on top of his, I whispered, "Thank you."

The front door burst open, and Kyle Goldstein appeared wearing an obnoxious Hanukkah sweater with flashing lights. "Hey, there's no mistletoe in this house, but I would never stop a man from kissing his wife."

Joe laughed, and he greeted Kyle with a handshake and a hearty pat on the back. "Thanks for the invite."

"Of course!" Kyle said, still grinning ear to ear.

A smile finally found its way to my mouth. "Hi," I managed.

Kyle's wide grin softened into a smile. "Hey, Carly, come on in. The ladies have all been expecting you."

I inwardly sighed, bracing myself to see Lauren Fein with Ari in tow, Abigail Goldstein with Isaac and a growing new baby bump, Rebecca Margolin with her girls and new baby, Max, and even Jessica Ballinger with a toddling Aria.

Poppy saw me first and pulled me into a motherly hug. "There you are!" she exclaimed. A Hanukkah headband sat atop her curls, and the felt dreidels swayed on their springs with each bob of her head.

"Hey guys," Jared said, approaching us. Like Kyle, he also donned hideous Hanukkah outerwear.

"Happy Llama-kah," I said, reading the design. "I had no idea they made so many ugly sweaters for Jewish holidays, and that is definitely ugly. *Mazel tov!* I think you might win the contest."

Poppy and Jared both laughed.

Joe joined my side. "I thought Kyle had us all beat until I saw Ted. The mighty Margolin is actually wearing a dreidel sweater that says, 'rollin with my homies.' If I hadn't seen it with my own two eyes, I never would have believed it."

My husband finally got a laugh out of me, especially as I spotted Culver's top, east coast producer with one of the ugliest sweaters I had ever seen, regardless of the holiday.

"Remind me how this is different from a Christmas party," I said close to Joe's ear.

"Just wait," he replied. "We haven't even gotten to the celebration yet, let alone all the food."

Poppy and Jared excused themselves to go mingle with some other guests, and Joe led me toward a row of tables covered in holiday fare. The buffet included fried potato *latkes* with accompanying dishes of applesauce and sour cream, jelly donuts called *sufganiyot*, a bowl full of chocolate Hanukkah coins called *gelt*, and various platters of more traditional party food.

"You'll have to settle the age-old debate about sour cream or applesauce," Joe said, his eyes twinkling. He fixed a plate for both of us with several latkes and a scoop of applesauce and another of sour cream beside it.

"Am I supposed to mix this?" I asked. "And this looks like a giant hashbrown. Smells amazing though." I inhaled the scent of fried potato, onion, and garlic. "Why would you put applesauce with this?"

Joe grinned. "Don't knock it until you try it."

I looked dubiously at him. "No ketchup?" I asked.

He pulled a face. "It's a latke, not a tater tot."

I stuck my tongue out at him and laughed. "Fine, fine." Realizing the latke was room temperature, I used my hand to dip it first in the safer of the two condiments. The fried potatoes and sour cream paired as deliciously as expected.

"And the other," Joe prompted with a slight flick of the wrist. He dumped a heaping spoonful of applesauce on his latke. He cut a piece with his fork and lifted it toward my mouth. "Here comes the choo-choo," he teased.

Rolling my eyes, I humored my husband and let him feed me the second bite of latke. My eyes widened in surprise and delight.

"See?" he said with a flourish. "It lightens up the latke. The sour cream tastes good, but it always feels like such a heavy bite to me."

Cutting off my own piece, I tested the combination a second time. "Wow, you're right. This is definitely unexpected."

"And yummy," Joe said, smiling down at me. "Want a latke kiss?"

"Make room," Rose Margolin called, carrying a massive oven tin as she stepped between the two of us toward the buffet table.

The scent of apples and cinnamon wafted toward me, and my mouth watered.

"Apple raisin *kugel*," she said over her shoulder. She placed the heavy dish on top of a table trivet. "I only make this once a year," she announced to no one in particular.

Rebecca Margolin walked over to meet her mother-in-law and pass along her sleeping newborn son. Greeting Rose with a kiss on the cheek she said, "Where's Dad?"

"He's looking for a place to park the car," Rose answered, her eyes all for baby Max. "Oh, this boy," she said, nuzzling close to his neck. "Come find me when he needs to eat again, honey. I'm not letting him go."

Rebecca laughed as Rose absconded with her grandson. "Hi there," she said, reaching out her arm to hug me. With baby Max still in view held by his grandmother, I didn't linger long in the embrace. I glanced at Joe with longing and then down at the floor.

"It'll happen, Carly," Rebecca said, pulling me away from my familiar, dark thoughts.

"How do you know?" I asked.

"It's a season of miracles," she replied with her infectious smile. "On the first night of Hanukkah, we add a special prayer when we light the *hanukkiyah*." Reciting the prayer in English, she said, "Blessed are you, Lord our God, King of the Universe, who performed miracles for our forefathers during those days, in this season."

"Meaning what?" I said.

"Meaning that God has been making miracles for His people for a long time, and He's not done yet."

Joe set down his empty plate and grabbed mine too. He put a comforting arm around my shoulders and ran his hand up and down my arm.

Withdrawing into myself once again, I said, "It's easy to have that kind of faith when you have everything you've ever wanted."

Rebecca's eyes darted to Joe and the hurt look on his face. "Stop acting like you don't, Carly. Your grandparents are outside on the patio chatting with Kyle's mom and dad. You have a *lot* to celebrate this year. Don't lose sight of the blessings and answered prayers you already have. God gave you the family you've waited a lifetime for. He gave you a wonderful husband. If He's been faithful to do all of that, you can trust that He'll give you a child one way or another."

Tears stinging my eyes, I felt Joe's arms around me before I even asked him to hold me. Rebecca offered a sympathetic smile before she rejoined her husband and children spinning dreidels by the hearth.

"That was some tough love," Joe said into my ear. "You took it well. I know that wasn't easy for Rebecca to say either."

From the depths of my soul, I heard the same words that Robbie Zendler had proclaimed from the bima of Beth Tefillah more than a year earlier, only I had memorized them from a different translation.

"Sing, barren woman, you who never bore a child; burst into song, shout for joy, you who were never in labor; because more are the children of the desolate woman than of her who has a husband," says the Lord.

In an instant, the hissing, tormenting voices were silenced in my head. The shackles broke from me just as they had on the floor of the Reform synagogue. The peace of God washed away the fear, filling me with hope and peace instead. I breathed in a deep sigh of relief. It would be okay. No matter what God chose to do, I knew *I* would be okay too.

"Carly?" Joe asked, watching me. "Everything all right?"

"It will be," I said, lifting my eyes to meet that beautiful gaze.

My husband beamed at me, his winsome smile and jade eyes reminding me of all that God had brought into my life. As the Goldsteins told the story of Hanukkah to the children listening with rapt attention, I felt an assurance that this same Hanukkah blessing would be shared with my own children. Abigail Gold-stein served as narrator for our party.

Unlike other versions of Hanukkah I'd heard, Abigail focused on the military victory of the Maccabees over the evil King Antiochus rather than the oil burning. She explained how the celebration of miraculous, eight-day oil was a tradition created by rabbis and the reason for our fried foods, but the recorded miracle was God delivering His people from annihilation. She mentioned something called the *apocrypha*, or extra-Biblical texts, that recorded events in between the end of the Old Testament and the beginning of the New Testament.

With dramatic flair and expert storytelling for the children, Abigail talked about the Jews' dedication to worship their God and their refusal to bow down to the idols of the Greeks. "Even if it meant they had to die, they refused to bow down to the evil king or his fake gods," she said. "They obeyed God's command to love the Lord with all of their hearts, all of their souls, and all of their minds."

The wide-eyed children took it all in, and Rebecca chimed in how God's people throughout history were challenged to trust in God more than their own lives. She reminded the children of the biblical stories of Purim, Passover, and Daniel and his friends who refused to bow to idols. With a side glance over at me, she added how God could take any hopeless situation and turn it into a miracle that brought Him praise.

Rose Margolin held up a dreidel and pointed out the four different Hebrew letters on each side. She explained how each letter, *nun, gimel, hey, shin*, formed a sentence, and she recited the Hebrew phrase, *"Nes gadol hayah sham,"* meaning "a great miracle happened there." I received another meaningful look and confirmation that my present circumstances had not sealed my future destiny.

Each family brought their own hanukkiyah to light, and my grandparents gave Joe and me the pewter menorah I had first spotted in the Beth Tefillah gift shop. I had mentioned it in passing one day before Shabbat services, and by the following week, they had purchased it for me along with a set of candles.

"*Hag Hanukkah Sameach,*" Joe said, staring at me through the flames of the burning candles. His jade eyes had never been more luminous. "You're *my* miracle, Carly."

"Happy Hanukkah to you too," I said, smiling back at him.

EPILOGUE

 I called from the bathroom, "can you come here, please?" My hands shook, hardly believing they'd lit the final Hanukkah candle one night before. Now, they held what felt like an even greater miracle.

"Everything okay?"

"Um, can you just come here?" I said, my voice trembling.

He was by my side moments later, his eyes searching mine. "What's up?"

No longer shielding the pregnancy test against my abdomen, I turned around and showed it to Joe.

Those jade eyes lasered onto the dark blue plus sign. He exhaled a half laugh, half sob. "That means what I think it means, doesn't it?"

I beamed at him through my tears. "Did we really make a baby? Is this actually happening?"

He pulled me into his arms and cried against my shoulder. I sobbed with him, placing the test down on the bathroom counter so I could fully embrace my husband.

He leaned back, cupped my face, and kissed me soundly before wrapping me in his arms once again.

"I'm so happy," he whispered.

I paused to silently pray, thankful beyond measure for a second chance. Joe dug his fingers into my hair as he continued to hold me.

Six weeks later, we saw our baby's first heartbeat.

Six weeks after that, we discovered we would be the proud parents of not one, but two babies due in early August.

When we announced the news to Joe's family, I had a feeling word would somehow travel back to my father. What I didn't expect was a phone call, an hour of tearful apologies, and my father to sit in the waiting room along with his ex-girlfriend, my in-laws, and my grandparents as I brought forth two little Hanukkah miracles.

Cuddled next to me in the tiny bed, Joe held our sleeping son while I burped our newly fed daughter.

"Congratulations," Adam said, eyes full of admiration amidst the throng of family members.

My grandparents shared his sentiments, alternately snapping pictures and weeping. My grandmother hugged me tightly and murmured words of thanks against my shoulder.

"Can I hold her?" Diana asked. "Oh, it's been so long!"

"Of course," I said, beaming at her. I placed my daughter in my grandmother's arms, and I noted the look of longing on my father's face.

Joe noticed it too, apparently, and he offered to let Adam hold our son.

"Are you sure?" he asked.

Joe nodded. "He's your grandson, Adam."

"My first," he said, his face uncharacteristically showing

emotion. He inclined his head toward Joe as he took my sleeping son into his arms. "Thank you."

"Thank you for coming," I said to my father.

Adam glanced over at me, his face glowing. "Thank you for allowing me to be here. I'm so proud of you, Carly."

My heart squeezed, not knowing how badly I'd needed to hear those words my entire life. Pausing for a moment, I glanced into my father's aquamarine eyes now shared with my son.

"God did it," I said. "He did it all."

ACKNOWLEDGMENTS

My precious Maggie. You were the inspiration when I started this book in 2020, and it was an honor and a privilege to know you. Your memory is a blessing, and I pray you are basking in the light of God's unconditional love for you. I wish you were here to hold this book in your hands, but I'm so thankful I got to tell you I love you and that this book was dedicated to you. You deserved so much better than this world. I love you and I miss you.

Kasea, thank you for always being just a text away. Your unwavering support and humor during my darkest days have been a blessing beyond measure. I'm so glad I can call you my sister.

Stephanie Cotta, you have made my day more times than I can recount. I am so proud of all your accomplishments—they are well deserved!

Barbara Kellyn, thank you for being such an amazing author, friend, and honest beta reader. Your feedback has truly made my writing better.

To my work fam, thank you for making it a joy to be in the office and for all the laughs (even the ones at my expense). The pool is still closed (for now!)

Hannah Linder and Catherine Posey. As always. You guys are the best. Thank you for helping my vision become reality.

To my beautiful babies, it is the highest honor in the world to be your mom. You three light up my life, and the world is better because you guys are in it. Don't worry, one day, you'll beat me at *Clue*.

Jesus, Yeshua, my beautiful Savior who took God's wrath upon Him so that I could be made clean, whole, and completely healed. Thank you for delivering me from darkness, from trauma, and from the belief your love for me has to be earned. Thank you for my freedom.

COMING FALL 2024

BOOK 5 IN THE BEAUTY FOR ASHES SERIES:
B'RIT HADASHAH: ALL THINGS MADE NEW

LAUREN FEIN'S TROUBLED HISTORY HAS BEEN chronicled within the published memoirs of her friends, but no one knows the true horror more than her longtime friend, Aaron Davis. While Aaron remains steadfast during her messy divorce, his romantic feelings cause confusion for both of them. Lauren believes her heart is as dead as her marriage, but when she encounters Jewish co-worker Grant Kaplan, their instant attraction presents even greater problems. Despite an equally complicated love life, Grant's fascination grows. While he seeks more information about Jesus and the New Covenant (*b'rit hadashah*), Lauren wonders if the end of her own marital covenant has ruined her forever. Will Lauren hide behind her pain, or will she entrust her future to the One who loves her more than any man ever could?

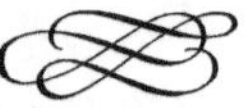

"POPPY LEVINE, ARE MY EARS BURNING?" MISS BELLE called from beyond the open door of the conference room. "I *know* you ain't telling people who don't even work at Culver all of my business."

"Come on," Poppy said to me, "let me introduce you to the natives."

I followed her toward the front desk, unsure of what to make of my first job interview in over eight years. The collection of people currently gathered together transformed from characters within the memoirs of my friends to flesh and blood individuals.

"This is Lauren," Poppy said. "She's interviewing for Carly's old position."

"Do you write books?" Culver's CEO, Phil Robbins, asked me. His blue eyes sparkled with mischief. "Apparently, that's how we know if we should hire anybody around here."

"You must be Phil," I said, warmed by his sense of humor. "I've heard and read a lot about you."

"And it's all true!" he said laughing. "Actually, Poppy and the rest of the girls were probably too kind to me. Miss Belle says I'm going senile."

"You hush your mouth, Phil Robbins, I never said nothing like that!" Culver's Mama Hen exclaimed, swatting at him. "But you're fixin' to drive me crazy with all of the carrying on you do around here."

I couldn't help but smile.

"Don't scare her before we hire her," the receptionist added with a laugh. She flipped silky black hair over her shoulder. "I'm Brooklyn, by the way, and I hope you *do* write books. I've read all the Culver ones, and they're *so* good," she said. "Do you have some hottie who's been secretly stan-ing you too? I love a good, slow-burn romance!"

I blushed and looked away while Poppy coughed. "Okay, guys, I think that's enough hazing for today. If Lauren even wants to take the job at this point, it won't be because of the three of you."

Miss Belle tried to look affronted, but Phil and Brooklyn seemed proud of Poppy's remark.

"Oh, put your pearls down," Phil chided Miss Belle. "You know you cause more trouble around here than anyone."

While a playful argument broke out, Poppy brought me back to the conference room.

"Sorry," she said, closing the door. "I hope I didn't scare you off the job by introducing you to the gang."

I shook my head. "No, they're pretty true to life. I just hope that I'm the right fit for you guys. Bonnie said my resume was thin compared to the other candidates you're considering. I will definitely work hard and do my best here, but I want you to go with the person you think will really do the best job. If that's not me, you won't hurt my feelings."

"Lauren, you do *want* this job, don't you?"

"Of course!"

Poppy smiled. "Then, quit trying to convince me I should go with someone else and let's talk about how this can work. If I don't think this is a good fit, I'm going to be honest with you. I don't want things to be weird at Bible study if they get weird at work. Been there, done that," she said, referring to a fight she'd had with Carly Trautweig, the woman whose role I hoped to fill at Culver Incorporated.

Poppy spent the next thirty minutes describing her daily work routine, and I found myself intrigued and intimidated. The balance of administrative and creative design felt like an ideal situation for me, but I also knew I'd have a huge learning curve navigating the ArtHut Design Suite. Poppy showed me some sample designs asking if there were things I would change. Feeling like it was a test, I eyed the documents critically. I pointed out some misaligned objects and typos and asked questions about changing some of the lengthier bits of copy into information graphics. Poppy's eyes held a warm glow the entire time.

Bonnie rapped on the door and exchanged a quick conversation with Poppy outside. Turning back to me, she said, "Lauren, thank you for coming in today. We'll let you know by the end of the week if we'd like to proceed with a second interview."

"Thank you for the opportunity," I said, shaking her hand.

Bonnie smiled warmly. "You're very welcome."

I picked up my folder and purse and waved past Brooklyn as I exited the Culver office suite.

"Nice to meet you!" she called from behind the front desk.

I pushed the elevator door button not sure if I had aced or failed my first job interview since my early twenties. I sighed and prayed.

"Going down?" a male voice asked.

"Yeah," I replied.

"I'm Grant."

I glanced over, surprised the man was still talking to me. I encountered chocolate brown eyes under thick brows the same color. Immediately, I was reminded of my favorite iteration of Peter Parsons from the Spider Guy movies, and I did a double take. If Peter had grown up, grown a beard, and taken a job at Culver Incorporated, this guy would have been a dead ringer. My pesky hormones reminded me that even though my marriage was dead, I most certainly was not. I wondered if his cropped curly hair would be anything like my son's if he grew it out longer.

"Are you new here?" Grant asked.

"Possibly," I said. "I just had an interview."

"CID or Benefits?"

Smiling, I felt flattered he assumed I'd been interviewing for a position with the commercial insurance division or employee benefits department rather than their support staff. "Marketing department," I replied.

He leaned in closer as if sharing a private joke. "Apparently, you have to be an author in order to work there. I've read all of the books written by the past and present members of the department. Are you ready to tell your story to the world?"

Rising to the challenge I held his gaze. "I have enough writing material to make your head spin. Whether I ever publish it or not remains to be seen."

Half of Grant's mouth cocked into a smile. Dimples appeared underneath his beard along with an approving gleam in his eyes. "Well, I hope you get the job. It'll be nice seeing you around here. What did you say your name was?"

"I'm married," I blurted out.

His eyes zeroed in on my empty wedding finger.

"And I don't do office dating or anything like that," I added.

Grant held up his hands in innocence. "I was just saying 'hello' to a new face, that's it."

I raised two suspicious eyebrows, but Grant maintained his surprised expression. Unfortunately, the dancing butterflies in my stomach did not abate after my awkward outburst. Part of me wanted to crawl into the nearest hole, and part of me wanted to challenge Grant's quick denial. Instead, the elevator doors dinged open, and Ted Margolin stepped out.

"Lauren!" Ted exclaimed. "I thought I'd missed your interview. Rebecca just texted me that your son wants to marry our baby girl."

"Oh," I said, embarrassed. "Yeah, he mentioned that this morning while we were getting ready."

Grant watched me closely, and I inwardly cringed.

"Kaplan, do you need the elevator?" Ted asked, assuming the "mighty Margolin" persona everyone knew and feared at Culver Incorporated.

"Just meeting a potential new recruit," he answered. "Lauren, it was nice meeting you. I hope you get the job." He offered a salute and headed to the reception desk beyond the glass entry doors.

I didn't like how Grant Kaplan knew my name or that I felt a small thrill at the sound of it on his lips. I immediately felt guilty—as if I was cheating on my best friend, Aaron, rather than my ex-husband. I sighed at the ridiculousness of that thought.

"Kaplan is new around here," Ted said quietly. "Not sure what I think about him yet. Did he make you uncomfortable, Lauren? Things seemed a little tense."

The answer was yes, though not in the way he supposed.

"Lauren?" Ted prompted.

"I'm fine," I said. "It's awkward talking to any man these days. He didn't do anything wrong. Sometimes, it's hard to tell what's just friendly conversation."

"Well, from the way he was looking at you and the fact you're still blushing, it does concern me a little bit."

I met Ted's golden gaze. "It's fine, I promise. You don't need to play father figure with me."

The mighty Margolin looked taken aback but didn't comment further. Clearing his throat, he said, "Did the interview go well?"

"I think so."

"Glad to hear it. I'm sorry for interfering, Lauren. You know we all care about you."

Mollified, I smiled back. "I know. I'm sorry I snapped at you."

"Apology accepted. Go give my wife a hug when you see her, and we'll be praying God opens the doors for you to get a job—whether it's here or somewhere else."

I patted his arm. "Thanks, Ted. I appreciate it."

He nodded and then stepped through the front double doors as I got into the elevator. I had a sudden urge to text Aaron and clear my mind of chocolate brown eyes and dimples.

OTHER WORKS BY ANA WATERS

BEAUTY FOR ASHES SERIES
Book 1: Tabula Rasa: Writing a New Story
Book 2: Ex Nihilo: Learning to Live Again
Book 3: Tikkun Olam: Restoring What Was Lost